MOUNTAINS OF FIRE

K.E. POTTIE

BookLocker

Saint Petersburg, Florida

Print ISBN: 978-1-64719-603-5
Ebook ISBN: 978-1-64719-604-2

Published by BookLocker.com, Inc., St. Petersburg, Florida.

Printed on acid-free paper.

The characters and events in this book are fictitious. Any similarity to real persons, living or dead, is coincidental and not intended by the author.

BookLocker.com, Inc.
2021

First Edition

Library of Congress Cataloguing in Publication Data
Pottie, K.E.
Mountains of Fire by K.E. Pottie
Library of Congress Control Number: 2021908475

ACKNOWLEDGMENTS

For my beautiful wife, Kim, who was always there to patiently listen to me ramble on about the book, bringing me glasses of wine.

Scott Goodall, author of *The Freedom Trail*, wrote the foreword. He also verified the route the characters took in the book.

Thank you, Gary Deslauriers, for the beautiful cover art.

FOR MY PARENTS,

LAREN AND ELEANOR POTTIE

INFINITY TITLES BY K.E. POTTIE

CODE NAME SONNY

Honorable mention—2012 Hollywood Book Festival.

Code Name Sonny is a brilliantly written story of World War II and the valor of people in the French Resistance. The suspense is first-rate as the plot unfolds to the story's end and will have the readers on the edge of their seats. *Code Name Sonny* should be on everyone's reading list as it is a remarkable, memorable book that will stay in people's minds for a long, long time.

—Alice D., Readers Favorite

Honorable mention—2012 Beach Book Awards.

The book, an engrossing spy thriller, masterfully interweaves past and present with the story of "Sonny" who idealistically joins up in 1944, the experiences he encounters and the fictional story of Sonny's son Jack who discovers surprises and pursuer's from his father's past almost too late to save himself and his family.

—Stacy Trevenon, *Half Moon Bay Review*

Excellent! The plot is rife with duplicity, action, and an ironic twist at the conclusion. The author has woven an intriguing story that will keep you looking forward to every chapter, whether it is behind enemy lines in France or on the quiet streets of this small American town.

—Bookreview.com

CONTENTS

INTRODUCTION

BY SCOTT GOODALL

AUTHOR OF

THE FREEDOM TRAIL

Let's face it, apart from a few gray-haired crag-rats like myself, the Second World War means very little to our modern generation of happy hikers. Dimly remembered pages in a school history book perhaps, or *The Guns of Navarone* belching flame and smoke for the umpteenth time on television. All something from Grandpa's era, a succession of noble deeds embedded in a savage past, annual ceremonial events to be remembered and paraded on certain specific dates such as Memorial Day and Veterans Day.

But to walk Le Chemin de la Liberté, or "the Freedom Trail," from beginning to end is to bring part of that school history book to life and to experience in a very personal way at least some of the dangers and hardships faced by those men and women who used this high mountain escape route during the last war.

More than sixty years have passed since those far-off days, and sixty years is a helluva long time. To understand how and why Le Chemin came into being, it is important to know certain

1

historical facts, so for those who came in late, the scenario went something like this...

In the late summer of 1939, a small but particularly nasty German Nazi by the name of Adolf Hitler set out to conquer Europe. Like all megalomaniacs, Hitler was not only bold and ruthless but also extremely efficient. In less than a year, his armies had overrun and occupied Poland, Norway, Denmark, Belgium, the Netherlands, and France. By June 1940, the German swastika was flying on every flagpole from the Pyrénées to the Arctic Circle and from the English Channel eastward to the Russian border.

After the invasion of Great Britain (which was expected to take place in a matter of weeks), and a later invasion of Russia, which the German generals were already plotting in secret, Hitler intended to draw up what he called a "New Order" for the ruling and governing of his vast Nazi-dominated empire.

The blueprint was diabolically simple. All Jews and the Slavic races of Eastern Europe were considered by the führer to be the *Untermenschen*, or subhumans, and therefore had no right to live. They would be exterminated. Other conquered peoples, such as the Dutch, Belgians, and French (and eventually the British), would be employed as slave labor for the benefit of the German master race and shipped out to work in factories, mines, and farms.

In France, however, during the early days of occupation, the Germans decided at first to try a velvet-glove approach to their forced labor plans. Using the Vichy French collaborators and public officials as front men, they began by asking for young, able-bodied volunteers to leave home and work in the German-run factories of Eastern Europe. *La relevé* (which means literally a changing or taking over from someone or something) was a deal in which one prisoner of war would be set free in exchange for every hale and hearty volunteer workman who traveled east. Official, long-term contracts were offered, plus good food, wages, and accommodation.

Although the vast majority of Frenchmen refused point-blank, a few did rise to the German bait, tempted no doubt by the prospect of earning enough to feed their starving wives, children, and families back home. But soon the real truth about working conditions began to filter back.

Although all mail between Germany and France was heavily censored, one unemployed tradesman from Toulouse who traveled east to work in a Berlin factory made a special arrangement with his wife. "If," he said, "you receive a letter from me written in black ink, you can believe every word I say. If, however, I write the letter in red ink, you will know I'm lying, and that everything is exactly the opposite of what I have said."

A few weeks later, the man's wife received a letter written in black ink. Her husband, it seemed, was fit, well, and happy. In glowing details, he told his wife how pleased he was to be in Germany. The food was excellent, the pay was good, his overseers were kind, considerate, and helpful, and the work stimulating and not too hard. He had plenty of time off for leisure and shopping. "Here in Berlin," he added as a footnote, "one can buy everything one needs... except red ink."

But in February 1943, off came the velvet glove and down came the iron fist. Infuriated by the near total failure of their volunteer scheme, the Nazi authorities introduced their infamous STO (Service du Travail Obligatoire) decree—in other words, the deportation to German labor camps of all able-bodied males over the age of twenty.

Two million prisoners of war were already toiling for the Third Reich, and the STO decree added millions more. Husbands were separated from their wives and children from their parents, all rounded up by force and shipped out in railway wagons, usually with very little food or water and certainly no sanitary facilities.

Conditions in the labor camps were appalling. Food was desperately short, winter clothing nonexistent, and the hours of work long and hard. Doctors and other medical staff and supplies were rarely, if ever, made available, and as a consequence, disease was rife. It was against this background of hate, misery, and despair that Le Chemin de la Liberté came into being.

All over France, thousands of young men were thinking only of escape. Britain had still not been invaded and was carrying on the fight alone. Although its army had been crushed and humiliated, France still retained the will and the courage to resist its hated German masters. Le tricolore continued to fly with the Free French Forces in North Africa, and in London, General Charles de Gaulle was doing all in his power to urge his fellow countrymen to join him in a new fight for freedom.

The direction for the vast majority of would-be escapees was south to neutral Spain. Once across the Pyrénées, there was the possibility of easy access to London or North Africa via British-held Gibraltar. After the fall of France, a network of escape lines had sprung up all over Europe. These were designed to help not only escaping civilians but also the ever-increasing number of Allied airmen being shot down during missions over Nazi-occupied Europe.

Several of these major lines were in operation throughout the war (the Comete Line, the Pat O'Leary Line, and the Marie-Claire Line, to name but three), and in each case the procedure was the same: evading aircrew were passed from link to link in the chain by a succession of local "helpers," who clothed, fed, and hid them, usually at great personal risk to themselves.

Having reached the mountains, the men were then hidden in secret collecting areas and formed into groups ready for the final night ascent to the Spanish frontier. Official statistics tell us that during the wartime years and along the entire length of the Pyrenean chain, there were 33,000 successful escapes by Frenchmen alone. Of these, 3,000 never returned home. Approximately 6,000 Allied servicemen (mainly aircrew) also made successful escapes.

Although the main evasion routes used by the Pat O'Leary Line were centered on the Mediterranean coast at Marseille, and the Comete Line concentrated on the Atlantic coast near Bayonne, many other evaders were filtered down through central France to Agen and Toulouse and then on to the central Pyrénées and the starting point of Le Chemin de la Liberté, in the small town of Saint-Girons. Naturally enough, as the war progressed, many other escape trails sprang up in this part of the Ariège, each one known only to its particular guide or *passeur*. Neighboring towns and villages like Foix, Tarascon, Aulus-les-Bains, Massat, Castillon, Seix, and Seintein all had a network of invisible mountain routes leading upward to the Spanish frontier. Of the 33,000 French *évades* during the war, 782 of them escaped over the mountains of the Ariège, the high point being in June 1943, when there were 113 successful evasions.

But at the beginning of 1943, due to increased German surveillance and often betrayal by Frenchmen who worked for the feared and hated Vichy-run paramilitary force known as La Milice, ambushes along many of these trails became more and more common. In all, more than a hundred *passeurs* were arrested and deported or shot out of hand as they tried to flee across the mountain slopes.

But even during the years of high surveillance, our Saint-Girons–Esterri escape route via the soaring massif of Mont Valier, stayed operational and remained so until the end of the war.

It was reopened and inaugurated in 1994 as an official way-marked hike with a difficulty rating of grade 3 (British equivalent, grade 5).

Bonne chance, bon courage, et bon voyage!

Scott Goodall
Saint-Girons, Ariège, France

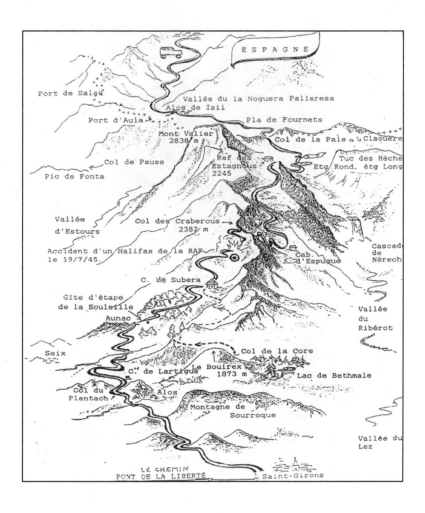

IRISH BLESSING

May the road rise to meet you,
May the wind be always at your back.
May the sun shine warm upon your face,
The rains fall soft upon your fields.
And until we meet again,
May God hold you in the palm of his hand.

PROLOGUE

What has come to pass…

Joe Turner, a.k.a. "Sonny," had taken off from a humble pea field in northern France. His mission to deliver radios to the partisans in France as part of Operation Bodyguard was a success, but it came with a price. He had left Henri, a man he had come to consider his adopted father, behind to await his death in that very same pea field from which his plane had lifted off.

Sonny returned to New Hampshire, joining the navy as a medic. He had seen enough killing, and at an early age. His desire to heal was now much stronger than his desire to kill.

But the past is a hard thing to escape, and Sonny occasionally found himself called back into the spy business by his former liaison, Major Scotty Smythe. Major Smythe called upon him time and again to help MI-6 with his expertise in biological warfare and parasitology. He was one of the few specialists in his field during the Cold War.

Sonny spent his time analyzing the different methods used by their Communist opponents and offered suggestions for defeating them. He traveled from South America to the barren deserts of Egypt looking for clues and meeting with double agents. In the end he was successful in preventing countless deaths.

He had lost Charlène, the little girl he swore to protect, during his mission in France. It wasn't until years later that he discovered she had survived. The truth was even hidden from him, to protect her.

Sonny's mission to destroy evil, which began with Charlène as a little girl, would lead to events that would change their lives in unpredictable ways.

At present, Henri has let himself into a trap to save Sonny's life. He is wounded and surrounded by SS soldiers bent on revenge that war engenders in those who are forced to fight in them. Henri had committed the worse offense—he had killed one of their own.

HENRI

This was the eve of the D-Day invasion, June '44. Henri Gibert knew he would die on this night before the Allied landings. Waffen-SS soldiers, elements of the Leibstandarte Adolf Hitler Division, were hot on his trail, meaning to kill or capture him. He would not be taken alive. Death was preferable to torture by the Gestapo.

His intent was to sacrifice his life so that his young protégé, Sonny, could escape. They had made their way into the enemy positions in order for Sonny to board a plane for England.

Henri watched as the plane struggled through the pea field, bouncing on the uneven terrain. The mists swirled violently around the single-engine plane as if trying to hold it on the ground.

Come on, Henri thought, get out of here.

Finally lifting off, the small plane dragged the mist with it, slowly gaining altitude. In the distance he could hear shots being fired. Bullets were ricocheting off the craft's wings.

The pilot pulled the yoke back sharply, and the plane rose in altitude and slowly disappeared from view. Henri could see the enemy's tracers follow the plane, but luckily no more bullets found their mark.

Good, Henri thought. I will die knowing that young man will make it.

The SS soldiers burst through the woods and fired at Henri, wounding him in the leg. The force of the bullet hitting him threw him to the ground. He crawled over to a downed tree and examined the wound. It was deep, and it was bleeding profusely. Henri pulled a handkerchief from his pocket and stuffed it into the wound as best he could. The pain was debilitating, and it sent shock waves through his entire body. Henri passed out for a few moments but came to as the SS started to cross the pea field in his direction.

***

Henri had just lost two of his best partisans, Marie and Sergio. Marie died caught in a trap, betrayed by Sergio. They were assigned the mission to gather intelligence on the V-2 rocket complex located at Foret d'Éperlecques, near Watten, France.

Sergio and Marie spent many hours together during Operation Bodyguard delivering radios to the Free French and Maquis partisans. Marie had revealed too much to Sergio during those missions. Thinking him a friend, she tried to help by giving out safe house locations and those involved in the resistance. It was a terrible mistake.

In truth, Sergio was gathering intelligence for the Nazis, and Marie was a pawn to him. In the end, Sergio shot his former comrade in the back.

The Abwehr had bought his allegiance and asked him to hunt down and help capture Henri and his team.

After Marie's death, their contacts in MI-6, a British intelligence group in charge of Operation Bodyguard, warned them of Sergio's betrayal.

British intelligence had already broken the German Enigma codes and had intercepted an Abwehr agent's radio transmission referring to a Spaniard and his successful mission.

Major Scotty Smythe of MI-6 immediately knew who they were talking about. MI-6 had long suspected that Sergio was a double agent but needed more proof. Sergio had volunteered for Operation Bodyguard because he knew MI-6 was closing in on him. His team of Nazi Abwehr spies were scattered among the coastal English ports. Their mission was to report on any invasion preparations by the Allies. But, unfortunately for Sergio, they were all quickly caught, before they could report their findings.

For the time being, Major Smythe's superiors argued it was best to keep him under a watchful eye. Perhaps to the allies advantage?

Nevertheless, Major Smythe, against orders, sent a single-engine courier plane to bring Sonny and Henri safely back to England. Luckily for Sonny, the major did. Had it not been for Smythe's disobedience, Sonny would not have survived.

Henri had refused rescue. This was his home, and he wasn't going to leave on the eve of its liberation from Nazi occupation.

Sergio had followed and confronted Henri and Sonny on their way to rendezvous with the plane, seeking to capture them and turn them over to the Gestapo. A short fight ensued, and Sergio was trampled by Henri's horse and left to die.

Henri had picked up Sonny and other members of MI-6, who were part of Operation Bodyguard, an operation that was used to make the enemy believe the invasion of France was to take place in Pas-de-Calais. Henri first met Sonny in England and brought him by boat across the English Channel, traveling into France south within Pas-de-Calais.

While traveling at dusk to deliver radios, the team came across a scene where two enemy soldiers had just shot a man and woman and were about to shoot their daughter, a little girl about nine years old. Sonny had jumped up from his hidden position behind the hedgerows and killed both enemy combatants.

Henri felt a deep sadness about Sonny, only seventeen years old, a young kid from America, arriving in France only to be thrown into that terrible situation just minutes after landing.

Running over to the little girl, Sonny picked her up and carried her into the forest. It was at this time that he was changed from a young kid to a young man who was destined to have many days of terrible memories.

At that moment a very strong bond was formed between the girl, Charlène, and Sonny, a bond that Sonny would carry in his heart for many years.

***

Henri Gibert was cornered; the Waffen-SS had reached the forest on the far side of the pea field, surrounding him. They fired in his direction with deadly precision as they moved forward, pinning him behind the tree. Thinking he could escape into the darkened woods behind him, Henri tried to stand but collapsed as a surge of pain shot through his leg. It felt like the bullet had cut into tendon and bone. His only option was to take as many of les bosch as he could, before they killed him.

"*Que Dieu me guide*," Henri mumbled as he braced his rifle as best he could on the old tree stump, returning fire on the approaching soldiers.

Henri realized in horror that he had been outflanked when he was suddenly pinned down by two Germans who were approaching from his left.

In response, Henri yanked two hand grenades from his tunic, pulling the pins.

"I see *Der Führer* has sent his finest to me," he shouted as two Germans closed on his flank. "Come and get me, *cochons!*" he yelled as the grenades flew from his hands.

The blinding blast and shock wave of the explosion showered Henri with dirt and small stones as the two enemy soldiers crumbled to the ground, one screaming in pain and the other torn apart by the blast, only a few feet away.

Henri aimed his rifle at the screaming German and put a bullet in his chest, killing him instantly.

Pivoting his rifle back toward the approaching soldiers, Henri took out two more, but as he aimed at a third, the rifle replied with an audible click, his magazine empty. He reached for his extra clip but realized it lay out of reach.

If only I could reach those weapons, Henri thought, gazing at the MP-40 machine guns several feet away by the dead soldiers.

His wound prevented him from moving at all, and as the Nazis closed in on his position, Henri was resigned to his fate; the enemy would show no mercy. He slowly slid back into a sitting position, letting his rifle slump to the ground. Henri gazed up at the night sky, bright with red tracers and blinding bursts from ack-ack guns that silhouetted planes and parachutes, descending on Pas-de-Calais.

L'invasion du Pas-de-Calais, Henri mused, I hope *les bosch* believe it!

Henri considered crawling to the wood line, but the attempt just sent waves of pain through his body. *C'est fini*, I will die here, he thought.

Henri had been part of the French Forces that had come to the rescue of Belgium when Germany invaded that country in a ruse to trap the Allies. German general Heinz Guderian, commander of the XIX Corps, personally led the attack that traversed the Ardennes Forest, crossed the Meuse River, and broke through the French lines at Sedan. Guderian's panzer group then raced to the coast, splitting the Allied armies in two, thus depriving the French armies and the British Expeditionary Force (BEF) in northern France and Belgium of their fuel, food, spare parts, and ammunition.

Henri and the rest of the Allied forces fought a losing battle, but they fought nevertheless. Henri was ordered to evacuate, even though he wanted to stay back as part of the delaying force to allow the Allies to escape to England. Two French divisions remained behind to protect the evacuation. They fought valiantly to defend their homeland and to allow the bulk of the trapped forces to escape to England. Although the lead French divisions halted the German advance, they were soon captured. The remainder of the French rear guard, protecting the beaches, surrendered on June 3, 1940.

Suddenly behind Henri the dark forest exploded brilliantly with gunfire. Turning, writhing in pain from his leg, he could see American paratroopers and French partisans emerging from the wood line, cutting a swath through the enemy formation. They brandished Thompson submachine guns and .45-caliber pistols. The firefight was quick and brutal, catching the Germans completely off guard.

When the firing stopped, the field was littered with the dead and dying enemy.

Lieutenant Robertson led this team, consisting of Sergeant Billy Waldron, a medic from Iowa, and Sergeant Tony Rizzo, an explosives expert from New Jersey, out from the cover of the forest.

A single paratrooper ran over to Henri when the fighting was over. He had with him a medical bag with a red cross over white that he tossed to the ground by Henri's feet. "Do you speak English, sir?" the young man asked.

"*Oui*," Henri informed the young American. "My name is Henri. I am with the Free French. You are here in time to join my little party." Henri managed a pained smile.

"What do they call you?" Henri continued in his best English.

"My name is Billy. I am the team's medic and can help you, Henri." Opening a packet of sulfur, Billy sprinkled it over the wound. "The sulfur will prevent infection."

"*Merci, merci beaucoup.* Perhaps you have some Cognac in your pouch?" Henri joked, knowing full well that having a bottle of Cognac would be a miracle. "I could use that *maintenant.*"

"I have something better," Billy stated, pulling out another small packet. Removing the paper wrapping, he gave Henri a shot of morphine. "That should kick in shortly."

Billy then retrieved two small branches from the tree line and tied them to each side of Henri's leg with cloth bandages, immobilizing it.

Sergeant Billy Waldron started the war as a medic in his local National Guard unit in Iowa. His father, a widower since

Billy was three, was a well-respected doctor and did not want William to enter the service before finishing his degree in medicine at Des Moines University. Billy had been adamant though; he wanted to be where his country needed him, as a medic treating the wounded. Since his enlistment, his relations with his father had soured. Waldron's father wanted his son to be the doctor he had become, powerful, a pillar in the community. Billy had seen his enlistment as his duty to his country and despised his father's status. After Billy's enlistment, the two no longer spoke.

Lying there, a familiar figure appeared above Henri.

"Ah, Madeleine," he said.

"*Oui, mon chéri,*" Madeleine replied. "Did you think I would leave you in a pea field?"

"I see you brought friends." Henri smiled broadly.

Madeleine continued with a sparkle in her eye, one Henri had not seen in a very long time, "Henri, I heard the first lines of Verlaine's poem, *'Chanson d'Automne,'* on the radio."

"Les sanglots longs des violons de l'automne, Bercent mon coeur d'une langueur monotone," she recited.

"It has begun, *mon chéri!*" she exclaimed.

"*L'invasion, enfin!*" Henri said.

"This Jedburgh Team is working with the Special Air Service under the same mission we have been conducting to fool the Nazis. We are to guide them to rejoin their comrades,"

Madeleine continued. "We need to get you to my house to recover. You are in no shape take care of yourself."

With that assertion, Madeleine went over to the lieutenant she had been talking to and pointed at Henri. There seemed to be some kind of argument, but in the end the lieutenant acquiesced to Madeleine's request.

Sergeant Waldron returned to Henri, commenting, "Sergeant Rizzo and I fixed you up a makeshift stretcher. The lieutenant and that Madeleine lady want to get you to safety and out of harm's way immediately."

The lieutenant approached the two men. "Henri, my name is Lieutenant Robert Robertson. Call me Robbie," he said with a thick Texas drawl.

"*Bonjour*, Lieutenant," Henri answered back curtly. "But we need to leave *immédiatement*! This is a very dangerous area. I have been told that the bosch Fifteenth Army and a Waffen-SS division have been positioned north of the Seine."

"Yeah, we know the German Fifteenth Army and the SS Division are there to counter against any Allied landing in the Pas-de-Calais. But, I reckon, Mr. Henri, they never met the likes of this Texan," Lieutenant Robertson said. "Case in point over yonder." He nodded to the field of dead.

Henri continued solemnly, "They will be looking for these bosch you have killed. Your courage cannot stand against their panzers and their weapons. Can you take me to my farm? There you and your men can hide while I tell you more about the bosch and their positions."

"You're right, Henri; I just hate to leave a fight," the lieutenant said.

"*Oui*, I agree," Henri replied.

"Well, if the krauts are gonna have conniptions and throw a hissy fit, I reckon we should be moving, Henri," Lieutenant Robertson replied.

"Madeleine will lead the way. She knows their patrols," Henri instructed, wincing in pain as Sergeant Waldron and Sergeant Rizzo placed him onto a makeshift stretcher.

"Everyone follows the lady," Lieutenant Robertson ordered. "Keep your spacing, gentlemen. I don't want the krauts taking us out in one blow."

The going was slow, and they proceeded as if every rock and tree hid the enemy.

Madeleine led the eclectic group on a path that ended up behind the farmhouse. The paratroopers fanned out to secure the area.

Lieutenant Robertson gave the all clear to Madeleine, who led this unusual team into a cave whose entrance was cleverly hidden behind dense vegetation.

JOB OFFER

Jack Turner surveyed the scene in silence. The cemetery was serene and peaceful after the fresh snowfall. Jack had just visited his father's grave and had slowly made his way back to the parking lot.

He had been the only visitor in the cemetery on the cold winter day, when he saw a gray limousine drive in and pull up to his father's grave site.

He watched as an old woman with an obvious limp in her right leg knelt at his dad's grave. What the hell? Jack thought. Just who is this woman? She certainly wasn't at Dad's funeral.

He watched as the woman cried at his father's headstone. My dad must have meant a lot to her, Jack thought. But I've never met her. The woman looks like she'd be about ten years younger than Dad. She looks very chic, very French, like a petite Jacqueline Kennedy.

He watched as she got back into her limo, the driver helping her in.

The limo slowly maneuvered around the narrow paths making its way to the exit.

Wait, she's French! Jack raced through the parking lot to his father's grave just as the limousine entered the main road. Several rose petals had floated onto the pathway leading to the grave site. A gift card was lying in front of a vase of roses. Jack picked up the red petals and rubbed them between his fingertips. He glanced down at the card. It read: "Thank you for keeping your promise to take care of me, Sonny. My love always, Charlène."

Jack unconsciously rubbed the scar above his right eye. Charlène was not dead? The biggest secret had never been told. Maybe his father was right two years ago, and the secrets should have not been revealed.

Jack held onto the card as he walked back to the parking lot. I have to find her, he thought, but how?

Pulling out his keys, Jack was about to get in his SUV when a black sedan pulled up next to him.

Nothing unusual for a cemetery, he concluded, but the hairs on his neck stood on end.

A man wearing a black fedora and woolen trench coat stepped out of the car.

"You Jack?"

"Yeah, sorry, and who might you be?" Jack replied.

The man in the black coat removed his wallet and presented Jack with a badge with the word "CIA" written on it.

"The name is Jean, Jean Aubrac," he revealed.

"Nice to meet you, Jean," Jack stuttered. "Am I in some kind of trouble?"

"Not in the least, my friend. As a young man in France, I knew your father and his companions. I am now semiretired, but it helps to show off the badge to get one's attention." Jean laughed, diffusing the tension.

"How did you know my dad?" Jack inquired tentatively.

"Let's get out of this cold and into my warm car, and I'll explain everything," Jean offered.

Tentatively, Jack went around to the passenger door, opened it, and got inside.

Turning to Jack, Jean began. "I was an orphaned farmhand working for my aunt during the war in France. My parents were killed by the Nazis, and she kindly took me in. I met your dad at her farmhouse in 1944 during the occupation. The woman you just saw drive away is my boss; her name is Charlène. After the war she joined the CIA and was a very effective operative during the Cold War. I met her after some time in the service myself," Jean said.

"My father talked about Charlène and what the Nazis did to her during the war," Jack commented.

"Did he tell you the whole story?" Jean asked.

"My dad was very cryptic, but now that I understand his secretive background, I can see why. Can you tell me more about her?" Jack asked.

"I can tell you what I know," Jean said. "Charlène's father, Maximilian Shemesh, was a tailor by trade, and her mother, Rita Falcon, was once a famous chef who ran a patisserie in

Versailles, but after she married her husband, she gave up that life to help in the tailor shop. She also worked part time at the *bibliothèque* there, or as you call it, the library, because she loved books and history. They lived upstairs in the brick building that housed her father's tailor shop.

"Charlène attended the local convent-run school until the Germans bombed it. After that, her mother stopped working at the library so she could tutor Charlène at home. Charlène once told me that her family had fled Versailles in the back of a run-down truck five weeks before she came to live in Bergues, where she met your father in those unfortunate circumstances. Her father made very stylish wool and silk suits for Manon Vuitton, a local banker. He came to their home one night and handed her father a list with his name and Charlène's on it. Mr. Vuitton said the Germans were rounding up Jewish families and taking them away in trucks and trains and they should leave immediately. Charlène said the Gestapo didn't care that her mother was French. But because her father was Jewish, she would be taken to concentration camps with other Jewish children and put to death."

"How sad," Jack commented. "Even the children?"

"Yes, especially the children," Jean answered. "She remembered that her father had told her that her grandparents died in Poland and that he had a brother who went to America before the war and lived on an estate in Virginia."

"Does Charlène still live there?" Jack asked.

"Yes, over the years we have worked together, hunting down Nazi war criminals and traitors to France from that estate in Virginia. We have been very successful."

"Good information. I understand now why Dad was so protective of her," Jack commented.

"She has had a tough life, but it has steeled her for the job at hand," Jean replied.

"What job is that?" Jack asked.

"Jack, your father was right; *they* are still here," Jean answered. "You saw what happened with Gisele. Her grandfather was a butcher, and she carried on the fight against you and your parents."

"What do you want from me?" Jack asked. "I have done my part."

"I understand you are still unemployed, correct?" Jean asked.

"Unfortunately, I can't find a job with the way the economy is these days." Jack grimaced.

"Your father and mother served our country well, and I understand this may be a bit fast, but I can get you a job with the CIA, as a last favor to your father," Jean remarked. "You of all people understand how these people think and operate. We need new blood to continue the fight against this evil."

"I appreciate the offer, but after my father's passing, I am not sure I want anything more to do with this whole spy thing," Jack responded.

"Believe me, I understand, Jack, but if you should change your mind, here is my card. Call me anytime." He handed Jack his business card.

"Is it possible to meet Charlène?" Jack inquired hopefully as he got out of the car.

"Consider the job offer, Jack, then we can talk about that," Jean said.

Jean started the black sedan, backed up, and hit the gas. The car left in a hurry, circling around the granite cherub fountain, and was lost quickly from sight among the gray mausoleums and sculptured head stones of the old cemetery.

Jack was inspired; in one day he found Charlène and got a job offer. Would wonders never cease?

REFUGE

Madeleine moved forward in the cave, motioning for the group to join her. The lieutenant recognized the familiar sight of wine bottles stacked in racks and others laying flat in long rows on the dirt floor. Madeleine pushed at a rack of wine bottles and the wall sprung forward a crack.

Pushing her way through the wine rack doorway, Madeleine guided them into Henri's secret cave. She led everyone through the darkness, lighting a lantern that illuminated the carved stone. Strange shapes and the grotesque forms of their bodies danced on the walls as the light reflected throughout the cave.

As they moved, the Americans spotted enough food supplies to outfit a company of men. In other areas, storage spaces had been carved out of the rock to house weapons, ammunition, beds, and linens provided by local farmers for resistance groups needing a place to hide.

The lieutenant eyed a strange assortment of weapons in the underground stash, dating from pre–World War I to the present day.

Henri explained that most of the weapons in the cave were from private collections. Some, he said, were from supply drops and downed Allied aircrews passing through the area.

Entering a large open area, Madeleine excused herself and disappeared through a wall into the farmhouse. She reappeared a few minutes later with Henri's sister, Antoinette.

"Henri, *mon Dieu!* What has happened? *Mais, tu est blessé!*" she exclaimed, rushing over to his side.

"*Fais attention*, Antoinette," Henri said. He winced as Antoinette hugged him furiously.

"*Mon Dieu*," Antoinette whispered. "What have they done to you?"

"I have done much worse to them," he said proudly.

"We must care for his *blessure séance tenant*," Antoinette said, turning to the lieutenant.

"*Messieurs*, I am Henri's sister, Antoinette," she announced. "I see one of you is a medic, *oui*? Can you help Henri? I am ready to help too."

"Ma'am, do you have some fresh water?" asked Waldron.

"*Oui, suivez-moi*," Antoinette replied, leading the medic past the wall of wine and through the fireplace.

"Quite the house of tricks ya got here, Henri," Lieutenant Robertson commented.

"It is necessary, *mon ami*. The Nazis are vengeful, ruthless pigs, or *cochons* as they are fondly referred to by we French," Henri replied. "A refuge when *les bosch* are hunting us down."

"I have heard of other hideouts being discovered, Henri. Why haven't they found yours?" Robertson asked.

"Actually they did, Lieutenant, from the cave side." Henri chuckled. "But they stopped at the wall of wine that hides the inner cave. I think the Bordeaux distracted them!"

"Where do you come from, Lieutenant? Your accent is quite interesting," Madeleine asked.

"I'm from Texas, ma'am," he said with pride.

Lieutenant Robert "Robbie" Robertson went on to explain he grew up in Big Spring, Texas, famously known for the crossroads of Highway 20, Highway 87, Highway 350, and the Missouri Pacific line. It was named for the big spring in Sulphur Draw, where for centuries coyotes, wolves, buffalo, antelope, and mustangs had come to drink, and which had been a source of conflict between Comanche and Shawnee Indians, as well as a stop for settlers on the Overland Trail to California. His colorful description of his home state of Texas fascinated Henri and Madeleine.

He went on to say that he helped on his father's farm, rising early each day to milk the cows before he headed off to school. Standing six foot three, Robbie was a good kid who worked hard on the farm and at school. And one day he expected to take over the family farm and continue the tradition of passing it on to the oldest son.

That all changed on December 7, 1941, when America's and Robbie's innocence were shattered, Robbie's and the country's ire peaking while President Roosevelt gave his "a date which will live in infamy" speech.

Robbie enlisted the very next day. That was 1941. Now, three years later, he was a lieutenant in the Office of Strategic Services, the OSS. The lieutenant and his team had volunteered to be part of a three-man Jedburgh Team to be dropped by the Carpetbagger air force behind enemy lines for Operation Titanic in the Pas-de-Calais. They worked with the British Special Air Service, (SAS) on this mission.

The SAS had the main part of the operation, but during the initial stages of the operation, they had lost two planes, along with their teams, on the crossing.

Under orders from Major Scotty Smythe, MI-6, Lieutenant Robertson and his team were to contact Henri and Madeleine, organize them into a greater force, and redirect their efforts to assist in the invasion of Normandy by delaying the redeployment of the powerful Fifteenth German Army stationed in the Pas-de-Calais area.

"We were dropped with some paratrooper dummies, nicknamed 'Ruperts,' to fool the krauts that this was the invasion site, and to organize the partisans in the area to delay the krauts. But we are scattered all across France," the lieutenant explained.

"LT, let's hope those Ruperts did the job!" Rizzo remarked.

"Let's hope so, Tony. I feel like all hat and no cattle surrounded by all these dummies." He chuckled. "Present company excluded of course," Robertson quickly offered in response to the dirty look Sergeant Rizzo gave his way.

Henri continued, "You may use my house as a base if needed, and Madeleine can help get you back to England. I have radio equipment here. I ask only that transmissions be less than thirty seconds. The Nazis are using radio tracking equipment and may monitor partisan activity."

Henri knew the Americans would pay a heavy price to liberate his country. The Nazis were well entrenched and had some of their best units in northern France. He hoped the many partisan groups could work together to make a difference in the upcoming battle.

Antoinette soon reappeared carrying a bundle of white sheets, followed by Sergeant Waldron carrying a pot of water, his medical bag thrown across his shoulder.

Sergeant Waldron immediately began tearing sheets into long strips, laying them down beside Henri. He carefully removed a packet of sulfur from his medical case and sprinkled its contents on Henri's wound.

"I need to get that bullet out before it festers in you," Waldron explained. "Has the morphine kicked in yet?"

"I am still feeling pain," Henri said.

"Perhaps I can help," Antoinette said. She got up and went over to the shelf to retrieve a bottle of eau-de-vie, a colorless distilled fruit brandy with a high alcohol content. "*Allez bois*, Henri," Antoinette said, holding his head up while administering the vintage drink.

"*Merci*, Antoinette. *Ca fait du bien*," Henri acknowledged.

Sergeant Waldron was able to remove the bullet, but Henri had lost a lot of blood. Waldron did note that Henri's leg wasn't broken; the bullet had just grazed the bone. He could recover sufficiently enough to leave in days, not weeks as first imagined.

Antoinette stayed with Henri as Waldron worked on his leg, holding his hand and comforting him through the pain. Madeleine was not far away, watching intently as Waldron finished stitching up Henri.

Wrapping the last bandage around Henri's leg, Waldron sat back on his haunches. "That's the best I can do in these conditions. He should rest for a least a week."

"We may not have that luxury," Madeleine stated. "The bosch will be searching this entire area for you. We should get him to my farmhouse, further south. We will be safer there."

Lieutenant Robertson said, "Billy, can we move him in twenty-four hours?"

"He's lost a lot of blood, LT. He'll need to regain his strength before he goes anywhere," Waldron explained.

Covering Henri with a warm woolen blanket and laying a cool wet cloth across his forehead, Antoinette stood up and said, "You must all eat. I will be back with food," adding as she left, "Henri, *repose-toi bien.*"

Sometime later, Antoinette appeared from the secret entrance to the house with a tray of breads, cheeses, and coffee that smelled delicious, which she placed on the table in the center of the cave. "It is not much, but please sit and eat," she said, offering a seat to her guests.

Sergeant Rizzo first looked at Lieutenant Robertson, and with a nod from him, he dove into the tray like a hungry wolf. "Forgive him, ma'am. He seems to have forgotten his manners," Robertson apologized. "Thank you for the fixin's," he added.

"No apologies, Lieutenant," Antoinette said. "It is I who apologize to you for not having a proper table setting for dinner, but please enjoy my fixeens, as you say." She laughed, returning through the secret fireplace exit and closing it behind her.

"Ma'am," was all the lieutenant could get out before Antoinette disappeared.

Sergeant Rizzo could sometimes be a bit brash and annoying, but he was the best at what he did. He had been in his father's construction business when the Japs bombed Pearl Harbor. His knowledge of explosives while working in the family business got the attention of the army unit he had trained with, and he quickly was transferred to an engineer unit. When the opportunity arose to be part of the new Office of Strategic Services organization, Rizzo joined as an explosives expert on the team led by Lieutenant Robertson. Rizzo constantly grated against the Texan, but Robertson soon learned how valuable and loyal Rizzo was to his team. He grew quite fond of the younger sergeant, in his early twenties, and took him under his wing.

Everyone in the group rested over the next day in the underground sanctuary. A few times German patrols searched the area, even once knocking on the door. Antoinette remained poised as they searched the farmhouse to no avail.

Madeleine walked up to Henri and spoke softly to him. "Henri, Charlène is still alive and will recover in time."

"How did you get her away from the Gestapo?" Henri asked.

"We removed her from the house in a coffin, so the bosch think she is dead," Madeleine explained.

"*C'est bien.* Will she be moved to your farmhouse?" Henri asked.

"*Oui*, I have already made arrangements," Madeleine replied.

"And Sonny. Did he fly back to England? Did Sonny get off OK?" Charlène asked.

"Yes, he did. Now we need to tell him about Charlène. He would want to know she is alive," Henri said, grabbing Madeleine's sleeve to emphasize his words.

"*Bientôt, mon chérie, bientôt.*" Madeleine consoled him. "*Alors, repose-toi bien. Ta blessure est profonde.*"

Henri had fitful, feverish dreams that night. He dreamed of Charlène, arriving too late to save her. His mind replayed the nightmare throughout the night:

Henri and Sonny entered quietly through the Portieres'
back door, careful not to be seen. At her kitchen table, Celeste
sobbed uncontrollably as Pierre grasped her in a hug to keep
her from falling.

"I could not protect her," she choked out through her
sobs. "Those monsters tortured her. They held me on the floor
and pointed their guns at me. I was thrown to the floor with a
gun to my head."

Sonny felt his entire body turn icy, as if all blood had
flowed out of his body. He and Henri rushed upstairs to find
Charlène in a small bed, her face so swollen and bruised she
was unrecognizable.

Pierre said, "They came when I was working in the fields
away from the farmhouse. They hit Celeste with a gun, tied her
mouth and hands, and threw her on the floor while they
tortured Charlène for information. Les bosch broke leg, arm,
and hit her face and head with rifle."

Celeste came up to gently push back the hair framing
Charlène's face that was matted with blood. "I tried to scream
for them to stop through the handkerchief they had pushed into
my mouth, but they would not stop," she said, whimpering as
she recollected the horror of that afternoon.

When Henri awoke the next morning, his fever broken and
his body soaked from sweat, the last words he heard from
Charlène that night were still ringing in his head.

"Je n'ai rien dit, je n'ai rien dit…"

Henri awoke to the beautiful face of his sister smiling at him.

"*Toute cette nuit*, we were worried about you, Henri," Antoinette said.

"You did not sleep, Antoinette?" Henri asked.

"*Non*, Henri," she replied. "And you talked during the night. But now I can tell you have no fever."

Sergeant Waldron, seeing Henri awake, came over to check on him. "You're a lucky man, Henri. I wasn't sure if the fever would break or kill you. Glad to see ya made it."

"*Merci*, Sergeant. *Pardon et merci*, Antoinette," he said as he grasped Antoinette's hand.

After feeding Henri some soup, Antoinette went up to the kitchen to prepare food for the Americans and Madeleine's partisans hiding in the cave. Waldron administered another dose of morphine to Henri, covering him back up with a dry blanket. Henri was soon asleep.

By the next day Henri attempted to sit up and move to the table, amid Sergeant Waldron's protests.

Waldron moved to assist Henri.

"I can move, Sergeant. *Je me sens beaucoup mieux*," Henri grumbled. "I cannot remain still anymore!"

Henri motioned for Lieutenant Robertson to sit at the table. "We should contact Major Smythe, Lieutenant; he'll probably want to know that my team has been compromised, and want to redirect your team," Henri said.

Henri pointed to the radio set up in the corner. "Remember to make transmissions short; *les bosch* have tracking equipment. If possible, send a message for Sonny that the little one is safe."

"Will do, Henri," Robertson replied, moving to the radio.

"Madeleine, get my maps in the drawer," Henri requested.

Madeleine moved over to an old beaten-up oak dresser and took out a roll of maps.

Spreading out the maps onto the table, Henri and Madeleine spoke softly to each other as the lieutenant dialed in the frequencies to MI-6.

Henri heard the familiar tones of Morse code as the lieutenant tapped out his message. Sharp tones sounded faintly through the speaker as the operator in England instructed the lieutenant in code. *Continue as planned; help Dada in whatever he needs.* Robertson replied, *Wilco, will keep you posted.* As per Henri's request, Robertson informed MI-6, *Tell Sonny the little one is safe.*

Turning off the radio, the lieutenant sat down at the table with Henri and Madeleine. "Major Smythe wants us to continue to help you, Henri. We are in your hands now. What would you like us to do?" Robertson asked.

"We have to leave. *C'est certain*," Henri replied.

Madeleine agreed. "If you stay the Nazis will find you. They always do. Bring Antoinette and your farm boy, André, to my farmhouse. They will be safe there, and you can recover properly."

"This is my home, *ma chérie*. I hate to leave, but I agree with you. We must go."

"But what if Madeleine's house is not safe from the krauts?" Robertson asked.

Madeleine said, "Then we must leave France and make our way to North Africa or England."

"But the fight is here, Madeleine, in France, and it is here I want to be!" Henri insisted.

"We live to fight—oh, how do you say in your language, Lieutenant? Ah yes, I remember—we live to fight another day, Henri. We will return to see the bosch thrown out of France!" Madeleine reassured him.

Madeleine, Henri, and Lieutenant Robertson turned their attention to the escape maps Madeleine had pulled from the oak dresser, which were now rolled out, pistols acting as paperweights to keep them from rolling back up. They discussed the safest route to get the group out of the country. The first option, Switzerland, was tempting, but they agreed that would put them out of the war for the duration.

"Switzerland is out of the question," Madeleine said as the lieutenant was tracing a route there with his finger.

"Why?" he asked.

"I want to return as soon as possible," Henri stated. "If we go into Switzerland, we won't be able to come back until France is liberated."

"I don't understand," Robertson replied. "It's much closer, and you are still free."

"*Oui*, but we will be useless to our France when she needs us most. The country is surrounded by Nazi-occupied territory and is filled with their spies. There is no way for us to get out, neither by walking nor by air—a prison in itself. If we go into Spain, and on to North Africa to fight with the Free French Forces there under General LeClerc, or make our way to England, at least we can return to the fight," Henri explained.

"Whatever you think best, partner. It's your backyard," Lieutenant Robertson replied.

"The best choice is one of the underground escape routes to Spain, through *les Pyrénées*. It is the escape route of American and British aircrews who have been shot down," Madeleine said. "The Germans may know some routes there, but many other routes are still good for those who need to escape. Especially now, since the Spanish government with Francisco Franco does not stop evaders from France crossing into his country. The Allies are beginning to win the war, and Franco wants to be a winner too," Henri said.

"And I have many contacts to the south to help us along the way, Lieutenant," Madeleine added.

Various escape routes to Spain were discussed over the next few hours. Henri's first choice was the Comète Line, on the western side of France, but it would be risky since the invasion had begun and Vichy and German forces would be watching the coastlines.

They ultimately decided to take the O'Leary Line through Saint-Girons. Even though that line had been compromised in 1942, it had recently reopened and seemed to be the best option. Once they made it to Spain, they could contact the British Embassy in Madrid and make their way to England, provided the Spanish did not arrest them. Even so, some escaping into Spain only spent six weeks at the most in jail before their embassies secured their release.

"It is decided then," Henri announced. "The O'Leary Line through Saint-Girons is our best chance."

Sergeant Rizzo entered the cave from his guard duty outside the entrance. "Fog's rolling in, LT; hard to see anything out there."

"Keep your head on a swivel, Rizzo. Use your ears instead of your eyes!" the lieutenant chided him.

"Right, LT, you're asking the explosives guy to listen," Rizzo smirked.

A glare from the lieutenant had Rizzo retreating outside.

Lieutenant Robertson checked over his gear for the trip as Sergeant Waldron attended to Henri, chiding him for not keeping still.

"You'll split those stitches, Henri. Take five, will ya?" Waldron preached.

"I will be fine, Sergeant. I have had worse days in the French army," Henri replied.

Madeleine excused herself to go upstairs to tell Antoinette of their plans and help her prepare for the journey. Studying the ceiling for a brief moment, she said, "Where is that latch?"

"On the left, ma chérie," Henri said.

"Ah, merci," she replied. Searching for the spot, she pulled a well-concealed latch downward. A trapdoor opened, and a rope ladder fell toward her.

Madeleine climbed the ladder. With a small thud, the trapdoor closed. Adjusting her eyes in the darkness, she pushed the wall in front of her, entering through the fireplace.

Closing the wall behind her, she paused momentarily to observe Henri's study. It was cluttered with books of every size and shape. They were pulled from the shelves and scattered everywhere. It was almost as if Henri had been trying to research something in a panic.

Walking into the kitchen, Madeleine greeted Antoinette with a kiss on the cheek.

"How is Henri?" Antoinette asked.

"He is in good hands with the Américains," Madeleine replied. "He is a strong man, Antoinette. He will be fine."

"He is a stubborn man," Antoinette said.

K.E. Pottie

"And right now, that is a good thing," Madeleine replied. "We need provisions for a five-day trip. We have to carry them, so we must take items that do not take too much space."

"*Oui*, Madeleine, let me get something to carry the food in," Antoinette said.

Gathering up what provisions they could, Madeleine helped Antoinette wrap the food in makeshift cloth bundles torn from the sheets in the house.

"I do not like to tear apart such fine linens," Antoinette said. "The bosch must pay me back!"

Madeleine smiled. "We all have our own ideas of how we will live after the war is over, *n'est ce pas*?"

"Just as long as I get my sheets," Antoinette said.

Hearing a commotion outside, Madeleine went back downstairs to open the front door, but André, the farm boy, burst into the room before she got halfway there, a look of panic on his face. "A unit of Germans with a listening truck is headed this way, *madame*!"

"They must have heard the Lieutenant's radio transmissions earlier. How far away are they?" Madeleine asked.

"Only a few kilometers down the road," André replied. "I was bringing the horse in from the fields when I saw the top of the listening truck through the fog. It is pointing to the farmhouse."

"We are out of time, Madeleine! We must leave now," Antoinette warned.

"André should come with us. He has no place to go and will be in grave danger if he stays behind," Madeleine said. "I'll go tell the others to get ready."

"*Oui, je suis d'accord.* André, go to your room and pack your bag," Antoinette instructed.

"*Merci, madame,*" André said, hurrying off to his room on the second floor.

Madeleine reentered the cave. "André has seen a German truck with radar a few kilometers down the road, and they are coming this way. We must leave now."

"The krauts must have picked up on the radio transmission," the lieutenant said.

"They have been monitoring the area for some time, trying to pick up on any partisan radio activity," Henri said.

"I am sorry, Henri. I tried to keep it short," the lieutenant said.

"Any transmission puts us in danger, Lieutenant. They have found us. Now we leave for Madeleine's farm," Henri said.

Madeleine, Antoinette, and André entered the cave carrying various items for travel: food, water containers, sheets shredded for makeshift bandages, and a small bag of clothes.

"We need to get out now!" Madeleine interrupted the men. "They are almost here!"

Everyone turned their attention to Henri and Sergeant Waldron, the medic.

"I bandaged him up as best I could, LT," Sergeant Waldron said. "He should be OK as long as we take it easy."

"Come hell or high water, it'll have to do," Robbie observed. "Rizzo, take point with Madeleine."

"Point?" Antoinette asked as she went past the lieutenant.

"Means he gets to go up front and lead, ma'am," Robertson said.

Madeleine and Rizzo led the group out into the foggy morning, followed by Robertson, Antoinette, and André, who led a packhorse with Henri mounted in the saddle. Finally, two of Madeleine's partisans brought up the rear.

The wispy morning fog intermittently obscured the small group and was a blessing. It hid them well from the advancing lights of the Germans.

As they proceeded southeast toward Madeleine's farm, they could hear the rumble of mechanized vehicles approaching Henri's farmhouse.

"We got out of there just in time, Madeleine," Rizzo whispered.

"We're not out of the woods yet, Sergeant. Keep pushing forward," Madeleine whispered back. "And be silent."

48

As they moved swiftly through the fog-shrouded fields of a wooded area, they saw the truck, its radar dish protruding from the fog and headlights barely visible.

"It's a good thing we have this cover," Rizzo whispered to Madeleine as they pushed closer to the wood line.

"*C'est sûr*. Any later in the day and we would have had to fight our way out," she quietly replied. "Sergeant, we need to be quiet. Please follow me and ask your questions when we are safely out of range." Under her breath she whispered, "Américains."

Madeleine guided the group onto a trail leading into the forest and out of sight from the approaching vehicle.

"This trail will take us most of the way to my farmhouse," Madeleine whispered to the Americans. "I have used it many times to move refugees south, and *les bosch* have not discovered it."

Safe under the cover of the morning fog, they moved deeper into the woods.

Behind them, SS storm troopers arrived at the farmhouse and kicked in the front door. After the room was inspected, they signaled the all clear to a man in a black leather trench coat. The Gestapo agent surveyed the room and barked at the soldiers, "Find that radio!"

The SS turned the house upside down, discovering nothing of consequence. With a shrug the Gestapo agent ordered the farmhouse be torched.

***

Antoinette walked beside Lieutenant Robertson. They marched through the overcast morning toward Madeleine's farm. She liked the tall Texan and felt safe in his presence.

"We'll be walkin' in tall cotton if the krauts keep their attention on your farmhouse," Robbie whispered to Antoinette. "You know, sometimes I wish I were back in Texas tippin' cows at Uncle Eddie's farm." He chuckled softly.

Antoinette didn't understand a word the Texan was saying but smiled politely and nodded anyway.

How did I ever git myself into this catty whompus? the lieutenant wondered.

STEAK AND A SHOT

Emily was late that night for dinner. She must be working on some major have-to-get-it-done project as usual, Jack mused. He was getting used to the idea of a nine-to-five with the CIA. It would be awesome! Even if it was just working in a field office surrounded by paperwork, however small the paycheck, it was better than being unemployed.

As Jack sat at the kitchen counter contemplating the possibilities, he saw Emily's car through the front bay window pull into their driveway. The sudden realization that he was supposed to have prepared the salad for that night's dinner sent him scrambling for the fridge. He simultaneously grabbed a head of lettuce and a bowl from a nearby cabinet. Tossing them at the same time on the counter, he grabbed a wooden cutting board and proceeded to rip the lettuce quickly with his hands, dumping an ample amount into the bowl just as the front door opened.

"Where is everyone?" Emily shouted into the quiet house.

Sassy, their German shepherd, suddenly jumped up from her nap, barking toward the front door.

"Some guard dog you are," Jack chided her before yelling around the corner, "In the kitchen." He grabbed some cucumbers and tomatoes, adding them to the pile on the cutting board just as Emily walked into the kitchen.

"Hey, sweetie," Emily said as she walked up and planted a kiss on Jack. "I see you forgot to make the salad again."

"Guilty as charged," he replied. "But well on my way to making a fantastic salad à la Jack."

"What do you do all day?" asked Emily.

"Sorry, I was at the cemetery today visiting Dad," Jack said. In the silence that followed, Emily noticed that Jack's eyes were moist, sudden tears welling up in his eyes.

She gave Jack a big hug. "It's OK, dear. I know you miss your dad. Here, let me help. The good news is that I brought home some london broil; it was on sale at the grocery store."

"My kind of salad!" Jack laughed.

For the next few minutes, Jack and Emily finished preparing the salad for the evening meal.

Jack said, "Mmm, and maybe some caramelized walnuts, dried cranberries and blue cheese as well in the salad?"

"Of course!" Emily said. "Pour me a glass of wine please?"

"What color?" Jack said.

"White, the chardonnay on the counter," Emily replied.

Emily turned to the cabinet by the stove and pulled out a variety of pans to cook the evening meal.

"How come you use so many pans?" Jack teased. "I think I wash more dishes than any man alive!"

"I never hear you complain about my cooking!" Emily retorted, giving Jack a peck on the cheek.

"Good point," Jack said sheepishly. "I'll go set the table."

Looking at the pans, she rethought how to prepare the meat. "I think I'll put the london broil on the grill, so you're off the hook tonight. But be a dear and light the grill for me, will ya?"

"And set the table too?" Jack mocked.

"Such talent," Emily said.

After quickly setting the table, Jack went out on the deck and started the grill. While it was heating up, he re-entered the kitchen, retrieving the chardonnay from the wine fridge and poured more into Emily's glass.

"Please watch the steak for me while I finish the salad," Emily said after placing it so it would cook to her liking.

"Of course, I get that job," Jack said.

Staring at the steak for several minutes, Jack called into the house, "When will it be thumb ready? It's cold out here."

"In two minutes," Emily said.

Only we would cook outside in the middle of winter, Jack thought.

Long ago, Emily had watched a cooking show that explained if the steak felt as if you were pressing on your thumb, it would be medium rare. Jack had always doubted that theory, but Emily's touch had been dead on every time.

Emily appeared once again by the grill carrying a large fork and platter for the steak.

Jack stepped aside to let the chef take over.

After a quick press of the meat, Emily pronounced the london broil ready. She placed the meat on the platter and then turned off the grill and closed the lid.

By chance, Jack chose that moment to bring up his encounter with CIA agent Jean Aubrac.

On hearing the word CIA, Emily lost her footing on the icy deck. With a look of sheer terror on her face, she dropped the steak platter into the snow.

Sassy, who had been lying in the snow nearby, a frozen puddle of drool on the ground before her, jumped at the opportunity. Before Emily or Jack could grab the london broil, Sassy was chewing on their dinner.

"Damn it!" Emily blurted out.

"Emily, are you OK?" Jack said. "I'm sorry. I should have told you when you first got home I had a job offer as a reward for Dad's service. I was approached by a guy name Jean Aubrac, and he offered me a job at one of the local offices."

"Jack, why would you do this to us again? The whole ordeal with Gisele has me jumpy," Emily said. "I don't think I can handle living that kind of life. It's already affecting my job. I'm afraid they are going to fire me."

Jack embraced Emily, kissing her forehead.

"I promise that won't happen again, Em," he whispered to her. "It will be a nine-to-five job.

"Promise?" Emily asked.

"Sure thing, kid." He smiled.

"When do you start?" Emily asked.

"I haven't told them yes yet. I wanted to make sure you were OK with the whole idea."

"I am all for two incomes again," Emily answered. "Just not one that involves shooting."

"I can always tell them no, Em," Jack replied.

"No, you should do this, Jack. I don't think we have much choice. Times are tough, and we are falling behind in our bills. We need the income. Just make sure it's office work, please."

"OK, I promise. Now can we go celebrate at the High Tide?" Jack asked, trying to lighten the mood. He thought they had the best prime rib anywhere, and Jack wasn't a salad only kind of guy anyway.

"Sure, why not," Emily acquiesced. "But only if you take that job. Eating out is getting expensive!"

"Deal!" Jack agreed. "I'll call them in the morning."

Heading out to the car bundled up for winter, the couple joked and smiled about what they would be able to pay off with the extra money in the house. Jack had an extra bounce in his step knowing he was finally going back to work, and it felt great.

The road to the High Tide had a sheen to it tonight. Black ice, Jack thought. He could hear his dad's warnings about the dangers of black ice echo in his head.

The High Tide in winter was always nice. The summer tourist crowd was gone and everyone knew each other. Jack and Emily were greeted by several patrons and the owners as they pulled up to their usual bar stools. They were greeted by the bartender Tommy as they sat down.

Tommy's real name was Tomas, a man of Spanish decent in his midfifties, but here at the High Tide everyone just called him Tommy. He was well liked by everyone who patronized the restaurant. He never did talk about his past, most folks just never asked. Instead Tommy always turned the topic back to current events.

"The usual, kids?" Tommy solicited.

"Yep," Jack responded. "Amber beer for me, and a martini straight up for Emily."

"Sounds like a plan," Tommy said, turning around to make their drinks.

"Prime rib tonight, the usual twenty ounce, Jack?" Tommy posed without turning around.

"Of course. Need you ask?" Jack replied.

"I'll take one too, but make mine the fourteen ounce, Tommy," Emily said.

She rarely ordered the prime, usually asking for a chef salad. Both Tommy and Jack were amazed at the change of routine.

"We're celebrating," Emily tried to explain. "Jack has a job offer!"

"Congratulations!" Tommy said as he handed the couple their drinks. "May I ask with whom?"

"I haven't accepted yet, but it's with that new finance company in their IT department—just up my alley," Jack replied.

"Oh I see," Tommy said. "Congratulations."

Jack slipped up, "I imagine I'll be stuck doing paperwork in some clerical office. Never been the spy type, Tommy."

"Nor would I want you to be, Jack. Too many whackos out there these days," Emily said, emphasizing the word whackos.

Tommy laughed behind the counter. "You may say that again, especially here during the summer." Turning solemn, he said, "I remember the English man. What was his name, Scotty? Sad what happened to him in the parking lot. It was the first time I can recall that anyone was murdered in this town."

"He was a good friend of Dad's." Jack stared into his beer. "I miss them both."

Emily rubbed Jack's back. "We all do, dear."

"You dad always complained there was never enough Jack Daniels in his drink," Tommy said as he turned to attend to another request further down the bar.

At the other end of the bar, Tommy paused and surreptitiously pulled out his cell phone. He typed in a message and pressed the send button.

An impatient patron at the bar yelled over to him, "Hey, Tommy, got my beer yet?"

"Be right there, Dave," he said, closing the cell phone and stuffing it in his pocket.

Jack and Emily ate their dinner, enjoying the company of old friends, everyone talking about how nice it was to get a bar stool at this time of year. It may have been a rough winter, but a nice meal sitting at the bar with a fire going was heaven as far as they were concerned.

The High Tide was emptying out early tonight as Jack and Emily stayed a bit longer, talking with Tommy and Linda, the owner of the High Tide, about the player trades for the Red Sox and Yankees and the upcoming wine tasting they always loved to attend.

Linda Zack opened the High Tide several years ago. When she bought the old run-down bar, it was filled with drunks and locals. It had once been the jewel of the town. Over time she resurrected the High Tide, and now tourists from all over New England stopped in to dine and enjoy her five star–rated restaurant.

Around eleven, Emily mentioned to Jack that they should be getting home.

The phone in Tommy's pocket began to vibrate. He pulled it out of his pocket and flipped it open. The message read "CIA." With a smile he closed it again and placed it back in his pants pocket.

At about the same time, Tommy announced to the group he was leaving soon as well.

"Great. Thanks, Tommy," Linda said. "See ya tomorrow!"

After a few moments, Jack and Emily headed outside, with Linda leaving by the front door. Linda slammed the old door shut and then locked it. They talked briefly as she got in her car and drove off, the couple waving to her as she drove down the icy road into the darkness.

Jack stood a moment taking in the winter sky, a backdrop of stars above their heads.

"Whatcha thinking about, dear?" Emily asked.

"How crazy the past few years have been. At least the stars remain the same," Jack said.

Jack grimaced as he thought back to that horrible night Gisele had kidnapped Emily. He had played those events in his head time and again. Jack wished he had had the courage to take matters into his own hands with Gisele. He knew she had been out to kill his father, but he had felt helpless and done nothing. Once again the scene replayed in his head.

They had finished their wine with Gisele at the High Tide, Emily declaring it was time to call it a night. "I have an early meeting tomorrow morning," she said, pushing her chair back.

As she stood up, Emily stumbled forward, knocking over the vase and the empty wine glasses on the table. "Whoa, guess I had too much to drink," she mumbled groggily.

"Maybe we should help her out," Gisele said to Jack.

"That's OK, I can get her," he said. But Jack was feeling light-headed, and his arm felt numb, so he accepted Gisele's help, despite his reservations.

They flanked Emily, holding her by her waist as they walked out of the restaurant to the rear of the parking lot where Gisele had parked. "Can you hold Emily for a minute while I open the passenger door for her?" he asked Gisele.

She nodded, and he walked to open the car door. When he looked up, he saw Emily slide from Gisele's grasp and drop to the ground. Jack raced around the car to rescue Emily.

He didn't get far. Jack felt his head explode as a hard metal object smashed the right side of his face.

Jack's last view with his left eye as he fell to the ground was Gisele's long legs in high-heeled shoes dragging a very still Emily into the backseat of her sedan.

Gisele opened the glove box, withdrew her grandfather's Walther PPK, and deftly screwed on the silencer. She walked to the rear of the sedan, where Jack was lying facedown in the mud, his hair matted with blood.

Jack was brought out of his daydreaming by Emily.

"Jack, I know what you are thinking, and there is nothing you could have done that night," Emily stated.

"I know, Em. It's just that I should have done something!" he replied emphatically. "Maybe now with this new opportunity I can do some good."

"I am pretty sure you won't be hunting down spies, dear," Emily said.

Seeing the hurt look on his face, she leaned against him and gave him a sweet kiss on the cheek. "But I am sure you'll do a great job for them."

"Thanks, gorgeous." Jack winked at her.

"Let's get into the car quick. It's cold out here!" Emily said.

The wind was beginning to whip around the parking lot, snow blowing in their faces. The leaves not cleaned up from the previous autumn were frozen into the snow and ice. They looked out of place in the wintery setting.

Grabbing hands to avoid slipping on the ice, they walked over to unlock the car. Jack noticed it leaning heavily to the left.

"Damn it!" Jack said. "Flat tire!"

Emily bent down to examine the tire more closely and stood up suddenly.

"Jack, I am scared. This tire's been slit," Emily said.

Jack looked around to see if anyone else was in the parking lot. They were alone and vulnerable, the blowing snow gradually covering the black pavement. Are we being watched? Jack thought. The High Tide bordered some railroad tracks, and a heavily wooded area was located on the far side. This was déjà vu for the couple. Jack was surprised and relieved to see Tommy behind the restaurant tossing some garbage into the dumpsters. He had thought the bartender had left a good quarter of an hour before.

"Thank God you're still here, Tommy! We need your h—" Jack started to say but then paused abruptly as Tommy approached.

Tommy stopped several feet away from the couple. He had pulled out a gun!

Jack instinctively pushed Emily behind him as Tommy raised the gun and pointed it at the couple.

"I am afraid this time I cannot let either of you go," Tommy said.

"Tommy, why, what's going on? I don't understand. Did we do something to you?" Jack asked. When Tommy did not reply, Jack got a bad feeling. "Did you slash our tire?"

"You killed Gisele, my partner, Jack. It's been hard to live without her and see you and Emily come into the restaurant and enjoy yourselves. Now it is time to take my revenge," Tommy said bitterly.

"Tommy, please don't," Emily cried out. But their answer was a blinding flash as the gun discharged, the bullet striking Jack in his left shoulder. Falling to the ground, Jack heard a second shot and a scream from Emily. Then the world turned black.

***

As Jack regained consciousness, his vision began to clear, and the bright, harsh light of a hospital room came into focus above him.

Beside the hospital bed were his mother Claire and the man he recognized from the cemetery, Jean Aubrac.

He was groggy and unable to make out his surroundings.

"Where am I? What happened?" he asked. "I can't think. Everything is a blur."

"It's the anesthesia," Claire said. "That will clear in a few days."

"Mom, is Emily OK?" Jack asked as he tried to rise from the hospital bed, pain immediately surging through his whole body.

"Jack, Emily is alive, and you must rest. You have a bad gunshot wound. You're lucky. The bullet just missed your heart," Claire explained.

"Where is she? Can I see her?" Jack said.

"I'll ask the doctor. I am sure we can wheel you in. But there is a problem, Jack." Claire paused before continuing.

"Jack, Emily has suffered severe trauma to her head." Claire tried hard not to cry, as she had done so frequently during the past few days.

"Oh no," Jack said. He was thunderstruck and was unable to rouse himself again for a few moments.

Claire moved closer to Jack's bed and let him bury his head in her arms, and she held him as they both wept. Finally, the pain in Jack's arm forced him to gasp, and he fell back into the pillows on the hospital bed, unable to move.

"How bad is the wound?" Jack asked.

"Jack, the wound is deep. It passed through your body," Claire explained. "You will come out of this, but it will take time to recover."

"Mom, I tried to protect her. I wish I had just pushed her out of the way."

"Jack, you did your best. If it wasn't for you shielding her with your body, she would be dead."

Jack was silent. He tried to think back, placing himself in the parking lot. He remembered.

After a while, when the pain subsided, Jack said, "All I can remember is that the bartender at the High Tide, a guy named Tommy, slashed our tire and then shot us. He said he was working with Gisele. I should have seen it. He must have been the one who slashed our tire a couple of years ago. Are the police investigating this? Who is looking for him?"

"Jack, we need to keep this quiet. The company will handle it," Claire said.

"The company?" Jack asked.

"The CIA, Jack," Claire whispered.

"Why not involve the police?" Jack asked. "They could help us. They investigated the last time our tire was slit. Maybe they can help."

"We will find Tommy, Jack," the man in the dark suit and overcoat said from the corner.

Jack focused on the blurry figure sitting in an easy chair. He slowly sat up to face him. It was Jean Aubrac, the CIA agent he met in the cemetery.

"Agent Aubrac? Why are you here?" Jack asked.

"We take care of family," Jean said.

Jack was stunned. He was now with the CIA, like it or not.

"And to answer your question again, we will find him. It's only a matter of time," Jean replied.

"How?" Jack asked. "He's probably long gone now."

"We have all the resources of the government, Jack," Jean said. "He's out there. We will find him."

Jack's shoulder ached painfully.

"Jack, you were shot in the shoulder. The wound is not serious," Jean said.

Claire glared at Jean. "Less clinical, please."

In truth the Frenchman just didn't know how to be tactful. He had been in the spy business too long.

"My apologies, but he has to learn to deal with this, Claire," Jean replied.

"He's right," Jack said. "I need to get past the pain and on my feet to help Emily."

The next few days were a blur to Jack. Although the wound was not life threatening, the morphine drip allowed him to rest. He was comforted by his mother, Claire, and Agent Aubrac being by his side, each taking turns watching over him. In the hallway two men in dark suits stood guard outside his room.

On the third day, the medical staff took him off the morphine. The doctor instructed the staff to put Jack on a steady diet of pain medications and antibiotics. The dressing was removed daily, his wound checked for infections and rebandaged.

Later that day Claire entered his hospital room and sat by the bed.

"How are you feeling today?" she asked.

"Better," Jack said. "But the staff won't tell me anything about Emily. Do you know anything?"

"I didn't want to say anything earlier, Jack, but she was in critical condition. She is doing better now, but she is not out of the woods yet," Claire replied.

"Please talk to the doctors for me. I would really like to see her," Jack said.

"I'll talk to the doctors today. I am sure now that you're in stable condition they will allow it," Claire said.

Jack closed his eyes for a moment, unable to process anymore. Claire grabbed Jack's hand and glanced over at Jean. "He should know, Jean."

Jack interrupted before Jean could speak. "Know what?"

"Jack, we suspected the bartender Tommy had been working with Gisele all along. After Gisele was terminated, we did not think he would reveal himself to you, not wanting to blow his cover. We knew he was probably sympathetic, but after her death we did not see him as a danger. So, instead, we kept on eye on him," Jean explained.

"After all that had happened, I would have expected you would tell me!" Jack said.

"I am sorry, Jack, but after what happened to your dad, we accepted the wisdom of your mother that it was best to keep this situation quiet. Do you remember anything that would make Tommy reveal himself to you?" Jean asked.

"I am not sure," Jack stammered.

"Jack, what is it?" Jean asked, seeing the torment on his face.

"I told him I had a job offer with a local finance company. I don't know how he could have connected me with your job offer to work for the CIA," Jack said.

Jean was about to explain, but it was Claire who spoke first. She looked at Jean.

"Jean, I believe we agreed that Jack was not going to work for the CIA. Didn't we agree it was just too risky for him? And for Emily? Now look at this situation! What have you started?" Claire said.

She was furious with Jean, and he knew it.

"Claire, I am sorry. I don't know how Tommy put two and two together. I should have told Jack not to say anything about his job offer."

"You have a mole," Claire said.

"That's possible, but everyone associated with this operation has checked out," Jean said. "I've known them all for years."

"Then you need to check again," Claire admonished, "because someone has betrayed us."

"I did. I felt it was time to bring Jack into the operation," Jean said.

"But why bring him in, Jean?" Claire asked. "The bosch would have left them alone. Jack and Emily were not worth taking the risk of being exposed.

Jean said, "When Jack was told that Charlène was alive, I thought it best to bring him in, before he said anything."

"Well, look at the result," Claire said. "Your timing is horrible, and I hope my daughter-in-law will recover from that mistake."

"Mom, how do you know Jean?" Jack inquired.

"Jack, have you heard of the Maquis?" Claire asked.

"Sure, when I was doing research on Dad, I ran across the name. The Communist partisans, right?"

"Yes. As you now know, I had been working for the Communists and was turned into a double agent by your father, with whom I fell in love. Jean's parents were Maquis and suffered greatly at the Drancy internment camp toward the end of the war. They did not survive. I met Jean's Aunt Liliane after the war while working as a Soviet spy. What I didn't know is that Liliane had turned her back on Communism and I was exposed. Luckily your father fell in love with me and helped me come to America. While I was being retrained, I met Jean."

"Did Dad know Charlène was still alive?" Jack asked.

"Yes he did, although he never told me," Claire said.

Jack glanced over at Jean.

"Your father got word that Charlène was alive after the war, Jack. Charlène was working with us at the CIA for some time before he found out. At first Charlène wanted to find your dad, but she was told that no records were ever kept of his whereabouts. It was Scotty Smythe who approached your father to give him the good news. It was a very emotional and joyful event when they met," Jean explained.

Jack fell silent. He had heard the story of her death from his dad but never imagined she was alive, or that they had met up years later. What a reunion that must have been, he thought to himself.

"Where is Charlène now?" Jack asked. "You mentioned that if I take the job I could meet her."

"She has an estate south of here in Williamsburg, Virginia. I intend to take you and Emily there as soon as possible, for your safety," Jean informed him. "You can meet her then, Jack."

"Jean, they shouldn't be moved. It's too risky," Claire said.

"Claire, I don't trust anyone here. We have our own doctors, and they will be safer at the estate. Arrangements are in motion."

At that moment a nurse came into the room. "Good, you're awake, Mr. Turner," the nurse said. "How do you feel?"

"The pain is a bit much. How bad is the wound?" Jack asked.

"Dr. Wainright said you will recover soon enough, but the wound is serious. He wants you to rest up," the nurse instructed.

"I want to see my wife, Emily," Jack said.

Claire spoke up before the nurse could respond. "I have told him of her condition, nurse."

"Oh, I see. Is Mrs. Turner your wife?"

Jack said, "Yes, of course she's my wife. Nurse, I need to know. Can I see her please?"

"I will have to ask Mrs. Turner's nurse to see what her doctor thinks. I'll get back to you as soon as I know," the nurse said as she turned to leave.

Jean, brandishing his badge, addressed the nurse before she reached the door. "Nurse, I am federal agent. The couple is to be moved to one of our undisclosed facilities today for their safety."

"I am afraid you cannot move either one of these patients without permission from their doctors. You may be risking their lives," the nurse replied.

"You have no choice. A medical team is on its way now to transport them both. Please get Emily and Jack ready now for traveling," Jean directed.

"I strongly object. I will have to tell my superiors about this!" the nurse said as she left the hospital room.

"You have such a way with women," Claire said.

"Je sais," Jean replied.

"Jean, what about my mother? She needs protection as well," Jack said.

"I am capable of taking care of myself, Jack. Besides, Sassy will be there for my protection as well as company." Claire smiled.

Jack was baffled. His mother seemed different somehow, but he just couldn't figure out why. Now how can Sassy protect Mom from danger? he thought. Sassy is an easygoing canine with a heart of gold. I don't understand. But then the pain slowly returned and distracted him from his train of thought.

Jack lay in the hospital bed in a daze. Emily, my God, what have I done? he thought. How could I have been so stupid to think this was all over after Gisele was killed? I should have never taken Dad to the lecture she gave at the Elks club. We could have all been fat, dumb, and happy, living out our ignorant lives. But Dad did tell us what happened, and how could I not go down this path? I can only pray that you are going to recover, because if I lose you, I've lost everything.

A man with a full head of shock white hair entered the room. He was wearing a US Navy tan uniform, covered by his white doctor's smock.

"Hello, Jack, I'm Dr. Matus, from Bethesda Naval Hospital. I was the surgeon who operated on your wife, Emily. We had her in the operating room for several hours, and she made it through. She has a serious head wound, and we need to watch for brain swelling. Also, I am afraid there may be some memory loss. When she came out of the anesthesia, she did not know her name. We are waiting for her to wake up fully, and even then we will not know the extent of her injury."

"Do you think her memory will return, Doctor?" Jack asked.

"Only time will tell. In most cases it does, but the bullet struck her in that part of the brain responsible for memory and cognitive thinking. She survived the surgery, and my hope is that she will make a full recovery." He accentuated his words by putting his hand on Jack's shoulder.

"Thank you, Doctor. Can I see her now?" he asked.

"Yes, I'll make arrangements to bring you to her. But you must understand that she may not know who you are. You have to be patient. If she awakens during your visit, you should not let her know who you are. Remember, when and if her memory comes back, let it be on her terms."

Half an hour later, Jack was lowered into a wheelchair by two nurses. His shoulder was throbbing with pain, but he willed himself not to back down from his visit. Maybe if he was lucky, he thought, she would be wake up and recognize him right away.

One of the nurses wheeled out him of the room and down the corridor toward Emily's room. Dr. Wainright joined them, and Claire and Jean followed.

Two nurses ran by them; alarm bells were going off. One nurse looked back at Dr. Wainright and said, "Room 258. It's Mrs. Turner!"

Dr. Wainright started to rush down the corridor but suddenly stopped, turning to the nurse pushing Jack. "Take him back to his room."

Jack tried to stand. "Let me up!" he shouted. "What's going on? Is Emily OK?"

Claire gave a worried look to Jean. "Jack, she is in good hands. We can visit her later."

That night Emily Turner, aged forty-two, passed away from complications of a gunshot wound.

FLIGHT!

The group traveled south through Tielt and Waregem, Belgium, and then moved on through the forested areas of Vieux-Condé and Denain, in France.

Just as the early mist was fading, the morning sun rose gloriously over the horizon. The partisans and the Americans arrived at Madeleine's farmhouse just southeast of Cambrai.

They were greeted by two young farmhands, who ushered them quickly into the comfort and anonymity of the three-hundred-year-old house. Gathering up the reins to Henri's horse, one farmhand disappeared behind the barn.

Madeleine's home was far removed from any major roads, and German activity was minimal out here in the country. Still, the hills have eyes, as Madeleine was always saying, and it was best to keep silent and unobtrusive in this part of occupied France.

Madeleine operated covertly from her farm and had been lucky enough to escape notice by the Gestapo. She had been extremely careful to ensure that she was not exposed by double agents, making sure she knew any who wanted to join her operation. Her country house was akin to Henri's, with the exception that her hidden place was just below the heavy dining room table through a trapdoor. From there a tunnel went on an east-west axis to a rise aboveground in the woods that opened into a small group of rock outcroppings. The entrance was hidden from view.

The tunnel had been used many times to ferry Jewish families, partisans who were compromised, and Allied pilots and their crews who had been shot down over France, passing them onward to the next safe house along their escape route, far to the south, through the Pyrénées Mountains and into Spain.

Her success at distributing radios and gathering intelligence for the Allied high command on German troop movements in the Pas-de-Calais area for Operation Bodyguard was only outdone by Henri and his team.

Henri had been a sergeant in the French infantry and was immensely proud of his service and his country's victory over Germany in World War I. That clouded his judgment; in fact, the whole army was certain they could not lose when France declared war on Germany after the invasion of Poland in 1939.

Things change. Wars and loves are lost. Henri did not surrender to the Germans in 1940 but instead spent time in England after rescuing dozens of men off of the beaches at Dunkirk.

One day in late 1940, he returned to France with the help of Major Scotty Smythe. Carrying his MAS 36 7.5 mm rifle, he arrived back at his farmhouse late one evening to the welcome arms of his sister Antoinette, who had waited for him since his departure. Henri at first wanted to be a recluse, as he was deeply affected by the death of his wife, Brigitte, and the utter defeat of the French army.

Antoinette was Henri's younger sister and looked up to her brother, whom she considered a hero. Their mother had died of cancer when Antoinette was very young, and her father had abandoned them after she was born. Henri was the only family she had known since childhood. Antoinette had married very young, but the marriage had not worked out, and her husband—not used to the farm life Antoinette loved so much—had moved back to Paris. Now in her early thirties, she was lonely and spent her time taking care of the brother she loved.

Then one day a young American lieutenant entered her life, and she felt something she hadn't in a long time. She liked that feeling and determined that she would do her best to get his attention once they were safe and free.

It was on June 18, 1940, when General Charles de Gaulle called for volunteers to fight the Germans from his exile in England. Many French, including Madeleine and Henri, were ignited by de Gaulle's passionate plea to resist, and they took up the initiative to form their teams and make contact with their English allies, especially the man they helped escape from Dunkirk, Scotty Smythe.

Major Scotty Smythe convinced Henri to help the Allies gather intelligence and hinder German troop movements in his area around Bergues in the Pas-de-Calais region of France in preparation for the invasion of France by the Allies.

At first Henri and Madeleine's partisan groups attacked German communications centers, railway lines, and headquarters, but the retaliation was swift and horrible, many innocents being brutally murdered by the Nazis. When their British and French counterparts in England found out about the sacrifice that the French people incurred because of these operations, they changed the mission of the partisans to gather intelligence only and wait for the day of liberation to strike. That was to come in June of '44, but for now the partisans would do what they could.

It was only recently that Henri and Madeleine were directed from Allied headquarters to support Operation Bodyguard, during which they met a wonderful young man by the name of Sonny. He was dedicated and intelligent beyond his years. Sonny taught them they were not alone or forgotten in their fight to free their country.

Now, after four long years, the liberation of France was finally at hand.

Together once again, Madeleine and Henri could make it through the coming storm to a new, free France.

Madeleine was in love with Henri. She visited him often after his return from England. Being a widow herself, she enlivened Henri with her weekly visits.

Seeing that she was pensive, Henri said, "You are deep in thought, *ma chérie*. What troubles you?"

Madeleine smiled softly at him. "*Rien, mon ami.* Just the idea of being free again. And that you called me *chérie,*" she said. Madeleine softly touched his cheek.

"As if you didn't know I love you," Henri answered playfully. "For the past four years you have watched over me after my wife's death. You brought me back to life, *ma bien aimée.*"

Madeleine was at a loss for words. Walking up to Henri, she hugged him tightly and gently kissed his forehead.

"You need to rest, *mon amour.* We must concentrate on escaping soon. When this is all over, we can lose ourselves in the moment. I cannot take you all over France on a stretcher surrounded by those loud *Américains!*" she said as she laughed.

Henri put his hand to her cheek and smiled.

Madeleine returned to the dining room, where the Americans had settled in for some hot tea, warm bread, and cheeses brought by Madeleine's housekeeper.

"I appreciate the hospitality, ma'am," Lieutenant Robertson said as Madeleine stood in the doorway.

"*Je vous en prie,* Lieutenant. We must take advantage of the food while we have the opportunity. Now you have informed us that the main landings in Normandy have begun, *oui?*"

"That's right. We're part of the diversion, designed to keep the German Fifteenth Army in Pas-de-Calais. In essence, Operation Titanic is part two of Operation Bodyguard."

"This is excellent news, Lieutenant," Madeleine said. "This will help us in the end, but we must remember we still have a dangerous journey to make through to the Pyrénées. We must remember *les bosch* are still on full alert."

"What will we run into in the mountains?" the lieutenant asked.

"The Austrians and the Vichy Milice units guard the border to Spain. They will be trouble. La Milice, as you know, is a paramilitary force created in 1943 by the Vichy regime. They are helped by the Germans, of course, to fight *la resistance française*. I believe they are like your State Guardsmen, Lieutenant. La Milice often tortures to obtain information. They are more dangerous to our resistance than the Gestapo or the SS because they are Frenchmen who speak the language and know the towns, the land, the people, and *les collaborateurs*. It will be a dangerous journey, and now that they know about the invasion, our journey will be more difficult," Madeline replied.

"We trust your judgment and leadership, Madeleine," Lieutenant Robertson said. "We will be ready for whatever happens."

"In the meantime, I suggest you and your men rest in my cellar. I have arranged for cots to be brought below so you can sleep with comfort tonight," Madeleine said.

"Thank you, ma'am," he replied. Turning to look at his team, he said, "All right, Rizzo. You can hit the sack if you wish. Waldron is taking care of Henri, and I can stay up a bit."

"If it is OK with you, Madeleine, I would like my men to stand guard with your people," the lieutenant said.

"Of course. Coordinate with Armand. Merci, Lieutenant," she said.

After Sergeant Rizzo retired to the cellar, the lieutenant stayed in the dining room to talk with Madeleine.

"We had always heard that times were tough in France. I am sorry we did not enter the war sooner to help you and your countrymen," Robertson said. "I only hope we can make up for the suffering the French people have endured during the occupation."

"No apologies, Lieutenant," she replied. "France has been through many wars. We shall be triumphant with this one as well. Our liberation is near. We finally have hope for our future and the future of France."

"Please call me Robbie, ma'am," the lieutenant asked.

"As long as you stop calling me ma'am," Madeleine retorted.

Smiling, Madeleine turned to walk toward the kitchen, almost bumping into Antoinette, who was carrying a tray with more bread, cheese, and hot tea.

Setting the tray down in front of the lieutenant, Antoinette explained, "I usually eat later than my guests. It is rude for me to eat in front of you, so I have brought food for us. Please join me, Lieutenant."

"Very kind of you, ma'am," the lieutenant said as Antoinette offered him a cup of tea from across the oak table.

"Please, Lieutenant, call me Antoinette," she said.

The pair from different worlds talked of their hometowns and upbringing, comparing farming techniques in Texas and France. Anyone observing the two trying to communicate with hand signals and drawings would have laughed at their attempt to break the language barrier they shared. Even with their differences, the two enjoyed the respite from the war by sharing stories of their homes. It was well past midnight when the couple excused themselves from the table to "hit the sack," as Robbie put it. He was excited and flustered at the same time, and did not fall asleep until it was almost dawn.

The group had decided to hole up for a few days once they arrived at Madeleine's farm. The delay was necessary to enable the partisans to transfer Charlène safely from a safe house in the region to Madeleine's farm.

On the morning of the second day, Madeleine approached the lieutenant.

"I have forged papers for everyone so you can get into Spain. They are without pictures, but with luck and bribery, you will not be stopped," Madeleine said, handing the lieutenant three documents.

"It'll have to do. Much appreciated," Robertson said.

He turned and went over to Waldron and Rizzo, handing them their papers.

Later that evening, a small partisan group arrived in a farm wagon. In the back was a coffin that carried their precious cargo—Charlène.

Battered and bruised from her recent torture by the SS and Gestapo, she had a patch over her left eye. A wicked scar ran across the right side of her head. Her left leg was in a makeshift cast as was her right arm.

Pauvre petite, Madeleine thought as she approached the stretcher, but Charlène's smiling face brought Madeleine out of her dismay.

Charlène spoke first. *"Je suis heureuse de vous voir, Madeleine."* After a short delay, Charlène spoke up again asking if anyone had information about Sonny.

Replying with a sad smile, Henri said, "Sonny has left for England, *ma petite*."

Charlène grasped Madeleine's hand, and tears began forming in her eyes. *"Qui le protégera maintenant?"*

"The English will take care of him now, *mon choux*," replied Madeleine. "Now we must get you to safety as well."

Madeleine directed the men to place Charlène in her bedroom on the second floor. Carefully lifting her off the back of the truck on her stretcher, the partisans made their way into the farmhouse as Charlène softly sang a familiar tune, recently taught to her by Sonny.

Close your eyes, little Charlène
Do not be afraid
Sonny's here, little Charlène
I won't let them hurt you
Do not be afraid
Close your eyes, little Charlène
Do not be afraid
Close your eyes, little Charlène
Do not be afraid
Sonny's here, little Charlène
I'll take care of you
They can never hurt you
Go to sleep, little Charlène
Close your pretty eyes
Go to sleep, little Charlène
Sonny's here; I'll take care of you
They can never hurt you

Antoinette helped place Charlène in bed, propping up the pillows and covering her with *un soft edredon.*

"Where did you learn that song, *ma chérie?*" she asked.

"Sonny taught it to me when I was hurt. *Ça me soulage,*" Charlène replied.

"Could you teach me to sing it to you?" Antoinette asked.

Sitting all evening, Antoinette rocked gently in the corner of Charlène's room, watching and humming Sonny's song until Charlène fell asleep.

Early on the third day, Sergeant Rizzo and his partisan counterpart, Armand, saw some movement off to the east while on guard duty outside of Madeleine's farmhouse.

"The Lieutenant and Madeleine need to hear about this. Watch the krauts. I'll go let them know," Rizzo said to Armand.

Moments later Sergeant Rizzo rushed to the makeshift bunk of Lieutenant Robertson.

"LT, wake up," Sergeant Rizzo whispered. "There's a kraut patrol a few clicks from here."

"Get everyone up and ready to go," Lieutenant Robertson commanded groggily.

Silently, Sergeant Rizzo turned back to inform the others.

As the Americans filed out of the cellar and into the farmhouse, Robertson was met by Madeleine.

"*Les bosch* are nearby. They must suspect something, Lieutenant," Madeleine stated.

"Maybe we should give them what they want," he replied.

"That would be unwise. There are too many, and we cannot fight for long without help," she explained.

"Do you think we can get out by plane?" the lieutenant asked.

"Before the invasion, I would say yes, but now…" Madeleine's voice trailed off.

Henri hobbled into the room on a crude set of crutches.

"Henri, you should not be up," Madeleine said.

"*Mais si!* I know *les bosch* are near, so I want to show you that I can come with you, Madeleine," he said. "I am feeling much better. I can keep up."

"But your leg, Henri. It will become painful to use during our escape," she said while examining his leg and locking eyes with Sergeant Waldron. "It will be a long, dangerous journey," Madeleine said.

"And this is something I do not already know, Madeleine?" he said, a bit irritated. "*La libération* is finally here. I cannot lie in bed and wait for it to come to me!" Henri emphasized his statement by hitting his crutch against the door, almost falling over in the process.

Madeleine was there in a flash, standing Henri against her body.

"I wouldn't dare keep you out of this fight, *mon chérie*," Madeleine responded. She bent to kiss his cheek.

"I am sorry, Madeleine," Henri apologized. "But we have been waiting for so long for this to happen."

"I feel the same," she replied. "But now you will have to be careful and wise," Madeleine said.

"Sergeant Waldron, are Henri and Charlène able to travel?" she said, still gazing at Henri.

"His wound will heal in time, but if I had my way, he would rest up for a few more days before getting up and moving around." Waldron continued with his clinical observation. "The leg is not broken as we first suspected. The bullet just grazed the bone. Henri and Charlène are able to travel, but we need to be careful with them."

"I do not believe we have a choice, Sergeant Waldron," Madeleine replied. "*Les bosch* will kill him if we leave him behind. I am not capable of having this on my conscience. So I will ask again, will he be well enough to travel, at least to the next safe house on our journey?"

"Yes, ma'am," replied Waldron. "I'll be at their side the entire time to help them."

"Thank you, Sergeant," Madeleine replied.

Madeleine said to the lieutenant, "Robbie, we will travel southeast to the next safe house in Saint-Quentin. There my friend and fellow partisan Liliane Aubrac will meet us. I will lead the way. Please have your men maintain silence unless it is absolutely necessary to speak for our survival," Madeleine said.

"Will do. All right, men, you heard the lady. Keep those weapons ready and get moving. Rizzo, take point up front with Madeleine."

"Again? I love you too, LT," Sergeant Rizzo said with a smirk.

"Feeling's mutual, Rizzo," Robertson replied.

Turning to the gathered assembly, Madeleine stated matter-of-factly, "I would have rather started our adventure at night, but it seems the enemy didn't like my plan. *Que Dieu nous bénisse.*"

Opening the trapdoor of the farmhouse, Madeleine led the group toward the wood line of a distant forest. Once out by the rock outcropping, their farmhand gave the reins of the horse to Madeleine. Lieutenant Robertson and Sergeant Waldron helped Henri and Charlène onto the horse. Antoinette took the reins, leading the horse. Henri sat high in the saddle with Charlène in front of him.

"LT, that Henri guy stands out like a sore thumb. The krauts will spot us," Sergeant Rizzo complained.

"We ain't got much of a choice, now do we, Rizzo?" the lieutenant said, glaring at the sergeant.

"Nope, but sure will be nice when we get where we are going," Rizzo said. "Shoot, LT, hard to take point when I don't know where I am heading!"

"This way." Madeleine smiled as she pointed down the forest road.

"Plain as the nose on your face, eh, Rizzo?" the lieutenant said.

Rizzo turned a bright red as he followed Madeleine down the path.

The first part of the journey was uneventful. The group made their way into the forest as rivulets of fog danced about their feet. On more than one occasion, someone in the group tripped on a tree root or took a misstep into a depression. About midday they came to a road bordered on each side by hedgerows that hid their movement should anyone be watching.

As they approached a forest, their goal to rendezvous with a partisan group that would guide them to Liliane's house fell short. A German motorcycle patrol was headed their way.

Henri, looking startled, whispered to Madeleine urgently, "I think they have seen me, Madeleine."

"Quickly," she whispered, motioning for everyone else to follow her into the forest.

"Henri, stay where you are. We will take care of them," Madeleine said.

The Americans and partisans blended into the flora of the forest. Madeleine turned toward Henri, holding her finger to her lips for him and Charlène to be quiet.

The audible click of safeties coming off was drowned out by the loud engine of the German motorcycle.

The motorcycle rounded the corner, a cloud of dust behind it.

A German soldier sprung from the sidecar of the motorcycle as it skidded to a halt on the dirt road. The other German stayed mounted.

In the forest Madeleine instructed her partisans with hand signals, designating who should fire on which German on the road.

The soldier walking toward Henri and Charlène eyed the pair with suspicion.

"Documents!" the German commanded.

"I am afraid in my hurry to get my granddaughter to a doctor, I have left them back on my farm," Henri replied. "She has had a bad accident on a horse this morning."

The German soldier was about to let them pass, but he noticed the blood staining Henri's pant leg. He had been told to look out for a wounded partisan and now thought he had found him.

"Descendez!" He pointed to the ground, lifting his MP-40 submachine gun toward the two.

From a distance, the crack of a rifle split the air, echoing from deep in the forest. The German soldier suddenly stiffened and fell to the ground; a bullet piercing the back of his head.

The mounted German soldier swung his MP-40 around, but a short burst from the lieutenant's tommy gun cut a swath across his tunic. The soldier slumped down across his handlebars, blood staining the fender, dripping into a puddle on the ground.

Charlène did not scream. She stared at the dead soldiers with disdain.

Madeleine turned to face the direction of the attack and saw another partisan group coming toward them in the forest. She smiled. It was her friend Liliane.

At the same moment, Henri and Antoinette moved into the forest, and Lieutenant Robertson ordered his men to hide the bodies and motorcycle in the forest.

"Hey, LT, can we keep the motorcycle? It might come in handy," Sergeant Rizzo asked.

"Too much noise," Robertson replied.

"Hey, it was worth a try. It would have been nice to have this baby for the trip south," Rizzo said.

"Too much trouble, Rizzo," Robertson said. "Now git 'er behind those bushes."

A group of four partisans, one woman and three men, made their way toward Madeleine. When they came close, Madeleine gave the woman a kiss on her cheek and spoke softly to her for a moment. The woman squeezed Madeleine's arm affectionately, and tears formed in her eyes as she nodded back.

"Lieutenant, this is my good friend, Liliane," Madeleine said, introducing a woman with beautiful wavy blonde hair that was partially hidden by a black beret. Her beauty was in stark contrast to the wicked Mauser Karabiner "Kar" 98k sniper rifle she had strapped over her left shoulder.

"Pleasure to meet ya, ma'am," the lieutenant replied. "That was quite a shot," he said, nodding to the dead German lying in the ditch nearby, adding, "and with their sniper rifle, too."

"I am giving them back their bullets." Liliane smiled. "One at a time."

"How kind of you," the lieutenant said.

"I do what I can, Lieutenant," she said.

Madeleine and Liliane whispered to each other briefly before Madeleine turned back to face Lieutenant Robertson.

"We need to leave this place now. The motorcycle patrols travel in pairs, and there will most definitely be another motorcycle nearby," Madeleine said. "Will Françoise meet us at the next rendezvous point?" she asked Liliane.

"She will be there. Even with her loss, she knows what she must do."

The Americans finished quickly covering the bodies with brush from the surrounding area. Liliane led them all down a trail at a brisk trot, deeper into the forest. Sergeant Waldron took the reins of the horse and followed the group.

After covering several kilometres, they halted briefly to ensure that the Germans had not followed. As they rested, Liliane brought a metal bottle containing water over to Madeleine and Henri. "And what of you? You and Henri cannot stay in France."

"We are not staying. Henri and I have agreed that we should take Charlène out of the country, possibly to America, where she will be safe. We will also guide the Americans into Spain to their embassy," Madeleine added.

"I am unhappy to leave before France is liberated," Henri said.

"You have accomplished much. You are much more valuable to France as a living patriot, and not a dead one," Liliane remarked.

"We will cross into Spain as soon as we can. Are supplies available for our journey?" Henri asked.

Hearing the conversation between the three, the lieutenant approached them.

They all turned to face the lieutenant.

"Lieutenant, I have ammunition at my farm if you need it," Liliane said.

"Much appreciated, ma'am. We are running low," he replied. "We need to go. When they find those bodies, this whole area will be crawling with krauts.

"I agree. We must leave this place," Liliane said.

"Who's got point?" Sergeant Rizzo butted in.

With a sigh, Robertson replied, "Who else?"

Sergeant Rizzo shot back with a wink, "We are a team, LT, come hell or high water!"

Henri did not miss the smile that flashed on his sister's face as she gazed at Lieutenant Robertson.

"Mon Dieu," Henri mumbled.

DARK SECRETS

It was a cold and damp January morning. With his mother, Claire, by his side, Jack watched the pallbearers lift Emily's coffin from the hearse and carry it to the gravesite. He was silent, too upset to talk.

The cemetery workers placed the coffin on a set of bands that was lifted by a hoisting device and placed hovering over the grave. It was then lowered so that the bottom of the coffin was just inches below ground level.

Claire was dressed in black. A veil, flowing down from a small round black hat, covered her face. She held on to Jack for support.

The priest intoned his words slowly as several friends stood nearby.

"Through faith we know that Jesus is at work among us even though we can't see it or measure it. Emily now sees and knows the mystery we are unable to find the words for. Someday we will know for certain the everlasting life that Jesus died to win for us. Holding onto that reality gives us the strength to carry on, if just for one more day."

In the distance, a man spied the group through binoculars, his breath creating icy rivulets in the air as he watched the coffin being lowered into the ground. Satisfied, he turned to get back into the limo.

"Vamanos!" he directed the driver.

"Adonde vamos, Señor Garcia?"

"Take me to the airport," he instructed the driver.

"Is your business finished here, Señor Garcia?"

"It is finished," Tomas replied. "Now go before someone spots us."

"Si, señor," the driver said as he put the car in gear and it lurched forward.

Garcia's car slowly moved down the icy back road, eventually disappearing into a wooded area.

When the funeral rites were completed, Jean escorted Jack and Claire to the waiting limousine.

Closing the door behind Claire, Jean spotted a glint of metal on the horizon. Can they never leave us in peace? he wondered.

Smiling sadly, he climbed into the limo and settled back in his seat as they headed over to Jack's house to get some belongings for his journey.

"Jack, I will have a moving company gather up your belongings and put them into storage," Jean explained.

"Thanks, Jean," Jack said. "I don't know if I'll ever use anything in the house again. Too many memories."

"You will someday," Jean replied. "I will make sure everything is taken care of."

Gazing out the window of the limousine, Jack was sad to think that everything he and Emily collected would now gather dust in some warehouse. He vowed someday to settle back into his home, once all this nasty business was over. Would it ever be? he wondered.

"How's Sassy?" Jack asked his mother, concerned about his dog because they had never been separated before.

"She's fine, Jack. She's getting used to my house," Claire maintained.

"Take care of Sassy, Mom. She is a good dog," Jack replied.

"Are you sure it's a good idea to go back to your house, Claire?" Jean asked. "I think you should come with us for your safety."

"I am too old to go traipsing around the country like the old days, Jean. If they want me, they know where to find me. Besides, Trudy will be spending some time at the house, and the company will be good for me," Claire replied.

"Are you sure that's wise to stay where they know you are?" Jack asked his mother.

"It doesn't matter where I go, Jack," Claire responded. "If they wanted to kill me, I would already be dead."

"Regardless, if you run into any trouble, call it in!" Jean said.

Claire nodded her head in agreement.

Everyone was silent for the remainder of the drive to the house, each person recalling fond memories of their lost loved ones.

When they arrived at Jack and Emily's house, it seemed hauntingly empty and quiet. Jack had tears in his eyes as he gazed at the landscaping that Emily had given him as a present to keep him busy. He thought back to that happier and blissfully ignorant time.

Every evening when Emily opened the car door in their driveway, Jack prepared for the first words out of her mouth, "I brought you something!" to which Jack would reply only half teasing, "Great! More work!"

"Wouldn't want you to get bored," Emily said, kissing him. Usually, he chased her around the yard with a garden hose. That ritual made her squeal and run into the house for cover.

Jack entered his house to gather up his shaving kit and one suitcase as instructed by Jean. An agent greeted him as he walked up the stairs to the second-floor bedroom. Some security, Jack thought. Where were you when we needed you? He chided himself for blaming a stranger, going to the closet to gather his belongings for the trip. He spotted Emily's favorite shirt, which she had bought for him, and took it off the hanger. I hate this thing, he thought, but it was Em's favorite. Grabbing a wedding photo off the dresser, he finished packing.

Jack took his time as he walked around the property before getting back in the car. As the car pulled away, he stared out the window wondering if he would ever see his home again.

Almost as if reading his mind, Claire said, "Don't worry, Jack. Someday you'll be back here planting away."

"It won't be the same without Emily, Mom," Jack replied. "I did this all for her."

"That is precisely why you must return," Claire emphasized. "Memories are a powerful thing, Jack."

As they pulled up to Claire's house to drop her off, she noticed a van parked in the driveway.

"I told you I would be OK, Jean!" Claire snapped.

"I am not taking any chances until we are sure we know who is behind this new threat, Claire," Jean remarked curtly.

"Just tell them to stay out of my way," Claire said as she got out of the car.

Jean turned to Jack. "How did you survive growing up?"

Jack answered, "I learned to duck at an early age."

Inside the trio sat down for some coffee and desserts, delivered from friends after the funeral. Everyone was hungry, and the food was delicious, but their hearts were not into it.

"Mom, I am little worried about you being all alone," Jack said.

"I'll be fine. Just ensure you keep an eye over your shoulder at all times," Claire said, kissing him on the cheek.

Claire had made cookies for Jack's trip to Williamsburg and had packed her famous pink bag full of other goodies. It was the one she always brought on family vacations when Jack was growing up.

"Just what a new operative needs, Claire, a pink bag," Jean teased.

"This bag was good cover back in the day," Claire said to Jean.

"It works for me, Mom," Jack interjected. "It will remind me of all those fun family road trips we used to take."

"Just make sure you eat. Nothing is more important than a good, solid meal," Claire replied. "I know Charlène will take good care of you."

Mother and son parted with a hug and a kiss.

Claire took Jean aside to talk.

Remember to duck, Jack thought with a faint smile.

"Jean, I don't need these men hanging around to protect me," Claire said.

"OK, I will send the van away," Jean replied. "If you need anything, please call."

"I will, Jean," Claire said.

Jean went over to Jack. "Hand me that cell phone. We need to dispose of it."

"Why?" Jack asked.

"Because it's probably bugged, and we don't need anyone following us," Jean explained.

Jean took Jack's cell phone and handed it to two men from the van. After Jean gave some brief instructions to them, they jumped back in the van and pulled out of the driveway.

"Thank you, Jean," Claire said.

"I still don't like this, but you're as stubborn as a mule," Jean replied.

Claire kissed Jean on the cheek good-bye. "Still have a way with the ladies, don't you, Jean?"

"Just remember to call if you need something," Jean reminded her, climbing into his car and starting the engine.

Claire walked up to the top of the driveway, waving good-bye as they rounded a corner.

Later that day, the two men drove south along I-91 into Connecticut and then headed west along I-84 to New York. Jean decided on a route that would avoid New York City, Philadelphia, Baltimore, and Washington, opting for a country route to Harrisburg, past Richmond, and then to Charlène's estate in Williamsburg, Virginia.

"Why the detour, Jean?" Jack asked.

"It avoids tolls, and as you know, tollbooths have cameras, which are about as secure as that phone you carried around. Jack, one thing you must understand, as your father did, is that your life has changed forever," Jean said.

"I know, it's just been a very hard transition for me," Jack replied. "I wish it could all be back to the way it was."

Jean knew that look; he had seen it many times in France during the war. Jack was defeated; he had given up. In time he will recover, Jean thought. The human psyche strives to rise above the pain, and I will be there to help him.

For the next few hours, the two men were quiet. It was Jean who finally broke the silence. "Jack, the offer for the job is still open. I wanted to gradually wean you into the business, but it's obviously too late for that now."

"Is that why Mom was so mad at you?" Jack asked.

"Yes, she was a bit upset with me," Jean answered. "I must be slipping in my old age. I never thought they would make a move on you. Something must be in the works."

"Not your fault. I got sloppy myself," Jack replied.

"The offer is genuine, Jack, and with what you have been through, it will occupy your mind."

"What kind of work are you talking about, Jean?" Jack asked. "Are you talking spying?"

Jean replied, "Jack, what I am about to tell you is declassified and public knowledge. I work for a branch of the CIA that is not supposed to exist anymore. The organization is called The Pond. In 1942, General Hayes Kroner, the head of the War Department's Military Intelligence Service, was permitted to set up an espionage organization separate from Office of Strategic Services, the OSS. He selected US Army

Captain Jean Grombach to head the organization. We called him 'Frenchy.' In '55, *The Pond* was officially disbanded by the government. Frenchy admitted he had proposed to Senator McCarthy that his entire organization work for the senator in doing nothing but investigating employees of the United States government. I was new to the organization at the time, and I did not agree with becoming a political tool. In France, we had fought that type of oppression from the Nazis, and I wasn't going to do that for this government. When we were disbanded, the government didn't know what to do with the network of agents in The Pond, so they kept giving us missions, since we were already in place in many parts of the world. To this day, we are a black-ops organization secretly funded by the CIA. The majority of our funding still comes through fake corporations based in Washington DC and New York City."

"Sounds complicated," Jack commented.

"We are known as CIA, but we are in reality a separate and distinct organization," Jean explained. "We specialize in gathering intelligence about the current Nazi movement, so that it never surfaces again."

"But I was under the impression they were all gone," Jack said.

"I am afraid not, Jack. Look at what happened to you and your father with Gisele. They are still a threat that we must abolish."

"How did you meet Charlène?" Jack asked.

"Charlène and I worked together when the Cold War started. We knew each other in France and met again in Budapest in 1958 on her first mission," Jean explained.

"I didn't realize you two have known each other for so long," Jack said.

"I was an operative in Europe, and I was assigned to help her with a trailing mission."

"How did that turn out?" Jack asked

"The mission went well at first. The American diplomat we were tailing was eliminated before we could get enough evidence to convict him. We suspected the Russians had a hand in it but could never prove it. More than likely some element in the Hungarian intelligence took him out before we got close. A man by the name of Vargas led their spy activities at that time, and he almost got us too," Jean revealed.

"So, it was a failure?"

"Charlène was very nervous. Prior experiences with the SS and Gestapo affected her judgment at times, but she persevered. We eventually uncovered enough information to put out a formal protest to the Russians," he said. "That alone can be embarrassing enough to make them execute some internal adjustments, if you know what I mean." Jean chuckled.

Jean knew if he correlated his story with Charlène's, Jack would understand. Once he meets Charlène, he will come around, he thought.

Jack needed to know more before he decided. "Did my father work for The Pond?"

"No, he worked with MI-6 almost exclusively, but we did work together on a few occasions," Jean informed him.

"Can you tell me anything about his missions?" Jack asked.

"I can discuss the declassified ones," Jean said, "if you agree to the employment."

"What would be my part in this if I said yes?" Jack asked.

"If you say yes, you would be an operative gathering intelligence for the agency. Of course you will be given a new identity and report on things we want you to observe. It sounds simple, but it can be quite difficult to maintain a new identity. And if you are caught as a spy in a foreign country, you can expect no help whatsoever from the agency. It may seem inhuman and cruel, but we create policy according to what is in the best interest of protecting our knowledge. If one of our sources–for example, you, Jack—were to fall into enemy hands, we would detach ourselves from involvement to quell as much retaliation as possible that could erupt as a direct consequence of the failed mission," Jean explained.

"Sounds harsh. Will I be trained?"

"Some of the training you would go through consists of staged kidnapping, torture, and escape techniques, all meant to frame your mind and willpower for the real scenario, if necessary," Jean explained.

Jack was horrified. The life he had known was shattered, changed in ways he could never have imagined. "I need to think seriously about all of this," he said.

"Certainly, Jack. We will talk when you are ready," Jean commented. "But know this. You will first learn about the organization, and work inside analyzing data and studying our enemies. We won't throw you to the wolves, so to speak, at least not immediately," Jean said.

Seems no is not an acceptable answer, Jack thought.

"What would you like to know about your father?" Jean asked.

"What he did, where he went, whether he ever killed anyone," Jack rambled off his questions.

"Joe was assigned to many missions, mostly in support, but he did have one or two that come to mind that he led brilliantly," Jean replied. "The one I remember most is when he was sent into Egypt for medical research—a cover in reality."

"Wait, he was in Egypt? Wow, sometimes you think you know a person! Why was he there?"

"It was in the 1950s, and at that time, the Americans and Russians were at odds during the Cold War. There were several times we thought nuclear Armageddon was at hand. It was a scary time for everyone. Your dad worked with a German scientist by the name of Inga. He was very apprehensive about working with his former enemy, but she proved invaluable to the CIA.

Your father's mission involved parasitology. His expertise in that field was biological warfare. We found out that the Russians in the '50s were interested in a form of delivery that would infect our troops in Europe. They wanted to deploy malaria, and intestinal infections of dysentery and diarrhea by some ancient, undetectable delivery system. It was all designed to demoralize and disable our soldiers, just before an all-out attack. The Russians discovered an ancient Egyptian formula that supported their studies in creating those weapons. Your father was there to find and destroy that link."

"Did he?" Jack asked.

"He did, and everything worked out in the end. Mostly," Jean said.

"Mostly?" Jack inquired.

"That's a story for another day," Jean replied.

Jean suddenly got quiet, and Jack dared not probe any further. It was obvious that the Egyptian mission had some difficulties.

For the next few hours, Jack sat quietly thinking how much his life had changed since that eventful New Year's Eve when his dad revealed his war service and the girl who supposedly died in his arms.

Jack remembered bits and pieces of his father's story from that New Year's Eve. He could hear his father's voice clearly as he related the tale:

"Her name was Charlène. She was eight years old. The Nazis were tipped off by someone in our camp about Charlène's true identity. The Nazis broke her leg, her hand, hit her in the head with a gun.

"Through all their torture, that brave little girl never ratted on us."

Jack remembered his father's reasoning echoing in his head:

"I could never tell anyone of all the killing and torture, because if I'm still alive, so are they, and I didn't want to expose my family to danger."

And suddenly Jack was back in the present knowing that his dad knew she was alive. He told everyone Charlène had died, he thought. That was very odd. Maybe he knew I would be curious. Jack felt sick. He wanted to throw up but held on to his composure. I caused his death, he thought.

He would have to make this right, and the decision was obvious. Jack turned to Jean in the car.

"Jean, I'll do it," Jack declared.

"Good. You won't regret it, Jack."

Let's hope not, Jack thought.

For the next few hours, Jack listened to Jean describe Charlène's estate, where the operations center was located and where for the next several months he would live and train.

"Jean, what if I had said no after all you have told me?" Jack asked.

"The government would consider you, and now me, a liability, Jack," Jean said. "What I have revealed to you would get me into trouble too."

Jean paused a moment as if deciding whether to go on.

"What is it?" Jack asked.

"Do you remember Ben Townley?"

"The *Globe* reporter in New Hampshire?" Jack looked puzzled.

"You are his replacement," Jean said.

"Wait. Ben was a spy?" Jack asked.

"Yes. He was working with Scotty Smythe when Gisele murdered him in the parking garage."

"Are you serious?"

"Jack, the intelligence community is a small world. Ben was to help Scotty and your father find Gisele. That interview he did with you was a trap to root her out. We figured she would be following you to find your father. Unfortunately, she was one step ahead of us and killed Ben before we could get to her."

Jack felt sick to his stomach. His fantasy adventure to be an award-winning writer got a man killed. I should have never started this whole research into Dad's war service, he thought. So far four people are dead because of me!

Jean recognized the look on Jack's face. "Jack, it's not your fault. Ben was well aware of the risks."

"I know, but I still feel my curiosity has gotten people killed," Jack said. "How am I supposed to feel?"

"Jack, no one understands how you feel better than I," Jean answered. "My parents were killed by the Nazis, and for years I blamed myself for not having saved them. There are those out there who want to destroy our way of life. Sooner or later, you would have run across it."

"I know. I guess with Dad's background you're right," Jack replied. "Maybe he should have told us sooner, so we would have been prepared."

"He did what he thought was best for his family," Jean pointed out.

"I guess you're right. Sometimes I feel like he would be alive if I had just confronted him instead of going behind his back like I did."

"We can't escape our past, Jack," Jean added. "Your father knew that all too well."

Jack went silent, and Jean let him be for now. He had absorbed a lot of information the past few days. He drove on in silence to let Jack process this new information and his decision to join the agency.

Jack thoughts were a total jumble. It was a lot to take in, but with everything that happened to his dad, Ben, and Emily, he knew he did not want to give up the fight. He had to do this for them.

A few hours later, about halfway to Williamsburg, Jack was pulled from his reverie as Jean drove into a local diner's parking lot.

"Why are we stopping here?" Jack asked.

"I am hungry and need some coffee," Jean said. "And besides, the pie here is *fantastique*."

Jack felt all eyes lock on them as they entered the diner. We must be some sight, Jacked thought, an old man with a fedora and me all bandaged up. His paranoia was at its peak.

Jean ordered them a piece of cherry pie and coffee, joking with the waitress, whom he seemed to know.

"Nice to see you again, John," the waitress said brightly with a smile. "Who's your friend?"

"My sister's boy. He is joining the company, and I thought I'd show him some of my favorite places here."

"That's great," she remarked. Her gaze fell on Jack's shoulder. "What happened to your arm, hon?" she asked.

"Hunting accident," Jack blurted out a bit too quickly.

"Always told him, be careful around guns," Jean said.

"Don't have one myself," she replied. "Too many kids in my house."

Seeing the men finishing their coffee, she said, "Refill?"

"No thanks, Betts," Jean answered. "We have to get going."

"I'll get your bill," she replied.

Betts went back to the cash register and printed out the receipt, handing it to Jean. Jean handed her a twenty and said, "It was a pleasure as always, Betts. Keep the change."

"Thanks, hon. Be careful out there."

Walking back to the car, Jean pulled out the bill he had stashed in his front left pocket. Betts had written a note at the bottom of the slip of paper. *The package is safely on its way.*

Back in the car Jack felt better. "Thanks, Jean. That place has some great food," he said. "I would love to go back there sometime."

"I stop every time I come this way," Jean said. "We will get through this, Jack, I promise."

Later that evening, the black sedan pulled through an ornate gate guarded by cameras. There was a long driveway ending at a manor house belonging to Charlène Shemesh. Jack was convinced that the dark winter day gave the estate an ominous look as the car wheeled around the circular driveway to stop in front of a pair of large oak doors.

THE ROAD TO NEVERS

Madeleine and Liliane consulted briefly with each other on the escape maps and nodded in agreement on a course of plans. The group would travel southeast away from the majority of the German troop movement toward the invasion beaches, sticking to forests and swamps as they made their way to the border of the Pyrénées mountains. It was to be a long journey there and a difficult climb through the passes, so they had to prepare accordingly.

Madeleine walked over to the group. She said, "We will go to Liliane's farm a few hours from here. From there she has acquired motor transport to southern France. We will make our way south of Toulouse to Saint-Girons. I know of a safe house there that can outfit us for the climb through the mountain passes."

"At least the passes will be not be snowed in this time of year, Madeleine," Henri said.

"True, *mon chérie*," Madeleine replied, "but it will still be a hard journey."

Several yards away Liliane was motioning for the group to move. "We must leave, Madeleine. It is not safe here."

"*Oui*, coming," Madeleine replied.

"OK, gentlemen, fan out on the flanks," Lieutenant Robertson said.

"Got point," Rizzo said, joining Liliane, who was already leading the group deeper into the forest.

Rizzo openly flirted with Liliane but wasn't making any ground as they walked south toward her farm. Liliane pointedly told the brash Jersey boy she had no time for his silliness.

Liliane had lost too many friends and had too much to do with ridding her country of Nazis to lose her head to love. It would be a fatal mistake to fall for the handsome American.

Picking up the pace, she moved ahead of Rizzo. Defeated, he fell into formation behind her, concentrating on protecting their flank.

The group made their way deeper into the forest throughout the morning, thankful that the fog had not yet cleared. Liliane's place was only about a two-hour walk from Madeleine's farm, but the German Fifteenth Army was on high alert with strict orders from Hitler to remain in place. The megalomaniac Hitler still believed the invasion would take place in Pas-de-Calais, not Normandy. With the invasion in full swing, they had to take many detours, hiding in forests and old barns to avoid discovery. As the German units pushed northward toward the coastline, the group's escape south became increasingly easier to navigate.

Later that afternoon they were almost discovered when a German mechanized unit literally crossed their path moments after they had passed through an open area and into a thicker part of the forest.

By late afternoon, as the sun was setting, the group rested on the outskirts of the forest, just within sight of Liliane's farm.

"My men and I will go first," Liliane said. "When it is safe, Pierre will come back for you," she said, pointing to her fellow partisan.

Liliane, with two men from her group, Armand and Pierre, headed down the grass-covered slope toward the darkened farmhouse.

As Liliane and her men approached, they noticed the front door was ajar. Motioning for the men to circle around back, Liliane entered the front door with caution, pushing it open with the end of her rifle.

She heard a chair crash to the wooden floor, suspecting it came from her downstairs bedroom.

Looking past the foyer, she saw one of her men signal to her from a window on the far end. Opening the window, he climbed in and pointed his rifle into an adjacent room. Outside the third man stood guard at the back door that led into her garden.

Liliane carefully entered the room off of the foyer, the *salle de séjour*, her rifle leading the way. Making her way back to the bedroom, she saw a dark figure rush by her toward the front door.

The partisan Pierre ran from the back room, tackling the figure just as it reached the open door to freedom. Liliane rushed over pointing her rifle at the prone figure.

"Ne tirez pas! Ne tirez pas, Tante Liliane*! C'est moi,* Jean,*"* the figure shouted.

"Jean? Jean, what are you doing here? Where are your parents?" Liliane said.

"Les bosch took them away to Drancy," Jean said. He began to sob as he sat up. "I was playing in the forest when I saw the Gestapo car approach our home. I hid from them, but I was close enough to hear them tell my parents where they were going."

"Mon Dieu, why?" Liliane asked. "Help him up, Pierre."

"They said they were Communists and enemies of the state," Jean explained. "I stayed in the forest until they left. I didn't know what to do, so I took a few of my things and came here. I am sorry if I put you in danger, Aunt Liliane. I will leave if you want me to."

"You are not going anywhere, Jean. You are my brother's son; you will stay with me," she replied.

"Merci, ma tante," Jean said as they hugged each other.

"Jean, there are friends waiting nearby for my signal to come and spend the night here. Please go with Pierre and bring them back. *Allez, vas vite!"* Liliane said.

Pierre motioned for Jean to follow him out the front door.

Liliane watched Pierre and her nephew cross the field and head into the woods. Her brother and his wife were Communists, working with the Maquis partisans. Someone must have exposed them to the bosch. In time those traitors will pay, she vowed.

She turned and walked into her kitchen to prepare food and drink there for the weary travelers.

Within minutes Pierre and Jean headed back to the farmhouse, motioning for the group to follow. Sergeant Waldron assisted Henri and Charlène down from the horse just as Jean took the reins from Antoinette to lead the tired animal into the barn for the evening.

"Liliane, what's wrong?" Madeleine asked, seeing pain on her face.

"My apologies but I have just learned that my brother and his wife were taken away by the Gestapo. You have just met their son, my nephew Jean," Liliane explained.

"Why did they take them?" Antoinette asked.

"They were Communists. They had successfully hidden their affiliation with the party since the occupation, until now. Someone exposed them to the Gestapo."

"They will soon come for you," Henri said. "You should leave."

"Come with us," the lieutenant said. "Two more won't make a difference."

"*Merci*, Lieutenant, but I have a sister in Paris. Jean and I will go there," Liliane explained.

"I am truly sorry, Liliane," Madeleine said. "We will leave immediately if it is necessary."

"We understand," Henri said.

"We have at least until tomorrow morning. They will not come out at night in this part of the country. There are many partisans patrolling at night, you know," Liliane said.

She then addressed the group. "I will make arrangements for motor transport for the journey."

To maintain its appearance of being abandoned, the house was kept dark that night. If the Gestapo came back that evening, they would have the advantage of an ambush. Henri, Antoinette, and Charlène slept in Liliane's bedroom while the rest bedded down on the floor in the *salle de séjour*, taking turns on guard duty.

The next day was uneventful aside from the occasional distant German columns that headed toward the Allied invasion at Normandy.

That evening, sitting with his back against an inner wall with his Thompson submachine gun across his lap, Robbie watched Liliane standing at the window, gazing out at the starlit sky.

"Liliane, will we be OK driving south? There seems to be a lot of kraut movement in this area," he asked.

"*Oui*, Lieutenant, *les bosch* stay on the main roads, and your transport will be taking the back roads," Liliane replied. "They are more interested in attacking the Allies in Normandy. *Que Dieu les protègent.*"

"I hope the krauts don't decide to take the scenic route!" Robertson said.

"They will be busy worrying about the invasion force and not an old farm truck, Lieutenant," Liliane said.

That evening, a Renault AHS two-ton truck arrived with a canvas cover over the back. Liliane and Madeleine watched for any sign they were being observed as the men began to outfit the bed of the Renault for a comfortable journey for Henri and Charlène. Hay from the barn and blankets from the farmhouse were brought in to soften the ride, while Madeleine, Antoinette, and Liliane prepared provisions for the journey.

Charlène was stoic during the preparations, sitting quietly, watching everyone.

"What's the story with the little girl, Madeleine?" Lieutenant Robertson asked, referring to Charlène.

"The Gestapo and SS almost beat her to death to find Henri's group," Madeleine explained. "In her own words she told us that she did not tell anyone what she knew. She is a brave little girl, Lieutenant, but I am afraid the torture she endured will scar her for the rest of her life."

"The Nazis have done terrible things, Madeleine. I only hope we can pay them back for this," the lieutenant said.

"We will," Madeleine countered. "As you *Américains* say, in spades!"

Antoinette and Liliane brought out food and whatever medical supplies they could dig up.

Sergeant Waldron then supervised moving and loading Charlène and Henri into the truck. Once he was satisfied that they were comfortable and properly cushioned for the ride, he gave a thumbs-up to Liliane that they were settled.

Watching the horizon for any observation, Liliane motioned for the rest of the group to come out in twos.

The rest of the group jumped into the back. Charlène and Henri were all the way toward the back of the truck, with the American team closer to the tailgate of the Renault.

After the truck was fully loaded, Armand took over as driver, with Madeleine in the passenger seat.

With a sputter from the diesel engine, the truck coughed to life.

Diesel fumes filled the back of the truck, and Sergeant Rizzo had to throw open the flap. "Oh now, this is fun," he said, gagging on the fumes. "Smells like Newark in here."

"Adieu, mes amis," Liliane said, waving as the truck bounced down the dirt road heading southeast.

As the truck rocked slowly back and forth over the rough road, Liliane watched until it faded in the distance. Turning to Jean she said, "Have your things ready. We leave in an hour."

***

The route was simple but could change at any moment should the Germans suddenly appear.

The group would travel at night through the countryside, and during the day, through the more built-up cities. The Germans were focused on the invasion, but they still had to be extremely cautious not to be noticed. Henri explained their unusual route was one used by farmers delivering their goods, so this farm truck would blend in nicely.

The route would take them from Liliane's farm, southeast of Bergues to Reims, then onto Troyes, south of Paris to Bourges, onto Saint-Elienne, and then southwest to Toulouse and into the passes of the Pyrénées near Saint-Girons, depending on Vichy French and German troop concentrations. Once across the border in Spain they could work their way to Gibraltar.

The most dangerous part of the trip would be the initial move south, since the main highways leading north would be clogged with German troops headed for Normandy. Once past Bourges, about an eight- to ten-hour drive, they would have far less to worry about.

In the event they were stopped, Lieutenant Robertson had piled crates at the rear of the truck to give the impression that the truck was transporting only farm goods. Anyone searching the truck would be discouraged by the heavy crates.

Armand Godard had been a tank driver in brigadier general Charles de Gaulle's improvised Fourth Armored

Division, formed after the German breakthrough at Sedan on May 15, 1940.

On May 17, 1940, at Montcornet, Armand was taken prisoner, his tank upended by a bomb dropped from a JU-87 Stuka. Although the Fourth Armored Division had forced the German infantry to retreat to Caumont, the war was over for Armand Godard.

After spending two years in a prisoner of war camp, Armand received good news. He would be released to return home.

On June 22, 1942, Prime Minister of France Pierre Laval announced the institution of la relève, whereby French workers were encouraged to volunteer to work in Germany to secure the release of French prisoners of war. For every three workers who volunteered to work in Germany, one POW would be released.

In reality, the *Service du travail obligatoire* was a forced enlistment and deportation of thousands of French workers to Nazi Germany to work as laborers for the German war effort. As time went on, the French factories were required to send over their own workers if the monthly quotas had not been met.

Armand's brother had been deported to Germany to become a worker for the Nazis in their factories and had died trying to escape back to France.

With his brother dead, and his parents gone as well years earlier, Armand was alone. Madeleine, whom he had known before the war, gave him work on her family's farm near

Cambrai. It was soon after that he enthusiastically joined the resistance along with Madeleine and Henri, instead of being a pawn for the Nazi industry.

Armand's service in the French army served the partisans well. He trained them in the use of firearms, and his knowledge of German tactics saved many during these years of occupation.

The first two hours were uneventful as they passed Saint-Quentin and approached Reims, the major east-west route into Paris. They stuck to the old farm roads most of the way. The rough roads made the journey unbearable for the passengers in the bed of the truck, but it was better than the alternative. Even now they still had to avoid elements of the Fifteenth Army group that was spread out defending Calais. It was lucky for them that the German eye was turned toward the sky and sea, and not on the old farm truck.

They made their way around Reims, but just south of the city, they ran into a checkpoint.

The checkpoint, luckily, was manned by Vichy French police. But with a small bribe to let Madeleine deliver "her farm goods" intact, the Vichy let them go without a full search of the vehicle.

They ran into a similar checkpoint at Troyes, but the Vichy police were checking the papers of every vehicle there.

"Vos papiers s'il vous plait!" the police asked Armand.

Armand produced the fake papers Liliane had given him, and the officer went back to consult with his counterpart in their booth. They discussed the papers for a few moments, occasionally looking back and pointing to the truck.

"Prépare-toi, mon gars," Madeleine whispered to Armand as she withdrew a pistol and placed it by her side out of sight.

The Vichy officer approached the truck, smiling as he handed Armand back his papers.

"Vive la Liberté," he whispered, winking at Madeleine.

The Vichy officer then waved the truck on through the checkpoint.

"That was lucky," Armand whispered as they passed through the checkpoint.

"I suspect they know our liberation is soon and want to be on the winning side," Madeleine said.

They continued on for two more hours, past Joinville, Chaumont, Montbard, and Avallon, without incident, when Armand informed Madeleine they would need petrol. Madeleine consulted her maps and instructed Armand to follow the signs south-southeast to the small village of Nevers, near Bourges, in the Burgundy region of France. There they would stop the truck and refill from the extra petrol Liliane had provided.

Arriving at the east side shortly after midnight, they crossed a stone bridge that led into the village. Pulling up behind an old inn, Madeleine got out, tapped twice on the side of the truck, and pulled open the flap of the truck.

Simultaneously, Robbie moved one of the crates out of the way to talk to Madeleine.

"Lieutenant, we have arrived in Nevers, in Bourgogne, and we still have about eight hours before we reach the border," Madeleine said.

"Shouldn't we keep going?" Lieutenant Robertson asked.

"Most French do not travel after midnight. There is a curfew, and violators are arrested. This inn is used as a safe house, and we can stay until tomorrow evening," Madeleine replied.

"We all could use a rest. That was a bumpy ride," he admitted.

Armand and Sergeant Rizzo unloaded the petrol from the back of the truck and proceeded to fill up the gas tank.

Madeleine and Antoinette knocked on the back door of the inn. After a brief discussion with the innkeeper, they were brought quietly inside.

"They know him?" Rizzo asked Armand.

"*Oui*, this is one of our safe houses. Partisans in trouble or in need of supplies come here," replied Armand.

"I need a drink, Armand," Rizzo complained. "It's been a rough few days."

Armand, smiling, took out a small flask of eau-de-vie from his jacket and handed it to Rizzo. He then took the second can of petrol from Rizzo and poured it into the tank.

"Salute," Rizzo whispered as he pursed his lips and took a healthy swig of the amber liquid. Replacing the cap, he handed it back to Armand.

"Pas si vite, camarade," Armand replied, setting down the can of petrol. He unscrewed the flask's cap and said, *"À l'amitié!"* taking a healthy swig.

Robbie appeared from the alley where he had been talking to Madeleine. He hopped back into the truck to check on Henri and Charlène, bringing them some bread, cheese, water, and a chocolate bar he had forgotten about in his ammo pouch.

"It's all we have at the moment, folks," he stated. "Maybe Madeleine can get some fresh grub from the inn."

Charlène ate what she was given and, when finished, asked the lieutenant, "Did you know Sonny, Monsieur Robbie?" she asked.

"No, little one. Was he your friend?" the lieutenant asked.

"Oui. He took care of me while he was in France," she replied with a faint smile.

"I am sure he did, kid. I am sure he did," Robbie repeated, his voice trailing off.

"Madeleine says we will be safe soon in Portugal. It must be very beautiful there. I think I will like because there is not war there," she said, tears in her eyes. "My mother always wanted to live by the sea."

Seeing Charlène's tears, Robbie clammed up. He held her hand for a few moments before exiting the truck and then took a brief moment out of sight from the others to wipe his eyes so no one would notice his own tears.

Inside Madeleine and Antoinette were informed that a Vichy Carlingue agent, a French affiliate of the German Gestapo, was staying at the inn and it would be unwise for them to remain there.

Heading back to the truck, Madeleine informed them of the urgency of their situation.

"The truck makes a helluva racket when she starts up, Madeleine. We should push it far enough away so we won't alert that Vichy agent."

"Oui, bien sûr," Madeleine agreed.

The back door to the inn opened up, and the innkeeper's wife came out into the courtyard. As she walked around the corner, Madeleine could see the terror in her eyes. A man dressed in a black coat and trousers came around the corner behind her holding a Luger pistol.

No one had a chance to get to a weapon when the Vichy Carlingue agent appeared brandishing his Luger 9 mm pistol. The Carlingue worked very closely with the Gestapo in rooting out partisans, being very successful and very much feared at their job since they were French.

"Do not move! I will shoot anyone who moves! What are you doing outside after the curfew? I do not recognize any of you!" the Carlingue agent said, glancing at the truck.

"We are delivering farm goods to market, and our truck broke down," Madeleine said.

"I suppose that is excusable," the Carlingue agent said. "Show me the farm goods in the truck. Everyone, please step aside so I can see all of you," he commanded.

The Carlingue agent opened the canvas flap and stepped on the back bumper of the truck, keeping an eye on the group outside.

The lieutenant was frantic. His weapon lay on the floor of the truck. They could be compromised!

As the Carlingue agent shined a flashlight into the truck, all he saw was the butt of Robbie's Thompson submachine gun as it hit him square in the face, knocking him backward and unconscious onto the muddied road.

Henri slid on his rear to the edge of the truck bed, his legs hanging over the side, and said, "He will have quite the headache when he wakes up!"

"Armand, tie him up. No need to be gentle," Madeleine said.

"Avec plaisir!" Armand said as he proceeded to hog-tie him with pointers from Sergeant Rizzo.

"Learned that at basic training from a farm boy," Sergeant Rizzo revealed with a wink to Armand.

Both men chuckled softly in the alleyway.

"Madeleine, we should kill him. He will alert the Vichy authorities in the area," the lieutenant said.

"You cannot stay here," the innkeeper's wife said. "His Carlingue friends will be looking for him when he does not show up tomorrow at headquarters."

"Is there another safe house nearby?" Madeleine asked.

The innkeeper's wife tilted her head and thought briefly. Suddenly she smiled. "Go to Saint Gildard's convent, and bring him with you. La Révérende Mère and the Sisters of Charity will take you in. They will know what to do with him."

"Oh my God," Rizzo spoke up, "if they're anything like the sisters back home, I'd hate to be him when he wakes up."

"That convent sounds familiar to me," Sergeant Waldron said.

"It is the resting place of Sainte Bernadette de Lourdes. La Vierge Marie spoke to her," explained the innkeeper's wife.

"That's it!" Billy Waldron said. "One of the holiest sites in France. I read she is buried in a crystal coffin. We shouldn't bring this scum into that sanctuary."

Madeleine spoke first. "That is exactly why we will take him there, Sergeant—to face God in the form of a saint. He will provide some useful information once we have him inside."

Since there was no need to push the truck away from the inn, Armand started up the Renault, which grumbled and gave off a puff of black smoke, while everyone climbed in.

With directions to the convent and a note from the innkeeper's wife, they proceeded down the road to Saint-Gildard.

A few prying eyes spied the truck as they passed the small village houses along the road to the convent. Everyone in the town knew the "visitors" would be safe there. The Germans would not dare desecrate one of the holiest shrines in France. Rumor had it that Himmler, a believer in the power of the occult, gave the order to steer clear of the Lady of Lourdes.

So it was on this cobblestone road that the small group of *évadés* made their way, motoring undisturbed, to the convent.

THE ESTATE

Charlène's Uncle David and Aunt Judith took her in after the war on their Williamsburg country estate. She spent her days riding horses and playing the debutant, thriving on the attention bestowed upon her by them. David and Judith were childless, and her presence gave them a fulfillment that had been lacking—the sound of a child's laughter. They officially adopted her in 1958, the sole heir to their estate.

There, Charlène grew up in a French household with the same food and living styles she was accustomed to in the Pas-de-Calais. She grew up with a loving family, and the memory of the Gestapo torture slowly faded away. The only reminder was the slight limp and the patch over her eye that covered a horrible scar.

Her mind on occasion would drift back to the memory of that day:

The children were kicking André's soccer ball around in the field behind the farmhouse when Simon began barking, alerting them to a truck pulling up to the front of the house. The children stopped playing and started to walk to toward the house when they heard two German voices calling out in French to Celeste to meet them on the front porch.

The children joined hands and listened intently. They held their breath as they heard the door open and Celeste greeted the

Germans. Overhead the bluebirds chirped, joyously unaware of the tension on the ground.

A few minutes later the back door opened, and Celeste, with an ashen face consumed with fear, called, "Charlène, come inside, my darling. There are two soldiers here who would like to speak with you."

Charlène stiffened. Pleading with Caryll and Francesca to loosen their tight grip on her hands, she walked quietly into the house, tears beading up in her eyes.

The other three children stood paralyzed. Only Simon's barking and the bluebirds' chirping broke the silence outside the house. Inside the house, yelling, threats, and the sound of breaking glass gave way to screams and then silence.

On occasion she would receive a letter from her foster sisters, Caryll and Francesca, in Burgues, France, updating her on the status of family affairs. She missed her adoptive family in Bergues.

In the 1960s, Charlène visited the family in Bergues. The reunion was joyous, and her foster parents were still alive and happy to see her. But the reunion was cut short. Charlène would wake up screaming from the nightmares that haunted her relentlessly in the Portieres' home. Her adoptive parents knew very well what the problem was, and they came to her one morning and told her she must leave, for her health. The house reminded her of the torture she endured while staying there during the war.

"You will never be at peace in this house, *ma petite*," her foster mother, Celeste, told her. "The memories of what they did to you will only leave when you go away."

"But I love all of you. When can I see you again?" Charlène asked.

"We will visit you in America, *ma fille*. Find your peace with your aunt and uncle in America," Celeste responded.

Aunt Judith and Uncle David greeted her back when she returned to the Virginia estate. She had intended to stay awhile in Bergues with the family that took her in during the war, but her past would not let her.

"You must walk your own path," Aunt Judith said. "It does not always travel in the sunlight."

Her aunt and uncle traveled often, leaving her in the care of their butler, Georges. He treated her like his own daughter, doting on her every need. When they returned, Charlène was overjoyed, forgetting Georges.

Georges was raised in a middle-class family on the outskirts of Paris. He was the youngest of five children, with two older sisters and brothers.

In his early twenties, he had grandiose plans of starting his own business, having fallen in love with a girl from a higher class in society. Georges wanted to impress her and her father, but in the end, the girl rejected him. He just wasn't part of their world.

His father, a butler, suggested that he learn the trade. Penniless and heartbroken, Georges became a servant for the very same people that had rejected him as an equal. He was very bitter and almost quit the trade before he met a Jewish couple, David and Judith Shemesh.

David and Judith had lost their staff when they moved to Paris, buying an apartment from the influential Parisian designer and decorator Jean-Michel Frank.

One evening, invited to dinner at an upscale event, they met Georges. It was an instant connection.

Rumors of atrocities against Jewish families began to filter back to David and Judith. A great uncle had purchased property in America at the turn of the century, when immigrants flooded America with its promise of freedom and riches. The uncle had purchased a large tract of land in Virginia and built a stunning estate.

They decided to move to America, foreseeing the disaster to come. They brought Georges with them.

Georges dedicated his life to the Shemeshes but longed for a family of his own. When Charlène arrived in the late '40's, he saw the daughter he had always wished for. But he was a servant, and so he buried himself back into his duties of running the estate.

It was on a dark and gloomy winter day when Charlène, but a teenager, learned that her Aunt Judith and Uncle David had perished in a plane crash. The news devastated Charlène, and the memories of her parents being murdered by the Nazis came flooding back. Had it not been for the longtime friend of the family and butler, Georges, she would have gone insane. Georges raised her as his own child.

Georges ensured that Charlène stayed on track, helping her decide on the finest Ivy League college, majoring in psychology. He became the proud father, watching her grow from a girl into a woman.

She buried herself in the books, graduating near the top of her class. Georges ensured she had the finest tutors to complete her education.

Her life experiences enthralled and horrified her classmates and professors alike.

At twenty-four she received her master's degree in psychology, and at twenty-seven, her doctorate.

She opened a practice in nearby Williamsburg, spending a few years listening to the woes of the local residents. She hated it!

One day would blend into the next. Her time as a child in France was filled with sad memories of the loss of her parents and the torture she received by heartless monsters. Charlène felt disdain for the petty complaints of her patients, longing for something more. She found herself flashing back to her childhood, and hatred for the evil she experienced welled up inside her. Eventually she became a recluse, closing up her business and staying within the comfort of her estate. She knew she had a higher calling but was unsure what that might entail.

Back at the estate she felt secure, safe from the outside world. Her rock was the butler, Georges. He was always there with a comforting smile and good food. He would listen to her patiently and provide fatherly advice. Over the years they grew very close.

Once, in the early 1960s, while in her early twenties, her "sisters" came to visit for the summer. They encouraged her to get out of the estate more often and live life. They reminisced on their childhood and on playing after breakfast, skipping rope in front of the house and taking their dog, Simon, for a walk through the farm to a small stream where they fished. There they had spent time playing with Simon, throwing sticks for him. It was fun to recall how he would race and retrieve them until they were too tired to throw another stick. And then when they had returned to the house, flushed and satisfied, they were surprised to see Simon had beaten them back and fallen asleep with exhaustion. It was hilarious to recall him sunbathing on the porch.

They had a wonderful time filled with good and sometimes bad memories of the occupation years, but they never discussed her torture. They even discussed Sonny, hoping to help Charlène find him one day.

It wasn't until 1969 that a man with a British accent, named Major Scotty Smythe, appeared at the door, talking briefly with Georges. As she spied the conversation from the lead-paned windows of her uncle's study, she spotted a man in his late thirties to early forties step out of the car. She recognized him immediately. It was Sonny!

Sonny's new wife, Claire, a stunning brunette, had accompanied him on the journey. Charlène welcomed them both into her home.

That evening they celebrated their reunion with a culinary feast *à la française*. And it was *arrosé* with the best French wines and Champagne. Afterward, in the den, they enjoyed sipping Cognac by a blazing fire.

They discussed much that evening. Not once did either Sonny or Charlène mention that horrible evening in 1944 when she had been tortured by the Gestapo.

Sonny and Scotty made a proposition that changed Charlène's life forever. They wanted to use the estate for their headquarters. Ever since the CIA had "officially" shut down The Pond and evicted them from the public eye, they had needed a new place to work from. At first Charlène objected, until Georges informed her that her aunt and uncle had been part of the organization as well. In fact, their plane crash was no accident. It was a botched mission.

Charlène went numb with shock. But determined to change her life, she agreed to the proposition with one condition: she wanted to be part of the organization as well. They tried to argue, but this wasn't the helpless girl they once knew.

"You'll need my services as a psychologist," she said.

"How so?" Scotty asked.

"I can tell you what someone is thinking before they know it themselves." She chuckled.

Neither Sonny nor Scotty could argue her credentials.

"Charlène, you will have to undergo the rigorous training all CIA agents must endure before they become agents," Scotty said. "Are you sure you are up for it?

"I am tougher than you think, Major Smythe," Charlène said. "What will I have to do?"

"You will train at nearby Camp Peary. It has been the CIA's training camp since 1951. You will learn driving techniques and navigation," Scotty explained.

"Sounds easy enough," Charlène said.

Sonny glanced over at Major Smythe, a worried look on his face.

"What's wrong, Sonny?" Charlène asked.

"Charlène, there might be an area of concern," Major Smythe said.

"Which is?" Charlène asked.

"Part of the training to become an analyst is to endure staged kidnapping and torture," Major Smythe explained. "Based on your previous experience during the war, this might be a problem for you."

Charlène went numb. The memories of that torture in 1944 all came flooding back at once. She was almost in a panic, wanting to flee the room, the memories. But when Sonny's hand grasped hers, her world stopped spinning. Everything came back into focus.

The look in Sonny's eyes was the same as all those years ago. She could hear him say, "It's OK, I will protect you."

"I can do it, Major," Charlène said, looking at Sonny, grasping his hand tightly. "I will find the strength."

Charlène excelled in her training with the CIA. It was the kidnapping and torture that almost caused her to fail. At midpoint in that exercise she found her strength; she sang the song Sonny had taught her as a child. She removed herself from her body and sang to the dismay of the instructors,

Go to sleep, little Charlène
Close your pretty eyes
Go to sleep, little Charlène
Sonny's here; I'll take care of you
They can never hurt you...

In the end she passed her test. She also buried the nightmares of that past torture during the war forever.

That reconnection with Sonny had been long overdue, marking a turning point in Charlène's life. From that joyous reunion, Charlène dedicated herself to fighting the evil that still lurked in the world.

Over the years she rose through the ranks, eventually leading the organization from her family estate. She oversaw the training of each new operative, tailoring their training based on her psychological profile of them.

Now in her late seventies, she watched from her drawing room as a young man, the spitting image of his father, stepped out of Jean's car. The fond memories of those early days with The Pond came flooding back.

Jean rang the doorbell as Jack waited behind him.

Charlène smoothed out her white dress as the butler opened the door to greet the visitors.

"Right this way, please," he said. "Madame Shemesh is in the drawing room waiting for you."

The two men were silent as the butler, the aged, but still loyal butler, Georges, led them down the hall and to the left, drawing apart the sliding doors to where Charlène awaited.

The room was filled with hundreds of books. As a child, Charlène spent hours here, poring over the great novels of the time, books by F. Scott Fitzgerald, Hemingway, and Raymond Chandler, to name a few.

Charlène turned from the window to greet the two men. "Welcome to my home, Jack. It's very nice to finally meet you!" she said as she kissed Jack on both cheeks.

"And you as well," Jack replied. How odd to be in the presence of Charlène, the person responsible for my "adventure" and my dad's ultimately death, Jack thought.

"Jean, you look dashing as always!" Charlène said.

Charlène had always admired Jean from afar. It was not quite a crush, but throughout their careers, as they crossed paths more than once working on different projects, she had grown fond of him. Jean, on the other hand, teetered on love for Charlène; but her detachment from emotion, perhaps as a result of her ordeal in France at a very young age, had left her irreparably scarred, keeping their relationship distant and always professional.

"A pleasure as always, Charlène. You look stunning as ever," Jean replied.

"Charmer," Charlène said. She then addressed Jack. "I am sure you are exhausted from the trip but none the worse for the wear—or wound as it may be. We have prepared a room for you, and the agency has provided you a nurse. I am sure you will find your stay very comfortable."

"Thank you, Charlène," Jack replied. Turning to Jean, he began to say, "What about—" but was interrupted.

"Charlène, our other guest should arrive tonight. I assume you have made all the arrangements?" Jean asked.

"I have," Charlène answered.

"Georges, please take Jack to his room and make him comfortable," Charlène directed her butler.

"Oui, madame," Georges said.

"Jack, dinner is at 5:00 PM sharp. If you need anything, please let Georges know," Charlène said.

"Thank you" was all Jack could muster. In truth he was exhausted and devastated by what had happened to Emily, and he just wanted to sleep. Georges guided him down the hall to a first-floor room.

Jack marveled at the beauty of Charlène's home. Unlike the painted walls of his house, this was truly magnificent. The cherry wood floors were covered by beautifully woven oriental rugs. Dark, rich cherry panels covered the walls of the hallway. High above, crystal chandeliers hung from ornate encasements.

This reminds me of the mansions in Newport, Rhode Island, Jack thought. "Beautiful," Jack said, following Georges.

"Merci, monsieur," Georges replied.

"Have you been with Charlène long?" Jack asked.

He did not receive a response, only a dirty look from Georges.

Jack was perplexed. "I am sorry. Did I say something wrong?"

"Monsieur Turner, it is impolite in my country to call the head of a household by her first name. I refer to her as Madame Shemesh," Georges said.

"I am sorry. I will remember to be respectful," Jack said.

They entered Jack's room. Georges withdrew the curtains to reveal large, ornate lead-paned windows. A beautiful view of the outside grounds opened up to Jack.

"It's beautiful here," Jack said.

"Oui, monsieur," Georges replied. "Should you need anything, *monsieur*, please ring for me." He pointed to the

intercom by the door. "Remember, dinner is at 5:00 PM sharp. Please dress appropriately."

"Thank you, Georges," Jack replied.

Georges excused himself from the room, closing the heavy oak door behind him.

The room has a Louis XIV look about it, Jack thought as he lay on the bed, instantly falling fast asleep.

Some hours later he awoke, Georges by his side. "Monsieur Turner, dinner is in ten minutes."

***

Earlier in the study…

"Jean, please have a seat. We have much to discuss. Cognac?" Charlène offered.

"*Merci*, Charlène," Jean replied.

The two old friends sat down in Queen Anne–style chairs, turned slightly and opposite one another to a stunning view of the courtyard and beyond.

It was Jean who spoke first. "The organization is in need of fresh blood, Charlène, and Jack is quite capable."

"We agreed with Claire to leave Jack out of this," Charlène said.

"We have no choice. He was already involved with the butcher's granddaughter, and elements of that group have known of his whereabouts. If we left him in New Hampshire, he might be dead by now. Look at his wife."

"It seems that you were already too late, Jean," Charlène replied. "I don't know how effective he can be at this point."

"You and I have been through much worse in France. I expect he will come through," Jean reasoned.

"Those were different times, *mon ami.* We had no choice, but he does," Charlène said. "Sonny's death has affected me, and now you want to place his son into my hands as well? I am not sure I can handle that."

"Let time tell. I am sure he will want to participate after what has become of his family. Revenge is a powerful motive," Jean said.

"That is not a good reason, and it is a dangerous one," Charlène snapped back.

Jean decided to change the subject. "How are your Aunt Antoinette and Uncle Robbie in Bergues?"

"They are doing very well, thank you for asking," Charlène answered. "Even though they are in their late nineties, they still get around town, but the trips to the United States are a bit much for them these days. I plan to visit them soon."

Jean did not respond, thinking of years past in France as he stared out onto the well-manicured courtyard sipping his brandy. For the next few hours the old friends sat quietly taking in the view.

That evening a guest arrived at the estate in a large black van. Charlène was there to greet its passenger.

"It is quite cold outside. Please come in. You must be tired after that long journey. My name is Charlène Shemesh," she said.

Charlène brushed aside Georges's attempt to guide the guest, explaining she would get her settled in herself. The new guest was carried on a stretcher to the same guest quarters as Jack, both in the same wing of the estate, in nearby rooms.

Doting over her new arrival, she said, "I spent much of my teen years in these guest quarters, as I did not feel much like family then, having lost my parents at an early age. It was a few years before my aunt and uncle could coax me out from here to stay in the main house with them. Over the years I have made this place a haven. I am sure you will find your suite quite comfortable and spacious. If you need anything, please use the intercom to summon Georges."

"Thank you for your hospitality, Charlène," the guest offered sincerely.

That evening, *le dîner* was superb. The table centerpiece was set with all types of fruit, and the smell of hot, fresh bread, piled high in baskets, filled the air. Butter from Normandy sat in crystal dishes. There was a superior selection of fine French wines, each sitting in an individual silver cooler, to accompany the meal. Georges stood by, ready to serve whatever each guest desired.

Dinner was utterly delicious.

Jack dug into the meal like a starving wolf before he realized his impropriety. He had never tasted such fantastic cuisine before.

Jack said, "I am sorry. I seem to have forgotten my manners."

"*C'est pas grave*. It is not important, Jack," Charlène replied. "It's been a long day for you. Please enjoy."

Finally, coffee and brandy were served simultaneously, depending on each person's palate. Jack chose the coffee, while Jean and Charlène enjoyed brandy.

"That was quite a meal, Charlène," Jack said. "I am not so sure I could eat this well every day and not gain weight!"

"*Merci*, Jack, but I do this for my guests. I find as I get older that I, myself, cannot normally eat like this anymore." Charlène laughed.

***

Over the next several weeks, Jack healed well enough to get around the estate. He walked the grounds, enjoying the cold, crisp winter air of the Virginia estate. Jack would now train to be a spy, something he only dreamed of in the past.

Ah, Emily, Jack thought, I miss you so much.

The days were spent in the secret operations center Charlène had under the estate. She told him it reminded her of the cave beneath Henri and Antoinette's farm in Bergues, France.

It reminded Jack of the Bat Cave!

"Jack, the training we will give you here is the same as the CIA agents have received at nearby Camp Peary since 1951," Charlène explained. "You will receive everything from driving techniques to navigation and tricks of the trade."

Although he was to go through training for staged kidnapping, torture, and escape techniques, it was mutually decided by Jean and Charlène that his real-life experiences with Gisele were enough to prepare him for his job.

Jack thought back to the day he finally captured and eliminated Gisele, the granddaughter of the Nazi butcher SS Sturmbannführer Gustav.

The sun was rising on the horizon when Gisele awoke in the passenger seat.

They were driving down a winding dirt road, but Gisele had no clue where they were. His SUV had skidded to a stop, causing gravel and dirt to fly everywhere and the passenger door to fling open on its own, as it was prone to do.

He propelled the SUV into a sharp U-turn. Gisele was catapulted from her seat and rolled into the chasm. Her screams could be heard only for a few moments.

Jack had played that scene over and over since the death of his father and Gisele. As the weeks went by, he buried himself in the training; his hatred for Gisele and her comrades drove him to train long hours.

Seeing Jack continuing to be emotional from his encounter with Gisele, Charlène took him aside to her study late one afternoon. "Jack, I can see why you are doing this, why you may want to train so hard, but you need to place those emotions of hatred aside. One day it will get you in trouble, if not killed," she said.

"I understand, Charlène, but that's what drives me. A part of me can't let that go," Jack replied.

"Once, I was the same as you. I had lost my parents and almost lost my own life to the Nazis during the war. Even when I moved to the United States and to this estate with my uncle and aunt, I was a recluse, afraid to go outside. Sonny brought me back to life, and from that day I vowed not to let my emotions rule me again," Charlène explained.

Jack instinctively gave Charlène a hug, and they both sat down and shared a glass of brandy, watching the setting sun light up the stained glass window of the study in a brilliant kaleidoscope of colors.

Jack's training began the very next day.

Jean's first goal for Jack was to train him to field strip and reassemble the firearms used by the organization.

Jean took him to an outdoor range on the property and had him assemble and reassemble those same firearms in different levels of light and weather conditions.

Jack's favorite part of training was learning how to safely handle and detonate explosives, especially the C-4.

After the basic firearms and explosive course, Jack was given training in severe driving techniques, from stealing a car to running blockades and fending off attacks on his vehicle. This training was followed with instruction in evasion techniques with high-speed turnarounds and precision stopping.

Jack was also given basic compass navigation through a variety of terrain, such as swamp and forest. As his instructor explained, "Jack, you must be able to navigate obstacles in the wilderness as well as urban environments under different conditions."

Jack took it all in with gusto. He had a new beginning and was going to see it through for his parents and, especially, as revenge for Emily.

Six months after Jack arrived, he was introduced to the last and most important part of his training. He was to learn how to trail suspects and detect if he was being followed himself. He was taught breaking and entering techniques, telephone bugging, and dropping off information in secret locales.

Last, and definitely not Jack's favorite, he learned the finer details of report writing.

In August, Charlène approached Jack. "Congratulations on completing your training, Jack. You have honored your father. The CIA actually does a final test of role-playing and hunting down the graduates, but Jean and I feel you are ready without going through that."

"Charlène, you have given me new hope and purpose, and I pray I can continue to honor his memory and make you proud," Jack said.

"I am sure he is smiling down on you now, Jack," Charlène replied. "I owe your father my life. It's only fair I prepare his son properly!"

"If you'll pardon me, I would like to pay a visit to our guest," Jack requested, excusing himself from Charlène's presence.

"Certainly, Jack. I will see you at dinner."

Jack went to his room and showered and shaved. Afterward he put on the shirt Emily loved. It was never his favorite, but it reminded him of better times with her and the many fond memories together.

Stepping out of his room and closing the door, he took the fifteen steps he counted every night to the room adjacent to his. Knocking softly, he heard a woman's voice say, "Come in."

Entering, he saw that the bandage covering her head had been removed; her soft blonde hair was gradually growing back.

"It's nice to see you again, Jack. How are you feeling these days?" the woman asked.

"Much better. My therapy here is finished," Jack answered.

"Oh... does that mean you will be leaving?" the woman asked.

Jack smiled. "For a time, but I will be back to see you walk out of this place."

"I love that shirt on you, Jack. That would be something I would pick out," she remarked, speaking her words slowly and deliberately.

"You chose this shirt for me. Look at it. Can you remember buying it?" Jack said, hoping the shirt would spark Emily's memories of their life together. He was almost desperate.

"No, Jack, I don't," Emily said. "I wish I could remember."

"You will, Em." Jack smiled.

As far as the world was concerned, Emily, for her own protection, was dead. Jack agreed with Jean and his mother that a fake funeral for Emily would throw off Tommy from carrying out the rest of his vendetta against their family. To him, she was dead. In time, I will exact my revenge on him, Jack thought, but he must never discover Emily is alive.

Even though she still did not recognize him, the doctors felt certain that she would recover most, if not all, of her memory. She had, after all, the best doctors in the country working on her rehabilitation.

"Jack, she may not remember the shooting; that trauma could be buried forever," Dr. Wainright told him one night.

"Maybe it's for the best then," Jack said.

Ever since Emily was secretly whisked away to Charlène's estate, Jack had visited her every night, sometimes waiting until she had fallen fast asleep. Her recovery had been a long and arduous experience, but he was there for her every step of the way. As per Dr. Wainright's orders, Jack did not reveal that he was her husband; instead he pretended to be a patient as well.

Charlène grew close to Emily. She was the daughter she never had. She did everything to promote Emily's recovery. Once Emily was well enough, they took walks around the grounds of the estate. She brought in the best therapists to recover her strength and movement. Emily had to be retrained to walk and to speak normally again.

As the months went by, with Jack busy with his training, she slowly and steadily grew stronger. Charlène was with her every step. She recognized the pain and desire to become well again.

When Jack could get the time off from his training, he would go on walks with Emily. On one such occasion, Charlène appeared with a small German shepherd puppy in tow.

Emily laughed as the puppy did its best to remove itself from the bonds of its leash.

She turned to Jack laughing. "Remember when Sassy was in puppy training? She was such a bad student!"

"Emily, you remember Sassy?" Jack asked.

"Yes I do," Emily said. "Were we married, Jack? I am starting to remember."

Emily suddenly felt like she was going to pass out. Images she recognized and remembered swirled in her head. The world around her spun out of control as she blacked out. The last thing she remembered was her husband's arms catching her as she fell.

JEAN AUBRAC

Jean Aubrac was born in the village of Saint-Quentin in the year of our Lord 1935 to Danielle and René Aubrac. He grew up with loving parents, who spoiled their only child.

Jean's grandfather was killed in 1918, in the trenches not far from their country farm. Although he never knew his grandfather personally, Jean would spend hours going through his trunk, which was kept tucked away under his parents' bed. His uniform, helmet, and medals were a source of fascination to the young boy, who loved to play army.

Danielle was a vivacious French housewife and mother, who treated her son like the daughter she could never have. After a very difficult pregnancy with Jean, the doctor warned that a second pregnancy would kill her.

Her husband, René, accepted this. When Jean reached the age of eight, René assumed most of his son's upbringing by having him help with the farm animals. René would also take him hiking in the woods, showing Jean how to survive on the edible plants in the forest.

Jean learned how to pick, dry, and grind ivy to be used as a spice as well as handle stinging nettles and dog roses. He learned to recognize the difference between hogweed, which can be boiled and eaten, as opposed to giant hogweed, which is poisonous.

The outdoors became his classroom, and his father taught him how to survive if the need arose. The occupation of their country was a very rough time for the French, and René knew that someday they might have to flee the country, especially given their recent activities with the Maquis partisans.

Jean learned how to find roots that would make a delicious soup he could cook in a pot of boiling water over a fire made with just two stones. He learned to capture, skin, and cook rabbits and squirrels by creating traps from nature.

Jean would always ask, "Papa, why do we have to kill the animals?"

René would always reply, "We are not killing them, Jean. We are harvesting them for survival."

It was a good point to Jean, but he never did like to kill the creatures of the forest, even for food.

They camped out under the stars. Another survival skill his father showed him was how to trap rainwater and dew by using his ciré to set up a makeshift shower. These were skills he would carry within him, using them often while on missions for French intelligence, and later, The Pond.

After France fell in 1940 to the invading German army, Jean was terrified when the occupying forces passed through their serene village, taking what they wanted and imposing strict curfews on the villagers. The Nazi regime was getting revenge for the oppressive sanctions placed on them by the Allies, especially the French, after World War I, the Great War. Jean's father, René, did not serve in that war, but his grandfather, André, did. Twenty-two years later, their home was still surrounded by what remained of the trench network of the French army of 1918. Jean would play army in those trenches with his friends, arguing who would play the victorious French over the bosch! When Jean would come home, proudly telling his father of his victories over the bosch, he would be scolded by his mother on the dangers that still lurked, buried in the ground. Millions of artillery shells were fired during that war, she reminded him, and not all of them had exploded.

"You are not to play there. *Jamais!*" she warned him.

"Oui, Mamamaman," he always said, knowing that he would venture there again the very next day.

Life in occupied France was no picnic. Several times a truck loaded with German soldiers had come and looted their home, taking their remaining cows, chickens, and horses. Any food they had would be split into what they had hidden and those items they would "allow" the bosch to take.

It was puzzling to Jean that this great mechanized army would need horses, but his father informed him that the Germans used thousands of them to move supplies and equipment to the rear areas on the battlefield.

Jean was present one beautiful summer afternoon in the nearby village when a Jewish family was taken away. A German man in a dark suit led the soldiers into the family's house.

"Gestapo," his father whispered and then hurriedly gathered up his wife and Jean and headed back to their *chaumière* on the village outskirts. For the most part, the Germans did not bother the Aubracs for the next few years, but eventually their affiliations with the resistance brought them under suspicion.

Jean's parents were avid Communists, belonging to the French Communist Party—*Parti communiste français*, or PCF—founded in 1920 by those in the French Section of the Workers' International (SFIO) who supported the Bolshevik Revolution in Russia and who opposed the First World War. The death of Jean's grandfather solidified their resolve.

Adolf Hitler's access to power in 1933 and the destruction of the Communist Party of Germany following the Reichstag fire on February 27, 1933, assured Danielle and René Aubrac that Fascism must be stopped at any cost, and they enthusiastically joined the party.

After the occupation, in May 1941, the young couple helped the PCF organize more than one hundred thousand miners in the Nord and Pas-de-Calais departments in a strike. It was very risky for them to get involved, but the oppression on the people was so intense, they felt a need to revolt against the occupiers.

When Germany invaded the Soviet Union in 1941, Danielle and René Aubrac joined the Maquis partisans, advocating the use of direct action and political assassinations.

By 1944 the PCF had reached the height of its influence, controlling large areas of the country. René and Danielle were very active in resistance activities with the Maquis partisans.

On several occasions René and Danielle had gone out with local partisan groups, sometimes headed up by Henri Gibert, other times by a woman named Madeleine. Their targets in the early years of occupation were communication lines and railway tracks, to disrupt the movement of German troops. They avoided killing the Nazis outright, as the risk of repercussions to French civilians was too great. The Germans, especially the feared SS, would exterminate entire villages for the death of even one German soldier.

One evening the couple met up with Henri on a mission to disassemble a rail track in the hopes it would look like an accident.

"René, Danielle, *Comment ça va?* How is that boy of yours?" Henri asked.

"He does what boys do, always in trouble!" René chuckled.

"He should study more," Danielle said, "before *les bosch* take an interest in him!"

"I don't think they would bother with a boy," Henri said.

"*Oui*, but these days, remaining silent and unseen is a good thing. Jean is too curious for his own good," Danielle said.

"*Comme tous les garçons!*" Henri replied.

The group nodded in agreement, René and Henri exchanging knowing smiles as they moved into a forested area opposite the railroad tracks that passed on the fringes of their village. René and Danielle were outfitted in their usual garb of dark clothes, René wearing a black woolen watch cap, and Danielle, her beret. They both carried Fusil Berthier Mle 1916 model rifles that René's father had kept from World War I. Each team member had a shovel or pick to move the rails.

"I just received a shipment of Lee Enfield rifles," Henri commented. "We should replace those old relics you two are carrying."

"They are reliable," René said. "I am not so sure the British ones are."

"Agreed, but the ammunition stocks are getting very low," Henri explained. "It's time to change while we can."

Entering a clearing, the railway tracks appeared before them. The partisans went to work. Working the rusted bolts with a sledge hammer, Henri was able to loosen one track.

"Use your picks and shovels," he instructed the other partisans. "Make it look like an accident, like the bolt snapped by itself."

Working in unison, the group was able to move the rail.

With a satisfied grunt, Henri said, "That should be enough to send the train off the tracks. *Maintenant, partons vite!*"

Packing up their gear and smoothing out the ground around the rail to hide their activities, the partisans blended back into the forest, going their separate ways.

The next day, the occupiers rounded up villagers and demanded to know who derailed their supply train. Everyone stood firm in denial, but *les bosch* were not satisfied. There were too many "accidents" of late. The German high command decided to bring in the Gestapo to investigate. Many villagers were interrogated, some never to be seen again. René and Danielle suspected someone talked, as the Gestapo questioned their activities on two different occasions over the past few months. Each time, they seemed to be appeased with the account of their activities in the village.

Realizing they were running out of time, René and Danielle made preparations to leave for southern France, possibly to cross into Spain, to save their family. Danielle and René were in contact with the Maquis partisan leader Madeleine, planning out a route of safe houses, supplies, and transportation to get them to the border.

A few days before their departure, the Gestapo caught up with René and Danielle Aubrac. Jean had been watching a rabbit as it entered its burrow in the woods near their small cottage when he saw a black sedan arrive with a German truck full of SS soldiers following behind. He knew what this meant. In the past, when his parents thought he was asleep in bed, he would sneak down the steps that led to his bedroom to listen to them talk at night. He heard his parents whisper many times of friends in the resistance movement who were taken away, never to be heard from again.

Jean froze, hidden from view in the dense forest by their house. Tears welled up in his eyes, and he want to cry out to his mother when he saw his parents beaten by *les bosch* and forced into the back of the truck. They would be taken to the internment camp at Drancy, a suburb of Paris. Few survived the savage interrogations, and if they did, they would either be executed or sent away to die in one of the many Nazi concentration camps. If they were fit enough, they could be sent to Germany to work in one of the wartime factories, helping the Germans defeat the Allies. Some chose to die.

Jean stayed in the forest for hours afterward. He was terrified the Gestapo had set a trap for him. He almost wanted to be taken away, so he could see his parents again. It wasn't until hours later that he had the courage to approach the house.

His legs resisted moving, but he put one in front of the other, forcing himself forward. Tentatively he pushed open the door, its hinges broken and creaking. It fell to the floor with a loud crash, and Jean instinctively rushed inside, his heart pounding.

The scene was horrific; furniture and family pictures were broken and strewn across the room. Droplets of blood led from the middle of the room past the front door, coagulating in a small puddle in the dirt outside. Jean sat in the middle of the carnage and wept uncontrollably, and at some point during the evening, he passed out from grief. It was well after midnight when he awoke, shivering from shock, in a fetal position on the floor.

With some effort he got to his feet and slowly went upstairs to his room, his brain unable to process what had happened. We should have left earlier, he thought as he began to cry again. We could have been happy and free!

Time became a blur as Jean lay in his bed. He was delirious from the horror he witnessed, devastated by the loss of his parents. He managed to get out of bed on the second day, determined to clean up the house. They would return, he thought. They must! When they do, *Maman* will be proud that I straightened out the house and cleaned up the blood.

Going outside, Jean grabbed an old wooden bucket. Working the pump at the well, he filled it halfway and marched decisively into the house, determined to make everything right again. Working through the day and into the night, Jean cleaned the blood from the floor and straightened out the furniture the best he could.

Later that night he lay in bed exhausted. If they are already dead, he thought, I want to die too. Tomorrow I will find Papa's rifle and take my revenge. Jean didn't remember when he fell asleep, but he awoke to a beautiful morning. The sunlight streamed into his room as it always did, and the birds were chirping outside his window.

Maybe this was all a dream, he thought hopefully. That was until he looked down at his clothes, still streaked with blood. Tears filled his eyes as he made his way downstairs hoping to see his parents getting ready to start their day. The house was silent, and Jean stood in the kitchen for a long time before deciding what he must do.

Searching the basement, he found his father's rifle wrapped in a blanket and buried in the dirt under the foundation of the house. I can use this, he thought, looking at the old rifle. I'm glad Papa taught me how to shoot. I can kill many bosch before they get me.

Walking with the rifle still wrapped in the blanket, Jean suddenly stopped in the *salle de séjour*. Although he had rinsed the majority of the blood off the floor, the visible outline of the blood pool had been absorbed into the wooden floorboards and would not come out.

It took only a few moments to make his decision. If he attacked *les bosch*, he would die, and until he knew for sure if his mother and father were dead, he would wait to take his revenge.

Placing the rifle back in its hiding place in the basement, he went to his bedroom, grabbed his *sac à dos*, and began to pack some clothes. I must hide in the woods, Jean thought, because *les bosch* will come back for me. They will use me to force information from my parents. I must hide for their safety, but where? His mind raced for an answer.

Jean sat for hours trying to decide what to do. He wished his parents were here to guide him to a decision. It was at sunset, as the shadows deepened in the house, when he made his decision.

Mais oui, I will find Tante Liliane. She will know what to do. Taking his ciré off the back of his bedroom door, he put it on and threw his *sac à dos* over his shoulder. Going into the kitchen, he grabbed a box of matches from the cabinet near the stove and went outside.

Jean grabbed the walking stick his father had often used on their hikes in the forest to learn about edible plants. He went over to where his mother had been hanging laundry when the bosch arrived to take them away and pulled down a bed sheet. Tearing it into strips, he wrapped it around the walking stick, tying it securely into a knot.

Moving to the side of the house, Jean lifted the petrol can filled with kerosene and poured some of the liquid on the makeshift torch. He methodically splashed his home with the flammable liquid, as tears streamed down his dirty face. Dropping the empty can of fuel to the ground, he struck a match against the tinder box and set the walking stick afire.

The torch lit up the night as Jean set the only home he knew ablaze. He knew that the Gestapo would return for him and search the home for any evidence they could find to incriminate his parents. He vowed they would find nothing, only a burned-out skeleton. By doing this I stand a chance of seeing them one day, he thought with sadness, tears running down his dirty face.

Jean stood in the front yard of the once beautiful *chaumière*, the flames engulfing it, The burning cottage, surrounded by the purple lilies his mother loved so much, made a surreal sight.

***

Liliane Aubrac was widowed at an early age when her husband died of a typhoid epidemic that struck her village in 1943. She barely lived herself but managed to survive the terrible disease by having her gallbladder removed.

Liliane recovered in time, with the help of her brother René and sister-in-law Danielle. Danielle stayed with her for a few months, helping her recover. Jean stayed with his mother, helping his aunt tend to the farm animals.

Aunt Liliane lived nearby, and Jean always looked forward to weekend visits to her farm. There she taught him how to ride and take care of her horses, milk cows, and feed the chickens.

It was a quiet, serene life, even in the occupation, but that all changed that fall when the SS Adolf Hitler Division arrived in Pas-de-Calais. They were much different than the regular German soldiers, very often cruel and ruthless. Stationed nearby, they commandeered her farm animals, leaving Liliane with only an old horse. Life after that was very difficult for Liliane, and she was very bitter.

It was then that her brother told her of his involvement with the Communist Maquis partisans. René explained that he could introduce her to the leaders in their area if she wanted to take revenge on *les bosch*. Liliane did not hesitate in aiding the resistance. She had heard Charles de Gaulle's resistance speech, in June of 1940, but that all seemed distant to her on her secluded farm. Now it was personal.

In 1944, Liliane was involved in partisan activities to disrupt Nazi troop movements. Her group destroyed railroad tracks and radar installations and reported troop movements to the Allies whenever the opportunity arose. It was a dangerous and risky existence, but the adrenaline of taking revenge on the bosch was addicting. She knew her chances of being caught were high, but the situation at hand demanded that each French man and woman do what they could to free their beloved country from Nazi hands.

Jean made his way toward his aunt's farmhouse, several kilometers away. He was on his own for the first time in his life. He knew these woods well, making his way along trails his father had shown him. Jean had no trouble finding the landmarks. They were well concealed from German eyes, but every partisan knew them.

His world was ripped away by *les bosch*, and he vowed on that long walk that he would dedicate his life to destroying that evil. It wasn't until the predawn hours that Jean arrived at Aunt Liliane's farmhouse. Normally, it would have taken him a matter of hours, but he hid often, seeing farmers and Germans alike passing nearby. He trusted no one.

Exhausted from his ordeal, he longed for a warm meal and the consoling arms of his favorite aunt. Still, as he spied her darkened farmhouse, the hairs stood on the back of his neck. Had they arrested her too?

No, he thought, it was like when his mother would go out at night to procure food for us from *le marché*. Mother and Father would leave around midnight on foot to walk to the village unseen. They kept to the wooded areas so as to not attract attention after the curfew. Tante Liliane must be going to other people to get meat and other *produits alimentaires* she needed. I will wait for her return.

Sneaking to an outcropping of trees nearby, Jean watched the house for many minutes before he decided it was safe to approach. The house was dark and Jean went to the back door, figuring he wouldn't be seen by anyone who might be watching the house.

Luckily the house was unlocked, something that was common in the farm country. Not wanting to make any noise, Jean softly closed the door behind him and stood still for a few moments until his eyes adjusted to the darkened house. He kept deathly still, his senses on overdrive as he scanned the pitch-blackness for any danger lurking within.

The dawn was still hours away, and he made his way into the darkness to find his aunt. Searching the house, he saw no sign of her, but luckily there was no sign that she had been taken away, either. Tante Liliane must have gone to town yesterday to stay overnight like she had many times before, complaining that her old horse took forever to get there! She should return by midmorning, Jean thought. I am exhausted and want to lie down, just for a little while. Finding his way to a tiny *chambre d'ami*, he settled down on the bed fully dressed and instantly fell fast asleep.

Jean did not recall how long he had slept, but the house was still dark when he heard the front door open. Jumping out of bed, he was about to shout out to his aunt when he thought better of the idea and peeked around the corner into the hallway. What he saw terrified him. He recognized a German sniper rifle slowly pushing open the front door as a shadowy figure entered *la salle de sèjour*.

Jean froze. They have come for Aunt Liliane! They will certainly kill me too, he thought. He knew he must find a way to escape and warn his aunt. Moving swiftly and silently toward the back door, he skidded to a stop when he caught sight of a figure entering the window. He was trapped! Turning and doing the only thing he could think of, Jean bolted for the front door, hoping to knock down the German and quickly make his way into the forest.

Jean saw his opening. Running as hard as he could, he raced for the front door. The figure with the sniper rifle had already made its way toward his aunt's bedroom.

He didn't get far. Someone tackled him from behind, hands grasping his jacket and dragging him to the ground. He fought viciously to escape but was pinned to the floor.

Looming overhead, the figure with the sniper rifle aimed at his chest.

Luckily for Jean, the figure was that of his aunt, not *les bosch*.

Years passed by as Jean grew up, helping his aunt until she died on a cool fall evening from complications of the typhoid epidemic she had previously survived.

By then, Jean was a young man in his twenties who had graduated from engineering school and was working in an agency within French intelligence. While hunting down Communist spies, he met a young man named Joe with the code name of Sonny. They worked together to capture a particularly clever Russian agent known only as Claire.

To his perpetual amusement, he would have never guessed that, upon her capture, Sonny would fall madly in love with her and marry her.

For years after, Jean showed no mercy to the former Nazis he hunted, avenging his parents' death time and again. He was well known in the intelligence community for his cold heart, but that softened one day in 1960 when he once again met Charlène on a mission to Budapest. He was to guide her into Communist Hungary to provide intelligence on a diplomat with ties to the Kremlin.

During that mission they shared their stories and experiences during the war, realizing the common ground they had when children lose their parents in wartime. Over the years, a special bond formed between the new friends, each seeing the world in a new light. For years they worked together like a well-oiled machine on high-level top secret missions for French Intelligence and The Pond.

After the mission in Budapest, Jean was assigned to The Pond as a liaison by French intelligence, eventually becoming an American citizen working for the same organization. Over the years, Charlène and Jean rose through the ranks to eventually run The Pond jointly.

Jean had not worked with Joe or Scotty on the recent encounter with Gisele but had sent a promising young operative by the name of Ben Townley to help find the woman. Unfortunately, she got to him first, murdering him in a newspaper's parking lot. At the estate's operations center, while talking to Ben on the phone, Jean had heard the unmistakable sound of a pistol's silencer pop in the background. His best and most promising operative was gone. It was a mistake to send the unseasoned spy into that situation, and he made a promise to himself to ensure Jack would be ready.

Now, in 2002, Jean did the best he could to train Sonny's son Jack in the fine art of espionage. Jack seemed at first to be an unwilling student, but Jean recognized the same desire for revenge that struck him as he burned his home to the ground, the same desire to pick up his father's old rifle to kill *les bosch*!

Revenge, he judged, is a powerful weapon.

WAKE UP CALL

The next evening, Jean and Charlène requested that Jack come into the study after dinner. Georges, the butler, poured them all some Cognac and left them closing the wooden doors together with an audible click.

"Jack, we feel it's time for you to go on your first mission," Jean spoke first. "We have been tasked with providing intelligence on a foreign businessman in New York City." Taking a small sip of Cognac, he produced a picture from a folder. "This man is a Hungarian, Vilja Vargas, and we believe he has ties to terrorist groups in Europe and the Middle East."

"We want you to tail him in New York," Charlène continued. "Our sources tell us that he will meet with a terrorist leader sometime in the next two days. We have secured a room for you at the Ritz-Carlton in Battery Park."

"All you have to do is get us proof of his activities. We will provide you with everything you need to record his actions," Jean said.

"That's all?" Jack was a bit disappointed at such a seemingly menial task.

"Jack, I know this sounds a bit simple, but in our line of work, there are a lot of mundane missions that need to be accomplished. Being the new kid on the block, so to speak, you're not going to get the more complex missions until we feel you can handle them," Jean explained.

Jack smiled at the pair of seasoned spies. "Actually, I am quite excited to get out there on my first mission, whatever it may be." Secretly he thought, No sense pissing them off now, or I'll be following people forever.

"That's the spirit!" Charlène said.

Over the next few hours, the two briefed Jack on the particulars of his mission: the flights he would take in and out of New York, his papers, and emergency contacts.

"It would be wise to get some sleep, Jack," Charlène intoned. "You won't get much over the next couple of days."

"Thank you for everything. I'll see you in the morning. *Bonne nuit.*"

"*Bonne nuit*, Jack," Jean and Charlène replied.

After Jack had left the room, Jean whispered to Charlène, "Do you think the mission is too dangerous for his first time? He seemed a bit nervous."

"If he is, I didn't see it. In fact, he seemed a bit disappointed on our choice of missions," Charlène said.

"He needs to build up his confidence; a simple trailing mission should help," Jean said.

"Vargas can be a dangerous man if provoked. We need to keep close tabs on Jack," Charlène said.

"He will be fine, *ma chérie*," Jean said as he lifted his brandy snifter. "To Jack's first!"

"À Jack et son premier succès!" Charlène replied.

Jack was excited and disappointed at the same time. I didn't know that was possible, he thought. I should see Emily before I leave. She may miss my visits. I sure will.

That evening Jack sat with Emily discussing her progress.

"Jack, when I dream, images float in and out. I saw a house with a matching shed, lots of flowers, and beautiful trees all around. Sometimes I dream I see you but can't make out your words," Emily said.

"Those images are of our house in New Hampshire, and when you can travel, I'll take you there. Hopefully it will jog your memory some more."

"That would be nice," Emily replied. "I have grown fond of you, and if we were happily married, I want to know what kind of life we had, Jack."

Jack hung his head, hiding the tears welling up in his eyes. After a few moments to compose himself, he said, "I should be getting to bed. I have an early flight tomorrow."

"Where are you going?" Emily asked.

"I have a training mission to complete, nothing serious," Jack said.

"OK, good luck. Come back soon," Emily replied.

Lying in his bed later, Jack stared at the ceiling. It was almost midnight, and he needed to get some rest. But his thoughts were racing about his mission. He would have to find a way to trail Vargas without making his presence known. Jack reflected on his training, albeit accelerated over the past six months. He knew he was up to the task. He unconsciously rubbed the scar on his chest and vowed, Someday I'll pay back that bastard Tommy!

The next morning came early for Jack. Georges woke him at 5:00 AM by bringing him a hearty breakfast of coffee, hot rolls and butter, fruits, and cheeses.

"Madame Shemesh has requested that you be ready at 6:00 AM in the front courtyard. Her chauffeur will take you to the airport," Georges stated.

"Certainly. Thank you, Georges," Jack replied.

"By your leave, Monsieur Jack," Georges remarked as he left the bedroom and closed the door behind him.

Jack, feeling too excited and nervous about the upcoming adventure, didn't eat much. He dressed in a blue business suit and a patterned red-and-blue tie that Emily had given him a few years ago at Christmas. He gathered up his small suitcase and satchel filled with bogus documents relating to computer technology. Jack's cover was to be a computer salesman on a trip to New York.

Walking down the hallway, he was met by Jean and Charlène.

"Jack, here is your wallet. Your name is John Willingham, from Qwertycom, based in Rhode Island. We picked John as your new first name just in case you slip up with your own real name." Jean instructed.

"Thanks," Jack replied. "That makes things a bit easier when I do."

"Let's try not to, Jack. This is a very important mission," Charlène said. *"Bonne chance, bon courage, et bon voyage!"*

"Thank you for all the help and confidence in me," Jack replied.

"We will wait for your nightly communiqué at the hour we designated," Jean said.

"Will do," Jack answered, striding through the open door and into the awaiting limousine.

Jack was to catch a small commuter jet from the Newport News-Williamsburg Airport to JFK. He was no stranger to New York; having been a New Englander, he had visited the city several times in the past. Once, on New Year's Eve, he even witnessed the ball drop in Times Square.

At the airport, the plane was parked in front of the gate when Jack arrived. It was an early-morning flight, and he breezed through security without any issues to await the go-ahead to board.

The hour-and-a-half flight was a bumpy ride, the summer winds playing with the small jet. At JFK, Jack recovered his belongings from baggage and hailed a taxi.

A yellow cab pulled up beside Jack, and the cabbie yelled though the open passenger-side window, "Where to, buddy?"

"The Ritz-Carlton at Battery Park," Jack shouted back, buses and taxis driving by, drowning out any chance of talking normally. Jack hopped into the back of the taxi, and the driver headed out onto the Jersey turnpike.

Pulling up in front of the hotel, the doorman opened the taxi door just as Jack was paying the fare. "Welcome to the Ritz-Carlton," the doorman greeted Jack. "May I take your luggage?"

"Thanks, I think I can manage," Jack said. Despite the fact that he carried in his own luggage, he slipped the doorman a ten, the smallest bill he had after he had paid the cabbie and given him a tip.

"Have a nice stay, sir," the doorman said. A ten, the doorman thought. Cheap bastard.

Jack was pleased he was able to get a room at the Ritz-Carlton in Manhattan. I've always wanted to stay by here, since it overlooks New York Harbor, Ellis Island, and the Statue of Liberty. I wish I could visit the SoHo and Tribeca neighborhoods, but I don't have time for that now. Maybe when Emily fully recovers, we can spend a nice weekend here, he thought. If we can afford it!

Jack strode up purposefully to the main desk to check in.

"How may I help you, sir? Do you have a reservation?" the man behind the desk asked.

Looking at the clerk's badge, Jack answered, "Yes, Don, I do. It should be under my name, Jack Willingham," he said, catching his mistake too late. Red faced, he decided to let it go.

"Ah, I have a reservation for two nights for a *John* Willingham. I assume that is you?" the clerk asked.

"Yes, sorry. Jack's my nickname."

"Are you here on business?" the clerk inquired politely.

"Yes, I'm in town for my computer company," Jack answered a bit too quickly. Calm down; you're too nervous, Jack thought.

The clerk gave him a quizzical look.

"Sorry. A bit much to take in. My first time in New York," Jack lied.

"Well, if you need any help during your stay, the concierge desk over there is at your service," Don replied. "We also have a wonderful spa for you to relax. Would you like help with your bags today, Mr. Willingham?"

"No thanks," Jack replied. "I have just one bag. I think I've got it."

"Fine," the clerk replied. "Here is your room key. I am sure you will find the view spectacular."

Jack took the envelope containing the key card and headed to the elevator. Off to one side, a man was sitting and reading a newspaper. He was also quietly observing Jack.

Jack's room was nicely furnished. The living room was decorated in pastel yellows. On the glass-topped coffee table were a bottle of pinot noir and a silver platter holding a variety of cheeses. There was a card beside them.

Opening the card, Jack smiled as he read the typed note: *Good luck, John.*

"Nice touch," Jack said aloud as he dropped his bag on the floor and placed his satchel on the coffee table next to the wine bottle.

Popping the cork and pouring himself a glass, he helped himself to a few pieces of cheddar cheese. Afterward, Jack took his bag and walked into the spacious bedroom, decorated in the same yellow pastels and dark wood accents. Wandering over to the window, Jack was greeted by a spectacular view of the Statue of Liberty and the Hudson River. The sun sparkled on the rippling water as tour boats passed his room on their way to Liberty Island. Beside the window was a telescope that Jack thought might come in handy. Peering into it, Jack quickly realized this was one of those decorations you find in hotels, not a telescope with any usefulness.

Jack ventured from the snug haven of his room onto the balcony, enjoying a breathtaking view along the scenic esplanade of Battery Park.

I better check in with Jean and Charlène, he thought, reaching into his inner suit pocket and pulling out the phone they gave him.

Opening the phone, he pushed the call button.

Jean answered. "I see you have made it, Jack. Any problems along the way?"

"None. It went smoothly," Jack said. "But then again, all I did was check in at the hotel."

"You would be surprised how many missions fail at the most mundane moments," Jean said. "Keep eyes in back of your head at all times."

"Will do. Have you any news about our friend?" Jack asked.

"He has made reservations for 8:00 PM tonight at the Two West restaurant at the Ritz. I would make reservations before that so you're already seated to observe him," Jean said.

"Great idea. Thanks, Jean," Jack replied, chuckling softly. He knew this already from his training. It reminded him of black ice for some reason.

"The *madame* gives her best," Jean informed Jack.

"Same." Jack held onto hope. "I'll talk to you after I have completed the task at hand."

"Till then," Jean said.

Jack ended the call and placed the phone on the desk. Exhausted from the lack of sleep the previous night, he set up a wakeup call for 6:00 PM after making dinner reservations for 7:45. Removing his jacket and placing it on the desk chair, he kicked off his shoes and lay down on the bed. And fell fast asleep.

The world came back slowly into view as Jack woke up to find his room dark. He glanced over at the phone, and a red light was blinking. Damn it, he thought as he looked at the alarm clock. 8:15!

Jumping up, he grabbed the phone and pushed the button for the restaurant. The clatter of dishes and conversation almost drowned out the voice of the woman who answered the phone.

"Hi, this is John Willingham. I am sorry, but business kept me from arriving on time for my reservation. Do you have any openings?" Jack asked.

"One moment, let me check, Mr. Willingham."

After a short pause, she said, "Mr. Willingham, I can fit you in. When can you be here?"

"Give me ten minutes," Jack said.

"Certainly. We will see you then," the hostess replied.

Jack rushed into the bathroom, splashing cold water on his face. Wetting his hands, he ran them through his hair to get rid of his bed head and then quickly gargled with the mouthwash by the sink.

Jack hurriedly put on his shoes, knotting one lace terribly, which took a few moments to fix. He grabbed the suit jacket off the chair, placing the phone in the inner pocket, and headed out the door.

Damn, how could I screw up my first mission on the first day? Jack thought. Jean and Charlène spent so much time on me, and I fall asleep!

Coming off the elevator, Jack followed the hallway around to Two West. As he walked in to be seated, he recognized Vargas, who was sitting at a table facing him in a corner of the restaurant. A man he couldn't make out was facing the other way.

"Welcome to Two West. Do you have a reservation?" the hostess inquired as Jack approached the hostess stand.

"Willingham," Jack responded.

"Ah yes, I have the same table you requested earlier in the evening," the hostess said as she took a menu from behind the stand. "Please follow me."

Seated at a table at the opposite side of the restaurant, Jack was still able to observe Vargas but could not see his accomplice clearly.

After water was served, and declining any alcohol, Jack ordered a nice New York strip for dinner. While in Rome, he mused.

Pretending to check his phone, Jack snapped a picture of Vargas and the unknown man, careful to ensure the flash was off. At least I didn't screw that one up, Jack thought.

Jack's steak was brought to him just as the two men were paying their bill. As the men started to get up to leave, Jack waved the waiter over, told him he had to leave, and asked for the check.

Annoyed, the waiter took his time.

The two men were walking to the exit.

Can't wait, thought Jack as he quickly got up to leave.

Thinking he was leaving without paying, the waiter attempted to stop Jack, but Jack would have none of it.

"Charge it to my room, 258," Jack said. "I am sorry. I have to go."

Jack rushed through the ornate doors at the front of the hotel. He stopped suddenly, spotting the two men directly in front of him. He pulled out his cell phone and turned away, as if he had just received a call.

Jack also noticed something else.

"Tomas, I am looking forward to our partnership," Vilja said to the other man.

"As long as it is as lucrative as ever, Vilja," Tomas replied.

Jack recognized the other man's voice. It was Tommy, the bartender from the High Tide.

"I have the funding, my friend." Vilja chuckled. "As long as your people can get the supplies I have requested."

"It will be done as you have asked, Vargas. I will have everything delivered to your warehouse in a few weeks. Just make sure the money is transferred tonight, or else you put everything in jeopardy," Tomas warned.

"You will have your money, Tomas, but I expect everything I requested, including Prussian blue," Vilja said. "Otherwise we aren't touching that stuff."

The men then parted into separate taxis, and Jack was at a dilemma.

The doorman approached Jack. "Cab, sir?"

"Yes and quickly," Jack replied, handing the man a twenty.

More like it, the doorman thought, and blew his whistle for a cab.

Jack thought, I know this is Vargas's connection that Jean and Charlène have been trying to find, but which one should be followed?

***

Tomas was the son of Sergio Garcia, and a comrade of Gisele Toffler. He was born to Sergio and María Muñoz Garcia in the Catalan city of Barcelona during a hot summer in 1952. Sonny's former nemesis, Sergio, had been a double agent in World War II and had served on the side of Fascism. Sergio Garcia was an accountant in the Spanish Republican government when the civil war started. He immediately volunteered in the Republican army and fought against the Nationalists until 1938, when he fled to France.

In March of 1938, when the Republican forces surrendered, ending the Spanish Civil War, Sergio was at a refugee camp with his wife and son. He hated Fascism and especially Franco, who consolidated his power over the Spanish people. After the fall of France in 1940, Sergio fled to England, contacting MI-6 to volunteer his services as a spy.

MI-6 rebuffed his attempts to become one of their agents, but when Sergio passed along troop and equipment concentrations about the occupying forces in France and Belgium, they took notice. Major Scotty Smythe interrogated Sergio Garcia in the spring of 1942 and determined he could be used as a viable spy for MI-6. With the permission of MI-6, Sergio was parachuted back into France to organize local partisans into teams, conduct sabotage, and report German troop movement back to the Allies.

Over the next two years, Sergio Garcia led Major Scotty Smythe to believe he was a valuable asset to MI-6, but nothing could have been further from the truth.

His arrival in France was compromised when Abwehr agents intercepted a message from him to Major Smythe. When given the option of being executed or serving the Nazis, he turned against his English allies. In April of 1944, as an SOE team was crossing the channel to deliver radios to the Free French partisans, Sergio Garcia relayed that information to his Abwehr contacts, which dispatched a bomber to dispose of the team. A month later, with agents closing in on his operation, Sergio Garcia volunteered to deliver radios with Jack's father, Sonny, and Marie into occupied France. He remembered the last time he saw Jack's father during the war. He had tried to capture him and Henri for a reward. Sonny's quick action caused him to fail.

"Over my dead body will you get us dead or alive, you bastard," Sonny had yelled at Sergio.

Sonny had jerked the reins of his horse, causing the mare to rear up, legs kicking. The horse kicked one of the men in the head, killing him instantly.

In the end Sergio was trampled by the horse Sonny was riding at the time, but he managed to survive with just a broken arm.

Tomas Garcia grew up hating the English and Americans, whom he felt were responsible for turning his father away from his Republican ideals. His mother, María Muñoz Garcia, had raised her son to appreciate the fine arts; music was his escape from the streets of Barcelona. He learned to play piano and thoroughly enjoyed listening to great composers such as Isaac Albeniz, one of Spain's musical treasures, and Manuel de Falla, the quintessential Andalusian, who ranked as one of the most important Spanish composers of all time.

Manuel de Falla was his favorite. He often played his pieces "Nights in the Gardens of Spain," the ballet *El Amor Brujo*, and "Ritual Fire Dance" while interrogating and torturing agents with Gisele Toffler.

In Tomas Garcia's twisted mind, Jack and Emily were enemies of his father's ideology, and they had to be disposed of for what they did to his friend Gisele. When Gisele contacted him about the boy who had trampled his father in 1944, Tomas Garcia enthusiastically volunteered to help her. After Gisele found Jack and Emily, Tomas Garcia acquired a job at the High Tide when the bartender Donny Sinclair was found dead of an apparent heart attack, courtesy of Tomas.

Jack had not gone unnoticed at Two West.

When Tomas and Vilja had gotten up to leave, Tomas saw Jack out of the corner of his eye.

"Vilja, we are being followed," Tomas had whispered quickly to Vargas.

"Who is it?" Vilja asked.

"Someone I thought I killed," Tomas replied. "I don't know how he found me, but that is his mistake. Take separate cabs. Whomever he follows, kill him."

"Easy enough," Vilja said, turning around just in time to see Jack turn away to check his phone.

Jack made his decision. "Follow my friend in that cab," he said, pointing at Tomas's taxi."

"Busy streets, buddy. Where is he going?" the cabbie inquired impatiently.

Irritated, Jack handed the cabbie a one hundred dollar bill. "I don't know. Just don't lose him."

"You got it, bud," the cabbie said as he grinned at his newfound wealth. "You with government or something like that?"

"Yeah, something like that," Jack replied.

By Jack's request, the cabbie kept a safe distance away from the cab Tomas had taken so as not to alert him.

"He's heading into Spanish Harlem," the cabbie said. "Not so bad anymore, but wouldn't go wandering around alone at night."

"Good to know," Jack replied.

The cabbie dropped Jack off on a side street a block up from where Tomas had gotten out, by an abandoned warehouse. Quickly rounding the corner to the main street, Jack watched as Tomas entered the warehouse through a side door. Can't be just one entrance, Jack thought, seeing that the main door was barricaded. I'll have to see if there is another way in.

Walking past the main entrance with a small crowd of people, Jack came around to the backside of the warehouse. Good, he thought. More than one way in.

The back of the warehouse had a series of windows on one corner, near a ramp and a large rusted garage door. Next to the garage door was an entrance into the warehouse. Jack tried opening that door, which had been broken into before, but it wouldn't budge. Even if I can get this door open, the racket would alert Tomas. Jack pondered his dilemma.

Glancing over at the line of windows, Jack tried to raise the glass panes of the first two unsuccessfully before the third window finally creaked open. Raising the window slowly to minimize the noise, Jack got it open just enough to climb in. Boosting himself up and into the warehouse, he landed softly on the cement floor inside, but not without tearing his pant leg. Great, he reflected, momentarily gazing at the small tear in his five-hundred-dollar suit. Wait till Charlène sees that. Loosening his tie and wiping away his sweat, Jack wondered how they kept so neat in those famous spy movies.

Somewhere in the distance, Jack could hear a radio playing faintly. He heard a woman's voice singing in Spanish. Sounds like some kind of opera, Jack thought.

Sneaking around a corner in the direction of the voice, Jack could clearly make out the room the radio was in, a flickering fire casting eerie shapes on the wall. The door stood ajar, and Jack deliberated his next move. I could rush in and take him by surprise, or wait and ambush him. The design of the building offered no chance for an ambush, so Jack decided to go for it. Pulling out his 9 mm pistol, Jack burst into the room, gun at eye level, only to find the radio perched on a chair in the middle of the room.

Behind him Tomas swung a heavy piece of wood at Jack's head.

REVELATIONS

The Révérende Mère addressed Madeleine, "I have received news of you, Madeleine, in advance. You are welcome to stay the evening if you desire. Soeur Michèle will provide for your needs. Is there anything you desire, *mon enfant?*"

"*Merci, ma* Révérende Mère. *Mes compagnons* and I need to rest for few days, if that's possible," Madeleine said.

"*Certainement*. May you find peace during your visit," the Révérende Mère replied.

"Révérende Mère, two of our companions need medical attention. Do you have any supplies we can use?" Madeleine asked.

"I will see what can be done. The sisters here will attend to everyone's need. Now follow Soeur Michèle, *je vous prie*," the Révérende Mère replied.

"We have another problem, *ma* Révérende Mère. We had to detain a local Carlingue agent who tried to stop our group in town."

"Ah, that would be Mainard. He has lost his way," the Révérende Mère said. "He was an altar boy once, but now he avoids the church. Where is he?"

Lieutenant Robertson spoke up. "Detained in the truck, ma'am."

"Bring him in. It is time I had a talk with that young Frenchman," the Révérende Mère said to Lieutenant Robertson.

"Yes, ma'am. Bring him in, Rizzo," Lieutenant Robertson commanded.

After a few moments, a groggy Mainard was brought before the Révérende Mère, hands tied behind his back.

"*Merci, messieurs.* That will be all. Please untie him," the Révérende Mère said to the two men.

"Maybe we should stay with you. He is a dangerous man," Sergeant Rizzo said.

"Not in God's house, Sergeant."

The Révérende Mère and Mainard left through a side door.

Everyone exchanged glances and mischievous smiles.

Two of the sisters had already been out to the truck, driving it behind the convent to the carriage house to hide it inside.

In the meantime, Henri and Charlène were carried out of the main foyer and into the infirmary toward the back of the convent. Sergeant Waldron, the team's medic, had asked if he could be of assistance, but the sisters politely refused, suggesting he needed rest as well.

The men were escorted to a room where beds, fresh clothes, boots, and a water basin were placed neatly at their disposal. A small table in the corner held a meager amount of bread, cheese, and fruit, along with a pot of steaming tea and cups. They all settled in knowing they really had no other choice.

"Never imagined I would be cloistered in a convent, LT," Rizzo commented.

"I am right there with ya, Rizzo." Robertson chuckled.

The men washed up, leaving their filthy clothes outside the door as instructed by the Révérende Mère and changing into those provided for them. The fit wasn't exact, but the clothes were clean.

"Got ya some high waters there, Rizzo?" Robertson asked, seeing that the sergeant's pants ended just below his knees.

"Yeah, LT, but at least they're clean—something I haven't seen in a week!"

The men were hungry and ate with concentration the food the sisters provided. Waldron even remembered to say grace before the food disappeared.

"Hey, Armand, still have some of that Cognac?" Rizzo asked.

"*Oui, mon ami.* Do you want to spice up your tea?"

"Damn straight," Rizzo replied, holding out his cup of tea.

"You boys be careful with that stuff," the lieutenant said. "We have a long way to go before we can relax."

"Aw, LT, it's just one sip. Besides, I think we are out anyway," Rizzo said, pointing to Armand, who was frowning as he held the flask upside down to show that it was now empty.

Sated with good food, and Armand's last drop of Cognac, the men settled down on the soft horsehair mattresses and fell instantly asleep.

At some point in the night, amid the snoring, the men all awoke to a bloodcurdling scream that had them sitting bolt upright. While the rest exchanged worried glances, Sergeant Waldron, still lying on his bunk and smiling at the ceiling, finally said, "I believe Mainard has met his match."

The Révérende Mère had broken Mainard. The young man who had once been an altar boy had collaborated with the Nazis. In his mind he saw it as an easy way out of a tough situation. At first he just wanted to feign allegiance, but his Nazi masters saw right through him. As time went on, he had to prove himself time and again, betraying his fellow countrymen to stay in favor with the Gestapo. Any wavering now on his part would bring their instant wrath. Over time he became one of the hated French Vichy Carlingue agents who spied on their own countrymen. There had been several attempts on his life, but he always received information beforehand and thwarted the partisan efforts.

The Révérende Mère's plan was simple. She prayed. She prayed all night in front of him, and that drove him insane. Eventually he broke down screaming. It was almost as if she had exorcized the demons from the wayward young man.

A few days after his exorcism through prayer, the Révérende Mère was able to coordinate his escape into Switzerland, where he spent the remainder of the war. She argued with local partisan leaders that he had not actually caused any deaths and that she had successfully ridded the young man of the Nazi masters' grip on his soul. Mainard would never return to his native France; he had made too many enemies. He eventually settled in the United States, working for various government agencies before passing away of a heart attack in his sixties.

The men spent the next day in the convent library examining old texts that filled the room. It was a much-needed respite for the travel-weary combatants, and they did not complain about their reprieve. No one spoke to each other louder than a whisper; such was the peace and solitude of the convent.

It was Madeleine who found a large, ancient scroll tucked away in a metal tube. Removing the cap, she slid its contents into the palm of her hand. Rolling it out, she noticed an odd pattern of geometrical shapes cut through the vellum. Written in fading ink was the date 1152 AD.

Funny, she thought. This parchment feels odd to the touch, almost like metal.

"Whatcha got there, Madeleine?" Robbie asked.

"A very old scroll, but instead of being dust, it's in perfect condition."

"Those patterns are some kind of engineering design," Robbie commented, gazing at the scroll.

"I don't know what it is, but it gives me the creeps," Rizzo commented, looking over their shoulders. "I've been in the construction business with my dad before the war, and I ain't ever seen anything like that!" he exclaimed a bit too loud.

That got the attention of the Révérende Mère, who was passing by the room after finishing her morning prayers. Holding out her hand, she received the scroll and case from Madeleine.

"*Mon Dieu*. Please follow me, everyone," she said.

Gathering the small group into her study, she explained the rolled-up parchment.

"Let me begin with a historical reference," she explained. "A man named Hans Talhoffer lived in the fifteenth century. He was a fight master who was employed as master of arms to the knight Leutold von Konigsegg of Württemberg, in southern Germany."

"Ah, I have heard of him while studying military history at West Point," the lieutenant said. "He was a *Fechtbücher* and the author of at least six discourses describing methods of fighting. The instructors told us that the rumor that the *Fechtbücher* was tied to a book written by Nostradamus. The book consisted of drawings, or plans, of destructive machines that could destroy the world as they knew it then. It was rumored that Nostradamus had the book, which he referred to as *Magicks*. Some say it was also known as the Doomsday Book. He was supposed to have given it to the Pope for safekeeping. Are you telling me it's real?"

"*Oui*, Lieutenant," the Révérende Mère said.

"LT, how do you know all this stuff?" Rizzo asked.

"I read, son," the lieutenant replied.

"Wait, are you telling us that these scrolls are related to that doomsday book? The one that I heard was a legend?" Waldron asked.

Everyone turned to the Révérende Mère.

"In order to use the book, they would need this scroll. But there are many others, each different, that are hidden in places I cannot reveal to you. The location of Nostradamus's book is only known to the Vatican, who received it from the mystic personally. Each scroll, and there are seventy in total, were distributed to minimize the danger should the book fall into the wrong hands."

"Forgive me for asking, Révérende Mère, but why isn't this locked up or buried somewhere?" Waldron asked.

"It is, my child." She smiled.

"You're in a convent," Rizzo whispered to Waldron.

"But why even tell us about the scrolls?" Robertson inquired. "You could have played it off as some old puzzle."

"Because you found the scroll by accident, and if you discussed it in front of the wrong person, we would be in great danger," the Révérende Mère answered. "High-ranking Nazi officials such as Heinrich Himmler, Rudolf Hess, and Walther Darré are known to have been interested in mysticism and the paranormal. If word reached them about these mysterious scrolls, they would destroy convents across France to find them. Then they would do the same to every church in the occupied countries."

She continued, "Father Gabriele Amorth, an exorcist of the Vatican, is convinced that the Nazis, especially Hitler, are all possessed by the devil. Reality is that the Nazis are criminals."

"They are the epitome of evil," Henri stated, "but how could they use the scrolls?"

"If they found the connection to *Magicks* by Nostradamus and the scrolls, they would eventually find the key to unlocking the weapons."

"Wait, these are keys to weapons?" Rizzo asked. "Why doesn't the church give them to the Allies?"

"Because, Sergeant, as a famous man once said, absolute power corrupts absolutely," the Révérende Mère answered.

"She's right, Rizzo," Robertson said. "Could we stop with Hitler?"

"But why do they need this anyway?" Rizzo asked. "They have a powerful army."

"You have to understand, Sergeant, that the National Socialists are evil, demented people. At the core of their philosophy is occultism. So you see, any means of winning by supernatural powers, the Nazis will try to obtain. Whether the scrolls and *Magicks* by Nostradamus will work together or is just a matter of fiction, we cannot take a chance. Since this was entrusted to the Vatican hundreds of years ago, we have kept it a secret to all but a few. I trust it will stay that way?" the Révérende Mère asked, looking at each person in the room.

"Now," she said before anyone could answer, "I have received word that the invasion of Normandy experienced difficulties at first, but a beachhead has now been established and the Allied armies are moving into the countryside."

Everyone was relieved to change the subject to more earthbound topics.

"That's great news, ma'am!" Robertson exclaimed.

"What were those difficulties, *ma* Révérende Mère?" Madeleine asked politely.

"On Omaha Beach the Americans almost failed, and many lives were lost," the Révérende Mère replied.

"Forgive me for asking," the lieutenant interrupted, "but how did you come by this information?"

A faint smile crossed the Révérende Mère's face. "I, too, Lieutenant, have volunteered."

"Volunteered? For what?" Robertson asked.

"I worked with MI-6," she explained.

"You're a spy?" Rizzo exclaimed.

"We all do what we can, Sergeant. The Nazis have been merciless to the church and clergy as well," the Révérende Mère explained. "The last place they will look for spies is in a convent."

"Well, I'll be," Robertson declared.

Later that day, the group requested and received permission to view the tomb of Bernadette Soubirous of Lourdes.

The Révérende Mère explained the miracle of Bernadette. "The visions of Bernadette began in 1858, when she was a fourteen-year-old peasant girl from Lourdes.

"She told her mother that she had seen a lady in the cave of Massabielle, near the town, while gathering firewood with her sister Marie-Toinette and a friend, Jeanne. To her amazement, she saw a lady of small stature and incomparable beauty. The lady was surrounded by light and inclined her head, inviting Bernadette to approach."

"She saw the Virgin Mary?" Sergeant Rizzo said.

"Yes, Sergeant," Révérende Mère answered. "She then took out her rosary to recite her prayers. The vision lasted about a quarter of an hour, and as Bernadette finished the rosary prayers, the lady disappeared."

"Didn't she have a bunch of visions, sister?" Rizzo asked.

"Eighteen in all, Sergeant," she said. "During one, Bernadette was asked by the lady to drink at the spring and wash in the water, although there was no spring to be seen."

"Bernadette scratched away at the surface of the earth and found water rising, which she was able to drink," Révérende Mère explained.

"I guess miracles do happen," Rizzo said. "We could use some against the krauts."

"Rizzo, show some respect," Robertson said.

"Lieutenant, he is right. A miracle is what we need at the moment to defeat *les bosch*," the Révérende Mère said.

"Didn't she die here?" Waldron asked.

"In 1879, in the infirmary. She was thirty-five," she explained. "In 1862, Pope Pius IX permitted the veneration of the Blessed Virgin Mary in Lourdes," the Révérende Mère finished.

Entering Bernadette's chamber, La Révérende Mère addressed the group. "And before you see Sainte Bernadette, allow me to read to you, or translate as best I can, a passage written by a priest, a Jesuit, André Ravier, who experienced much joy when he saw the saint. It is inspirational. May I?"

Everyone was silent and eager to have the Révérende Mere read his words.

We taste some of this delight when we see Bernadette in her shrine. Her eyes are closed, but she is there! Intact, that face upon which was reflected the marvelous light of the virginal mystery, the Immaculate Conception. Intact, those lips which conversed with the Virgin Mary. Intact, those hands which, guided by the hands of Aquero, painfully scratched the soil of Massabielle and opened for us the miraculous spring of penance. Intact and present, this heart so tender and so strong which beats for the love of Jesus and His Mother, and on their account for all the sinners in the world. Intact, as if she had just gone to sleep, and awaits only the angel's call to rise to her feet. God did not want her to escape totally from our human wretchedness, nor leave her brothers and sisters for whom she gave her life. She is still among us. A. Ravier, S.J.

"I never heard that," Sergeant Waldron said.

"It is famous here in France, Sergeant," Révérende Mère replied.

No one spoke further, and each went to pay their respects to Bernadette. They were all awed by the experience.

They all came away with peace of mind and a renewed spirit to carry on the fight.

Henri sank to his knees. "*Mon Dieu*, it is true what they say about her," he said. Henri cried out as he made the sign of the cross.

"Henri, your leg!" Madeleine said.

Henri grabbed at the wound on his leg. It still hurt, but its healing had definitely accelerated.

The others knelt in prayer. It was a surreal and peaceful moment in a very real and dangerous world.

The last to enter Bernadette's chamber was Charlène. While the others stayed for only a few minutes, Charlène was inside with the Révérende Mère for well over two hours. Charlène came out changed not only in mind; she was walking with only the aid of her crutch! The brace on her arm was removed, and she had full movement.

Charlène was walking with a limp, but she was walking. The doctors had expected her to be handicapped for the rest of her life. None could deny the miracle of Sainte Bernadette. Charlène limped gingerly to the Révérende Mère, who gave her a warm hug and kissed her cheeks.

Charlène's whole demeanor had changed; she was smiling for the rest of the day, a willing and helpful charge of the Révérende Mère.

Years later Charlène would recall the peace that had settled over her when she viewed the body of Bernadette Soubirous of Lourdes in her crystal coffin.

It was on this day that Nazi occultism gave way to the power of prayer.

It's a Helluva Town

The world came back into view with shards of flickering firelight accentuating the throbbing in the back of Jack's head. The whole place smelled like something was rotting, combined with a dusty, wet odor Jack couldn't identify.

He had walked into Tomas Garcia's trap; Garcia must have known he was following him. I should have reported my findings instead of chasing this madman, Jack thought. As the room spun into focus, he could see the Spaniard standing before him with his hands in his coat pockets, watching him with a cool demeanor.

"Welcome back, my friend," Garcia commented. "You shouldn't have followed me."

Jack decided to play dumb. "Tommy, what's going on? Why did you shoot us at the High Tide?"

"Because I was seeking revenge for my friend Gisele!" Garcia growled.

"That insane bitch was your friend?" Jack blurted out.

The unintended comment got Jack a wicked slap across his face, blood running down his chin from a cut lip.

"Yes, Jack. My name is really Tomas Garcia. Gisele's grandfather and my father had much in common. My father, Sergio Garcia, was part of Sonny's team; he did the right thing by turning them in. Henri trampled my father with a horse, thinking him dead, but as you can see through me, he survived."

"The right thing?" Jack cried out. "He betrayed them!"

"They were nothing," Garcia spat.

"They were fighting to free their country!" Jack defiantly responded.

Laughing, Garcia turned to his boom box and pressed the play button, sending the inserted CD into a whirling spin.

The soft sounds of a piano filled the room. Jack noticed a small fire made up of broken boards from the warehouse flickering nearby.

"Quite relaxing, don't you think, Jack?" Garcia intoned. "This is the great nationalist Spanish composer Isaac Albeniz, one of Spain's musical treasures. I have enjoyed playing his music since I was a boy."

"Seems a bit out of place, Tommy," Jack replied sarcastically.

Pulling out from his coat pocket a Spanish .32-caliber Luger, reminiscent of the German World War II version, Garcia angrily pointed it at Jack.

"The name is Tomas. Say that name once more and I will end your life."

This guy is insane, Jack thought. I'll have to figure out a way to keep him calm.

"What do you intend to do with me, Tomas?" Jack softly said, trying to diffuse the Spaniard's anger.

"I want to know who sent you to follow Vargas," Garcia replied as he removed a needle filled with a clear liquid from his satchel.

"Vargas? I was following you, Tomas, to find out why you shot us," Jack lied.

Garcia approached with the needle to Jack's left side. Jack tried to squirm away, but to no avail, as the needle punctured his carotid artery. Jack felt the icy-cold liquid flow into his body.

"What was that?" Jack choked out.

"Just some truth serum," Garcia replied. "I don't believe you were just following me. How did you find me? Now let's get to the truth, or the next needle will leave you dead."

Over the next few hours, Jack was subjected to grueling questions, to which he was able to bend the truth, but Garcia did not give up. Jack was beaten and cut, all to destroy his will and give Garcia the information he wanted.

"You're a stubborn one, Jack Turner. I would have expected you to have spilled your guts by now. Have you visited Emily's grave lately?" Garcia chuckled.

Jack's gaze spoke volumes to Garcia.

He's hiding something, Garcia thought, or why would he follow me to New York? Was Vargas his target, or was he after me? There's no way he could have known I would be in New York.

Beaten and bloodied, the hours of torture and mind games passed by. Jack wasn't about to betray Charlène as Garcia's father had done. If I am to die, let it be now, he thought. At least I die with honor.

"I'll ask one more time, Jack. Who sent you to follow us?" Garcia remarked bluntly. Turning, he increased the volume on the boom box, the piano concerto drumming loudly in Jack's ears.

"Tomas, I was following you," Jack affirmed in a haze, concentrating on each and every word as he was trained to do when it came to truth serum. I can't let Garcia know, he thought over and over, no matter what might happen.

Garcia walked over to Jack and placed a handkerchief in his mouth, knotted in the middle, viciously tying it to the back of his head. Jack winced as the knot cut into his head wound.

Going back to his satchel, Garcia pulled out a blood-caked surgical saw and approached Jack. Reaching down, he grabbed Jack's right arm and began sawing at Jack's wrist. Jack screamed loudly as pain like he never felt before surged all the way up his arm, but Garcia held on and finished cutting through flesh and bone. Blood flowed onto the chair's arm, running down on the floor. Garcia then grabbed the flaming board and cauterized the wound, the smell of burning flesh filling the air around them. Jack passed out from the excruciating pain as Garcia tossed the board back into the fire, along with the detached hand.

After a moment, Jack regained consciousness, the severed nerves in his right arm sending signals of pain to his brain.

Removing Jack's gag, Garcia said, "If you won't tell me then, Jack, you'll just become a meal for my friends." Garcia pointed to the rats rummaging behind some boxes.

"I told you everything I know, Tomas. I wanted to kill you for what you did to Emily," Jack struggled to say. He didn't care, as pain filled his entire being. Death now would be better than what Garcia had planned for him.

"I guess you're going to be disappointed then, Jack." Garcia snorted. "I have work to do, so... good-bye. I am sure you will make a fine london broil for the rats!"

Jack's trepidation was tenfold. He had failed to follow his orders or get his revenge on Garcia for shooting Emily. He struggled uselessly at his bonds.

"I'll leave the soothing sounds of Isaac Albeniz as the rats gnaw on your bones," Garcia whispered in his ear, deftly retying the gag in Jack's mouth.

In moments Garcia was gone, the rats slowly closing around Jack, excited by the smell of fresh blood. His whole arm throbbed, and he was unable to move his uninjured arm to release himself. He was still groggy from the truth serum but calm in the thought that he had not betrayed Charlène or Emily.

God, if I am to die, let me bleed to death before these damnable rats eat me alive! Jack prayed, envisioning the horror.

Over the next few hours Jack grew steadily weaker, and the rats made several attempts to get to him. Each time, Jack was able to scare them away, making loud noises and shaking his body in his restraints. But after each attempt, he began to lose consciousness from the loss of blood from his cauterized wound and the smaller cuts inflicted by Garcia during his torture.

Weak and distraught, Jack gave up as he slowly lost consciousness, and the encircling rats drew closer.

Inside his suit lapel, a red dot began to flash in rapid succession.

The light grew brighter as Jack tried to focus. Am I dead? He wondered. Jack squinted his eyes to avoid the bright glare of a white light.

***

"Georges, get Charlène! He's awake," Emily said.

"Oui, madame," Georges replied. He walked down the hall, trying not to run in his excitement.

Jack's vision slowly cleared, his first image that of his beautiful wife, Emily.

"Em, it's good to see you," Jack said. "I guess I got into a bit of trouble on my first job."

"At least you're alive, Jack," Emily said as she kissed his forehead.

"What was that for?" Jack said. Was this *his* Emily?

"You stood by me while I was lost and badly hurt, Jack. I will be here while you recover from your injuries," Emily said.

The couple was interrupted by Charlène, standing in the doorway. "It's good to see you awake, Jack. You had us worried."

Jack winced. "How did you find me?" he inquired. "I thought I was a goner for sure."

"We had a tracking device installed in your suit. I would apologize for not having complete trust in you, but looking back on our decision, it did save your life," Charlène admonished.

"I know, I failed you and Jean, but when I saw Tommy— I mean Tomas—" Jack said, glancing at Emily, her face aghast in recognition, "I wanted revenge. Now I have failed my mission, and I am sorry."

"Jack, I remember! Tommy shot us!" Emily gasped.

Charlène lay her hand on Emily's shoulder. "He is a dangerous man; Jack will not go after him alone again."

"Alone? Again?" Jack asked. "I thought I was done as an agent, especially with my hand chopped off."

"No," Charlène clarified. "Garcia won't stop until he kills you. You must finish this. When you are rested and feeling better, we will brief you further, but for now, you need to rest and regain strength. There is much to do before I let you on another mission."

"Yes, Jack, rest. I'll be back later," Emily repeated, kissing Jack's forehead again.

When everyone left the room, Jack took stock of his wounds. He was cut and bruised all over his body, a result of Garcia's torture, and the worst of it being his missing hand. If only I had followed the mission, I would have been fine, he thought, angry with himself. Steeling himself, he reasoned that this was inevitable, and better to be alive without a hand and with Emily than rat food in New York.

Jack was exhausted; he could almost feel the fingers move on his right hand as he stared at the massive bandage hiding his view. He was tempted to rip the bandage off to see his hand, move his fingers, but he remembered the excruciating pain as Garcia's saw cut through his skin. Slowly, inevitably, Jack drifted off to sleep haunted by nightmares filled with rats.

Two months passed. As Jack recovered, he spent time in the briefing room studying the intelligence reports on Garcia and his father's activities during World War II. Charlène had made it her mission to find and eliminate this evil once and for all.

Poring over Charlène's collection of letters and intelligence reports from World War II, Jack began to see a story unfold before his eyes—a story of his own father leaving France without knowing she was still alive. He was amazed at

Charlène's escape through the Pyrénées Mountains to avoid capture and certain death at the hands of La Milice. In the end was their reunion and collaboration to keep this evil at bay.

"I see you are a history buff, Jack," Jean said, seeing the documents strewn across the large oak briefing table.

"It's all coming together now, Jean," Jack replied. "My father, Charlène, how they escaped death by fleeing. It must have been a horrible time for everyone."

"To survive, Jack, to survive," Jean stated, his voice trailing off as he thought about the painful memories of the occupation of France.

Jean Aubrac had not taken the journey south through the Pyrénées with Henri, Madeleine, and the Americans. He had stayed with Liliane and her sister after they had fled to Paris. It wasn't until after the war, when Henri returned to France, that he was adopted after the death of Liliane. Jean was grateful to Henri for taking him in and spent his life fighting the man's cause of bringing the remaining Nazis to justice. The young man had reminded Henri of himself, so dedicated was he to bringing the monsters down, never to rise again.

"Jean, how does Charlène afford to do all of this?" Jack asked, looking around the elegant room.

"Charlène inherited the estate from her Uncle David and Aunt Judith. They had an import-export business. During the war her uncle did his best to smuggle Jews fleeing Europe, and the business allowed that to happen. When he passed away, the reins of the company were handed to her. With our connections in The Pond and CIA, we are able to funnel the money, legally, into the organization. Her family's estate is hers alone, but she allows its use so we can concentrate on our mission without all the red tape," Jean explained.

"And the government is OK with all of this?" Jack asked.

"Only as long as we are not an embarrassment," Jean emphasized, glaring down at Jack's stub.

"It won't happen again." Jack glared back.

"No, Jack, because I can't let you out into the field. Your cover is blown. They *will* be looking for you!" Jean reprimanded.

"But you can't let him get away with this!" Jack pleaded. "All the other agents are out in the field. I know this guy; he served us drinks every Friday night."

Jean lowered his head, eyes moving up to gaze at Jack. "No, Jack, you're not the only one."

"Who?" Jack's voice trailed off as Emily entered the room. "No. She can't do this. Let me finish the job," Jack said.

"Jack, I have been training too. I can do this. My torture and kidnapping by Gisele taught me to be strong, and I too want to settle the score," Emily insisted. "I have been through all the same training as you, Jack, and passed with flying colors. Let me do this."

"I am just worried about you, Em," Jack said.

"I'll be fine," she said.

"I don't want this to happen to you," Jack said, showing her the bandaged stump.

Emily was about to say something, but Jean interrupted her. "Emily, we should let Jack rest."

Jack lay in his room all day trying to grasp the magnitude of the situation. His lunch, consisting of a roast beef and roquefort sandwich and a raspberry tart, sat on the tray by his bed untouched. He sipped at the cold coffee contemplating the situation. He almost lost Emily once, and now she was taking his place? That madman Garcia will eat her for lunch, he thought disparagingly, gazing down at the bandage covering his right wrist.

That evening, Jack joined them for dinner.

"I have a confession," Jack announced.

"And that is?" Charlène asked.

"I was selfish. Emily is an intelligent and strong woman. It was wrong of me to try and prevent her from going into the field. That is her decision to make without me being condescending. I must apologize to Em. But if she is to go out into the field, I want to help if I can," Jack said.

Emily grabbed his left hand across the table, her grip strong, a soft smile appearing on her face.

"Agreed," Charlène declared. "I will brief everyone at 7:00 am tomorrow morning. Now let's eat before our delicious dinner gets cold."

The four enjoyed their evening meal: soufflé au fromage, followed by gratinée de coquille St Jacques, and clafoutis aux abricots, an apricot batter-pudding, for dessert.

If I were to die tomorrow, Jack thought, at least I will have eaten well.

Later that evening in the study, the fire low and crackling, Jean and Charlène discussed the current situation.

"Are you sure she is strong enough to handle Garcia, Charlène?" Jean asked.

"She has been ready for a long time. Her experiences with Gisele's torture, surviving a brain injury, and taking care of Jack on his return have helped in preparing her. She is more than ready to handle this," Charlène said with pride.

Charlène was right; Emily's experiences had toughened her from a corporate scientist. And her training had been intense, but she had made it through. In some areas, such as weapon training, she had excelled even beyond Jack's accomplishments.

Musing over the possibilities as she sipped her Cognac, she thought, She is Jack's equal.

"Jean, we have been going about this all wrong. Together, as in their marriage, they are rock solid," Charlène asserted.

Lowering his glass slowly, Jean proclaimed, "Why didn't I see this before? Of course! Just like we were in those early days."

"We weren't married," Charlène said, lowering her eyes to the crackling fire.

"We should have been, *ma chérie*," Jean responded, clinking his glass to hers.

"Ah, but we had no time for that, did we?" she said, her eyes fixated on the flames.

For the rest of the evening, they sat quietly by the fire, silently enjoying each other's company.

The next morning, Jack's alarm announced its presence way too early for his liking. Over the past months, while recovering, he had the luxury of sleeping in. The 5:00 AM alarm was unwelcome.

Autumn was in full swing, and the trees on the estate were turning bright gold and red colors. As Jack swung his feet off the bed and stared out the lead-paned window, he thought, Winter will soon be here. Rising up and walking barefoot on the cold floor to his bathroom, he unwound his bandage to examine his wound. I always figured I'd cut this thing off with my table saw back in New Hampshire, he brooded, not have it cut off by some psycho Nazi Spaniard! All things considered, the wound was healing nicely and he was ready to get back out to the field again, if only they could trust him.

Washed and dressed in a black shirt and khaki pants provided by Georges, Jack left his room, making his way to the elevator that led down to the operations room below the house.

***

Getting ready in her room, Emily was terrified, but she dared not show it. Over the past few months while Jack recovered, she was trained by Charlène and Jean in the nuances of the spy craft she had entered unwillingly. Emily had been a rising star in the corporate world until Gisele destroyed that. Even after things had settled down and they buried her father-in-law, Emily's posttraumatic stress caused work problems. When Tommy, a.k.a., Tomas, had shot her, the chances of returning to that corporate world vanished forever.

Emily's ordeal with her memory loss was a long, hard road to recovery. She had progressed, but slowly. The incident with the puppy had jogged only a portion of her memory.

It wasn't until a nurse came in with a syringe while Jack was away on his mission that the memories flooded back. It was at that precise moment that Gisele's kidnapping became foremost in her thoughts. Images swirled in her mind as she screamed out Gisele's name. The nurse, frightened, ran out to retrieve Charlène, who, upon entering Emily's room, found a babbling, incoherent woman. It only took a moment for Charlène to recognize the emotional stress of remembrance. She had been there before.

Leaving her room for the elevator, Emily thought, I have got to get a grip. I can't let Jack do this alone. I am stronger than this!

After washing up and getting dressed in a black pullover shirt and khaki pants, Emily bumped into Jack as she headed to the elevator leading to the conference room. They were both wearing identical outfits.

"Morning, dear," she said as she smiled, kissing him.

"We've been married too long Em," Jack laughed.

"What?" Emily asked, suddenly realizing they both wore identical clothing.

"I guess we both have good taste," Jack said.

"I guess you're right," Emily said.

"Emily, are you sure you're OK with all of this?" Jack asked, changing the subject.

"Do we have a choice, Jack?" Emily calmly answered, touching Jack's cheek in the process.

Jack said, "No, you're right, sweetie. This isn't going away unless *we* do something about it."

As the elevator descended and opened into the conference room, the couple walked out in unison, together as partners, a team. Jean glanced knowingly at Charlène; he had seen that demeanor before when they finally clicked as their own team.

Welcoming the pair of budding spies, Charlène cheerfully said, "Good morning!"

"Morning," Jack and Emily said in unison.

"We have a lot to discuss today, *mes amis*," Jean injected into the conversation. "You'll find folders on the table in front of you."

"Georges, coffee please," Charlène said to the butler.

"*Oui, madame*, right away," Georges said.

"Our CIA counterparts have requested that we follow up on Tomas Garcia and his connection with Vilja Vargas," Jean enlightened the couple. "We have heard through the CIA's sources that Vargas was inquiring about a dirty bomb."

"After the terrorist attacks on September 11, 2001, concerns about the safety and security of these radiation sources and devices have grown considerably, as I am sure you both know, particularly amid fears that terrorists might use radiation sources to make a radiological dispersal device or dirty bomb," Charlène said.

"I've obviously heard the term, but how would he get the devices to make a bomb?" Jack asked.

"One way is to purchase or steal them on the black market, Jack," Charlène replied. "We have been in contact with the U.S. Centers for Disease Control and Prevention, the U.S. Department of Homeland Security, and the U.S. Agency for Toxic Substances and Disease Registry to see if they have heard of any unusual inquiries for purchasing these items."

Jean explained, "Such materials are commercially available within the medical and agricultural industries, in oil drilling equipment, and even in very small amounts in household smoke detectors. Cesium-137, cobalt-60, and americium-241 are considered to be the most likely materials for use in a dirty bomb due to their availability and their relative ease of handling. Several thousand devices are licensed for use today in the United States. The devices are used for cancer therapy, sterilization of medical devices, irradiation of blood for transplant patients and of laboratory animals for research, nondestructive testing of structures and industrial equipment, and exploration of geologic formations to find oil and gas deposits. So you see, as there are industries that make use of these materials, it is imperative we find Garcia and Vargas."

"What about uranium and plutonium?" Emily asked.

"While they are much stronger and more lethal agents, they are also significantly more difficult to acquire and control," Jean explained.

"Where do we look for these clues?" Jack asked.

"Cesium-137 and cobalt-60 are both found in cancer treatment radiation machines. I want both of you to look for any recent purchases in the New York area for radiation treatment machines used at cancer treatment facilities. I believe that is our best shot at locating these purchases," Charlène said.

"What kind of transactions do I need to look for?" Jack asked.

"Cobalt-60 used in food irradiation takes the form of small, radioactive 'pencils.' They are shipped in special hardened-steel canisters that have been designed and tested to survive crashes without breaking. Look for those kinds of deliveries within the greater tristate area. Since those kinds of transactions have to go through Homeland Security, I have given you access to their database, with their permission of course," Jean said.

"What about americium-241?" Emily asked.

Jean replied, "That is a man-made radioactive agent used in oil drilling and surveying equipment and in very small amounts in household smoke detectors. Check on any purchases or theft of surveying equipment around the area. I highly doubt they would purchase smoke detectors, because they would have to be at it a long time, and time is not on their side!"

"Looks like we have our work cut out for us," Jack announced.

"Yes, but listen to me carefully, Jack," Charlène said. "This is no game as you now realize, and every step you take needs to be approved by Jean or me, understood?"

"Understood," Jack replied.

"You two are now a team. Watch each other's backs, and report everything you see," Jean chimed in, looking at the couple. "Now start researching, and let us know what you find."

During their training, Jack and Emily had learned how to bypass computer security systems with specially coded software provided by the government.

"Feels odd, spying on our own government," Jack said.

"It's not spying, Jack. We're just cutting through some red tape," Emily replied.

They sat in the operations room and hacked into numerous state and government databases all that day to find nothing unusual with stolen or purchased materials of cobalt, cesium or americium-241, or the purchases of radiation equipment by any cancer treatment facilities.

Emily found herself reminiscing on her time at the pharmaceutical company, wondering if she could, or would even want to, go back to that life, when it hit her like a Mack truck—laboratory animals for research!

"Jack, I've got it! Check on deliveries to pharmaceutical companies. I think I know how they are going to get the materials!" Emily excitedly announced.

"How?" Jack asked.

"Lab animals are used in cancer research. The materials used in that type of research are shipped in bulk," Emily explained.

Typing the key words into his computer, he received a list of recent purchases by two pharmaceutical companies.

Jack turned to Emily. "Bingo!"

SAINT-GIRONS

The group had spent a week resting at the convent, waiting for the most opportune moment to complete their journey across the border and into Spain. The Sisters of Charity had been very kind to them. Their clothes were washed, and they ate well, even though the convent was short on food.

Soeur Michèle covertly handed Armand his flask, filled with an eau-de-vie from the region from Révérende Mère's medicine cabinet.

Meanwhile, farther to the north, the invasion was fully under way, with the Allied armies making good progress against the Germans. The beachhead had been secured, and it looked as if a breakout was imminent. Already parts of France had been liberated from their oppressors.

To everyone's surprise the Révérende Mère announced the convent had a well-equipped radio room that would enable Lieutenant Robertson to make contact with England.

During his conversation with his superiors, he was ordered to stay behind and gather intelligence, *not* to escort Henri and the others. With a disheartened sigh, he was about to acknowledge his orders when the radio went dead.

"What happened?" he said, looking at the Révérende Mère, who was holding a plug in her hand.

"It would appear we had a power failure, Lieutenant," she said with a mischievous smile. "I think your friends here need your help."

So I either ignore orders and help them, or obey orders and let them go it alone, Robertson thought. Can't help those power failures, he mused.

The lieutenant slowly walked back into the hall where his friends were waiting.

"What did HQ say, LT? We a go for taking these folks to Spain?"

The lieutenant glanced over at Révérende Mère, who commanded his gaze. Not taking his eyes off of her, he said to Henri and the others, "We have been instructed to help you, Madeleine and Charlène, across the border to Spain."

The Révérende Mère smiled at the young lieutenant and said, "I will have the sisters prepare supplies for your trip, Lieutenant. Come, Charlène." She held out her hand to the girl.

Madeleine spoke first. "I know of *passeurs* in Saint-Girons who can help us across the Pyrénées, but we might have to talk our way past the Spanish border guards."

"Then I'll let my Thompson do the talking," the lieutenant said, patting his submachine gun.

"Let's hope not, for her sake," Madeleine said, nodding to Charlène.

The group adjourned to their spartan quarters to pack what belongings they had for the trip.

After an hour the Révérende Mère entered the great room where they all waited. She informed the group that their truck was ready with supplies for the journey over the mountains.

Each of them thanked the Révérende Mère for her kindness and hospitality. Charlène was given a gold cross, blessed from the water of the grotto in Lourdes. The farewell was especially heartening to the group.

Outside thick clouds of black smoke rose up and away from the courtyard as Armand started the truck and it sputtered to life.

Henri looked into the back of the truck to find fresh supplies of food, plus clothing for the mountain trip and petrol for the truck.

As they left the building, Madeleine turned to the Révérende Mère and asked, "What happened to Mainard?"

"He has seen the light, *mon enfant*," the Révérende Mère replied simply.

"I bet," mumbled Sergeant Rizzo.

"Then I shall leave him in your capable hands, *ma* Révérende Mère," Madeleine said, returning her smile.

Lieutenant Robertson took Madeleine and Henri aside. "I received terrible news when I talked with HQ," he said as he gazed at the cobblestone courtyard.

"The SS Das Reich Division in Normandy has massacred those living in the towns of Lidice and Oradour-sur-Glane, near Limoges." He looked up from his downward gaze. "The

SS suspected the townspeople had hidden explosives. They herded men, women, and children into the church and a barn. They left no one alive."

Armand could barely speak. "My cousins live in Oradour," he said.

Madeleine was aghast, tears flowing from her eyes. "We should go there, Henri, and get our revenge," she said bitterly.

"No! We must cross that border, Madeleine, for Charlène," Henri said.

Madeleine said nothing and went to the back of the truck with Charlène.

"Lieutenant, we will go to Spain, but when this is over, the Nazis will pay for their crimes against my people," Henri said.

The Renault was thrown into gear and traveled along the cobblestone courtyard and through the front gate.

Their journey took them southwest through Moulins, then headed west to avoid the town of Vichy. Taking a direct line southeast to avoid German roadblocks, they stopped in Rodez, nestled in the Avéyron Mountains. This route should have taken them a few hours, but in avoiding Vichy and German roadblocks and checkpoints by winding their way along dirt and ancient back roads, it took more time, especially at night. The old Renault complained the whole time.

"I hope this old mule makes it to the border," Robertson said.

"Told ya we should have kept that bike, LT," Rizzo complained.

Lieutenant Robertson sighed and shook his head.

When they stopped outside of Saint-Girons, Lieutenant Robertson asked Madeleine, "Which way are we going through the mountains?"

Madeleine explained, "Near Saint-Girons, past Mont Valier. The escape route to Spain is not for the weak, Lieutenant. There are several secret routes over the central Pyrénées into northern Spain."

The lieutenant had heard of the escape route, being briefed at MI-6. This route was taken by hundreds of Frenchmen and Jews fleeing from their German oppressors, and by many RAF and American airmen who had either crash-landed or parachuted to safety after being shot down by the Nazis.

Another route used to smuggle downed airmen and others to freedom was the Pat Line, named after Pat O'Leary, alias of Albert Guérisse. And Mary Lindell, also known as the Comtesse de Milleville, had organized a new escape line, the Marie-Claire.

Madeleine continued. "*La Dame Qui Boite*, the Limping Lady," she translated to English. "She made that same crossing in '41 and was promptly thrown in the Figueres prison for six weeks by the Spanish. It would be helpful to have those papers, Lieutenant."

"MI-6 acknowledged they were working on it with the British Embassy in Spain. With a little bit of luck and a lot of gold, we should get those papers," the lieutenant replied.

"Who is the Limping Lady?" Sergeant Waldron asked.

"One of your best spies, Virginia Hall. She has done much for the cause of liberty," Madeleine explained. "She crossed the Pyrénées in the dead of winter with the Gestapo on her heels and with a wooden leg named Cuthbert!"

"Sounds like quite the lady," Sergeant Rizzo commented.

Henri continued where Madeleine left off. "Several well-organized escape lines are still safe, Lieutenant, and each has partisan helpers who will clothe, feed, and hide us, at great personal risk to themselves. We will be hidden in secret, ready for the final night climb into Spain. We will know more when we meet our contact in Rodez. Then we will know which route will be the safest," Henri finished.

Arriving in town around 11:00 PM on the evening of June 15, 1944, the group pulled up behind the local inn sympathetic to the resistance, La Toison d'Or.

"The Golden Fleece, how prophetic," Sergeant Waldron remarked.

Henri and Madeleine went inside via the front door to speak with the innkeeper while the group waited by the truck in a side alley. It was late and close to curfew in the small town, and they were worried that the local Vichy Carlingue or La Milice would be patrolling the streets very soon.

Madeleine appeared in the alley motioning to the group to follow and then escorted them to the back door of the inn. The smell of rotten food filled the enclosed area, encircled by a stone wall. Antoinette froze in terror at the sight.

"I am sorry, *mes amis*. I hate rats!" she whispered.

The innkeeper, a smallish man with shocking red hair, chuckled at Antoinette. "You should see the ones in the cellar!"

"Mes amis," the innkeeper addressed the group, "my name is Reynaud, but my friends call me Rousel."

The group entered the inn, leaving Armand to guard outside.

"Come into *mon salon.*" Rousel motioned to them as he pushed a wall open, showing secret stairs leading into a dark void.

"Said the spider to the fly," Rizzo recited.

Taking a candle from the table, Rousel motioned for everyone to follow him down into the darkness.

Rousel lit candles as he went down into the secret cellar, lighting the way for the group to follow. Once down the stairs, he also lit three candles that sat atop an eight-foot-long table strewn with maps of the region.

"Madeleine, I see you have brought *des Américains* with you once again, and a girl. They will be very difficult to get past the Vichy units in the area," Rousel announced. *"Les soldats Américains* should not wear their uniforms. They need to look like us, like they are French. I bring clothes for them."

"*Merci*, partner," the lieutenant replied.

"Rousel, we are all going on this journey," Madeleine said. "Our mission in le Pas-de-Calais was almost complete, but we were compromised by a double spy, a Spaniard by the name of Sergio Garcia."

"*Mon Dieu!*" Reynaud exclaimed. "This is difficult, but you have luck. *Les bosch* are on alert with Normandy. *Les bosch* are in Perpignan. The Saint-Girons–Esterri escape route, south of Toulouse near Mont Valier, may be *bien*. Southwest, La Milice, of Eaux-Bonnes, is watching the border with Spain, but we are watching them. I marked out passage to Saint-Girons. A guide will take you to the beginning of your escape route," Reynaud said.

He pointed to a map. "From here, you should go north of Montauban via Caussode, on to Agen, then south to Lannemezan, and finally west to Saint-Girons. This route will avoid La Milice and get you to our contact there."

"*C'est bien*, Rousel. *Merci infiniment*. You have our gratitude," Madeleine said.

"I have your supplies in the corner," Rousel said, pointing to a dark area in the basement. "There is extra petrol in the big tank against the wall. Take what you need. As for tonight, I am afraid this is all I can offer. I have some bedrolls for you. I am sorry, but it is the best I can do."

"You have done much for us already, Rousel. *Nous vous en sommes extrêmement reconnaissants*," Henri said.

"My thanks will be hearing that you made it to Spain," he replied. "Now I must attend to the inn before I am missed. *Dormez bien.*"

They all settled in for the evening, Antoinette doting over Charlène, ensuring she was comfortable before setting out her own bedroll, more to the middle of the room to avoid any possible contact with rats.

Armand appeared downstairs informing the group that all was quiet in town and proceeded to lay his bedroll out on the table.

The Americans leaned against one stone wall, using the bedrolls as pillows, while Henri and Madeleine lay next to each other, holding each other throughout the night.

Sometime early the next morning, Rousel brought down a breakfast of bread and cheese with hot coffee. The group ate the meal quickly, Sergeant Waldron exclaiming, "This coffee is like mud, but it sure tastes good!"

"It is French," Henri said proudly. "I have been told that our *café* is quite stronger than what you *Américains* call coffee, *n'est ce pas?*"

"I'll have to remember this stuff when I get back to the states," Waldron commented.

"Woo wee!" Lieutenant Robertson laughed. "That'll take the spots off a cow!"

After breakfast, Armand and Sergeants Waldron and Rizzo loaded the supplies into the back of the truck and filled the gas tank and cans with petrol. Armand and Rizzo shared their tradition of a eau-de vie toast with Waldron as they topped off the truck.

Later that day, Rousel came down to the cellar. "It's time to leave. *Et, que Dieu vous bénisse!*"

The group filtered out the back door of the inn in twos. Armand and Rizzo went first to start the truck, followed by Madeleine and Henri, Robertson and Waldron, and, finally, Charlène and Antoinette.

The Renault rumbled to life and left the alley heading southeast away from Rodez along the highway toward Albi. They blended in with the traffic of horse carriages and other farm vehicles traveling in the same direction. They did not notice the black sedan that followed them at some distance.

In the back of the truck, their spirits were high, knowing that they soon would be crossing the border into Spain. Even though the journey would be tough, it would lead to freedom.

"Hey, LT, how come we didn't cross the Swiss border instead?" Sergeant Waldron asked.

"Because we would be stuck there for the duration, and I have no intention of missing the big game. Besides, we can get a flight or sub out of Gibraltar and get back to England one helluva lot quicker," Lieutenant Robertson replied.

"Makes sense," Rizzo said. "Except my sore ass disagrees with you!"

Passing through Albi, Armand made the turn through the village of Gaillac on the road to Agen. A few moments later, the black sedan was again behind them.

"We are being followed, Madeleine," he said.

"I saw them too, Armand," Madeleine acknowledged. "Keep going. There is a bend in the road past Auch near Mirande; we can take care of them there."

Armand turned south at Auch and then headed toward Mirande. The sedan was still trailing them from a distance. As soon as they rounded a big curve in the highway and were out of sight of the sedan, Madeleine instructed Armand to stop the truck on the side of the road. Opening the flap to the back, she quickly explained the situation to Lieutenant Robertson.

"Are they Carlingue?" the lieutenant asked. "I had been keeping an eye on them.

"Most likely, or Gestapo," Madeleine said.

"What do you want to do, Madeleine?" the lieutenant asked.

"Kill them. When they turn that corner, we will be waiting for them."

Pulling her Sten submachine gun from its hiding place behind her seat in the cab, Madeleine strode out onto the deserted highway, the sun setting behind her casting an eerie aura around her. Lieutenant Robertson, Armand, and Sergeant Rizzo sought cover in the bushes on the side of the road. In the truck, Sergeant Waldron and Henri pulled the flap down and slid their rifles through a small opening on each corner.

The black sedan turned the corner, tires screeching in an attempt to catch up to the truck it had lost sight of, realizing too late that Madeleine stood in the road with machine gun in hand. The driver tried in vain to turn the car around, but it skidded off the road slinging gravel and dust in the air.

All hell broke loose as Madeleine and the men opened fire, riddling the car with bullets. The driver died instantly, but the passenger leaped out the passenger's side with an MP-40, shielding himself with the car door, and returned fire. Armand and the Americans dove for cover as bullets ricocheted off of the trees and rocks behind them. Madeleine was trying to outflank the Carlingue, but another burst in her direction sent her to cover behind the truck.

Desperate to finish off the Vichy, Madeleine withdrew a grenade from her jacket, pulled the pin, and rolled it under the car. The ensuing explosion upended the sedan, flipping it on its side and crushing the Vichy agent underneath, killing him instantly.

Madeleine ran over to the men to ensure everything was OK. Armand stood and nodded in her direction.

"Yeah, looks like we got lucky again, Madeleine," Robertson said.

"I don't think so, LT," Rizzo said.

"Rizzo, what? Aw, hell. Damn it!" Robertson cried. "Waldron, get over here!"

The medic leaped from the truck turning over Rizzo and ripping open his jacket.

Sergeant Rizzo was lying in a pool of his own blood; a bullet had pierced his chest.

Waldron frantically worked on Rizzo's wound, sprinkling a packet of sulfur on it and shoving a bandage into Lieutenant Robertson's hands, telling him to apply pressure.

Waldron could not stop the internal bleeding; the wound was fatal. He sat back and looked directly into Rizzo's eyes.

"Sorry, Tony, I can't stop the bleeding," Waldron said.

"That's OK, Billy boy. I want you to tell my dad I got fifty of them bastards before they got me," Rizzo requested.

"Yeah, buddy, maybe I'll make it a hundred," Waldron said, smiling.

Rizzo spoke in a weakening voice to Robertson. "LT, I'll be waiting for that motorcycle when we get back."

Tony Rizzo, the explosives expert from New Jersey, then took his last breath, head slowly falling back across Waldron's supporting arm.

Everyone was stunned. So far they had escaped unscathed, spirits high. They had seemed invincible. But now, Tony Rizzo, the Italian kid from New Jersey, was dead, and Lieutenant Robertson felt responsible.

"It was my fault. I should have had him back farther. We were too bunched up," Robertson said, disgusted with himself.

"Not your fault, LT," Waldron voiced, grasping his shoulder. "Tony knew the risks."

Robertson grabbed the dog tags around Rizzo's neck and gave a yank. Picking up the sergeant's body and placing it on a blanket Waldron had retrieved from the truck, Robertson wrapped him carefully and carried him into the woods by the side of the road.

Madeleine knew they couldn't stay long otherwise they would be discovered, but she did not dare stop the lieutenant.

"Armand, get the car and those bodies off the road, and get the truck started. We will leave shortly," she directed him.

Henri, who had been inside the truck guarding Charlène and Antoinette, had come forward when Sergeant Waldron leaped out of the truck. Gingerly jumping onto the road, he went to help the Americans.

Lieutenant Robertson and Sergeant Waldron used a shovel from the truck to dig a shallow grave. After digging down into the moist soil three feet, they gently placed the body of Sergeant Rizzo into the grave. Shoveling in the dirt, they gathered rocks and placed them on top to prevent animals from digging up his body.

"LT, do we have to leave him? Tony deserves better than this," Waldron said.

"After this is all over, we're gonna come back and give him a proper military funeral," the lieutenant said.

Madeleine was anxious. It was possible that more than one car of Carlingue agents had been following them. She paced back and forth on the road, torn between the need to flee the area and respect for burying the dead. She walked to the bend in the road and looked to see if any more vehicles were coming.

Satisfied with their work, Lieutenant Robertson stuck Rizzo's bayonet into the ground and placed his helmet on the blade.

Turning to Madeleine, who had waited nervously the whole time for them to finish, he announced with grim determination in his voice, "Now let's get across that border."

The statement was punctuated by a rumbling and a crash as the sedan was pushed off a small ravine nearby, the two bodies falling with it. The smell of cordite mixed with petrol filled the air around the crash scene.

Relieved that they were on the move again, Madeleine was the last to climb into the front seat of the truck.

"Who were those guys?" Waldron asked Robertson in the back of the truck.

"Probably the Vichy Carlingue Madeleine and Henri referred to at the convent," the lieutenant said. "Those bastards weren't worth Rizzo's life."

Sergeant Waldron didn't say anything else. Tony was his friend, and they had trained together from the beginning. Rizzo could never keep his mouth shut, he thought, smiling secretly, but he was always there for you when you needed him most.

"I'm gonna miss that bum," he mumbled to Robertson.

The Renault grumbled to life in a puff of thick black smoke and sped back onto the road heading north toward the road that eventually led to Saint-Girons.

It was around 8:00 PM when they arrived in Saint-Girons, a quiet town nestled between rolling hills, the Pyrénées looming in the distance against a starlit sky. Madeleine had Armand pull into a side street near L'Hotel Souquet on the outskirts of town.

"So that's where we are going?" Waldron, pointing to Mont Valier, asked Henri as they climbed out of the truck. "It looks like it's snowing up there."

"We will take the pass on either side of Valier. The snow has melted where we are going," Henri replied.

Madeleine and Henri entered the inn first and returned minutes later with a woman named Françoise.

"*Bienvenue à* L'Hotel Souquet!" she said, warmly welcoming them. "*Entrez.*"

Once inside, she motioned for the group to take a table near the kitchen.

"I usually close at this time, so it will be fine for you to stay here until I get your rooms ready for tonight," Françoise informed them.

The inn is run-down, Lieutenant Robertson noted to himself.

Noticing Robertson's gaze about her establishment, Françoise commented to him directly, "I must apologize for the condition of my inn. My husband, you see, was killed by La Milice when he was discovered guiding a Jewish couple across the border. Since his death, I have not been able to keep up the inn. If I no longer wanted to help people escape, I would not operate the inn anymore," she said.

"My apologies, ma'am," the lieutenant replied in his Texas drawl. "When this whole mess is over, I would be more than willing to come back and help you fix it right."

Then, turning to Antoinette, he said, "I might have a hankering to visit France," and smiled his Texas-wide grin at her.

Antoinette smiled shyly, blushing a deep red.

"You are kind, Lieutenant," Françoise replied. "It would be good to see you and your wife again after the war is over."

"But—" Robertson stuttered.

"I prepare your food," Françoise announced. "I have rooms upstairs at the far end for the ladies and the girl. The men can stay in the first room to the right."

"Do you need assistance in preparing the rooms?" Antoinette asked.

"*Merci*, no," Françoise replied. "The inn has been empty for quite some time."

Françoise excused herself.

Waldron had a wide grin on his face.

"What, Billy?" The lieutenant asked.

"Got ya married already, LT." Sergeant Waldron chuckled.

"Shut up, Billy," Robertson growled.

Changing the subject, Lieutenant Robertson questioned Madeleine. "So what enemy forces are we up against in the crossing?"

"The *Milice Française*. We call them *Les Souris Grises,* the Gray Mice," Madeline told him. "There are our war veterans, organized by the Vichy government of Pétain. They keep watch over us and report signs of resistance."

"They are traitors to France," Henri said.

Madeleine continued, "Some partisan groups have targeted the leaders and members of the Milice, shooting them in the streets, at their homes, while Milice offices have been attacked with grenades. The times are hard, Robbie, *n'est ce pas?*"

"You do what you have to do," Robbie answered.

"Robbie, can you tell us about the invasion?" Henri asked.

"The German units in the area are not paying attention to the border and are expecting another invasion to capture the port of Marseilles and the lines of communication leading northward," the lieutenant explained.

"Then we have only to fear *Les Souris Grises*, and some of them may be having second thoughts," Madeleine said.

"Well, no sense in getting them all worked up if we don't have to. I'd rather avoid them, given the status of our little group," Robbie stated.

Françoise moved around the dining room with grace and ease as she set the table with a savory stew. It filled the room with rich aromas of allspice, a hint of pepper, and beef broth.

She also opened up a few bottles of wine and placed them in the center of the table with several glasses.

The group dug into the meal immediately. The food smelled and tasted delicious. No one investigated its contents, as it didn't matter.

Antoinette raised her glass and proposed a toast.

"To Sergeant Anthony Rizzo. *Que le bon Dieu le bénisse.*"

"To Rizzo!" they toasted.

The lieutenant picked at his food. "I'm gonna miss that bum."

The rest of the evening was spent quietly sitting by the fireplace sipping wine and discussing the particulars of the escape route.

Sitting by the crackling fireplace, the lieutenant inquired, "Madeleine, will Charlène be able to make it through the pass?"

"She is a very strong girl for her age, Robbie. I have seen women with babies walk across the Pyrénées to escape. Charlène will surprise you," Madeleine commented.

"Ever since we left that convent, she has seemed to gain strength. Not that I wholly believe in miracles, but I can't argue this one," Robbie admitted.

"Truly that was a miracle. Now we should get some rest. The next days will be very difficult, even for the strongest of us," Madeleine replied.

A yawning Robbie replied, "Well, it's time to hit the hay. *Bonne nuit*, folks."

"*Bonne nuit*, Robbie," Henri and Madeleine said.

Prussian Blue

"Emily, it looks as if there was a recent investigation by the FBI on the purchase of Radiogardase, Prussian blue insoluble capsules, in bulk, but no information or company names are given," Jack said. "What is that stuff?"

"Prussian blue is a commercial product to remove cesium-137 indirectly from the bloodstream by intervening in the enterohepatic circulation of cesium-137, reducing the internal residency time and exposure by about two-thirds," Emily said matter-of-factly.

"English?" Jack asked.

"It cleans the chemical from the blood," she answered.

"Ah... how is this connected?" Jack asked.

"Jack, if the FBI is investigating bulk orders of Prussian blue, then they already suspect that someone intends to make a bomb. Look for any listing of cesium-137 as well," Emily said.

"So then logically if we find orders from companies linking both, we find the dirty bomb," Jack reasoned.

"Exactly, and we should check pharmacies because a prescription is needed to get Prussian blue," Emily said.

A few hours of searching later, Emily stopped typing on her keyboard and sat back in her chair, thinking for a moment. "I may have something here, Jack."

"Do tell," Jack said.

"There have been payments to Toffler Chemicals by a radiation scanning company in Spain, with assets going through the Caymans," Emily declared.

"As in Gisele?" a visibly shocked Jack asked rhetorically. "What was that woman into?"

"Apparently more than we knew. It's a shame we killed her before we could find out more," Emily said. "It would have been easier to find out what's going on here."

"I am glad she is dead after what she did to us, Emily. I would do it again," Jack solemnly said.

"I know, dear; I wanted her dead too. But hindsight being twenty-twenty here, having her alive would have made this a lot easier," she commented, turning back to her screen.

"Toffler Chemicals is sole US distributor of Prussian blue in the greater metropolitan area," Jack revealed.

"I'll check on the FBI database to see if they have anything on Toffler Chemicals," Emily said.

After a few minutes of scanning through the files, Emily said, "Looks like there are several case files that the FBI and Homeland Security are currently investigating."

"On what?" Jack asked.

"Toffler Chemicals has reported theft of product—to be more precise, Radiogardase!" Emily said.

"We should brief Jean and Charlène. This is the link we've been looking for," Jack said.

Jack sent for Charlène and Jean, notifying them of the intelligence they had gathered. Emily explained the situation with her understanding of drug practices and procedures with Prussian blue.

It's a good thing you have the background that you do, Emily," Charlène said. "Otherwise we might have missed this piece of the puzzle altogether."

Jean walked in at that moment talking to no one in particular with a folded note in his hand. "A message was intercepted by the CIA, originating from Vargas to Garcia. It's a line from the poem 'Hibakusha' by the poet from Hiroshima, Sankichi Toge. He witnessed the destruction of that city," Jean said. "Hibakusha means A-Bomb survivor."

The sun shone, and nothing moved but the buzzing flies in the metal basins, reeking with stagnant odor.

"Interesting line," Emily observed. "I know what it means."

"What are you thinking, Emily?" Charlène asked.

"There're refineries and chemical plants all around this area. We should concentrate on the words 'metal basins' and 'stagnant odor.'"

"That could be anywhere around New York," Jack said. "It's the proverbial needle in the haystack."

"Anywhere just might be Newark or Linden," Emily replied. "The proximity to the highway would make the refineries a perfect target."

Jean said, "I suspect the lines from the poem will kick off key events on their timeline. The CIA and FBI are in agreement. They want us to take the lead on the investigation. You two find them and quickly. I fear we are running out of time."

"Does the FBI or CIA have any information we can use?" Jack queried.

"No more than we do, Jack. Any good intel we receive we will pass along to them," Jean said. "Talk to me first."

"Will do," Jack affirmed.

Charlène looked to Jack. "Please come with me. I have something for you."

While Emily studied maps of the Newark area, Charlène took Jack to a small side room, weapons from various wars and eras lining the wall. On a small wooden table in the room was a metallic box, which Charlène unlatched and opened. Inside lay a prosthetic hand on a red-velvet cushion.

"Not sure I could get used to something like that," Jack said. "I've seen people walk around with those fake hands, and always thought, why bother?"

"This one is different, Jack. It was developed for the military," Charlène explained.

"OK, I'm game. What does it do?" Jack inquired.

"In this case, the hand will bond to what you have left of your wrist. It's very high-tech stuff. From what I understand, it reconnects nerves to your arm and you can *feel* your hand again," Charlène said.

"Well, brushing my teeth with my left hand is a bit awkward, and showers are awkward," Jack said nervously. In truth, he was scared of the thing.

"I guess I should just go for it, huh?" Jack said.

"It's up to you, Jack. Your choice," Charlène said.

"All right, here goes then," Jack said.

Taking the prosthetic with his left hand, Jack held it in position.

"How does it go on?" he asked.

"The first time you put it on, open this compartment," Charlène said, pointing to a barely visible outline under the hand's wrist. Charlène pressed on the bottom side of the wrist and a small compartment opened. Inside was a keypad and digital readout and what appeared to be an on/off button. Pressing the button the hand came to life, and Jack almost dropped it as the fingers slowly opened up. The opening at the other end also increased in size.

"The four-digit code is 7227, Jack. Don't forget it," Charlène warned. "Once the end opens wide enough, you can slide your wrist in."

Carefully positioning the prosthetic over his wrist stump, he slid the prosthetic on. At first the sensations were pleasant, almost a soft tingling, but moments later pain shot up through his arm. Jack grasped the hand to try to remove it, but Charlène stopped him.

"Jack, it's only a moment of pain. The prosthetic is adjusting to your DNA," Charlène said.

Jack was on one knee from the jolt, but the prosthetic was already calming down, and he was no longer feeling pain in his arm.

"It will take a few weeks for the nerve endings to rebuild and your hand to regenerate," Charlène explained.

"Wait, come again?" Jack said.

"The military has spent millions on stem cell research. They are now able to regrow severed limbs, hearts, and many parts of the body. Your body actually does the work," Charlène said.

"Wait, I remember something about this on one of the prime-time news shows, about a guy who cut off his finger. So this is the same?" Jack asked.

"It's better. That process took a month to grow a finger. This improved version will take a month to grow a whole hand, Jack," Charlène said.

"I don't know how to thank you," Jack said.

"After what happened with Garcia, it's the least I can do," Charlène acknowledged. "In the meantime, you need to stay here and monitor Emily's movements. Be her eyes and ears while she is looking for Vargas and Garcia."

Jack saw no use in arguing the point; his stubbornness had gotten him into this position, and he could easily help Emily from operations.

"Tomas thinks she is dead, Jack, and we can alter her appearance enough that he won't recognize her. We will be right there with her," Charlène reminded him.

Jack was astounded. If this thing actually works, he thought, looking down at the oversized hand, I'll be golden!

Jack walked out and showed a surprised Emily the medical device attached to his arm. She was as dumbfounded as he by this incredible technology.

Emily beamed. "Seems like we will both get back to normal, dear."

The rest of that day was spent tracking down any purchase, reports of theft, or deliveries of Prussian blue to and from Toffler Chemicals.

"Maybe we are looking at this all wrong," Jack stated.

"How so?" Emily asked.

"Well, what's the best way to hide something?" Jack asked, grinning.

Emily said, "Occam's razor. The principle that generally recommends that, from among competing hypotheses, selecting the one that makes the fewest new assumptions usually provides the correct one, and that the simplest explanation will be the most plausible until evidence is presented to prove it false."

Jack countered, "By *shaving away* unnecessary assumptions or cutting apart two similar theories. Brilliant, Emily!"

Emily typed several keywords onto the computer, easing back into her chair.

Turning to Jack, she said, "Vilja Vargas and Associates, a biotech company that stores and ships compounds to major pharmaceutical companies."

"You're kidding." Jack laughed. "I was just trying to impress you!"

"OK, I'll track the shipment records in and out of Vilja Vargas and Associates, and you concentrate on Toffler Chemicals," Jack replied.

"I'll bet we find a connection," Emily promised.

Not just one connection but several came up between the two businesses, for shipments of class 4 noncontrolled chemicals. They had enough evidence by the end of the day to present the FBI with a valid argument to start an investigation on the two companies.

At the afternoon briefing with Jean and Charlène, Jack and Emily gave the new information.

"Nice work, you two," Jean commented. "The FBI will need more evidence before they can get a warrant to check them out. It's funny how we sometimes miss the obvious."

"We will need surveillance on Garcia and Vargas," Charlène said to her team.

"You're right, Charlène. Emily, are you ready?" Jean asked.

"Definitely," she replied.

Jack was about to object but was interrupted before he could embarrass himself.

"I'll be all right, Jack, and in touch the whole time," Emily said.

"You won't be alone, Emily," Charlène repeated. "We have another agent, Marie Sinclaire. She will go on this mission with you."

That evening over a delicious dinner of beef bourguignon sautéed with onions and mushrooms, Marie Sinclaire arrived at the estate and was introduced to Jack and Emily.

Introducing her, Charlène tapped her wine glass with her spoon. "This is Marie Sinclaire, one of our best agents in Europe. Her grandmother died in France in 1944 while working with your father, Jack."

"I remember him and Scotty telling me the stories. Now I know why they seemed upset when they discussed her. I am sorry for your loss," Jack apologized.

"No need for apologies, Jack," Marie said. "She gave her life for France in that horrible war and will always be remembered as a hero."

"Just as your father was, Jack," Charlène added.

The conversation turned to lighter topics as they enjoyed the delicious dinner provided by Charlène. After dinner the group retired to the study to sit by the fire and discuss the upcoming mission over a savory glass of Grand Marnier.

"Vargas and Associates is located in the heart of Newark, and not far from the oil refinery and storage tanks in Linden—a perfect place to start a dirty bomb," Jean informed the group. "If they were to set the bomb to explode into one of the tanks and it caught fire, the radiation would spread exponentially."

"Ladies, I want you to be acutely aware of my strictest orders concerning the mission at hand," Charlène said as she looked at Jack's mechanical hand. "You will be surveillance only, and there will be no onsite investigation at Vilja Vargas and Associates. Are we understood?"

"Understood," both women said simultaneously.

"We would like to know who comes and goes, the amount and type of vehicles that do business with Vargas," Jean instructed.

"What about Toffler Chemicals?" Jack asked.

"We believe that our real target here is Vilja Vargas and Associates. I suspect that we will find both Garcia and Vargas at his business. Once we confirm they are on-site, the FBI will close in and arrest them," Jean said.

"After the death of Gisele, it looks like Toffler Chemicals is under new ownership and has turned away from this venture. But there is still a historical trail there, and the FBI will gather evidence from them once Vargas and Garcia are captured. They wouldn't want to tip off Vargas or Garcia by raiding that facility," Charlène added.

"I would hate to be in that audit," Emily said. "They can be brutal!"

"Hopefully," Jack said, chuckling at the thought of Gisele's former business going down hard.

After finishing up some detailed instructions on where to park the car and how to act if approached, the group settled in to finish their Grand Marnier and retire to bed for the upcoming surveillance mission the next morning.

Georges sent the limo driver around in the morning, and the two ladies climbed in back for the trip to the airport. The flight was short, and thankfully uneventful. After renting the four-door black sedan they requested, and refusing the upgraded red sports car with disappointment, they headed out to the business site of Vilja Vargas and Associates.

Entering the business park, they parked the car in a large lot with an overview of the biotech firm in the distance. Positioning the camera, they sat quietly in the car recording the comings and goings of personnel and trucks at Vilja Vargas and Associates.

"Seems to be a helluva lot of activity for a small biotech," Emily observed.

"Way too much," Marie agreed. "Maybe we should get a closer look?"

"Charlène was strict about our hands-off approach for now, Marie. After what happened to Jack, I think we should follow her orders," Emily said.

"I guess, but if they are going to catch this guy, it's not happening from here," Marie commented.

Marie was right, but Emily pondered that she was not ready for the same kind of treatment Jack got when he was captured by Tomas Garcia. Even worse, what if Charlène found out? But she's right, Emily thought. We have to get a good look at what's happening in there.

"I am not comfortable with getting a look inside, but you're right. How about if we check it out tonight when they're closed?" Emily asked.

"Sounds like a plan," Marie replied.

"If we can get physical evidence they are storing mass quantities of Prussian blue, cesium, cobalt, or americium, we've got them," Emily said.

The rest of the day was spent gathering information on trucks and people who did business with Vargas and Associates. License plates were recorded, and the two women took turns sleeping throughout the day to rest up for the night's prying into the biotech company owned by Vargas.

Back at the estate, Jack monitored the GPS tracking devices implanted into the phones of both women. The devices were top secret and also checked on body heat surrounding the phone. Not much use in the daytime, Jack observed, but at night it was a handy feature.

Emily checked in with Jack every three hours and reported any suspicious movement that might have indicated illicit activity. Emily raised her camera as one truck entered the facility, clicking a picture. She woke up Marie.

"What's up?" Marie asked.

"A truck from Toffler Chemicals just entered the shipping yard," Emily said.

"They supposedly stopped doing business. Did you get the license plate number?" Marie asked.

Calling Jack, she reported the incident and gave him the plate number.

After a few minutes searching the DMV records of Toffler Chemicals, Jack found something interesting.

"Emily, that truck was reported stolen last year, along with its cargo," Jack said.

"I bet I know what's in there," Emily said. "We need to get a look at that truck, Jack."

"You know Charlène's instructions, Emily. Let her contact the FBI and get them in there," he said.

"It'll be too late if we have to wait on the FBI, Jack. Get Charlène's permission for us to get into that truck."

"I'll ask, but she's not going to like this," Jack said.

Jack found Charlène and Jean in the study, enjoying a quiet dinner together.

"Hi, Jack. Join us?" Charlène asked politely.

"No thanks. Georges brought me a sandwich earlier," Jack replied. "I have some good news from Emily and Marie. They spotted a Toffler truck that was reported stolen last year delivering goods to Vilja Vargas and Associates."

"Interesting," Jean said. "And I'll bet that it's filled with the makings of a dirty bomb."

"So that's it then," Charlène said. "The truck is the bomb!"

"Wait, do you mean the truck is rigged to go off?" Jack blurted out. "Charlène, Emily and Marie sent me here to ask if they could break into that truck to find evidence!"

"Jack, you must stop them. That truck is probably booby-trapped to go off if it's tampered with!" Jean said.

"Which is exactly what will happen when it's parked outside of the intended target," Charlène said.

"Jean, call the FBI. It's time to move in and take out Vargas," Charlène instructed her lieutenant.

"Jack, get Emily and Marie out of there. If the dirty bomb is detonated, they will get lethal doses of radiation."

***

"Leave the phones in the car," Marie said.

"Why?" Emily asked.

"Those phones not only detect objects around us but can give away our position as well," Marie explained.

"You know we're going to catch hell when we get back about leaving our phones," Emily said.

***

Running back to the operations center, Jack immediately got on the secured phone line and dialed Emily's phone, but she did not pick up. He tried Marie's with the same results.

Back in the parking lot, the two phones lay on the front seat of the car as Marie and Emily worked their way toward the truck.

"Let's go around back via that empty building," Marie said, pointing to a blind spot in the security camera coverage. "It looks like the cameras don't cover that section in the back."

"Let's get some pictures and get the hell out of here," Emily said.

Heading out of sight around the empty office building, Emily picked the lock on a side door, turned the knob, and walked inside, pistol drawn, followed by Marie.

Making their way around to the back of the empty building, they opened a door to the shipping room. Much to their surprise, it was bustling with activity, with armed guards overseeing men in protective suits moving around boxes marked "Prussian Blue" with chemical MDA stickers on them. Their entrance attracted unwanted attention.

"Crap, move!" Marie yelled, pushing Emily back into the room they came from as the guards fired on an exposed Marie, bullets scattering all around her in the entrance. Marie, unable to get out of the way, took one bullet in the chest and was thrown back into the room beside Emily.

Emily grabbed Marie and dragged her away from the entrance, bullets flying past her head. Slamming the door shut, she shot off the doorknob and pushed a nearby desk in front of the door.

"Marie!" she screamed, awaking the unconscious woman. "Thank God! I thought you were dead," she stammered.

Pulling open her shirt, Marie revealed the bulletproof vest as Emily helped her up. "You should get one of these. They are all the rage in Paris!"

"Who wears a bulletproof vest on a surveillance mission?" Emily asked, lifting her up.

"We have to get out of here. We are compromised," Emily said.

Running back toward the window they broke in through, they climbed out but soon realized that the guards had cut them off from their retreat to the car. Marie dropped to one knee and shot, killing one guard instantly. More of Vargas's men began firing in their direction, pinning them behind a dumpster. The only escape route was to go back in the building, but one guard was inside blocking them.

"We have two choices: sit here and die, or take our chances and shoot our way out," Marie said.

"I'd rather go out shooting if that's my choice," Emily said, thinking about Jack as they were about to make a break.

Suddenly, the sound of sirens and screeching tires could be heard approaching the area. Men in dark suits jumped out of several cars and drew their weapons.

"FBI, hands up or we will shoot!" one shouted.

The two guards out front dropped their weapons and raised their hands in surrender.

Looking over at the two women, one agent called out, "Drop your weapons and identify yourselves. Keep your hands raised!"

Dropping their weapons, they raised their hands.

"We are CIA. We have identification," Emily said.

Producing their badges, the FBI agent lowered his gun. "I am Agent James Wilson. We got a call from your handler Jack, said you were in trouble."

They both retrieved their guns and stored their badges.

"We were. Thanks for the save, James," Emily said. "But there is one more guy inside that buil—"

A shot rang out from the building, and a bullet grazed Emily's left arm.

Marie spun with alarming speed while pulling out a small, flat pistol hidden in the small of her back. There was no hesitation as she aimed her gun toward the window and fired, placing a bullet into the chest of Vilja Vargas.

Agent Wilson followed Marie into the building.

As they approached Vargas, Marie kicked his gun away from him and grabbed his bloodied shirt.

"Where is Tomas Garcia?" she yelled at Vargas, laying face up, a pool of blood spreading beneath him on the cold cement floor.

Smiling at her, he garbled out two words, coughing up blood. *"Ockhams Messer."*

He died moments later.

Outside, Emily felt a burning sensation from the bullet that hit her in the arm.

Running to her side from watching Vargas die, Marie examined Emily's wound. "You'll be OK, and you're lucky; the bullet just cut your arm."

"Remind me to buy one of those Parisian vests. And where did you get that pistol? You have an incredible aim," Emily said. "What about Vargas?"

Marie looked perplexed. "He's dead, but he said something strange when I asked where Garcia was."

"Which was?"

"Ockham's Messer," Marie said.

"Ockham's Messer? Marie, we have to get back. We have a mole!" Emily exclaimed.

"How do you know?"

"Because Jack and I were discussing this in operations before," Emily said.

"You two know what Ockham's Messer is?" Marie asked.

"Yes, but I'll explain later," Emily said. "We need to get back to the estate."

"Shame Garcia wasn't here too," Marie said.

"We'll find him eventually," Emily said. Her arm felt like someone had poured hot grease on it. I can't imagine Jack's pain when Garcia sawed off his hand, she thought.

"She OK?" Wilson asked Marie.

"She'll be fine. Do you have a first aid kit we can use?" Marie asked.

"Sure, let me get it for you," Wilson said.

As he left to get the first aid kit, the police arrived along with more FBI agents.

Men and women filed out of the company, and each was questioned and released or taken downtown for additional interrogation by the FBI.

Walking over to the women, Wilson handed Marie the first aid kit, which she proceeded to open in order to find a bandage with which to tend Emily's wound.

"Yeah, and just between you and me, I would have hated to have had to arrest that SOB," Wilson said. "You know, it's a good thing you didn't get into that truck," he said, pointing at the vehicle as the other FBI agents cordoned it off.

"Why?" Emily asked apprehensively.

"Because *that* is our dirty bomb," Wilson answered. "We are handing the truck over to the military as soon as they arrive to dispose of it."

"How come the FBI didn't warn us of this before?" Emily demanded to know.

"I am sorry, but we weren't sure until we got that call from Agent Jack Turner. It was then that we put everything together," Agent Wilson said. "Besides, we couldn't rush in until we had more proof."

Emily and Marie stayed while the FBI questioned them on their observations of Vargas and Associates. Retrieving their phones from their car, Emily called Jack and informed him of the events.

"Emily, Charlène wants you on the next available flight back," Jack said.

"Oh great, am I in trouble?" Emily asked.

"I would consider a king-sized bottle of Grand Marnier if I were you, dear." Jack chuckled.

An hour later a black Humvee pulled into the parking lot towing a trailer. Men in black uniforms got out and tied heavy straps with hooks around the truck, securing them tightly.

"What are they going to do with the truck?" Emily asked.

"Dump it in the ocean," Wilson explained.

"You Americans are not very concerned with the environment," Marie said.

"Better than thousands of dead bodies to clean up," Wilson shot back.

The drone of rotor blades slowly filled the air and a Sikorsky CH-53K Super Stallion helicopter hovered overhead. Everyone in the vicinity of the truck scurried for cover as debris, rocks, and sand were kicked up into the air. One black-suited soldier stood atop the truck and used a hook to connect the straps to the undercarriage of the chopper. Checking his work, he jumped down and signaled the crew chief with a thumbs-up. The pilot slowly guided the helicopter upward, easily lifting the truck off the ground. He paused momentarily to ensure that the deadly cargo was secure, and then, pulling on the collective, the powerful helicopter rose into the air with the truck dangling beneath. The pilot turned the chopper out to sea.

Arriving late that night at the estate, Marie and Emily were summoned to Charlène's study. Jack gave his wife a hug and kiss as she entered.

"Good to have you back, sweetie. Your arm OK?" Jack asked.

"I am fine, dear. Just a scratch," Emily said.

"Jack, you'll excuse us for a moment," Charlène said.

Jack closed the study doors behind the two women, Charlène's arms crossed, reminding him of the sisters' office at the Catholic middle school he attended.

"God help them!" he thought.

LE CHEMIN DE LA LIBERTÉ

Françoise prepared the group for the tough ascent. She supplied them with warm clothes and, most importantly, good footwear, and cheese, bread, and sausage as their staples for the journey over the Pyrénées.

"Françoise, are there water sources through the passes?" Sergeant Waldron asked.

"*Oui*, Sergeant," Françoise said. "There are many places where small streams flow out of the rocks to feed the rivers in the valleys below. There are also two large lakes along the way."

"We could use some of Armand's brandy," Waldron said. "It would help our wounded with the pain."

"The *passeurs* in this area have hidden eau-de-vie along the route at the usual overnight stops," Françoise said.

"Eau-de-vie?" Waldron asked.

"I believe you Americans call it moonshine," Armand said.

"Rizzo did enjoy his moonshine," Lieutenant Robertson said.

"*Oui,*" Armand replied with a sad smile. "My flask of brandy is low. I will need a refill."

"*Mon ami*, the eau-de-vie is to help *évadés* to freedom, not to fill your flask for pleasure," Françoise chided him.

"*Excusez-moi,*" Armand said. "I meant no disrespect."

Saying nothing further, Françoise turned away to attend to some supplies. Flustered, she dropped the cheese on the floor and then quickly bent to pick it up.

"Françoise, are you OK?" Madeleine asked. "Is something troubling you?"

Françoise sighed. "My twenty-year-old nephew André will be taken to Germany as part of *le Service du travail obligatoire.*"

"That sounds like a prisoner exchange," the lieutenant said.

"You are right, Lieutenant," Françoise said. "The Vichy Prime Minister, Pierre Laval, instituted *la relève*, where French workers are encouraged to volunteer to work in Germany in exchange for the release of our prisoners of war."

"Why doesn't he just fight back?" Sergeant Waldron asked.

"How do you when a gun is pointed at you?" Madeleine said.

"We intend on fixing that," Lieutenant Robertson said.

"Françoise, how many have been deported to Germany?" Sergeant Waldron asked.

"About six hundred thousand of our countrymen work for a German victory. The Vichy also operate concentration camps and have deported many Jews to Germany," Françoise said.

"*C'est dégoutant* what the Vichy government has done to our countrymen," Henri said. "We can take your nephew with us to Spain."

"I am afraid you are too late, Henri," Françoise said. "The Vichy have him in the town jail, and there are many guards. A truck drives through the area and picks up young men who are deported each week. They will pick André up tomorrow."

"What stops anyone from overpowering the driver, or running away?" Waldron questioned.

"The men are told their families will be held responsible if they try to escape," Françoise said.

"In other words, they would kill them," Waldron said.

"*Oui,*" Françoise said. "But I am his only family left. The rest have been deported to concentration camps or are already dead. You see, André's family was sent to the Drancy camp, an internment camp for Jews. The camp is under direct control of a ruthless Nazi SS officer named Alois Brunner. From there his family was sent to Auschwitz."

"We have heard the rumors of Auschwitz," Antoinette said. "No one returns."

"Why wasn't he sent to the concentration camp at Drancy?" Henri asked.

"André is a healthy young man, useful to the Nazi cause. The Vichy have not told the Nazis he is Jewish. They apparently want to fulfill their quota this month," Françoise said.

"Maybe we should do something about that, Henri," Robbie said. "Our team has the expertise to make a jailbreak for the young man. It's a shame we lost Rizzo. He was good at blowing stuff up."

"A rescue would be very risky for you. It will not be easy," Françoise said.

"Madeleine, you've been quiet on this. What do you think?" Robbie asked.

"It is risky, as Françoise has said, but I am in favor of not allowing *les bosch* to claim another Français," Madeleine replied.

"I agree," Henri said.

"But I must say again that trying to get him out of jail would be too dangerous for you and might get you all caught," Françoise stated.

"We already are at risk, Françoise," Madeleine said. "One more will not make a difference in our chances."

"Then I will guide you myself," Françoise said. "If we are to rescue him, my life is worth his. They will kill me in reprisal for his escape in any case."

"Then you must escape France with us," Madeleine said.

"We will take the path leading from here in Saint-Girons through the Pyrénées and into Spain," Françoise said.

"We have some planning to do, Françoise. Do you have any maps of the town?" Lieutenant Robertson asked.

"*Oui*, I will get them for you," she replied.

Sitting down at a back room table, out of view from the main room of the inn, the group planned out how they would free André from the Milice.

That day they should have been preparing for their own departure through the mountain passes, but not a single one in the group could have lived with themselves if they had left the young man to be sent off to die in some forced labor camp.

"How many guard him, Françoise?" the lieutenant asked.

"Only three, but their barracks is just outside of Saint-Girons, and they could have many more soldiers here in very little time," Françoise explained.

"Anyone have a horse and a nice sturdy piece of rope?" Robbie asked.

"I do," Françoise answered. "Why? A horse would attract too much attention and would not make it through the passes to Spain."

"Oh, just thinking of a good ole-fashion Texas jailbreak!" Robbie declared.

"How did I know that was coming?" Waldron laughed.

Seeing the confused looks on the others, Robbie briefly explained what always happens in western movies.

"Let's hope the Vichy haven't watched one of your westerns," Henri said with humor.

The rest of the day, the group rehearsed the attack plan and the route to be taken once they freed André.

Robbie said, "Françoise, you should wait with Henri and Charlène with the supplies while we conduct the attack. We can rendezvous after we rescue André from jail."

"There is a run-down barn just outside of our village that we often use for preparing *évadés*," Françoise said, pointing to the map. "André knows the place. We can meet there."

"We'll be coming fast, like the dogs are after us," Robbie expressed. "Be ready."

Henri glanced over to Sergeant Billy Waldron.

"Don't ask." Billy laughed.

That evening around 7:30, the group quietly left the inn and gathered in the shadows of a nearby barn with a full view of the mountain peaks of Ariège to await their escort, Françoise.

As evening fell over the quiet town of Saint-Girons, two groups left in separate directions from Françoise's inn. Henri, Antoinette, Charlène, and Françoise walked southeast toward the rendezvous point looking like a family going on an evening stroll.

Sergeant Waldron, Lieutenant Robertson, Armand, and Madeleine crept slowly through the town and approached the Pont de Fer, an old iron bridge spanning the Salat River.

The evening was deathly quiet. A dog barked in the distance, piercing through everyone's nerves and making the midnight-black horse skittish.

"Probably a cat," Lieutenant Robertson whispered.

"Let's hope so," Madeleine answered.

The lieutenant spoke softly to the horse, calming it down, and they made it across without incident.

Whispering to Robbie, Madeleine asked, "What did you say to him to make him calm down?"

"I told him to shut up or I'll send him to the German front," Robbie said.

It took all Madeleine had to not burst out laughing.

The group turned left and climbed a hill for about a half mile, passing a local restaurant, and then took a sharp right toward the town hall in the area known as Maison de Beauregard. Not wanting to be seen, they entered an alley to get around to the back of the jail where André was being held, as described by Françoise.

"Silencers," Lieutenant Robertson whispered.

As they reached the back of the jail, the lieutenant uttered softly, "Well I'll be damned. And where are the windows with bars?"

"Guess they didn't watch any westerns, eh, LT?" Waldron murmured.

"Shut up, Billy. OK, plan B," Robbie whispered back.

"Which is?" Madeleine asked, speaking softly.

"The horse becomes our distraction. Armand, take him around to the front and, on my signal, shoot a round in the air with that silencer off your Sten. Use your hand to hit the horse on his rear end hard," Robbie said.

"*Oui*, Lieutenant," Armand replied as he took the reins from Robbie.

"Billy, get out some of Rizzo's plastic explosives and a fuse," Robbie commanded.

Handing the lieutenant the Composition B and a roll of fuse, Billy and Madeleine went around the corner a safe distance away. Placing the explosives in a doorlike pattern, Robbie connected it all with a fuse. Laying the fuse around the corner, Robbie nodded to the others as he lit the fuse.

Signaling Armand, a shot was fired, and after a whack on its ass, the horse charged down the street.

A pair of Milice came out of the building just as Armand finished screwing the silencer onto his Mk II Sten.

Two Gray Mice fell silently in a heap in front of the door.

The Composition B blasted a hole through the old brick building. The explosion was loud, blowing dust and debris all over the rescue group. In fact, half of the back of the building lay on the ground in a huge pile of rubble.

Madeleine and Robbie laid down a burst of fire from their Stens as three more Milice fell. A fourth Milice was able to make it through the front door, but Armand finished him off as he fell onto the bodies of his comrades.

Kicking in a locked wooden door, Madeleine and Robbie stood in amazement. Two other men were with André, huddled in the corner.

"OK, gents, I am Lieutenant Rizzo with the American army. Consider yourselves rescued."

Madeleine explained the situation in French, and the three men followed her and Robbie out the back and over the rubble just as the rest of the back of the building collapsed.

"Whoa, LT," Waldron exclaimed. "I think you used too much. I can hear Rizzo now!"

"All right, let's get to the rendezvous point," Robbie said, "Madeleine, tell them to take us to Le Roc de Gabach."

Earlier, Françoise, Antoinette, Henri, and Charlène traveled along an alternate route from the rescue group. After crossing the Pont de Fer and passing the Maison de Beauregard, they quietly made their way through town to the fields that overlooked the outskirts of Saint-Girons and the approach to their first challenge, Le Roc de Gabach, an upward climb of about 600 meters.

They had almost made it to the fields when they heard someone approaching them from a nearby building.

A Milice guard brandishing a pistol approached the group. "Ah, Françoise," he said in relief, lowering his pistol. "It's almost curfew, what are you doing out this late? And who are these three," he said pointing at her guests.

"*Bonsoir*, René. This is my cousin Henri, his sister Antoinette, and her daughter Charlène, visiting from Marseilles. We stayed too late at a friend's house and lost track of the time," Françoise answered.

"I expect you have travel papers on you, Henri?" René asked.

"*Oui, un moment, s'il vous plaît.* Ah, I must apologize. I must have left them at the inn," Henri explained nervously.

"It is a dangerous practice to be out after curfew, Henri, and without travel papers—and with *des sacs à dos*? Going somewhere?" René said. "The clothes you have on are for traveling in the mountains too." René began to back up, raising his pistol.

"They are just visiting, René. It is late, you are correct. We should be going home," Françoise said, trying to diffuse the situation.

"Well then, please let me see the contents of your *sacs à dos*," René demanded.

As Henri slowly removed his backpack, a terrific explosion rocked the town below. René spun around to see the blinding flash and then smoke rising from the area of the jail. Henri seized his chance and swung the backpack at René, knocking him to the ground, the pistol discharging as it flew from René's hand and bounced on the ground. In a flash Henri had his knife out and struggled with René. Gaining the upper hand, he plunged the knife into René's heart.

"Something went wrong, Henri. What should we do?" Antoinette asked.

"It sounds like Robbie had to change the plans. We should wait at the rendezvous point anyway."

"Henri, will Robbie be OK?" Charlène asked.

"The Lieutenant can take care of himself, *ma petite*. We will see him soon."

Dragging René's body into some nearby bushes, the four started across the fields to their rendezvous at the barn in Eycheil, a small village containing a few houses and barns, just southwest of Saint-Girons.

No one noticed when Charlène picked up the pistol, wrapping it carefully in a handkerchief and sliding it into her backpack.

André led the expanded group through the streets, on occasion pausing to ensure they would not be seen. More than once a curious eye peeked from behind a darkened curtain to watch the group run swiftly by.

As they passed the last house on the approach to the fields overlooking Saint-Girons, a middle-aged woman wearing an apron stepped out, causing the men to raise their weapons, fearing an ambush.

They quickly lowered them when they realized the woman was no threat.

She softly whispered, *"Vive la Liberté! Vive la France! Vive les Américains!"* and handed Lieutenant Robertson a small parcel of food before disappearing into her house.

"Merci," Madeleine whispered.

The woman just nodded in her direction and silently closed her door.

No one spoke. The sacrifices made by the people of Saint-Girons and the surrounding towns along the French-Spanish border were immeasurable. The help they received was humbling to all those present.

They approached the building where Henri had stabbed René, and Madeleine saw the blood.

"Lieutenant, quickly," she said, motioning to him and fearing the worst.

Lieutenant Robertson ran over and, seeing the blood, followed the trail into the bushes. Signaling for Madeleine to come over, he pointed to René's body.

"Henri was busy. Let's get to the rendezvous point before this guy's friends come looking for him," the lieutenant said to the group.

"I think your little explosion has already alerted them, Robbie," Madeleine nervously said to the lieutenant.

"Either way, it's time to get the hell outta Dodge," the lieutenant said. "OK, folks, move out. We have a barn to find."

***

Françoise led Henri, Madeleine, and Charlène into the foothills and started their ascent, taking in the magnificent grandeur of the mountains among a myriad of stars.

The path ran through a forest filled with beech trees. Occasionally the path was lined with foul-smelling box trees.

Partway into their journey, they entered a clearing at 2,100 feet. A path lay ahead, but Françoise directed the trio to a smaller path to the right.

"The old barn is a short distance down this trail. We can rest and wait for the Lieutenant's group to arrive," Françoise explained.

"Can we sleep there tonight?" Charlène asked hopefully.

"*Non, ma petite.* We must keep moving to avoid capture," Françoise said gently, caressing Charlène's hair.

"*Je comprends*, Madame Françoise. I can walk fast," Charlène replied.

She is a brave girl, Françoise thought. Does she really know what lies ahead?

The four approached the barn, Henri scouting ahead to ensure they would not be ambushed. With the coast clear, he motioned them forward, entering the barn.

About fifteen minutes later, Henri met Lieutenant Robertson and his group outside of the barn and guided them inside.

"André!" Françoise exclaimed. "It's good to see you again, *mon petit.*"

"*Ma tante*, what's going on? Who are these men?" André asked.

"They are here to help us finally escape," Françoise said.

"So it is true then, we will go to America and freedom?"

"*Oui*, very soon, but we have a hard journey ahead of us, so you must have much courage to face whatever happens," Françoise warned.

"I will, *ma tante*, I will," André acknowledged.

Turning to everyone, Françoise said, "This time of year is very unpredictable. It could be a sunny day, and then suddenly a storm comes. The clothes and supplies I gave you are for the surprises we may meet. We must leave now. La Milice and Germans will be searching the area after the destruction we caused in town."

Everyone filed out of the barn slowly, trepidation setting in as the Pyrénées rose to the heavens before them.

The first night was the longest in miles, but the ascent was gentle. Moving through beech woods and across flower-filled meadows, they entered a very thickly wooded terrain of oak, chestnut, and black poplar as they hiked along the barely visible mountain trail.

The group made progress steadily upward as the town slowly faded from view.

Thankfully, they met no one.

"Stay close. We travel only as fast as the slowest person," Françoise explained. "Keep as quiet as possible. Do not use walking sticks to test the way, but follow in each other's footsteps."

After several hours of climbing, the sky had grown darker, as clouds covered up the starlight.

Neither Henri, who walked with a slight limp, nor Charlène complained about their injuries throughout that first night. It was evident that complaining would be useless, and even detrimental, to their flight.

Sergeant Waldron was astounded at the quick recovery of the pair since their visit to the convent and Saint Bernadette. Maybe miracles do happen, and now is the time for another, he thought, glancing at the pair again.

As Waldron thought about miracles, a heavy downpour set in.

"We should stop," Madeleine said to Françoise.

"Is there any place nearby we can hole up?" Lieutenant Robertson asked.

"Perhaps. There is a secluded farmhouse nearby owned by the Barrau family," Françoise answered.

Looking at the tired, ragtag group, the lieutenant nodded. "We will go there."

Françoise guided the band through a series of woodland paths, climbing above the villages of Eycheil, Lacourt, and Alos and on to the Col de l'Artigue at 2,600 feet. She had been to the small, secluded farmhouse many times before, and she knocked at the door to ask permission to spend the night.

They were met by Madame Barrau and her son Paul, who invited them to stay in their barn during the storm.

Before long Madame Barrau entered the barn carrying a steaming pot of hot soup, Paul following with half a loaf of bread, bowls, and spoons.

Lieutenant Robertson was astonished that the woman seemed used to having such strange guests.

As she distributed even portions in wooden bowls, she never inquired about their intentions, quietly going from person to person.

"Thank you, ma'am," Sergeant Waldron and Lieutenant Robertson both said to her as they received their steaming bowl of sausage in a warm beef broth.

"Il n'y a pas de quoi," Madame Barrau replied, pouring the soup. *"Finissez ce que vous avez dans vos bols et dormez*

bien," she told them all. "I will have my son, Paul, bring you some warm blankets," she said in English.

Looking at Charlène in her ragtag dress, she said, "*Ma petite*, come with me. I have clothes that will fit you properly."

Mistaking Madeleine for Charlène mother, she said, "Will you allow your daughter to sleep with me in the house tonight? You see, the Vichy killed my husband after he was caught guiding a group such as yours through the pass, so I have a warm bed she can share. She will not have another opportunity until you reach your destination."

"Mais oui. Merci infiniment, madame," Madeleine said. Not such a bad idea after all, she thought.

Taking Charlène by the hand, and holding the empty pot in the other, she led the girl through the side door, closing it tightly behind them.

Françoise explained, "Let me tell you about her family. Her husband and brother were arrested and died in a German labor camp because they were *passeurs*.

"Forgive me for interrupting, Françoise," Sergeant Waldron said. "What is a *passeur*?

"A guide, Billy," she answered. "Someone who guides others through the mountains to safety and freedom."

Sergeant Waldron nodded knowingly. Françoise continued.

"Her son, Louis, had replaced his father and uncle as a *passeur* after they were arrested, but he was shot by a German patrol while waiting to guide a party of *évadés* in 1943. *Les bosch* surrounded the barn he was in, and when he refused to come out, they set it on fire. He tried to escape through the smoke but was killed in a nearby field."

"It's sad what your people have gone through," the lieutenant said.

No one said another word as they finished the hot soup. Everyone settled down in the barn to sleep in the hay. Lieutenant Robertson, Henri, Madeleine, and Sergeant Waldron took turns standing guard outside. The rain was constant that night, which was a godsend to them. No soul would go out in this weather looking for *les évadés*, much less well-armed ones.

As the sky lightened, signaling dawn, the group awoke to Madame Barrau entering the barn with Lieutenant Robertson carrying a tray of fresh bread and cheeses.

Everyone ate the food without saying a word.

Shortly after breakfast, the two young men who had come with André spoke to Françoise quietly. When they were done, she gave the young men a hug, kissing them on both cheeks.

Françoise walked over to Lieutenant Robertson. "Lieutenant, they have to return home and face the labor camp. Their families are in danger if they do not."

The lieutenant looked at the two men who were saying good-bye to Madame Barrau. "I heard someone once say that courage is not the absence of fear, it is taking action in the face of it," he quoted to Françoise. They left quickly down a different path from which they came.

The rest of the group thanked Madame Barrau and her son for their kindness, leaving what little money they had on them, and everyone said their good-byes.

Back on the trail, they descended to the Col d'Escots at 2,100 feet; then they gradually climbed to the village of Aunac at 2,200 feet. The group was now fifteen miles into their journey.

The ascent was very strenuous; the path rose steeply, providing no shade. By 11:00 on the second day, having scrambled through more steep foothills, they were at the Col de la Core.

Henri was amazed at the tenacity that Charlène had shown while climbing in her condition. He knew that she was in pain, but the young girl did not complain once. When the going got especially difficult, Henri would ask for a short break because he knew Charlène would not.

While resting among huge granite boulders, Henri thought back to that eventful evening not so long ago when the partisan group entered the cave underneath the farmhouse, Charlène instinctively hiding behind Sonny, clutching his pant leg, obviously scared of the damp, foreboding tunnel.

Sonny had reached for her hand and whispered, "It's OK. I will help you," which comforted Charlène. Henri remembered her smile, her face streaked with dirt, her eyes swollen from crying, and the scratches on her arms and legs from running through the woods. Now here was this brave young girl again, ascending a foreboding mountain pass without a complaint!

After the brief rest, the group was once again under way. Madeleine and Henri helped Charlène through the rocky terrain of beech trees mixed with fir and, at the highest level, birch and pine. Broad-leaved trees of wild cherry, ash, maple, walnut, linden, and boxwood were also abundant.

Françoise would stop every now and then and retrieve a bottle of eau-de-vie hidden in a bush. "Have a sip, *mes amis*. It will make you strong for the rest of the journey," she said as the bottle was passed around. "I learned this trick from a friend of mine, a Basque *passeur* named Florentino."

Even Charlène took a sip, the heavy eau-de-vie burning her throat and making her cough. She missed her foster family in Bergues, Pierre and Celeste Portiere and their children, Caryll and Francesca. She concentrated on those good memories to forget the pain she was in. She thought of the day she skipped rope with Francesca in front of the house and then took Simon for a walk through the farm to a small stream where Pierre and André had taught her how to fish.

Her foster mother, Celeste, had provided each of the girls with a pastry and hot chocolate. After *le goûté*, or late afternoon snack, Charlène remembered sitting in a comfortable high-back chair in the small salon with a book near the comforting fire.

Madeleine's voice brought Charlène back to the mountainous landscape and difficult climb. "Are you feeling all right, *ma petite?*" she asked Charlène, thinking she was getting delirious from the exertion forced upon her.

"*Oui*, Madeleine, *merci*. I was just thinking of my family in Bergues. I miss them," she replied with some sadness.

"Don't worry. I will make sure you see them again someday," Madeleine said, kissing Charlène on the top of her head.

Walking over to Madeleine and Charlène, Sergeant Waldron exclaimed, "I heard some young lady likes piggyback rides!"

Frowning at the sergeant, Charlène proclaimed, "What is a piggyback ride?"

"Here, I'll show you." Sergeant Waldron said.

He scooped her up and onto his back to, at first, squeals of protest and then joyful acceptance. Billy Waldron carried her for the rest of that day.

During the afternoon and into the evening, Françoise led the group through very rough terrain, taking the path to the Cabane de Casabède, a quaint mountain pasture occupied by shepherds during the summer. They maneuvered their way through a flock of sheep, scattering the animals as they moved past. The shepherd nodded as they passed and then turned away, as if to acknowledge he never saw them.

They continued on and up to the beauty of Le Col de Soularil, at a staggering height of 4,700 feet. Below them and to their left, they spotted the sheer granite face of Le Rocher de l'Aube, "Dawn Rock." They made a steady and fairly level push to their night stop at La Cabane de Subéra. The rocky terrain was filled with brilliant green summer grass.

Exhausted, the group was happy to stop for the night, and they soon fell asleep in a small outcropping of rocks.

OCKHAM'S MESSER

The next morning a meeting was called in Charlène's study with the three agents. In no uncertain terms, Charlène laid down the law on future procedures when out in the field. A stricter sense of purpose was now in effect.

Concluding the long meeting, she said, "I want all of you to review the standard operating procedures I created and follow them!" Charlène got up slowly and walked to the elevator, leaning heavily on her cane as if the years had suddenly taken their toll on her.

Jean, who had been silent during the whole time Charlène was talking, said, "She is very worried about all of you and is disappointed on your handling of the last few missions. But since your efforts have stopped a major disaster, you are to be congratulated."

"What are our next steps?" Jack decided it best to move the conversation forward.

"From what we can tell, Garcia is in the wind, but we need to track him down."

"How?" Marie asked.

Jean explained, "We will need to know if Garcia tries to leave the country legally."

"Jean, I think we have a mole," Emily said.

"What makes you think that?" Jean asked.

"Vargas's last words to Marie were 'Ockham's Messer,'" Emily said.

"How does that pertain to a mole in our midst?" Jean asked.

"Because we were discussing Occam's razor in operations last week, and it just strikes me as too coincidental that those were his dying words," Emily said.

"I will get a team to sweep for bugs," Jean said. "Now check for Garcia on flights going to Spain and Mexico. That may not provide a viable trail, but in his panic to escape, he may get sloppy."

"You think he may head for Mexico?" Jack asked.

"It would be a good way to get to Spain indirectly, but he would be more likely to hire a private plane to Mexico, if he were to go that route," Jean explained.

"I'll check out all the small airfields in this area to see if Garcia has any record of activity," Marie said.

"The FBI will be watching the border for any suspicious plane activity, but our job will be to eliminate Vargas and Garcia if we find them," Jean said.

"Why not let the FBI take care of this?" Jack asked.

"Because they would give those bastards the due process of the law, Jack, and our superiors want him to disappear, understood?" Jean said.

"After what that son of a bitch did to me, I'll pull the trigger myself," Jack said, looking down at his metallic hand.

"Can you feeling anything yet, Jack?" Emily asked hopefully.

"You know, it's strange, but I could swear I can feel my palm sweating in there," Jack said.

"That's a good sign, Jack. When the LED goes from red to green, we'll take a look," Jean said.

Over the next three weeks, the team waited and watched for any activity from Garcia, but there was nothing.

Charlène was no longer furious with her agents, acknowledging that her team did the best they could given the circumstances. So young, so brash, she thought to herself. They remind me of my younger days with the agency!

Charlène always forbade any business discussion at the dinner table, as it was meant to bring everyone together at one time and one place. Discussions of famous authors, music, and the arts were the only topics allowed. But on occasion she did permit business to be included if it was tied to a historical lesson.

"Has anyone ever heard of Dušan Popov?" Charlène asked one night at dinner.

When no one answered, Charlène explained, "He was a double agent who worked with both the British MI-6 and the German Abwehr organizations in World War II. His loyalties were truly with the Allies at that time.

"Sounds kind of like Tomas and his father, Sergio," Jack said.

"Except they were and are working for the enemy," Charlène replied. "In '44, Popov became a key part of the same deception your father was on, Jack."

"Forgive me for asking Charlène, but why the history lesson?" Jack asked meekly.

"The spy business is a very tricky and most often dangerous business. You will lose a lot of friends before you are done with it," Charlène explained. "The events of the past few months have not gone the way I have expected. So you must forgive this old lady, for I have been ill of late, and if I seem a bit too harsh on all of you, it's because I want to keep you all alive. My trust in you has been regained, and in time you all will make your own history."

The next morning in operations, the group mulled over the disappearance of Garcia.

"Emily, I was thinking last night about Occam's Razor," Jack stated. "I think it can provide us the answer."

"How so?" Emily asked. "I know we found Vargas that way, but Garcia has no ties here in the US that we know of."

"Well, in German, *Ockham's Messer* translates to Occam's knife, and that refers to distinguishing between two theories either by shaving away unnecessary assumptions or cutting apart two similar theories," Jack explained.

"I guess you do listen to me," Emily said as she smiled.

"Only on Tuesday's, but I digress." Jack smiled. "So, let's shave away the assumption that Garcia has a company here, and he was not in business with Vargas, so how does he operate?"

The answer dawned on Emily. "How stupid of us!"

"Gisele," Jack said.

"But how does Gisele fit into this? I thought she was dead and her company sold off," Marie asked.

"Jack, Garcia *owns* that company!" Emily stated. "He bought it under a false name!"

From behind them Charlène, leaning heavily on her cane, spoke up. "I haven't told you this before, but you may want to also check in the town of La Línea, near Gibraltar, Spain."

"How is that connected?" Jack asked.

"The Garcia family owns a home in Spain. Sergio, Tomas's father, once had a sister there, and the home might provide us clues on his whereabouts," Charlène said.

"What about the company here?" Emily asked.

"I'll contact the FBI. They'll need solid evidence to get a warrant to get into Toffler Chemicals and tie Garcia to this whole thing," Charlène remarked. "You three will get us that evidence."

"How so?" Marie asked.

"Emily will pay a visit to Toffler Chemicals tomorrow," Charlène said.

All three were assigned to the Toffler mission that night. Jack and Marie would enter the building, break into the company's datacenter, and download any information that might be useful in finding Garcia. Jack was well suited for this mission, as he was in corporate IT before he was laid off. His job was to steal the data from the company's servers.

"I will notify the security company to shut down the cameras for routine maintenance between 11:00 PM and 2:00 AM. That's your window," Jean informed them. "We hacked into their e-mail system, specifically the IT schedule for datacenter personnel, and no one is scheduled to be on duty tomorrow night."

The next day at Toffler Chemicals, Lisa Wilson, the company's business manager, greeted pharmaceutical representative Kimberly Matus in her office. Lisa was excited at the possibility of securing a major contract for her company.

Lately, business was slow, and the unfortunate hiking accident of the previous owner and CEO, Gisele Toffler, weighed heavily on everyone's minds.

The new CEO of Toffler Chemicals was Thomas Gregory. He had a long track record of raising revenues and profit. He was a perfect fit. Ever since Gisele had passed away suddenly, Toffler Chemicals had lost its direction. Toffler Chemicals was fortunate to find Thomas Gregory so quickly. He had smoothly stepped in to fill Gisele's role as CEO.

Tom had met with all his managers a week before and established some tough goals. He was currently on a business trip to Spain, and Lisa saw this new venture with Kimberly Matus as an opportunity to impress her new boss and maybe get that promotion she had been hoping for under Gisele.

Emily wore a short dark-haired wig, tucking her long blonde hair inside. Charlène had makeup artists alter her cheekbones. She wore three-inch heels, a short pencil skirt, and tinted granny glasses.

Jack whistled at her as she entered operations.

Emily blushed.

"If Garcia shows his face, get out of there, Emily," Charlène said. "If he gets too close, he will recognize you."

"Will do," Emily replied, stumbling as she tried to navigate in the high heels.

"I hate these things," she said.

Later that day, Emily drove up to the security booth at the entrance to Toffler Chemicals.

"Can I help you?" the guard asked.

"My name is Kimberly Matus. I have an appointment with Lisa Wilson," Emily said.

The guard picked up his clipboard listing all visitors for the day. "Yep, you're on the list," he said. "You can park in the visitors' lot in front of the building. Here's your pass to get inside," he said, handing her a pass marked "Visitor."

"Thank you," Emily said.

"No problem," the guard replied, opening the steel gates that barred her way.

Emily parked in the visitors' lot and walked to the entrance of the building. So far, so good, she thought to herself.

On opening the front door, another security guard asked to see her pass, which she flashed at him.

"Where are you headed?" he asked.

"Lisa Wilson's office," she replied.

"Down the hall, room 178," he said.

Emily nodded to him and started to walk down the hallway. She stumbled again in her high heels.

Finding room 178, she knocked on the door.

"Come on in," Lisa said.

Opening the door, Emily introduced herself.

"Sorry the door was closed; I was on a conference call with the CEO," Lisa said. "I see you found your way, Kimberly. Was security helpful?" Lisa asked.

"No, they just kind of pointed in your direction," Emily said.

"I am so sorry, Kimberly. I will talk with them," Lisa said. "God knows anyone could walk into this place and take everything right from under our noses!"

"Can I get you some coffee? Our brew is actually quite good," Lisa asked.

"No thank you, Lisa," Emily answered. "I have had too much already!"

"So, how can I help you, Kimberly?" Lisa asked.

"Call me Kim, please," Emily said. "We have a list of compounds that we want to outsource the storage of and be provided plates back as we need them. We are downsizing our facilities due to this economy, and we need some help in that area."

"Have you put out a request for purchase?" Lisa asked.

Handing Lisa the paperwork, Emily said, "As you can see, it's a fairly simple request."

"Kim, I really appreciate this, but isn't it unusual for an onsite visit, without calling our business managers?"

"We have heard that your company is the best, and I wanted to give you a heads-up first, on a major project we need help on," Emily said. "Besides, I was in the area doing business with one of our clients, and I thought an impromptu business meeting would be OK."

"I have a training session I need to conduct for our new employees in an hour, so I need to let you go, but I certainly will look this over!" Lisa exclaimed.

"Thank you. We look forward to doing business with you," Emily said.

"Me too. Let me walk you out," Lisa said, motioning with her hand toward the office door.

Tripping on the chair leg, Emily fell against Lisa, catching herself on her arm. "I am so sorry, Lisa," Emily said.

"That's OK. I do it all the time. High heels are a liability, aren't they?" Lisa laughed off Emily's clumsiness.

Lisa made her way to the training room and reached down to grab her ID to swipe the security lock, but the badge was not there. "Damn I lost it again!" she thought.

She went to the nearby phone mounted on the wall of the hallway and called security to report her missing identification badge.

"So you lost your badge?" the man on the other end said.

"Yeah, I had it this morning. I must have dropped it somewhere," Lisa said.

"Well, I can have a temporary one made up for you now if you come down to the security office," he said.

Delays, Lisa thought. "Can you bring it to me? I have a training session I have to conduct in a few minutes."

"Sorry, my orders from our new CEO are to not leave security at any time. You'll have to come get it here," the man said.

"OK, I'll be right down," Lisa said, a bit annoyed, and slammed the phone on the receiver.

"Bitch," the security guard mumbled.

That's curious, Lisa thought. This new CEO has this place locked down like Fort Knox. What's he afraid of?

That evening the guard in the main security room was monitoring the cameras and watching television while eating his lunch. He glanced at the clock on the wall; the security monitors went to white noise at 11:00 PM sharp.

Right on time, he thought, turning up the volume on his portable television with his back to the security screens.

Jack and Marie were to enter the building using Lisa's stolen security badge—they all prayed it was still active—and Emily was to wait in the car to enable a swift getaway if needed.

At 11:05, with a sigh of relief, Jack swiped Lisa's ID on a rear door of Toffler's datacenter, and was followed in by Marie.

Outside, Emily, at a distance, observed the main gate security guard, asleep in the gatehouse. A roaming guard, walking around the building, checked all the entrances on thirty-minute intervals before going back to sit in the security car to read some magazines and listen to the radio until his next round.

Making their way inside the datacenter, Jack and Marie found the secured server room. Swiping the card, the red light turned to green, and Jack entered first. Marie followed and placed the backpack she was carrying on the floor. She pulled out a portable hard drive and placed it on the main console desk.

Jack had just found the console when someone outside swiped a card in the door.

"I thought no one was supposed to be here tonight," Jack whispered to Marie.

"No one was on the schedule," Marie replied. "Now quickly, get behind those servers."

The two hid behind a rack of servers as the door opened.

"Damn it, the hard drive!" Jack whispered.

An overweight man in his late thirties entered the server room. He proceeded to sit at the main console just inches away from the portable hard drive. The technician's belly covered his belt, and his ketchup-stained white shirt hung partially out of his pants. He set a large paper bag on a desk in the center of the room. Looking down at his stained shirt, he sighed. Popping open the top of the soda cup, he dunked in a napkin and dabbed at the stain. No use, he thought. I'll throw it in the wash tomorrow. He sighed and undid his belt, tucking in his shirt.

Your zipper is open, you idiot, Jack thought.

Eyeing his inbox, the technician picked up a security request for programming Lisa Wilson's new badge. Great, someone lost another one, he thought. I don't understand the sudden need for all this new security.

He shrugged and took a sandwich from the paper bag. Glancing down, beside his soda, the technician noticed the portable hard drive. He picked it up and flipped it over a few times to figure out where it came from. The technician put the hard drive down, picked up the phone, and started to punch in some numbers on the dial pad.

Jack started to sweat. He knew the man was calling security.

Marie carefully lifted a keyboard lying on the floor nearby and tossed it several feet away. The loud bang accomplished what she had hoped for, echoing on the floor.

The technician immediately placed the phone back on the hook, struggled to get out of his chair, and waddled around the corner. "Who's there?" he said in a loud voice.

The technician fell in a heap to the floor as Marie's pistol struck the back of his head.

"What do we do about him?" Marie asked. "Should we kill him?"

"Nah, I have a soft spot for those guys. He didn't see us, so he can't identify us," Jack said. "I have an idea."

Taking a server off the rack near the unconscious technician, Jack banged the corner of the server box against the heavy steel server rack, making a sizable dent. Over at the console, he grabbed the soda and spilled it around the oversized technician, concentrating on his feet. Carefully laying the server next to the technician, he stood back admiring his work.

"What a klutz," he said.

Nodding in approval, Marie patted Jack on his back. "Not too bad, you softy."

Jack and Marie got back to work, searching the database and transferring any files that were suspect onto the portable drive.

Concentrating on keywords in the European countries and transfer of chemicals, Jack stumbled upon something.

"I found something, Marie," Jack said. "When I did a search on Europe, France and Spain, I found flight tickets to Paris in the corporate travel accounts for a Mr. Tom Gregory, CEO."

"That's got to be him. Has the flight left?" Marie asked.

"Unfortunately it left yesterday at 1:00 PM, landing in Charles de Gaulle Airport," Jack said.

"Have you ever been to Paris, Jack?"

"It's on my to do list," he said. "OK, I think we have all we need for the FBI to raid Toffler Chemicals, and we can track Garcia now that we have his pseudonym."

Slinking down the hall, the two spies heard footsteps coming their way. A security guard was making his rounds and was headed in their direction!

Quickly, Jack thought, we must get out of sight! He motioned for Marie to follow him as he retraced their steps back to the datacenter.

Across from the datacenter, Jack pointed to a training room with a security lock on it. Fumbling in his pocket for the identification card, he inadvertently dropped it. Marie, in one motion, snatched Lisa's identification card off the floor and swiped the card in the security lock, causing the red light to turn green. Opening the door, they slipped inside just as the security guard turned the corner in full view.

"It's 1:30. The cameras will be activated in thirty minutes," Jack whispered.

"Can we leave by the window?" Marie asked.

Marie and Jack worked their way around the shadows of the room, avoiding the light streaming in from the hallway. At the window they observed a two-story drop to the ground that steeply fell away to a ravine. Large jagged stones ran around the building at its base.

"Well, that's a no go," Jack said. "I always thought those kind of stones were for erosion control, but that looks like some kind of defense and security system."

"Jack," Marie whispered, "look at the brick pattern. It's alternated, and every other one sticks out. We can climb down."

"You're kidding, right?" Jack asked.

"Would you rather go back out there?" Marie pointed to the door. "That's what I thought," she said when Jack remained silent.

"Besides, this wall is on the side of the building out of the sight line of the security office."

Pulling out a small pocketknife, Marie checked the window for any sign of security wires and found one that ran to the window latch; she folded it in half where there was some slack and sliced it in two, hoping that this would not set off the alarm.

"Standard window security, it's an easy design to bypass," Marie informed him.

Pushing open the window, the two could hear the sounds of an ambulance siren.

"They must have found your friend," Marie said. "Let's get out of here."

Marie deftly climbed out the window and started making her way down the brick face, hands and feet working with precision on the bricks that jutted from the facade.

Perching himself on the window ledge, Jack gingerly placed his feet on a brick, but his left foot slipped. Reaching out with his prosthetic hand, he grabbed a brick and broke it off. It fell noisily into the rocks below. Both Jack and Marie froze for a moment, hoping the noise would not draw anyone's attention.

He was so focused on escaping that he did not wonder how his prosthetic hand would handle this situation. No need to wonder now, he thought. I've got to be careful with this thing.

This time Jack gently took hold of a brick with his prosthesis and slowly began climbing down.

From below Marie whispered, "Jack, come on!"

"Did I ever tell you I am afraid of heights?" Jack said, finding his footing again and climbing down onto a set of bricks below.

Back at the car, Emily saw the ambulance pull up and started to panic. My God, I hope that isn't for them, she thought. Just then Jack and Marie appeared, running across the grassy field on one side of Toffler Chemicals.

"What happened? I was worried about you two," Emily asked, pointing to the ambulance entering the gate.

"The technician in the datacenter bumped his head," Jack said. "Let's get out of here."

Emily started the car and left the parking lot, leaving the lights off. When they finally were out of sight and on the highway, she said, "I thought no one was on shift tonight."

"It must have been an unscheduled update, or someone forgot to notify the company in the e-mail system as CIT is supposed to," Jack explained.

"That guy might have a slight headache when he wakes up," Marie said. "I can't believe his head put a dent in my gun."

"That was too easy," Jack said.

"Sometimes it is. I just wish all my missions were that easy," Marie said.

Across the globe, in a small village in Spain, Tomas Garcia, a.k.a., Thomas Gregory, watched Jack and Marie from his computer, which was connected to the company's security camera.

"Not so clever," Garcia said, switching off his computer and turning off the light to his office.

***

The next morning at the operations center, Jean informed the team of his findings. "We found a listening device tucked away behind one of the computers. It's definitely not one of ours," he disclosed.

"Did you destroy it?" Marie asked.

"No, we have it in a soundproof box. We figure we can use it to our advantage if we ever want to send out false information to whoever planted it."

"Who could have planted a bug in here?" Jack asked.

"Good question," Jean answered. "We have visitors from the CIA and FBI constantly; the list of suspects is endless. If we can trick them into coming back here to retrieve the bug, we may be able catch them."

"I have my suspicions," Jack said. "Get the bug. I have an idea."

That evening Georges served a scrumptious dinner that included many of Charlène's favorite foods. But she was continuing to feel unwell and could not join the group for dinner.

Jack spoke up as he was served. "Well, this is a pleasant surprise, Georges. I see that you are serving some of Charlène's favorite dishes and one or two of mine. I can understand your knowledge about Charlène's preferences, but how did you know about mine?" Jack said.

"Madame Shemesh must have told me, Monsieur Jack," Georges replied with a smile.

The next day, looking out the main entrance door, Jean watched an FBI agent push a handcuffed Georges headfirst into their car.

"How did you know it was Georges?" Jean said to Jack as he walked up to his side. "You had no concrete proof."

"He was the only one who knew of all of our missions. He was always there, an unobtrusive servant listening in the background."

"Could have been anyone," Jean maintained.

"I had a gut feeling," Jack said. "Besides, don't you know it's always the butler who did it?"

"But why would he do that?" Emily asked. "He raised Charlène as his own. He was a father to her all these years."

"Only he can answer that," Jean said. "Maybe he was resentful over not becoming part of the family. Charlène kept him as a servant for all these years."

That afternoon Jean came back down to the operations center, explaining that Charlène would take her meal in her room again. "Is she OK?" Emily asked.

"I was sworn to secrecy by Charlène, but I should tell you anyway. She is dying of a rare and rapid form of cancer," Jean said.

"Oh no!" Emily said.

"How did this happen?" Jack asked. "She seemed OK to me."

"She has always been a strong woman. She would never admit to the pain she has been going through. Not even to me."

"How long does she have?" Marie asked apprehensively.

"The doctors had given her six months to live last year, so nothing is predictable. I don't know what to tell you," Jean answered.

Everyone paid their respects to Charlène that evening. Later in the study they all shared a glass of brandy while Charlène slept. Jean shared fond memories of their friendship over these many years. No one interrupted him as they stared into the crackling fire.

Over the next few weeks, Marie, Jack, and Emily worked hard to discover more information that might lead them to Tomas Garcia. As they were toiling over flights in and out of the country, the red LED on Jack's mechanical hand turned green. For a few moments Jack just stared at it, not knowing what to do.

"Jack," Emily said, "should I get Charlène?"

"Yes, sure," he said nervously.

After several minutes, Emily returned pushing a wheelchair in which sat a sickly looking Charlène.

"Charlène, I am so sorry to see that you are ill. How do you feel today?" Jack asked.

"Thank you, Jack, for your concern. I've had better days. Now, I hear that your treatment may be finished?" Charlène said.

Jack was apprehensive. "Seems so, but I am a bit afraid to open this thing!"

"Jack, open the compartment I showed you and type in your code," Charlène said.

Pushing on the door underneath his wrist, the latch popped open. Damn, what was my code? Jack panicked.

Seeing his expression, Charlène said, "Think hard. This is all part of your training—to remember things after periods of time have elapsed."

Punching in the numbers, the mechanical hand released its tight grip on his wrist, and Jack could *feel* the air rush around his palm and fingers! Slowly pulling off the device, he was astonished to see a fully formed—albeit a bit black and blue and discolored—hand. It was stiff and a little awkward, but he was able to move his fingers with some effort.

Emily and Marie gasped.

"Jack, that's amazing!" Emily said. "Unbelievable!"

"Thank God for miracles." Jack smiled at Charlène.

"Jack I have been told that the discoloration will go away in time. You will gain full movement the more you use your hand. In time, you will never know you lost it," Charlène explained.

His fingernails had not grown out fully yet, and his movements were awkward.

"Jack, you'll have to start exercising to get your strength back," Charlène said.

"Hey, I'll do what it takes," Jack said.

She placed a black glove with the fingers cut out on the table.

"Here, use this brace. It's made for people with carpel tunnel," Charlène said. "At least until full movement returns."

"A carpal tunnel brace?" Jack asked. "Do I really need this? I hate those things."

"Jack, just use it," Emily said. "Be happy you got your hand back."

"OK." Jack smiled. "Just don't expect me to moonwalk like some pop star."

Jack put on the glove and adjusted the Velcro straps for a comfortable fit.

"See, was that so hard?" Emily asked.

Jack turned to Charlène. "Charlène, what about you? If this cell growth thing worked on my hand, couldn't it work on your cancer?"

"Ah, I see Jean has told you. That man never listens to me," she said weakly. "No, Jack, I am afraid at my age I would not survive any treatment."

Jack got up and gave Charlène a warm hug, thanking her for everything she had done for him and Emily. She held him close for a few moments.

"Forgive me, but I must go rest," Charlène said.

Jean walked to her wheelchair and guided Charlène back to her room. They talked quietly to one another for a few moments and then Jean kissed her gently. She lay back in her bed surrounded by down pillows and looked out her windows to the estate grounds beyond. She slowly faded, a smile on her face, holding the memory of Jean's kiss.

Jean quietly closed Charlène's bedroom door and returned to the operations center. "We have another issue that has arisen that is tied to Vargas and Garcia," he said on his return. "Have you ever heard of Hans Talhoffer?"

"*The Book of Fighting*," Jack proudly answered.

"Very good, Jack. You must be a student of history," Jean replied.

"Not really. I was just unemployed and watched the History Channel all day," Jack said as he laughed.

Jean continued, "Hans Talhoffer lived in the fifteenth century. He was a *Fechtmeister*. That means fight master."

Great. Another history lesson, Emily thought.

"He was the author of at least six illustrated treatises describing methods of fighting with weapons and on horseback."

Jean noticed Emily roll her eyes.

"Emily, this is very important. Please pay attention," he admonished her.

"Sorry, I am not a history fan," Emily apologized. "That's Jack's thing."

Ignoring her, Jean continued. "But there is one more book that no one knows about, the Doomsday Book. The book contained plans of machines that could destroy the world as it was known in medieval times. It was rumored that Nostradamus had this book, which he referred to as *Magicks*. The world thought that Nostradamus had either hidden or destroyed the book, because it was never found, until now."

"Are you saying Vargas or Garcia found the book?" Jack asked.

"Maybe. We think that the dirty bomb was just to test our security. There have been indicators from our agents in Paris that someone has found the book and wants to put it to use."

Marie spoke up, "Does anyone know what's in that book for sure?"

"No, only rumors, and they are not good ones. If the rumors are true, it's a medieval method of making a nuclear bomb," Jean warned.

"Obviously we are involved, so what do you want us to do?" Jack inquired.

"I am sending all of you to Paris to find out what our agents know about the book."

"Couldn't the agents in France let us know what's going on?" Marie asked.

"We need all the agents we have involved, Marie," Jean said. "I am sending you three in to help them, and if possible, to get the book and bring it back here."

"Shouldn't it be destroyed?" Emily said.

"Our military would like to see what it contains. I was instructed by the highest authority to bring it back intact," Jean said.

"The President?" Jack said.

"It doesn't matter, Jack. We have our orders. We must find that book!" Jean said.

"When do we leave?" Jack asked.

"Marie, I will send you on a flight tomorrow to meet up with our operatives in Paris and to pave the way for Jack and Emily's arrival in three days' time. You're familiar with the agents and the territory. I have made all the arrangements. You will all fly out of JFK," Jean said.

Waving good-bye to Marie that next morning, Jack and Emily watched the limo pull away through the ornate gates of the estate.

They spent the day in the operations center studying facts about the Doomsday Book, Nostradamus, and who they were to contact once on the ground in France. They both were nervous about the operation, as neither could speak the language. Finally, after a detailed discussion with Jean, they decided that they should pretend to be newlyweds in Paris.

"Paris, always wanted to go there." Emily chuckled. "But not to search for some doomsday book!"

Jack flashed a smile. "Ditto!"

The next evening while everyone was sitting down at the dinner table, their host's chair was empty yet again.

Jean had replaced Georges with a younger man named Pierre, a distant relative. He did not have the experience of Georges, but he was eager to please his new employers.

The dinner progressed awkwardly, but Pierre was able to make it through without too many mistakes.

When they had finished eating, they all sat quietly, observing Charlène's empty chair.

"Will she recover, Jean?" Emily asked.

"I pray she does," Jean said. "She has always been a fighter."

They sat quietly sipping on Cognac when Charlène's doctor entered the room, his eyes misty. "I must announce with sadness that Madame Charlène Shemesh has passed at 7:00 this evening."

***

Madame Charlène Shemesh was placed in an ebony-colored casket and buried near a small grove of trees, between her aunt and uncle. Everyone gathered at the small, solemn ceremony as a rabbi spoke softly above her coffin. "We weave or unravel a few more stitches in the garment of life; Charlène Shemesh has finished her heavenly gown. Do not say in grief that Charlène is no more, but live in thankfulness that she has touched your life. As it is said in Genesis 3:19, Charlène Shemesh, for dust you are and to dust you shall return."

When the ceremony was over, Jean approached the coffin, suspended over the open grave. He quietly spoke something no one could hear and laid forty-four long-stemmed red roses by her headstone. He knelt by the gravesite, weeping at her loss. No one could hear the words he was saying, but Emily thought she could make out the words "I love you."

Jean had adored Charlène and fallen in love with her. It was the profession that kept that love at bay. Jean slowly propped himself up using the headstone. He was tired. For many years they had been comrades, sharing a life of secrecy. Now she was gone. It is time I retire, he thought, and leave this business to younger, stronger men and women.

Seeing Jean struggle to get up, Emily approached him and wrapped her arm around him.

"Thank you, Emily," he said.

They all left the gravesite and walked slowly back to the estate talking about how kind and wonderful Charlène was in life.

Jack and Emily left Jean to grieve in private, while they went to operations. They could not find the energy to work, given the circumstances, and just sat quietly.

After a few hours, Jean entered operations, his eyes red and swollen.

He was the first to speak. "We haven't heard from Marie since her departure."

"Is that unusual?" Jack asked.

"Normally, no, but she never made contact with our operatives in Paris, and I am worried about her," Jean said. "Be cautious. I will have a trusted agent meet you at the airport on your arrival. Memorize this poem and destroy it. Whatever line he says to you, you'll be expected to respond with the next line.

Looking down, Jack and Emily read.

May the road rise to meet you,
May the wind be always at your back.
May the sun shine warm upon your face,
The rains fall soft upon your fields.
And until we meet again,
May God hold you in the palm of his hand.

"I know this poem. You always sent me lines from it while we were dating," Emily said.

"It was always a favorite of mine," Jack said. "I'm glad you're starting to remember."

"Excellent. Don't forget it," Jean said to the couple.

"No worries," Emily replied.

Jack and Emily boarded a plane that evening for Paris to find Marie, Garcia, and the Doomsday Book.

Emily and Jack settled in business class, preparing for the long flight ahead of them.

Shaking his head, Jack turned to Emily, in her seat. "This promises to be one helluva mission."

"Wouldn't want to get bored, now would you?" Emily said.

Jack paused a moment, getting serious. "Have you remembered more about us and the events before you were shot?"

"I see and remember more things each day, Jack, but still not the night I was shot," Emily replied.

"The doctors said people never remember severe trauma events, and my hope is that you don't," Jack said.

"I want to remember. I need the closure. It's hard to explain how a black hole in your memory can drive you nuts," Emily said.

"I get it," Jack said as he affectionately kissed her forehead.

"This is going to be a long flight." Emily yawned, laying her head on his shoulder.

"Hey, wanna join the mile-high club?" Jack asked.

"Jack, behave!" Emily's face reddened. She was hoping that no one else had heard this.

Jack softly chuckled as the plane lifted off the runway on its way to Paris.

Mountains of Fire

A morning of glorious sunshine and a stunning dawn greeted the *évadés* as they awoke the next morning in la Cabane de Subéra. The forests had given away to open fields of grass and boulders. The ascent from there became quite steep, and after two hours of climbing, Françoise pointed out the plateau of le Pic de Lampau.

The tree line began to fall away, and they emerged onto the open mountain negotiating some enormous granite boulders. It was a very difficult upward trek to le Col de Craberous. The group struggled up the almost vertical climb to the top, loose gravel slipping under their feet. Several times, one or two of the escapees had to avoid being pummeled by stones jarred loose by the person above them.

The pace was slow, and everyone in the ragtag group was tired.

"We must keep going," Françoise said. "The weather in the mountains can change very quickly."

The two Americans, although exhausted themselves, helped Henri and Charlène to climb the rough terrain. They almost made it to the pass at the top of le Col de Craberous.

Without warning the stone above their heads burst into shards as several rifle bullets ricocheted around them.

Scrambling for cover, they were able to get out of sight, behind some boulders.

Lieutenant Robertson peered down the valley, recognizing one young man from the jailbreak, leading a group of La Milice in their direction. They were literally only several meters from the top of the pass but couldn't move without being exposed to the enemy.

"Looks like one of our friends has ratted us out," the lieutenant said to Françoise.

Peeking past some boulders, Françoise said, "I would have never expected Maurice to betray us. They must have threatened his family."

"Either way we are trapped, between a rock and a hard place, so to speak," the lieutenant said.

"Armand, Henri, get everyone over the ridge on my command. Billy, help Charlène and Antoinette over the top. Madeleine, Françoise and I will lay down some covering fire. Once over the top, you two get ready to cover us when we move," the lieutenant commanded.

Madeleine and Françoise rushed down around the granite boulders to the lieutenant's position, a perfect depression behind a huge boulder. He signaled to spread out along the length of the path.

Françoise said to the other two, "Please do not kill Maurice. If he really is being forced to guide them, I don't want him hurt."

"OK. Let's concentrate fire on both sides. That way we can avoid hitting Maurice and force them to cover, much as I would like to mow down some Gray Mice," the lieutenant said.

On the lieutenant's signal, the three rose up from behind their cover and started firing to the sides of the oncoming enemy. One Milice went down with a bullet to his head.

Lieutenant Robertson pointed at Henri, Waldron, and Antoinette, and said, "OK, move!"

Seconds later, the trio climbed up and over the pass, briefly silhouetted themselves against the gray sky. Henri assisted Antoinette successfully over the top, as did Sergeant Waldron, carrying Charlène in front of him to protect her from any stray bullets fired from below.

The lieutenant, Françoise, and Madeleine laid down covering fire, sending the advancing La Milice to take cover behind some boulders.

Armand was the last to climb up the steep path. He slipped at the top and tumbled back the way he came in a heap. Standing back up, he silhouetted himself for a second too long while trying to regain his balance.

Even though the three below were laying down withering fire, one Milice was able to get off a shot that ricocheted past Armand, missing him by inches, but a piece of stone ripped through his hand, instantly causing blood to flow.

Scrambling over the top of the pass, Henri positioned himself to cover the escape of the three below. Sergeant

Waldron set Charlène down behind a boulder and immediately tended to Armand's wound.

"Looks like you got lucky, Armand," Sergeant Waldron observed, wrapping a bandage over the wound. "It's not that deep."

"*Merci*, Billy. Now I must help the others," Armand said as he grabbed his Sten. He shrugged off the pain and climbed into position at the pass.

Henri whistled in the direction of the three below, gaining the attention of Madeleine, who crept over and nudged the lieutenant and nodded in Henri's direction.

"OK, Madeleine first, then Françoise. I'll meet you at the top," the lieutenant instructed.

"Now!" Robertson exclaimed as Françoise rose with him to fire down below.

Madeleine sprinted the last few yards over the top, sliding down the other side, small rocks scratching her through her pant legs.

Henri and Armand placed a few rounds near La Milice, who didn't dare move.

Françoise was next. Lieutenant Robertson rose one last time firing above the heads of the Milice, who were now sufficiently pinned down below. Françoise climbed the path with Henri and Armand firing single shots on both sides, pushing her way over the top and sliding down next to Madeleine. Both smiled at each other at their success.

Madeleine went over to Charlène and Antoinette, hidden behind a boulder. Charlène was covering her ears with her hands to block out the sound of the shots. Her eyes were closed. Antoinette was beside her, shielding her with her body.

"Are you OK, Charlène?" Madeleine asked.

"She is afraid they will capture us and take her away," Antoinette stated.

"Oh *non, ma petite*. We will have our *café* in Gibraltar next week!" Madeleine said, straightening Charlène's matted hair.

"*C'est promis*, Madeleine?" Charlène asked, raising her head from Antoinette's protective embrace.

"*Oui, je promets,*" Madeleine replied.

Below, Lieutenant Robertson ran up to the pass, bullets bouncing all around him as La Milice took advantage of the group's loss of sustained covering fire. Ten feet, just ten more feet, Robertson thought, wondering if a bullet would make its mark on him. Henri and Armand did their best, but La Milice realized they had the advantage in firepower and opened up on the lieutenant.

Armand could not get a shot off lying down as he was. Without some kind of cover fire, the lieutenant would go down. Standing again, Armand fired down into the valley, wounding one Milice. As the lieutenant closed the gap to the top, Armand crumpled to the ground, a bullet lodging itself in his right leg. Seeing him fall, Sergeant Waldron grabbed Armand's jacket by the shoulders and pulled him back below the opening in the pass.

Taking out the last of his bandages, he quickly applied pressure to Armand's second wound. He picked up a small branch from the ground, tied another bandage higher up Armand's leg into a knot, and twisted the bandage into a tourniquet.

Robertson made it to the other side but, glancing down, saw three bullet holes in his jacket and pants. Patting himself down in a panic, he realized he had been lucky; not a single bullet had found its mark. Well, I'll be, he thought. Maybe another miracle from Bernadette.

"Billy, can he be moved?

"Robertson said.

"I am afraid not, LT. He would bleed to death. We need a few days to get him strengthened for continued escape."

"I am afraid we don't have time, Billy," Françoise replied. "By tonight La Milice will have reinforcements, probably many bosch and we, will never succeed," she said, looking at Armand.

The group was stunned. Everyone knew what had to be done, and it was Armand who broke the silence.

"Give me enough ammunition and I will hold them here as long as possible. You must all leave now," he said.

"We can't leave him here to die," Sergeant Waldron said.

"Billy, we have no choice," Robertson replied, turning to Armand. "If we can get you behind some of these boulders, then with luck they will bypass you when we are out of sight."

"Lieutenant, if La Milice do not shoot me, the weather will kill me," Armand said.

Turning to the group, Robertson asked, "How much ammo do we have left?"

The replies were discouraging. At best they had three magazines of Sten ammo, and Armand had three rifle bullets left.

"I have two hand grenades. You can have those as well," Robertson said.

"LT, I'm staying with Armand," Sergeant Waldron announced. "If I stay, I think we can hold them off long enough to allow for your escape."

"Billy, we need you for the trip. You're coming with us," Robertson said. "I can stay with Armand and hold 'em off."

"You can court-martial me when we get back, LT, but I'm staying," Sergeant Waldron proclaimed defiantly. "You don't have the medical experience to get Armand through. I'll see you back in England."

Lieutenant Robertson was about to object, but what Billy said was true. Armand was in no condition to slow the Germans for very long, and Waldron was the only person who could keep Armand from dying from his wounds.

Robertson handed Waldron his Thompson submachine gun. "I have one clip left, Billy. Use it wisely."

Charlène ran up to Sergeant Waldron and gave him a big hug without a word, tears in her eyes.

"Don't worry, kid," Waldron replied. "I'll see you in a few days."

Everyone said their good-byes, the knowing looks upon their faces acknowledging that they would almost certainly never see each other again.

Lieutenant Robertson took Sergeant Waldron aside. "Billy, is there anyone you'd like to send a message to?"

"My sister in Iowa, Kate," Billy replied. "Tell her that her big brother loves her, and please give her this," he said, taking a gold cross from around his neck and handing it to Robertson.

"Will do, my friend. Make them pay in spades," Robertson said grimly.

"They won't make it through this pass," Waldron replied.

"Let's go," Lieutenant Robertson said to the rest of the group.

As they made their way among the boulders, now and then one of them would glance back at the pair. Waldron helped Armand prop himself up to gain a better view of the valley down below just as the skies opened up in a steady downpour.

After about an hour the rain subsided, and a brilliant rainbow crowned the mountains. The rocky terrain was difficult to climb in the best weather. But now the path was slippery as well. It seemed as if they had not covered much distance since they left Armand and Waldron behind.

Behind them at the pass, Armand signaled Sergeant Waldron there was movement below. The heavy downpour had drenched the pair, but they dared not seek cover in case La Milice made their move.

"*Les Souris Grises* have found their courage, Billy," Armand said.

"Let's see if we can send them back into their holes," Sergeant Waldron replied.

With daylight waning, the two men prepared the remaining ammunition, setting clips beside them on the rocks. Each had two hand grenades, Waldron's two and the pair given to Armand by Lieutenant Robertson.

The two men waited nervously as La Milice slowly climbed the pass, and when they closed within rifle range, Armand glanced at Billy.

"Not yet. Let them get closer, then we open up," Sergeant Waldron whispered. "Maybe an ambush will send them packing down the mountain."

Armand smiled as he braced his rifle on a rock.

There were about fifteen men coming up the pass, the young French boy no longer in sight.

Armand knew the young boy would be shot or sent to a concentration camp if he did not tell them where their group was. It was betrayal or death for many young men in France. He tightly gripped his rifle, knowing his fate would be the same.

La Milice slowly closed the gap: 500 feet, 400 feet, 300...

Sergeant Waldron opened fire on the lead man, bullets from his Thompson ripping through the man's chest and sending him facedown to the ground with a sickening thud, blood splattering on nearby rocks.

Armand screamed, "*Les Souris Grises*, crawl back into your hole with *les bosch*!" and then fired two rounds into the next man in line, hitting him just above the left shoulder and severing his carotid artery. The man crumbled to the ground holding his neck, slowly and inevitably bleeding to death.

La Milice was quick to respond, as several lay down covering fire. The two men were pinned down at the pass, bullets whizzing above their heads and kicking up rocks in front of them. Sergeant Waldron grabbed one of his grenades, nodding to Armand to do the same.

"Now," Billy said, pulling the pin on the grenade. "One, two, three."

Releasing his hand slightly, the handle popped off with a clang, and Waldron lobbed the pineapple toward the militia. They could hear someone shout, "*Handgranate!*" as La Milice dived for cover on the opposite side of the path. A second later Armand did the same, but he threw his grenade on the opposite side from Billy's to catch anyone trying to escape the first one.

The strategy worked. The first explosion only wounded a few of the militia, but the second instantly killed four of them and left the rest dazed.

Their success was short-lived though, as when Armand stood up to fire, ignoring the pain in his leg, three Vichy militia were upon them. Armand was able to get off a round into the first attacker, killing him, but the second soldier shot Armand in the chest at point-blank range. Armand fell facedown over his rifle.

Billy Waldron stood up to meet the remaining two as he drew his Ka-Bar from his belt and stabbed a Milice in the stomach, kicking him aside. Taking on the third Milice, he swung the knife at his neck, only grazing him, a thin line of blood appearing by his carotid artery.

Just as Waldron was about to make the killing blow, two Milice made the pass and fired into Sergeant Waldron, the impact of a lone bullet hitting him in the shoulder, knocking him back among the rocks.

A blinding explosion rocked the pass, lighting up the night sky.

As the lead Milice raised his rifle to finish off Waldron, Armand, mortally wounded, raised his body slightly, pulled the grenade pin, and waited two seconds before slowly rolling the grenade between La Milice. In horror they watched as the grenade settled between them.

Faint reports of distant guns reached Robertson, who glanced back toward the pass and saw a dim outline of where his friend Billy Waldron was making his last stand. As he gazed in their direction, he could hear the far-off sounds of battle where La Milice, probably reinforced, had engaged the two men.

Anyone else, Robertson mused, would go down easily against such odds, but not Billy. Sergeant Billy Waldron had come to his team as a young, inexperienced medic in 1943. The young farm boy from Iowa proved to be a good soldier, keeping up with the tougher soldiers like Tony Rizzo. Rizzo took a shine to Billy, ensuring he made it through the demanding training exerted on them by the OSS. When Rizzo died on that barren roadside, Robertson could see the enthusiasm leave Waldron with the loss of his friend.

Lieutenant Robertson lowered his head as Antoinette laid her hand upon his shoulder.

"I should have gone back to help," the lieutenant said, not facing her.

"*Non, mon ami,* you only did what was right for everyone," Antoinette said. "They did it for you."

Françoise interrupted. "Lieutenant, we must keep moving until we are a safer distance away."

"OK, Françoise," Robertson said.

The group continued until they could no longer see the path, and then they stopped for the night.

It was a fitful night's sleep for everyone, after sore muscles and exhausted limbs made the trek even more treacherous. Each and every person there grieved the loss of their friends.

It started out as a perfect plan, but now, with the loss of Rizzo, Waldron, and Armand, the escape seemed to be a failure to the lieutenant.

Madeleine sat with her back against a boulder, unable to sleep. She wondered who would fall next. Antoinette? Her beloved Henri? The thought of losing another of their group kept her awake all night.

The sunrise was as beautiful as ever. Everyone was sore and disheartened by yesterday's disaster at the pass. They slowly and painfully packed their belongings into their rucksacks.

"I know we have lost friends and comrades," Françoise said. "We should not waste their sacrifice."

"You're right, Françoise," the lieutenant said, picking up his gear and walking down the rocky trail.

One of them should have been me, instead of Rizzo and Waldron, he thought to himself.

Everyone steeled themselves for the arduous day of climbing.

On the third day of their journey, the group continued to hike the mountains and covered twelve miles in ten hours.

The following morning, they descended over 600 feet to la Cabane d'Espugue. Rounding a huge boulder, the group saw a gorgeous mountain lake, l'Etang de Cruzous. The sight of the ancient glacial lake was amazing as it sparkled in the morning sun.

"Billy would have loved this," Lieutenant Robertson said.

"C'est trés beau," Antoinette said. "He will see it, Robbie."

Afterward, they resumed their climb to le Col de Pécouch, at 7,500 feet, which seemed unattainable. They spent most of the day negotiating the tough climb and helping each other along the way, taking short breaks.

Twice during the day's climb, Françoise pulled a bottle of water from behind a rock or under a log to refresh them for the climb.

A regular Houdini, the lieutenant thought. Where's the rabbit?

Finally they descended to 7,000 feet and slept under the towering rocks of the Refuge des Estagnous.

On their fourth day, they made an early start, eager to get to Spain, and freedom. They followed the trail from Estagnous, down past another sparkling lake, le Lac Rond, and then back upward to le Lac Long. Spain was almost in sight for the exhausted group of *évadés*.

That morning they negotiated the granite boulders on the flank of Mount Valier, going from rock to rock, helping Charlène and Henri over the rough ground toward the Spanish border.

Bracing their exhausted and battered bodies, they made the final push for the border along the steep, narrow trail.

The breathtaking views of steel-blue lakes, reflecting perfect images of sky and rock, distracted them from their continual pain.

"We should fill our canteens at the lake," Françoise said.

"Good idea," the lieutenant replied. "Everyone hand us your water containers. Françoise and I will fetch some water."

Gathering up everyone's containers, the two navigated the boulders, finally reaching the crystal-clear mountain lake.

Above them the lieutenant caught sight of a golden eagle soaring above the rock formations. "I wish I could fly," he said, looking up.

"Me too, Robbie," Françoise said. "Would make this easier."

Making their way back to the top of the trail, they handed back everyone's water containers.

Charlène began to drink the ice-cold water.

"Careful, *ma petite*," Antoinette said. "Drink it slowly, or you will get cramps."

Throughout the day they pushed forward. Freedom in Spain was only hours away. Renewed by the fresh mountain water, they made steady progress among the huge rock formations.

By midday they were standing atop the Col de la Clauere with one foot in France and one in Spain. Their earlier burst of strength was now sapped by the arduous climb. Even so, they exulted in the warm Spanish summer breeze.

It was Charlène who first found the letters *FE* carved into a rock, the sign that they had finally reached the border.

"What does this mean, Antoinette?" Charlène asked.

"La liberté et la paix, ma chèrie!" Antoinette said happily.

"France and España, Charlène," Henri said. "It means no one will ever hurt you again."

Charlène's Texas-wide grin needed no explanation.

Like so many *évadés* before them, the group was exhilarated at the sight of liberation from *les bosch*.

"Many of my countrymen are held in Spanish jails, Lieutenant Robertson," Henri said.

"Why, isn't Spain neutral?" the lieutenant asked.

"Oui, but jail is common. Can this be changed?" he asked looking directly at Charlène. "As *Américains*, your embassy will help you if you are caught."

"Unless we can reach the Portuguese border or Gibraltar, we are still in some danger," Madeleine said.

In the past, the Fascist regime of General Franco deported Jews back to Nazi-occupied France, and Henri was especially worried that Charlène's ancestry would be discovered and she would deported to a concentration camp.

"Gibraltar might be the best option. I know of an OSS team escaping to Portugal that was held for several weeks before being handed over to the American Embassy," Lieutenant Robertson said. "At least there, in Gibraltar, the Brits are on our side."

"*En tout cas*, we have a dangerous route to take, but no one will be shooting at us," Henri said.

"We need to take these final steps across the border, Lieutenant," Françoise warned. "La Milice will follow us relentlessly to here after the attack back at le Col de Craberous."

Checking his pistol, the only remaining weapon he had left, Robertson lamented as he counted three rounds left in his Colt .45. He said, "I would make them pay the price, if I had enough ammo."

"We all would, Lieutenant, but the time to fight will come again for all of us. The liberation of France will be soon, and we still have much to do before we can call our home free once more," Françoise said.

"You're right, Françoise, but it's hard for an ole hand like me to leave my buddies behind. Let's get this crew to Gibraltar," Lieutenant Robertson said as he started down the path to the River Noguera Pallaresa in Spain.

They reached the River Noguera Pallaresa, descending into a valley leading to the village of Alos d'Isil. Nearby, a small lake provided refreshment. There they were able to wash the dirt and blood from their bodies and clothes.

Lieutenant Robertson, red faced, turned away as the unabashed French took no heed in striping their clothes to bathe naked under a warm Spanish sun.

Having dressed again after a refreshing swim, Françoise approached Lieutenant Robertson. "Lieutenant, the track to our left is an old trail made by the Spaniards to drive their herds down the valley to Tabescan, and the nearest city, Lerida. Nearby is the village of Esterri d'Aneu, close to the prison in Sort. We should avoid that area at all costs."

Turning to look in the distance, Lieutenant Robertson stared up the mountainside trail they had just overcome. He had lost his men on this escape and mourned their passing. Blinking and rubbing his eyes, he caught a glimpse of a figure making its way down into the final descent. Slowly walking toward the figure, he was hit by a sudden recognition. It was Billy!

The others, in various stages of dressing after their bath, stared in awe as Lieutenant Robertson sprinted up the hill in time to catch Sergeant Waldron, who collapsed in his arms.

"Didn't think you could get rid of me that fast, did ya, LT?" Waldron said weakly.

"Good to see you, Billy," Robertson replied. "You're hit. Let's get that tended to."

Picking up Waldron and placing his arm over his shoulder, Robbie, with Madeleine helping him, walked the final steps to the lake. Everyone gathered around, joyful that Waldron had returned from the dead.

"What about Armand, Billy?" Madeleine asked.

"He saved me, Madeleine," Billy said. "La Milice were about to finish me off when he sacrificed himself. He is a true hero."

Madeleine, tears forming in her eyes, said nothing about Armand. She had grown close to him, and this hit her hard. Henri, seeing her in pain, embraced her, allowing the tears to flow.

Antoinette helped Waldron remove his shirt, telling him to sit down. She walked over to the river and washed out the blood stains, coming back to clean his wound with the wet garment. She took a small bandage from his medical pack and dressed his wound.

Françoise paced nervously, alternating watching the horizon for Spanish police and checking on Antoinette's progress with Sergeant Waldron.

Once Antoinette had finished, Françoise addressed the group. "I know a place where we can sleep tonight to help Billy rest for the final part of our journey," she said.

"Is it close?" Antoinette asked. "Billy cannot travel far."

"There is a cave a few kilometers from here," Françoise said. "Spanish goat herders live inside. They have helped me before."

"They live in a cave?" Charlène asked.

"*Oui, ma petit*, for many years," Françoise said. "Now come, I will take you there."

Holding out her hand to Charlène, she led her and the escapees down a dirt road to the herders' cave. Inside a man dressed in traditional herders' clothing greeted Françoise warmly.

He was followed by his wife, a short, heavyset woman in traditional Spanish clothes, a shawl covering her head.

Speaking in Spanish, she pointed to Sergeant Waldron in a pleading manner. The Spaniard nodded his head and turned to walk away.

When he reappeared, Françoise said, "He has a small barn around the bend, normally used for his sheep. We can stay there tonight, but we need to leave in the morning. They are taking a big risk by letting us stay."

"Shouldn't we get away from the border as soon as we can?" Madeleine asked.

"Billy's in no condition to travel at the moment. A day won't hurt our odds at this point," the lieutenant chimed in.

Even with the language barrier between the Spaniards and the group, they showed genuine hospitality. Like Madame Barrau, the Spanish couple seemed to be used to such visitors.

The group was totally exhausted, and their food had run out two days ago. The famished group was grateful for the meal of polenta and goat's milk the Spaniards shared with them.

The hay loft was heaven compared to the rocky terrain of the past few days. That evening, they never slept more soundly.

They were free at last.

CITY OF LIGHT

In Paris, Marie reached into her purse for her phone to make contact with Jean at the Virginia estate, but it wasn't there. I must have dropped it, or maybe someone stole it, she thought, retrieving her luggage. Eyeing a pay phone, she dismissed the idea of using it. Someone could listen in. I'll call him when I get to the hotel.

She was about to go outside to flag down a taxi when she saw a man holding a sign with her alias name on it.

"C'est moi," she said to the man. "I am Abella Hamlin."

"Mademoiselle Hamlin, Jean sends his compliments. He has sent me to pick you up, if it should please you?"

"Oui, monsieur," she said. "Please take me to the Hôtel de Sévigné on the Champs-Elysées."

"Bien entendu, Mademoiselle Hamlin, at once," the limo driver replied.

Climbing into the limo, Marie saw someone in the interior shadows.

"Who—" was all Marie got out, as a needle slid into her neck.

"Take us to the warehouse, before she wakes up," the shadowy figure said to the driver.

The limousine sped through the streets of Paris, arriving in a seedy part of the city thirty minutes later. Marie was lying unconscious on the seat.

The limo driver pulled up to a warehouse. The warehouse door was opened by guards inside. Marie was hauled unceremoniously from the back of the limo and carried into a room with a steel door, and the bolt lock was slammed into place.

She awoke some hours later weak and groggy. Her head was spinning in the pitch-black room. She stumbled around in the blackness, determining that she was in some sort of concrete bunker. There was nothing in the room, with the exception of a cot with a filthy-smelling mattress.

They want me alive for some reason, Marie thought, but why?

***

Jack and Emily had been briefed by Jean that Marie had gone missing.

"Does anyone know what happened?" Jack asked.

"No, only that she never checked into the hotel," Jean said.

"What about her phone? Is the GPS locator working?" Jack asked.

"That's the first thing we tried. Nothing is showing up on our tracking system."

"Shouldn't we abort this mission and go find her?" Emily asked. "She needs our help, Jean."

"No, you must go complete your assignment," Jean said. 'I will notify you if we find out anything of her whereabouts. If we find her, I will redirect you to get her."

Three days later, Jack and Emily's plane touched down at the Charles de Gaulle Airport in Paris. They had assumed the names of Bob and Barbara Wilson, a couple on their honeymoon in Paris.

They climbed into a taxi at the airport, instructing the driver to take them to the Hôtel de Sévigné. It was a small and intimate privately owned hotel in downtown Paris. It was full of charm and character, warm and welcoming to the couple.

Jack paid the cab driver, and they approached the desk clerk to check in.

Recognizing the couple were *Américains*, the clerk said, "Welcome to the Hôtel de Sévigné. Can I help you?"

"Thank you. We are here on our honeymoon!" Emily replied, showing off her ring.

"Mais, c'est merveilleux! Vous êtes ici pour votre lune de miel," the clerk replied.

"Ah, yes, I guess. I mean *oui*," Emily answered, not sure what "*lune de miel*" meant but too tired to find out.

After they were confirmed and given the room key, Emily discreetly asked the desk clerk if their friend Abella Hamlin had checked in. Scrolling through the reservations on the computer screen, the clerk replied that she had not checked into the hotel as they had expected.

Jack excused himself as Emily finalized the check-in process. Going outside, he pulled out his cell phone and immediately called the operations center in Williamsburg. The conversation with Jean was brief, and disturbing. Marie was still missing.

Entering the room, they were greeted by a sumptuous double bed facing three large windows that revealed a balcony overlooking the Square des Etats-Unis. Their accommodations were just what they needed after the long flight, and the view of the square below was beautiful. But because of the circumstances, it was not a sure bet that they would be able to enjoy these surroundings.

The *porteur* set their luggage in the corner of the room, waiting patiently.

Jack dug into his pocket and produced several francs for him. After the *porteur* excused himself from the room, Emily said, "I am worried, Jack. If whoever took Marie knew she was to come here, then they must know we would too."

"We have no choice. Our only hope to find her is to blow our own cover. Besides, we have a job to do." Jack grimaced.

They both knew this was a dangerous business, but now it was twofold.

Emily opened the french doors leading to the balcony and stepped outside to a spectacular view of Paris.

The cool autumn evening made her shiver a bit as Jack came to rescue her with a luxurious throw.

"Beautiful," she said, looking at the Arc de Triomphe, brilliantly lit against the night sky, and, off in the distance, the Eiffel Tower, sparkling like a guardian over the City of Light.

Below them on the street, unnoticed, a man in an alleyway dropped his cigarette on the sidewalk, crushing it with his toe, and disappeared into the darkness.

***

Marie lost track of time in her black prison. She was dehydrated from lack of fluids and disoriented from the darkness that surrounded her. She didn't know if she had been in this prison for days or just hours when the door opened. A blinding light framed two figures in the doorway as she was grabbed by each arm to keep her from bolting out the door. They didn't have to worry though; in her condition, she wasn't running anywhere.

The figure of a man pushing a woman in a wheelchair appeared next. "Well, one of Charlène's pawns finds her way to Paris. What are you looking for, Marie?" the woman said in a harsh accent.

Dutch, perhaps? Marie thought. Or is she trying to mislead me? "I don't know what you are talking about. I am Abella Hamlin, and on vacation in Paris. Who are you people?"

"Marie, Marie, please don't lie to me. I know who you are. Have Jack and Emily come to Paris as well?" the woman asked.

"I have no clue who those people are. Please let me go!" Marie said.

One of the woman's guards brought in a chair, a small desk, and a lamp. He placed the light on the desk, turning it on. Marie squinted at the harsh light as a second guard lifted her off the bed like a rag doll and tied her to the chair. The woman nodded to the men, and they left the room.

"Do you need to refresh your memory? I have someone capable of making you remember," the woman said nonchalantly, motioning her hand to someone beyond the door.

When the woman in the wheelchair was rolled out of the doorway, a man emerged holding a doctor's satchel in one hand and a boom box in the other. He walked into the room, setting the boom box on the desk, and closed the door behind him. Pushing the play button, the soothing sounds of Isaac Albeniz on piano filled the room. In a heavy Spanish accent, he asked, "Do you like classical music, *señorita?*"

***

Jack and Emily arose to a knock on their door. *"Service de chambre,"* the woman behind the door said. Peering through the door, Jack opened it, and they were greeted with a tray holding coffee, croissants in an elegant bowl, and a dozen red roses with a card inserted between the stems. The maid set up everything on the table outside overlooking the city and left discreetly. They sat down to eat breakfast, taking in the warm autumn air, with the Eiffel Tower jutting up and over the buildings, standing proud and tall in the distance.

Emily opened the card and read aloud, "Under the Eiffel Tower at 11:00 AM, I can't wait *until we meet again.*" The last line was written in cursive.

Jack recited the poem he had memorized, "'May God hold you in the palm of his hand.' I have always wanted to see the Eiffel Tower."

Downstairs after having eaten their breakfast, they asked the desk clerk for a cab to the Eiffel Tower. Ringing up the local cab company, she told the newlyweds that the cab would pick them up on the corner in a few minutes.

The cab took the long way to the Eiffel Tower, past the Arc de Triomphe and beautiful fountains and statues dedicated to past military victories and heroes of France, before finally reaching the landmark itself. They were caught up in the beauty of Paris. Paying the cabbie as the taxi pulled up to the Eiffel Tower, they made their way to a food vendor serving crepes.

"While in Paris?" Jack asked hopefully.

"Sure, why not?" Emily said.

Emily ordered food and drink for them both, and they made their way to a nearby bench, enjoying the view.

After about twenty minutes, a casually dressed man in slacks and a sport coat approached the food vendor.

The man ordered a crepe and paid the vendor. After consuming some of the crepe, he slowly walked up to the couple. "I think," he said in English with a French accent, "you have just been married?"

"Yes," Jack said. "How did you know?"

"It was easy," the man said. "You *Américains* are awed by our city, *oui?*"

"This is a beautiful city you have here," Jack said.

"*Merci, monsieur.* It is a place to reconnect with old friends. As my father used to say, until we meet again."

"May God hold you in the palm of his hand," Jack replied.

"Perhaps I could show you around the city? My name is Eugène, and our mutual friend Jean sends his regards."

"Thank you. That would be delightful!" Emily exclaimed. "Perhaps some local places where there are no tourists?"

"I know of a wonderful place," Eugène replied, hailing a cab.

Taking the cab to a private residence just outside of Paris, Eugène ushered the couple quickly inside.

"Eugène, have you heard from Marie Sinclaire? She has not contacted us since her arrival here in Paris," Emily said with anxiety.

"No, but we have agents in the city looking for her. We will find her if she is here," Eugene said. "Jean has asked me to report anything we find about her to him as soon as I get any information."

"Please keep us in the loop," Jack said.

"Eugène, Jean mentioned you have information on the Doomsday Book?" Emily said.

"*Oui*, Emily. My intelligence sources have come across a rumor about the Doomsday Book. Have you been briefed on it yet?" Eugène asked the couple.

"Just vague references to Hans Talhoffer and Nostradamus," Emily replied.

"Talhoffer was well known in Medieval Europe. His works were genius, but he had a more sinister side to him as well."

"The Doomsday Book?" Jack asked.

"Exactly, and it was rumored that Talhoffer had illustrated many machines that were more than ordinary weapons. They had the ability in the right hands to kill thousands in medieval Europe. By today's standards in population growth..."

"Millions," Jack answered.

Eugène disclosed, "A century after his death, Nostradamus was rumored to have had the book and channeled some of his prophesies based on the contents of it."

"So has someone found it?" Emily asked.

"We believe that Tomas Garcia is getting close to finding it."

"We did recover a message we believe is tied to the book. There are many fanciful drawings around, and one has to overlook some serious problems to think these were practical machines," Eugène stated. "We also believe that his *Book of Fighting* and the Doomsday Book are pieces of a puzzle. Apart they are meaningless, but together…"

"Where did the message originate from, and who sent it?" Jack asked.

"Between Garcia and a woman we have yet to identify. We call her the Dane," Eugène replied.

"Sounds like he has a new partner," Jack said.

"Maybe his new partner figured out the relationship between the two books," Emily said.

"That's not good. What was her message back?" Jack asked.

"This is the message we intercepted from that woman to Garcia: 'I speak not against masters of defense indeed, they are to be honored, nor against the science, it is noble, and in my opinion to be preferred next to divinity, for as divinity preserves the soul from hell and the devil, so does this noble science defend the body from wounds and slaughter. We must awaken that Greek goddess of fire, Pyrène,'" Eugène explained. "It is a variation of a similar text in one of Nostradamus's French quatrains, where he describes methods he used to treat the plague—none of which, not even the bloodletting, apparently worked."

"Pyrène, as in the Pyrénées Mountains?" Jack asked. "What are they planning?"

"I am not sure, but I think I know where the book is," Eugène replied.

"Where?" Jack asked.

"In 1940, when the battle for France took a turn for the worse, the Doomsday Book, which was stored here in Paris, was moved to HQ—MI-6, in Scotland—for safekeeping from the Nazis," Eugène explained.

"Who were they afraid of that knew how to use the book?" Jack asked. "They could have played it off as just an ordinary old text."

"The Nazis were smart, Jack. Himmler was interested in the occult. His network of spies surely found out its value as a weapon."

"Isn't the book still in Scotland?" Jack asked. "We could go there and get it."

"When an attempt to steal the book in Scotland was thwarted by MI-6, they decided to move it to a safer location," Eugène said.

"Where did they move it?" Jack asked.

Eugène continued, "A top-secret mission was to deliver the book to SOE agents in Algiers. Then they were supposed to hide it in a secret location, somewhere in Egypt."

"Why keep it? Why not destroy it?" Emily asked.

"It held possible secrets to help win the war, Emily, and the Allies were interested in using it against the Nazis," Eugène said.

"But that would make the Allies no better than the evil they were fighting," she said.

"You're right, Emily, but MI-6 never found out. The Halifax bomber crashed into the Pyrénées Mountains," Eugène conveyed. "The book was never found. All searches to find the book after the war were unsuccessful."

"I read about that crash site; the remains of the Halifax and its crew were found by a shepherd boy. After the crash the resistance members were able to recover many of the supplies in the shock-proof parachute containers. They then used those same containers to bury the crew members," Jack explained. "Maybe the book was buried with them."

"Jack, how do you know all this?" Emily asked.

"History Channel," Jack said.

"I guess all that time on unemployment wasn't wasted after all," Emily said.

"Wouldn't they have found the book with the crew members then?" Emily asked.

"No, because the area was still occupied, so the graves had to be kept secret," Jack informed them. "After the war a cemetery was built on the site, and the men were reburied in 1994."

"Jack, do you think the book was buried with them?" Eugène wondered.

"It's possible," Jack said.

"I can't imagine someone wouldn't think of that," Emily replied.

"They must have looked and did not find it; maybe they thought the book was burned up in the crash?" Jack said.

"Well there's only one way to find out then," Eugène remarked. "We need to examine that cemetery."

"I am not one for digging up war heroes," Jack said. "Are there any other possibilities?"

"Only one," Eugène replied.

***

Back in her cell, Marie was exhausted from Garcia's torture. It was all a mind game, she said to herself, trying to break my will to garner any information that might be useful to him. I won't tell these terrorists, she kept saying over and over in her head, *je ne dirai rien.*

Garcia closed the steel door behind him, plunging Marie into blackness once again. Garcia made his way down the hall, entering a plush office off to one side of the warehouse.

"She won't talk, and I am afraid that more torture will just kill her before we find out anything useful," Garcia informed the woman in the wheelchair.

"She has said nothing about the book?" the woman asked.

Garcia answered, "I don't think she knows where it is, and perhaps we should have followed her before kidnapping her."

"Do not question my methods, Garcia!" the woman replied. "Perhaps we can use her to get the book. Make contact with Aubrac's pawns. Tell them we will make an exchange."

"As you wish."

Jack, Emily, and Eugène caught a train from Paris to Toulouse the next day, with plans to rent a car to travel to Saint-Girons, the starting point of Le Chemin de la Liberté, which would lead them to the cemetery.

"We will get some warm hiking clothes and boots in Saint-Girons because they are much cheaper there than in Paris," Eugène informed them. "We also have a safe house in the village where we can get hiking equipment."

"Good. Feeling a bit naked without proper equipment," Jack said.

"Eugène, I am still not comfortable with digging up a grave site. I think it's disrespectful to dig up those war heroes," Emily said.

"I have no intention of disturbing those graves, Emily, because I am sure someone has already checked. That would be too obvious. There has to be something else. That book has to be close by," Eugène maintained.

"Makes sense, but where would someone hide it?" Emily asked.

"Occam's Razor!" Jack declared proudly.

Eugene was puzzled. "Occam's Razor?"

"Simple! If the book was not found at the graves, then the book or a clue to its whereabouts must be at the crash site," Jack said.

"The only thing located beside the plane there is a cross dedicated to the crew, Jack. That's it!" Eugène exclaimed.

Emily grinned. "Jack, sometimes you surprise even me."

At that same moment, in an abandoned warehouse in Paris, the woman in the wheelchair appeared in Marie's doorway. Marie's eyes could not adjust to the bright light to see her face clearly, but she did see the man who delivered a tray to her room. Walking to the table, he set up the small lamp as before and turned it on.

"Enjoy your meal, Marie," the woman said graciously.

"Why are you doing this to me?" Marie asked. "I don't know any of those people you are asking about."

"Stop lying, Marie. In the end the Doomsday Book will be ours," the woman said, instructing the man behind her to close the door. Marie heard the audible clank of the bolt set into place.

In Toulouse, Eugène arranged for transportation to Saint-Girons. Arriving late that afternoon, they acquired two rooms at Hôtel La Rotonde, meeting up for dinner that evening. Afterward, Eugène drove them to a vacation home—a safe house for The Pond agents. Inside there was a cache of weapons, body armor, clothing, and food.

"We don't make many trips through the mountains, as many people did during the war, but now and then this house supplies our agents for a border crossing," Eugène said to the couple.

A half hour later, everyone had hiking clothes, a backpack, a pistol, and a military-style tri-folding shovel. Eugène instructed them to leave everything here, and they would come back to outfit before making the hike up the mountain.

"Why don't we just stay here?" Emily asked.

"I agree," Jack said. "We could stay hidden until we make our way up the mountain."

"We have arrived in town. It would be suspicious for us to disappear and suddenly reappear. This safe house is used for equipment storage only. We have been instructed not to stay," Eugène said.

"Aren't the neighbors curious on the comings and goings?" Emily asked.

"No, *mes amis*. They work for us," Eugène replied.

Making their way back to the hotel, the group went to bed early, knowing that they had a difficult trek ahead of them.

They checked out of the Hôtel La Rotonde early the next morning and headed for the safe house to gather their gear.

Outfitted for the mountain climb, they crossed la Pont Le Chemin de la Liberté, over the Salat River, following the route that Charlène had taken many years before. They entered the fields that led upward to Le Roc de Gabach, on their way to the crash site, a three-day journey.

It was a grueling hike through the mountains, but the group was well equipped and slept each night under a blanket of stars. They encountered snow along the way, but the down clothing they wore kept out the chill.

On the third day, they reached the crash site and examined the cross.

"I don't see anything. This is solid rock, not even a line in it," Emily said, examining the granite cross.

"Maybe it's buried underneath," Jack said.

Digging around the base of the cross with his military shovel, Jack hit something hard and small a few feet down. Reaching in, he pulled out a small, rusty metal cigarette container. Opening the box, he found a stained aviator's silk escape map, folded into a small square.

"Looks like a map. Maybe it will show us where the book is," Jack said.

Opening the map, there was an x on an area in Spain, near Esterri d'Aneu.

"Why does that name sound familiar?" Jack asked.

"That was the first town in Spain where people who were escaping from the Germans entered after their dangerous crossing. It meant freedom for them," Eugène said.

"No, there was something else. Charlène once told me a story of goat herders near there who were very poor and living in a cave," Jack said, recalling the story of that visit in 1944 she had told him about one evening over a glass of Cognac.

"Let's make our way back to Paris and figure this out," Eugène said on the windswept plateau.

"Can't we just hike across the mountains into Spain?" Emily asked.

"No, without the required visas, the authorities would arrest us," Eugène explained. "We should go back to Paris and figure out how this map is tied to all of this."

"Any news on the whereabouts of Marie? I am worried about her," Emily said.

"We are closing in on her location. We have tracked some communication between Garcia and his new partner, they are somewhere on the west side of Paris," Eugène said.

With the map in their hands, the group made the three-day hike back to Saint-Girons. They were exhausted from their hike in the mountains, arriving in Saint-Girons very late at night.

They decided to stay in the safe house for the night, rather than check into the hotel at this hour.

The next day all three took the train to Paris, Jack and Emily arriving back at their hotel after parting at the station with Eugène.

"Eugène, do you think this is a treasure map?" Jack asked.

"To find the Doomsday Book? Possibly," Eugène said. "We can take a flight to Barcelona and follow the map to find out."

Jack could not understand why they had not remained in Saint-Girons to discuss the map. He found it strange that Emily had not questioned this either. What was Eugène up to? And when was the last time he had contacted Jean to tell him about their own progress? He just couldn't remember. What was going on?

They all agreed that would be the next appropriate step.

The call to Jean was disappointing. He had heard nothing from or about Marie.

On the balcony a vase of yellow roses sat on the table, a card tucked in between the blooms.

It read *I am sorry to inform you that Marie is not resting comfortably in our hands. We have a bargain for you: Marie for the book. If you want to see her alive again, meet a man in a gabardine suit at Café Francis tomorrow at 9:00 AM.*

"A gabardine suit?" Emily read aloud. "How melodramatic."

Jack called Jean. They took his advice and checked out of the hotel with the excuse of a family emergency. Jean was probably correct in assuming that Garcia knew of their whereabouts, and that they shouldn't stay in the hotel. It was odd that they weren't targeted there, but it was possible Garcia knew they would come to him if he had Marie anyway.

After making the phone call, Jack went back to the balcony. Now there was a vase of yellow chrysanthemums on the table with another card tucked in between the glossy green stems. Picking up the card, he read aloud: *I am sorry for your loss.*

Loss? Jack thought. Wait, aren't chrysanthemums for funerals in France? And how did I know that? Jeez, I am losing my mind. They just told us that Marie would be OK if we brought them the book. Whose loss are they talking about?

Emily appeared on the balcony next to Jack. "I love roses, Jack; you can never bring me enough of them," she said.

"But they're chrysanthemums," Jack said, turning to point to the vase.

"Jack, you never did know your flowers." Emily smiled, picking out a yellow rose from the vase and carrying it inside.

What the hell? Jack thought. It's gotta be stress.

They spent the rest of the day zigzagging across the city, changing taxis and making sure they weren't followed. As their new cab took the turn onto the street where Eugène lived, the flashing of police lights confronted them. They watched two French paramedics exit the front door carrying a stretcher with a bloody sheet over a body. The taxi driver pointed to the house, and Jack explained that he must have given the wrong address and asked, "Could you please take us back to our hotel?"

Emily gave Jack a look of horror at the sight of a body covered and bloodied coming from Eugène's apartment. She lay her head on his shoulder.

Back at the Hotel de Sévigné, they had no problems getting a room back, even with the clerk being a bit annoyed at them. The clerk left to have a talk with the hotel manager behind closed doors.

The hotel manager came out and checked on the availability of other rooms, telling them that they had a cancellation of a smaller room.

"We will take it," Jack said.

"*Bien, monsieur*. Will you be using the same credit card?" the manager asked.

"Yes," Jack replied.

Once back in their new smaller room, Emily said, "Jack, we have no choice. We have to meet with these people, but we don't have the book. What should we do?"

"We go find that book," Jack said.

The next morning they arrived at Café Francis for their rendezvous with the mysterious messenger. They sat down at a corner table overlooking the street, ordered *deux cafés*, and waited. At 9:05 AM, he arrived, wearing the gabardine suit as expected.

"I am glad you value your friend's life," the man stated with a French accent. "I'll be brief. Do you have the book?"

"We want proof that Marie is alive before we hand over the book," Emily demanded.

"She is alive," the mysterious man said. "Now, may I have the book please?"

"We don't have it, but we know where it is. We can have it to you in three days, but we want a guarantee she will come to no harm during that time," Jack said.

Pulling out his phone, the man tapped the screen, bringing up a live feed into Marie's room. Showing the couple, he said, "Three days is all you have before she is dead."

As the live feed was playing, Emily covertly slid her phone from her jeans pocket, opening it up and pressing a series of numbers.

The man closed his phone, terminating his connection, and placed it in his coat pocket.

"How do we get in touch?" Jack asked.

"You can contact me at this number," he said, handing Jack a number written on a small slip of paper. "I don't recommend losing it."

The man got up, walked out, and disappeared down the crowded street.

Jack was about to get up and follow him, but Emily stopped him. When he gave her a puzzled look, she said, "Jack, that's not a good idea. Marie is their captive, and there is probably more than one of Garcia's agents watching us.

Besides, we can find Marie anyway," she said. "Let's go back to the hotel. I've got something to show you."

Arriving back at their new room, Emily showed Jack her phone.

"I used our tracking software to pick up on the video feed that guy showed us of Marie," she said.

"Nice job, sweetie," Jack said, kissing her cheek.

"We need to get to Barcelona as soon as we can," Jack said. "Can you look up flights on the phone?"

"Sure, but why can't you do it?" Emily asked.

"You're just better at getting the deals than I am." Jack smirked.

With a sigh, Emily checked for flights to Barcelona for that evening.

"Jack, I can't get anything until tomorrow morning," she said, staring at the screen.

"We don't have much time. Should we rent a car?" Jack asked.

"No, that would take too much time," Emily replied.

"Maybe Jean can get an agent to assist us," Jack said.

"That would also be wasting time, Jack. We need to get moving. Wait, I can get us on an early-morning flight," Emily said.

Wow, Jack thought, that was fast. How did she do that?

The next morning they made arrangements with the desk clerk to return to their room in three days' time.

"Are you visiting outside Paris?" she asked.

"My hubby here wants to visit Berlin," Emily replied. "I don't know why, since I think we should stay in this beautiful city."

"Yes you should!" the clerk answered.

"Well, I am a book nut," Jack announced proudly. "I understand that the library in Berlin is filled with all kinds of exotic and interesting books!"

"He's a big fan of Nostradamus," Emily added.

"That's nice," the clerk politely replied. "I look forward to your return, Mr. and Mrs. Wilson!"

Later that day their plane landed at Aeroport Del Prat' in Barcelona.

VENGANZA

Otto Von Bismarck once said, "It is to Germany's interest to put the Spanish fly on France's neck."

The group of *évadés* awoke next morning full of hope for the coming day. The sun rose majestically on the eastern horizon as they made preparations to travel south through the Spanish countryside toward Gibraltar. In the loft everyone rose lazily, still battered and bruised from the long journey over the Pyrénées Mountains.

"I know of a safe house in the nearby village of Esterri d' Aneu and further west at San Sebastian," Françoise said to the group. "We should travel at night until we get to San Sebastian, where a British diplomat will meet us. From there we can take a train to Algeciras, in southern Spain, and then finally go by car or truck to Gibraltar. Remember, it can still be dangerous if we are caught."

"I thought we were safe now, Madame Françoise," Charlène said. "We are free of the bosch, *n'est ce pas?*"

"We may be free of *les bosch*, but the Spanish are Fascists too and do not like us," Françoise said. "They are looking for any excuse to send us back to please the Nazis and Hitler."

"I guess ole Adolf is going to be a tad disappointed if I have anything to say about it," Lieutenant Robertson said.

Antoinette walked over to Charlène, gently taking a hold of her hand, "*Viens, mon enfant.* Let's wash and see if we can find some fresh goat's milk and cheese."

The pair wandered off to find the herder's wife.

After a moment's pause to let the two pass out of hearing range, Françoise said, "Robbie, your courage is good, but we must all remember that, under the law, if we are caught by the Spanish, the only way they will release us is to say we have escaped from German captivity, not escaped from France."

"Or we will be sent to the concentration camp of Miranda del Ebro. It is terrible place. Some stay there for months before the British Embassy can save them," Henri said. "Spain is neutral, but they accept the German authority. If we are caught, Charlène will be deported once they discover she is Jewish."

"Now there's something for ya," Sergeant Waldron, commented. "No Jews are allowed to live in Spain, yet they are here, aren't they?"

"They have no choice, Billy," Madeleine said. "Either they die under Nazi rule or they hide that they are Jewish and live in Spain."

"From everything I have heard, Franco's government does not appear to have shared the rabid anti-Semitic ideology promoted by the Nazis," Lieutenant Robertson said to the group.

"You are correct, Robbie. They are probably trying to please both Hitler and the Allies, waiting to see who wins this war," Françoise replied.

"Someone told me that if you are caught in Spain, you must be at least five kilometers away from the border or you will be sent back to France," Henri replied. "Is that true? If so, we should move now instead of waiting for night."

"*Oui*, Henri. *Ta raison*. It is important that we get as far from them and the border as possible. We cannot wait," Françoise responded. "But if we leave now in daylight, we take a greater risk of being caught. We cannot risk that."

The group spent the day resting and preparing for the walk at night to the safe house in the village of Esterri d' Aneu.

"I am scared," Charlène said. "What if they find us? I do not want to return to France."

"We are safe here, *ma petite*," Madeleine said. "They will not find us as long as you do not move."

"*Oui, madame,*" Charlène replied. "I will stay inside."

It was a beautiful, warm summer evening, the wind blowing off the mountain range behind them as they proceeded into the village of Esterri d' Aneu. Entering the village, Françoise led the group down side streets of the town. She stopped at a nondescript single-story house.

"Follow me to the back door," Françoise said. "It is dangerous to wait here in the alley."

Drawing her pistol, Françoise entered the tiny courtyard at the back of the house. She knocked softly on the door, and it was opened by a tall man with ebony hair and a goatee. After a few moments' discussion, she waved the group around to the courtyard and introduced them to the man at the rear entrance.

"My real name is John Smythe, but here I am known as Emilio Diaz."

Bringing the group inside his home, he bade them have a seat while he went to the kitchen to prepare coffee for his guests. Coming back into the *gabinete*, Emilio explained his presence.

"As you know, many have escaped Nazi-occupied Europe, ending up here in Spain. I was sent here by MI-9, our escape and evasion section," Emilio explained. "My job is to support the covert actions of the British Embassy staff and aid escapees and *évadés* who had found their way across the border."

"I will send the code word to the British Embassy to let them know they will have visitors," Emilio said.

"Many thanks, partner," the lieutenant said. "But how do you plan to get us to the British Embassy?"

"I will get you to the next safe house, in the city of Huesca, by truck. From there you will be smuggled in to the British consulate in San Sebastián. Your documents will be provided by the British Embassy and will consist of British passports and boarding passes for the train. Depending on your arrival time, you will either spend the night there or take the train immediately to Algeciras. At Algeciras, you will be picked up by a diplomatic car driven by a British consulate official named Michael Cresswell," Emilio said.

"But enough for now, I can prepare some bread, fruit, and cheeses for you. I also make a very good cup of coffee if you like."

"I'm in for a cup," the lieutenant said. "And make it a strong one."

"We appreciate your welcome, Emilio," Madeleine said. "Whatever you can spare is appreciated."

Offering his guests seats in his house, Emilio made his way into the kitchen and prepared a tray for them. The inviting aroma of coffee brewing on the stove filled the house.

Emilio brought out the tray and set it on a small table in the middle of the room. "Please, enjoy," he said, motioning to the food.

Emilio had always purchased more food than most other people in town. He needed to stock up for any *évadés*, escapees, or *passeurs* staying at his house. The baker in particular was always suspicious of Emilio buying vast quantities of bread when he was such a slim man. Emilio always laughed off the questions, stating that his cousin, Javier, who usually ate him out of house and home, was coming to visit!

After everyone had their fill, Emilio refilled their cups. "Normally I would send you to the rail station of Canfranc, the main conduit for smuggling people and information to the

British consulate in San Sebastián, but with the invasion of France, it is highly unadvisable to disembark from there to England."

"Why?" the lieutenant asked. "That would be the fastest route."

"And now, the most dangerous, Lieutenant," he explained. "There has been increased U-boat and air patrol activity since the start of the invasion."

"That means Portugal is out of the question," Lieutenant Robertson said.

"Exactly, since the route to Portugal would put you in the same situation," Emilio said.

Charlène's heart sank at the thought of not being able to visit the sea and make her home in Portugal.

"Then where can we go?" Henri asked.

"Gibraltar is your safest bet, Henri. From there you can go to Algiers in North Africa," Emilio said. "In Gibraltar, you'll meet up with a man who goes by the code name Sunday. He is the main point of contact for those arriving Gibraltar and is responsible for their debriefing," Emilio said.

"Can you brief us on the route, Emilio?" the lieutenant asked.

"Certainly. From here we travel to Huesca, the halfway point. It will take about four to five hours travel time, depending on the weather," Emilio continued. "There is a safe house in Huesca, where you will spend the night. From there you will receive instructions on the next leg of your escape."

"Why can't you take us all the way?" the lieutenant asked.

"It would look suspicious for me to drive all that way. I am a tailor by trade and have conducted business in Huesca with my cousin Javier Diaz Gomez many times, so no one would notice. But going on further would arouse suspicions. I would be gone too long. It has taken many months for people in Huesca to become familiar with me," he said.

"Makes sense. When do we leave?" Lieutenant Robertson asked.

"In the morning. For now, enjoy my hospitality," Emilio said.

The group spent the remainder of the evening resting in the house of Emilio and sitting by the stone fireplace. They talked about their homes as the fire burned low.

Charlène asked about the cowboys and Indians in America.

Sergeant Waldron began to spin a tale of how the cowboys and Indians first fought each other fiercely but then learned to live together. Charlène visualized the tepees, how the Indians dressed, and their customs. She was especially curious about their dance, which Sergeant Waldron clumsily attempted to show her. Everyone had a laugh at his expense.

The next morning, while it was still dark, Emilio gathered the group in his *gabinete*. "Before you go, you must leave all of your weapons behind. If you are caught with them, you will be imprisoned, and it will be impossible for the embassy to free you. Anyone found with weapons is considered an enemy of the Spanish government. I know you will not feel safe without them, but it is not worth the risk."

Reluctantly each person gave up his weapon, and the group filed into the back of Emilio's old beaten-up 1927 Renault truck.

"She may not be much to look at," Emilio said, "but she's carried many *évadés* to freedom!"

"This ole gal will do just fine, partner." The lieutenant nodded in approval.

In the back Emilio had placed piles of cloth and wool for the long trip to Huesca. Antoinette made a small bed for Charlène, who settled in comfortably, using a sheepskin as a pillow.

The ride that day was uneventful. As they made their way along run-down, bumpy back roads to Huesca, the *évadés* were grateful for the respite from their ordeal.

As they entered Huesca later that afternoon, their four-hour ride stretching to several hours due to a flat tire, the group anxiously peered out of the back of the truck.

Huesca, chief town of its province, lay on the slopes of a hill above the Río Isuela. It was a teeming market center for the agricultural produce of the surrounding area. The group took turns peeking out the back of the truck now and then, catching sight of other trucks, carts, and wagons delivering their goods and returning from the marketplace.

Driving down a side street and stopping in front of a clothing store, Emilio went round to the back of the truck. "Please stay here until we can get inside. We will leave in pairs so as to not alarm anyone walking past."

After spending a few moments inside the shop, Emilio reappeared and brought the *évadés* inside in pairs.

Everyone was thankful that they made it inside without anyone seeing them.

Further back in a darkened alley, overlooking the clothier, a lone figure slipped back into the shadows unnoticed by Emilio.

The small store, set back from the main road, was dimly lit by a few lamps. The heavy lead-paned double doors in the front of the shop opened to a deep, rich mahogany-paneled room. The atmosphere was that of an Old World shoppe in medieval Europe.

A small man entered from a side door. "Welcome to my humble shop. My name is Javier Gomez. You are safe with me."

"*Gracias*," the lieutenant replied.

"Our leader, General Franco, has allied himself with Hitler, but I suspect that will all soon change. I was recruited by Emilio a few years ago to help those escaping Nazi-occupied Europe. I will do what I can for you," Javier said.

"Merci, mon camarade, merci," Henri said. "The journey to freedom has been long for us."

"There is still a long journey ahead, *amigo*. Tomorrow I will take you to the British Embassy in San Sebastian to get your documents," Javier said. "For now, though, I am sure you are hungry and tired from the trip. Down the hall is a bathroom, where the *señoras* may wash. Caballeros, please join me for a drink?"

"Javier, I'm afraid I must return home. I must not arouse any suspicions by staying away for too long," Emilio said.

"You are right, my friend. Safe travels until next time!" Javier said, shaking Emilio's hand vigorously.

Emilio bade everyone farewell and wished the group luck on their escape as he nonchalantly left out the front door.

Having refreshed themselves, the group settled down to rest for the next leg to San Sebastian. Javier hid them in the attic, two floors above the store. He provided them with pillows and blankets for the evening.

Javier excused himself to make a delivery around 4:00 PM. "Please stay here. You are still very much in danger."

The attic was small and humid, but everyone made themselves as comfortable as they could while they waited for Javier to return.

Upon his return, Javier entered the attic with a steaming bowl of chicken and vegetables.

"I am sorry for the meal. Chicken is the only thing I can serve in these difficult times," he said.

"We thank you for your food, shelter, and courage," Henri said.

"De nada, amigo," Javier said.

Antoinette and Charlène volunteered to clean up the dishes when Javier prepared himself to go out again, but he politely refused their help, asking them to stay in the attic and out of sight.

Later that evening as his guests slept soundly in the attic, Javier crept out the back door of the shop as a full moon lit up the streets like a white-hot sun.

Lieutenant Robertson, not trusting Javier, but careful to remain hidden behind window drapes, saw Javier leave the house. He woke Madeleine and Henri and said, "I just saw our host leave. I have a funny feeling about him. Hope that he is on the up-and-up," he said.

"He has a secret life," Henri replied. "He cannot be exposed. The darkness hides many things."

"Even so, we should not let our guard down until we are safe in Allied territory," the lieutenant said.

The next morning the *évadés* awoke to the smell of coffee and freshly baked bread. Making their way downstairs, Javier invited them into the kitchen, where a breakfast of sausage and farm-fresh eggs greeted them.

"Javier, *pardon*, but where is your wife?" Antoinette asked. "Could I help?"

"She is visiting her mother in Madrid. I expect her back anytime now, as long as she does not poison her against me!"

Antoinette was embarrassed, and, staring at her breakfast, she finished quietly.

Freedom tasted great, André thought as he ate his breakfast. The young man, who had experienced the ugliest sides of war, dreamed of freedom in America.

"We should be leaving before the streets get crowded for the morning market. I went out last night to send a message to the embassy in San Sebastian that you would be arriving today. You will be getting your papers there," Javier explained.

Glancing at Madeleine and Lieutenant Robertson, Henri replied, "*Merci, gracias, señor*. How can we ever repay you?"

Boarding Javier's Renault truck, the group settled in for the four-hour trip. Using the materials that Emilio had given Javier, Antoinette repeated the process to make Charlène a comfortable bed for the long ride.

About an hour into the ride, the lieutenant peered out the back of the truck. "A much different atmosphere from that of occupied France, wouldn't you agree?"

"*Oui*, Robbie," Henri said, patting Robbie's shoulder. "There is no boot of the bosch on their heads."

"Franco is not much better than the bosch, Henri," Madeleine said. "But at least these are his people. They are not murdered for who they are."

For the rest of the ride to San Sebastian, no one spoke, taking in the Spanish countryside and enjoying the warm summer breeze that flowed through the openings in the canvas.

Arriving in town, Javier wasted no time driving around to the service entrance in back of the British Embassy. When they were out of sight from the street, Javier pulled over and let out his cargo.

The *évadés* were quickly ushered inside the embassy. A British soldier led them down narrow corridors to a small briefing room outfitted with an oblong oak table surrounded by plain oak chairs. The room had no outside windows, and a single bare bulb hung from the ceiling, dimly lighting up the space.

As the *évadés* waited, a smartly dressed man in his fifties entered the room. The lieutenant noticed that guards were now posted outside the room.

"Ladies and gentlemen," the man said, "I am the *Chargé d'Affaires*, Nigel Willingham, and I understand you are in need of traveling papers to get back to jolly ole England. I have received news that there are three Americans in this group. Is that correct?"

"Yes, sir. My name is Lieutenant Robertson from the US Army, and this is Sergeant Waldron. We are working with MI-6."

"And the third soldier?"

"I am afraid we lost Sergeant Rizzo, our explosives expert, to the Carlingue before we could cross the border."

"I am sorry for your loss, Lieutenant, but gratified you have made it this far," the *Chargé d'Affaires* said. "From what I see we have our allies, the French, here as well?"

Henri spoke up first. "*Oui*, Monsieur Willingham. We had to leave France after we had attacked their SS headquarters near Bergues. We are in your hands."

"I must warn you that you are still in grave danger," Willingham said. "Jerry's intelligence activity has been on the rise recently. I suspect they are attempting to draw Spain into the war, providing them with a second front against the Allies."

"Would they?" Henri asked.

"Doubtful. General Franco may be a ruthless leader, but he's no dolt," the *Chargé d'Affaires* replied. "He knows we are winning and wants to be in a good position when the war's over."

"What kind of danger should we expect if Franco is coming to our side?" the lieutenant asked.

"The German spy network is deeply embedded in this country. They still look for those escaping from France. They would try to kill you," Willingham said.

Looking around the room, he saw Charlène. "Who might be this dashing young lady?"

"My granddaughter, *monsieur*. We could not leave her. She would have been killed," Henri said.

"Well, we couldn't let the Jerry do that, now could we?" he said, smiling at her.

Charlène blushed and hid her head in Madeleine's shoulder.

"I must apologize for the interrogation," Willingham said. "Since this war began, you never know just who you are talking to these days. We always have reason to worry about what happens on the other side of the Pyrénées. Even though Spain has claimed neutrality, we have been playing a game of cat and mouse with Jerry here."

"Sounds like a sticky situation," the lieutenant commented.

"It is, Lieutenant. I understand you have a bit of a sticky situation yourself."

"I know," the lieutenant replied. "I ignored my orders."

"It seems you may have made the right choice. You have been confirmed by MI-6 to proceed with the *évadés* to Gibraltar. Henri and the rest have paperwork to proceed to Algiers afterward and contact the Free French Forces there. I don't know if you have heard, but the Allies are making splendid progress on the invasion beaches and are now moving to the interior of France," the *Chargé d'Affaires* said.

"Well, that's welcome news. Thank you, sir," Robertson said.

"I guess my court-martial is off the table too, eh, LT," Waldron said.

"Shut up, Billy. You're starting to sound like Rizzo," the lieutenant said.

"Mon Dieu, c'est un miracle! Vous avez entendu?" Henri said to the others.

"Henri," Willingham said, "we have picked up messages from your former agent, Sergio. Apparently, he has gone to Madrid looking for you and Madeleine. I understand he is a double spy and in reality is working for the Gestapo."

"He is a traitor," Henri said.

A messenger appeared in the doorway, delivering a teletype to Willingham. He paused a moment, considering its meaning. Finally he spoke. "I believe this pertains to all of you."

"What's wrong?" Henri asked.

"It's a correspondence between the German Embassy and Berlin that we have intercepted. It says, 'Ref. Recent *évadés*: As you know, the German Ambassador has granted 2,500 pesetas for the appropriate handling of this case. We are proceeding.' Well now, it would appear that you are in grave danger, my friends, and must proceed with extreme caution," the *Chargé d'Affaires* warned. "I believe Sergio is on the hunt for you."

"He set a trap as I led MI-6 agent Sonny to the rendezvous plane last month; I think it is time we set a trap for him," Henri growled. "Sonny saved my life!"

"Henri, let it pass. The safety of the group on the whole depends on being anonymous," Madeleine said.

***

Sergio Garcia, a Catalonian loyal to the Old Spanish Republic, fought as an infantryman in the Spanish Civil War from 1936 until 1939, which had begun as an attempted coup d'état by a group of Spanish army generals against the government of the leftist-leaning Second Spanish Republic, then under the leadership of president Manuel Azaña.

Fleeing from the Nationalists to avoid prison, with his wife and newborn son Tomas, he joined ranks with the Marquis, Communist partisans while at the refugee camp in Vernet-d'Ariège, France. Soon after the invasion of Germany in May 1940, Sergio was captured and had suffered so much in a Nazi concentration camp that his once fine mind cracked. He became a double agent for the Gestapo and the Allies, serving two masters.

Sergio reported the situation to his Gestapo superiors in Paris. He requested to lead the hunt for Henri and Madeleine. At first the Gestapo refused to let him go, thinking it a waste of resources, but when he described the escape of the American agent, Sonny, and the possible link of Henri and Madeleine to code breaking activities, they decided that Sergio's request had merit.

Sergio had informed SS Sturmbannführer Gustav of the whereabouts of Charlène, a possible way to force the surrender of Sonny to the Gestapo, but he had not expected her to be so strong. He had failed to capture them and almost died in the process. He painfully remembered the night on the trail with Sonny and Henri.

He had flagged down Sonny and Henri.

"You cannot travel on this path; les bosch *have patrols along this route."*

"How many?" Henri inquired.

"They have an entire company out there, Henri," he replied.

He had walked out from the shadows, brandishing a German Luger. "Get off your horses and lie flat on the ground, or I will shoot him first," he said, pointing at Sonny. "Dead or alive, it doesn't matter, but you both are worth more alive to the Gestapo."

"Over my dead body will you get us dead or alive, you bastard," Sonny screamed at him.

Sonny had killed his comrade, and then trampled him with his horse.

When he awoke, Sergio had a fractured bone in his arm and some bruises. Hearing the sound of gunfire to the southeast, he was startled as a single-engine plane roared past him, just feet above the treetops.

He would have his revenge.

Now, a few weeks later, Sergio entered the German Embassy in Madrid on the same day the *évadés* were being briefed by the British. Producing his travel documents and orders from the Gestapo, he was escorted into a private office, where he handed a well-dressed man his papers.

"Señor Garcia, how can I be of assistance?" the man asked.

"Heir Bowman, as you can see by my orders, I am searching for a Frenchman by the name of Henri Gibert and his accomplice Madeleine. It would be quite helpful if you can provide me with weapons and contacts in the area to help me hunt them down."

"Señor Garcia, I will have them contact you. You are staying at the Hotel Ritz, are you not?" Bowman asked.

"Yes. I will be expecting them, Heir Bowman. Thank you for the assistance," Sergio replied.

"My spy network has uncovered a safe house in Huesca owned by a man named Javier Gomez, a clothier by trade," Bowman said. "The Abwehr are attempting to turn him. His family is being asked to convince him of the error of his ways.

"So the solution should be an easy task for you." Bowman chuckled. "I have allocated 2,500 pesetas for this job. Please see my clerk, in the office by the door."

Sergio got up to leave, thanking Heir Bowman for all his help, but was abruptly stopped by the German.

"Why are these people so important to you, Sergio? When the Third Reich conquers the world, they can be dealt with later," Heir Bowman said.

"Two reasons. My cover has been revealed, and I want to eliminate them before MI-6 discovers this. If they are killed now, at least they cannot counter my claims of innocence."

"The second reason?" Bowman asked.

"Personal vengeance," Sergio said. Excusing himself, he left.

Hours later, driving in a black Packard sedan given to him by the German Embassy, Sergio made his way into Huesca. Staying at a local Abwehr agent's house, he made his way to the clothier shop of Javier Gomez. He arrived through an alleyway just in time to see the *évadés* file into the shop in pairs, carefully scanning the main street for any signs that they were observed. They didn't check the alley as he slid back into the shadows.

It was after midnight when Javier walked into that same alley behind his shop to meet with Sergio.

"Why are you doing this to my family, Sergio?" Javier asked.

"Your family will be safe, if you do as I say," Sergio replied.

"What must I do?" Javier asked.

"I want to know where Henri and Madeleine are headed and who they are going to see," Sergio said. If I could catch more agents, the better my status will be in Berlin, he thought.

With no other choice, Javier betrayed the *évadés*. He explained that they were going to Algeciras via train from San Sebastian and then on to Gibraltar.

"See now, wasn't that easy?" Sergio said. "If you want your family alive when this is over, you will not say a word to any of your Allied contacts, *está claro*?"

"Sí," he replied.

"Now get back before they suspect anything," Sergio instructed Javier.

Bastardo, Javier thought, making his way back to the shop. His stomach was in knots. He was fearful for his family.

Sergio was proud of himself. Touching the bandages wrapped around his fractured arm, he thought, Now, Henri, you and your friends will die.

A COLD DISH

The man in the alley who spied Jack and Emily on their first night in Paris at the Hotel de Sévigné flew to Madrid. Contemplating the situation, he thought, Jean has trained a couple of fools!

Getting off the plane, he rented an Ebro Jeep Comando. They must be on the trail for the Doomsday Book, he thought. I'll head northeast toward Esterri d'Aneu for my rendezvous with them.

Emily and Jack landed in Barcelona and rented a four-wheel drive Land Rover for the drive to Esterri d'Aneu. The first priority was to find the Doomsday Book. The map they found in the mountain passes would guide them to its location. Riding through the beautiful Spanish countryside, they remained quiet, remembering Eugène, the Frenchman who had guided them to this point.

"This is a rotten business, Jack," Emily said.

"I know. But I can't see myself doing anything else, Em, not after Dad's death," Jack replied.

"Me either, actually, but it's still hard to watch someone die who you've made friends with," she said.

"Like Eugène? I guess then we shouldn't make friends," Jack said.

"Easy for you to say. I can't be that cold, Jack," Emily said. "Maybe I am not cut out for this."

"Well, the way I see it, Em, it's nice to work with you," Jack said.

Emily kissed Jack on the cheek. Looking down at her map and pointing to her right, she said, "Jack, there's the dirt road leading to the goat herder's cave."

Turning onto the dirt road, dust encompassing the car, they headed off in a northwesterly direction. The road was rough, but they managed to remain out of the deeper ruts.

"Thank God it's not raining," Jack said. "We would be stuck in knee-deep mud."

Glancing to his right, Jack saw a clown in yellow peddling alongside the SUV. The clown waved to Jack, laughing as he did so.

"What the hell is that?" Jack said, pointing to the clown.

"What?" Emily said, looking to her right. "I don't see anything, Jack."

Jack looked again. The clown was gone.

"It was nothing, just dust playing tricks on my eyes," Jack said.

I am losing it, he thought.

Traveling for about forty-five minutes, they saw an abandoned farmhouse in the distance.

"Jack, I think that's the place. Pull over," Emily said.

"That has to be the one Charlène talked about. She said the cave was around the bend from the lean-to where the farmers kept the goats."

"Certainly looks like it could have been a lean-to, but it's just a pile of rotted wood now," Emily observed.

Getting out of the car, they walked up to the broken-down lean-to to search for clues. Finding nothing of interest, they walked around back of the dilapidated structure to find overgrown shrubs in front of a rock face.

"It has to be behind the shrubs," Jack said, making his way into the thick growth.

"I'll wait here," Emily said.

"Gee, thanks," Jack replied.

Pushing through, Jack came to some boards, collapsed in front of an opening.

"Found it. Let me clear away the boards blocking the entrance," Jack said.

After a few moments of pulling away the shrubs covering the entrance, Jack began clearing a way into the entrance. Satisfied he had made a sufficient opening, he called back for Emily.

Inside the cave they could see various household items: cots, pots, pans, and old bags of grain that had holes chewed through them.

The cave was littered with old, broken furniture. Rusted pots and pans hung from a wall. On one side, books, intermixed with rusted cans, sat on sagging shelves. Cobwebs and a layer of dust covered everything.

"Great. Rats, I bet." Emily winced.

"And maybe a snake or two," Jack teased her, making her jump to his side. "See if you can find anything."

Looking around for any sign of the book, Jack did not know where to begin.

In the meantime, Emily began searching the kitchen area, and she saw something covered with grime that looked like a tube on one of the makeshift shelves.

Pulling the tube out from amid crumbling books, she popped open the latch, and a rolled-up parchment spilled out onto her hand.

"Jack, are we looking for a book or a scroll?" Emily asked, inspecting the metal tube.

"Anything that resembles a book, I guess," Jack said.

"I ask because I just found a scroll rolled up in a metal canister or something that looks like a tube. You know, the kind large enough to roll a poster into. But what I found, well, it's not a book. It just looks out of place in all of this junk. It's not a book, it's several scrolls." She grinned, holding an ancient parchment in her hands.

"Let's have a look at it," Jack asked, holding out his hand.

Slowly and carefully unrolling the ancient text, Jack looked perplexed.

"What's wrong, Jack?" Emily asked.

"This scroll feels odd, it feels new, not aged. It also has these weird holes in it, but they aren't random. They look like they were designed to be there." Jack thought for a moment, examining the parchment. "Of course! Remember, Eugène said that they fit together like a puzzle? I never thought he meant it to be literal!" Jack exclaimed excitedly.

Examining the other scrolls, they found the same designed holes, each with a different pattern.

"Jack, there are chemical structures on some of these scrolls, and from what I can make out, they are for very dangerous substances," Emily said.

"As in what, Em?" Jack asked.

"Neurotoxins and things that would make the Black Death look like a common cold. It would take too long to explain how all this works, but it's safe to say they are deadly."

"I think I know how they fit together," Jack said. "The machines that Van whatshisname drew up had odd patterns and discrepancies in their design too, and I bet these designs on the scrolls match up."

"So you're saying that these deadly chemicals go into his machines?" Emily asked. "Jack, we have to destroy these scrolls. In the wrong hands, they could be used to wreak havoc on the world."

"OK, that sounded a bit corny there, Em, but you're right. Let's start a fire outside and burn these things," Jack said.

Making their way outside, Jack piled some wood up tepee-style, stuffing twigs underneath for kindling. Taking one of their roadside maps, he tore it into small pieces, crumpling each one, and pushed them inside the kindling pile.

Removing a lighter from his pocket, Jack lit the map pieces on fire. The dry kindling caught fire quickly. Fifteen minutes later, the fire was blazing nicely.

Jack grabbed one scroll and tossed it onto the fire.

Nothing happened.

"Why aren't they burning?" Jack asked.

"Didn't you say they felt funny?" Emily replied, taking out another scroll and feeling the texture.

"You don't suppose they could be fireproof, do you?" Jack asked. "Because if they are, it makes sense that MI-6 never destroyed these scrolls—they couldn't."

"Jack, what do we do?" Emily asked.

"We get these back to Jean. In the meantime, we should replace these with some fakes. How's your chemistry, Em?"

"I am not sure I can re-create this, Jack, especially here," Emily said.

"Let's take a picture of this and send it to Jean," Jack said. "Maybe he can have some good copies drawn up for us."

Emily agreed. "Good idea. I have just the tools to do it myself. I hope it convinces whoever is after this. I haven't drawn structures since I was in the lab," Emily replied.

Jack rolled out the scroll and had Emily hold it in place on the ground while he took a picture. He typed in a message and sent the photo directly to Jean's phone. In a few moments, Jack received a reply that the papers would be delivered to their hotel room.

After scattering and stamping out the fire, Jack and Emily got in the car and headed back the way they came. The sun was setting on the horizon behind them, and shadows began to creep onto the dirt road. Rounding a bend in the road around a small rock outcropping, the sudden roar of an engine caught Jack's attention, but too late. Almost instantly after, a truck slammed into the side of their Land Rover. Jack recovered quickly, pushing the pedal to the floor as rocks and dirt flew all around them.

Speeding down the dirt trail, Jack saw the truck back up and turn in their direction. It spun out briefly, but the driver regained control. The unknown assailant was in pursuit.

"Jack, who is that?" Emily cried out, looking back but seeing only the outline of the truck in clouds of dust.

"I don't know, but I'll bet whoever it is, they aren't on our side!" Jack shouted above the roar of the engine.

They maneuvered as best they could down the rough, uneven road to get away from the pursuing truck, but the distance between them was closing fast. They rounded another corner with a deep gully to their right. The truck was able to get on Jack's left side and was nudging the Land Rover on the bumper, trying to cause a spinout into the ravine.

Jack remembered his training. He said, "Hold on, Em. I'm gonna try to flip him."

Jack waited until the truck was adjacent to them. He knew the driver was going to try and bump him again. Tapping the brakes, he turned the wheel left and hit the right rear of the truck. The truck spun perpendicular to the road and flipped over several times, skidding, and landed upside down in the ravine.

Jack slammed on the brakes. Both he and Emily jumped out of the Land Rover, pistols drawn. Making their way down the ravine, they cautiously approached the smoking truck. The man in the driver's seat slowly crawled through the broken window, dragging a broken left arm behind him. They recognized him immediately. It was Eugène!

"Eugène, we thought you were dead!" Jack asked. "We saw your body being removed from your apartment."

"How could you do this to us?" Emily screamed at him.

Dragging himself to an upright position, his left arm grotesquely out of position, he said, "Because Garcia paid me more. Give me the book and he will let you all go free."

"Eugène, who was on that stretcher at your house? We thought you were dead," Jack asked.

Eugène spat out blood. "That was a Pond agent. He had discovered my betrayal, so I killed him."

"Where is Marie, Eugène? Tell me or I swear I will put a bullet in your head," Jack shouted.

"You can kill me, but that will do you no good," Eugène said. "I am a dead already for failing to acquire the book."

"Where is Marie?" Jack raised his pistol to Eugène's head.

Eugène, ever the survivalist, quickly divulged the address in Paris where Marie was held.

"Thank you, Eugène," Jack said, raising the pistol once more, but Emily put her hand on his arm.

"I have a better idea, Jack," Emily said.

Alone in the cave, Eugène's good right arm was tied to one of the support beams that creaked with his every movement, a knife just out of reach of his broken arm. In the distance, the sirens of the Spanish police could be heard approaching the cave.

Later that evening, Emily and Jack arrived at the Barcelona airport, filled out the insurance papers for the accident, and flew back to Paris.

Skipping the hotel, Jack and Emily drove a rented car to the address Eugène had given them. As they approached the warehouse, Jack turned off the headlights. Then they waited.

Around 1:00 AM, the doors to the warehouse opened, and a limo drove away.

"Should we follow them, Jack?" Emily asked.

"No. They have no idea we got the address from Eugène, and he isn't going anywhere," Jack replied. "Marie has to be in there. Let's find a way in."

Sneaking down a side alley, they approached the warehouse with caution.

"Good, no cameras," Jack said. "Let's try that stairwell over there." He pointed to old rusty steps on the outside of the building.

Climbing to the second floor, they stood in front of an old door. Jack tried the knob and found it unlocked.

"Garcia's not much for security, is he?" Jack whispered.

"We still have to be careful, Jack. Marie is in there," she whispered back.

The second floor was a gangway that went around the entire warehouse. It was probably used by management to view the operations of the warehouse during business hours, Jack thought. A black sedan sat in the middle of the warehouse. A colorfully dressed clown on a bright-red tricycle was riding around the car.

Jack blinked his eyes in disbelief. A clown? he thought. What the hell is going on here? He turned to look at Emily and pointed to the clown.

"What, Jack?" she whispered.

"You see that?" he whispered back.

Turning around, the clown was gone. I must be tired, he thought. I'm seeing things.

He stared at the car until Emily tapped his shoulder, motioning for him to get moving.

Working their way around in the shadows on the walkway, they saw a man unlock a bolt on a steel door. He opened it and disappeared inside pushing a cart.

Jack pointed to the scene, motioning for them to circle around above the door. Moving unseen, the two got above the doorway to where Marie was confined just as the guard came out with the cart.

"Cover me," Jack mouthed to Emily, leaping over the rail and landing on top of the man. He knocked the man against the cement floor so hard that the man was killed instantly, his neck broken.

Jack spotted Garcia making a run for it to the black sedan. Garcia jumped in the car and started the engine, tires squealing as he hit the gas. Jack and Emily fired on the car, but the bullets bounced off and Garcia escaped, crashing through the old warehouse doors. I don't understand, Jack thought in the heat of the moment. Why are the bullets bouncing off? This car does not look like it's armored.

Jack quickly moved to Marie's prison and threw open the steel door. The shadowy figure of a woman stood beside a wheelchair, holding a knife to Marie's throat.

"Stop or I will slit her throat!" she warned. "Now drop your gun or she dies!"

"Just let her go," Jack said to the woman, focusing on the dimly lit room.

The sudden realization of who he faced hit Jack like a truck. It was Gisele!

"I thought you were dead!" Jack said.

Laughing, Gisele replied, "When you try to kill someone, make sure they are dead!"

"I should just shoot you now," Jack growled.

"You might get me, Jack, but more likely you will kill your friend. Are you willing to take that risk?" Gisele asked. "Now slide your gun over to me."

Jack had no choice. Dropping his pistol, he slid it to her. He watched it as it spun across the cement floor.

Slowly Gisele limped over to the gun, picking it up.

Jack said, "I have the book. Let her go and I'll give it to you."

"Let me see it, Turner," Gisele said.

Jack pulled out the faux scroll.

"That's the book? No one said it was a scroll," Gisele said. "No matter. Just set it down on the floor and back up. Now where is your wife, Jack? You two are never apart."

"She's outside in the car waiting for me," Jack said.

"A shame. I would have loved to see her face. But I have a flight to catch, so drop the scroll and move to the corner behind that desk," she said.

Pulling Marie along with her, Gisele grabbed the scroll and glared at Jack. Moving to the doorway, she looked at Jack. "This is for all the pain you caused me, Jack," she said. Pulling the trigger, Gisele put two bullets in Marie's back and then dropped her limp body onto the floor. Before Jack could respond, Gisele shut the door and locked the bolt in place.

Jack cried out, running over to Marie.

Coughing up blood, Marie said, "Jack, I am sorry."

Staring at the steel door, Gisele could hear Jack yell out to Marie. The thought of his pain made her smile.

Turning around, Gisele was startled to see Emily pointing a pistol at her head.

"Well, I see the housewife knows how to hold a gun," Gisele said. "But can she use it?"

"You bet I can, bitch!" Emily said as she emptied her magazine into Gisele. She was dead before she hit the floor.

Emily jumped over the dead neo-Nazi, slid the bolt, and threw open the door. Jack was on his knees inside, cradling Marie's head. He had his head buried in her shoulder, softly weeping. As he raised his head to look at Emily, he caught a glimpse of the clown on the bicycle, still riding around inside the warehouse. This is all too confusing and sad, Jack thought.

***

Marie was buried at her grandmother's estate in the French countryside. Jean flew in from Virginia to pay his respects.

Jack asked to speak at the funeral. He spoke of Marie's bravery and her service to her country. He told everyone that she lived her life her way, never compromising her integrity and always looking out for her fellow co-workers.

After paying their respects to Marie's family, Jean drove Jack and Emily to Henri's house in Pas-de-Calais.

Arriving in the evening, Jean stood near the entryway of an old cave. "This is where your father distributed his radios to the partisans."

"Hallowed ground for me, Jean. Those must have been tough times," Jack replied.

"I brought you both back here, to the beginning, so you could understand why I do this, why you should continue to do this. It was very important to your father to fight this evil. It is an eternal struggle, which you cannot give up."

"We have no intention of giving up, Jean," Emily said. "Don't think I could ever work in the corporate world again."

"I am glad to hear that. Now let's go inside. The stars may be beautiful, but it's cold outside," Jean said.

They sat by the same fireplace where Henri, Antoinette, and Robbie warmed themselves many years ago. Jean told tales of heroes and hard times in occupied France and stories about his father.

"*Les bosch* burned this house to the ground during the war," Jean said. "After we were liberated, Henri came back here and rebuilt it. This fireplace is all that remains of the original building."

"I can imagine my father sitting here, waiting to deliver radios for the partisans," Jack said.

They sat quietly and enjoyed the fire.

Around 11:00 PM, Jean said he was tired and going to bed. He got up and made his way upstairs to his bedroom. About halfway up, Jack stopped him. "What about Garcia?"

"We will discuss how to deal with him tomorrow, but for now, enjoy the fire and get some rest," Jean said.

Jack and Emily fell asleep that night by a crackling fire, her head resting on his shoulder.

The next morning, Jean led them into the faux fireplace that led to the cave below the house. It had been transformed into an operations center for The Pond. French intelligence and Pond agents used it frequently.

Picking up the scrolls, Jean studied them as if trying to decide what his course of action against Garcia would be.

"Garcia must never get his hands on these scrolls," Jean said.

"What's the plan?" Jack asked.

Jean explained, "I have information that he will be on a train out of Paris to Toulouse in a week on business. I want you two to be on that train and take care of him before he leaves the country. Once he is in Spain, he can disappear through his network of spies and safe houses."

They planned over the next few days, working out methods of terminating Garcia as well as alternatives. Jean had makeup artists come to the study and disguise both Jack and Emily, changing their appearances drastically.

Jack turned to Emily. "Does this nose make my eyebrows look too bushy?" He grinned.

"No, Cyrano, why?" Emily said.

"Are you both ready to go?" Jean asked. "Here are your tickets," he said, handing them two pieces of paper. "They were purchased right here in this farmhouse, using *mon ordinateur*. *L'internet* is something efficient, *n'est ce pas*?"

Emily quickly took the tickets from Jean and stuffed them in her purse.

Jack had a frown on his face, still holding out his hand to get his ticket.

She said to Jean, "He loses these all the time."

"Are you staying, Jean?" Jack asked.

"For a brief time," he replied. "I will monitor the mission from the cave. Call me as soon as you have taken care of Garcia."

"Will do," they both replied.

Jack and Emily got into the car provided by Jean and drove away from the farm.

Watching them drive down the paved road, Jean thought, This place has changed.

Jean smiled and turned to go back inside. "Go get 'em, cowboys."

Arriving at the train station in Paris, the couple made their way to their train.

A sudden bright flash of light momentarily blinded Jack. He blinked his eyes. He was in a brightly lit room.

"Jack," Emily said.

"Sorry, got dizzy for a moment," he replied.

"What are you talking about, Jack?" Emily said, turning around to face him.

"Um, nothing. I must be tired," he replied.

They boarded the train searching for Garcia but didn't see him. Making their way forward, Jack spotted him sitting in the first coach car after the locomotive. They sat in their assigned seats until the train began to leave the station.

Seeing that the seat beside Garcia was empty, Emily decided to make a move and motioned for Jack to follow. Garcia was in an aisle seat, and Emily asked if she could have a seat next to him. Garcia watched her take the seat, admiring her legs as she slid by him.

Garcia looked up and stared at Emily's face. He recognized her!

Emily reacted quickly. She knew she was compromised. She pulled the syringe from her jacket, but Garcia saw this and grabbed her arm, stopping the needle, just inches away.

Jack, seeing the struggle, quickly moved in with his syringe and punctured Garcia's carotid artery, draining the poisonous fluid into him.

Garcia shoved them down into the aisle. Jack and Emily were entangled on the floor. Garcia struggled toward the engine compartment and banged on the door.

No one moved on the train. That's odd, Jack thought. They all calmly watched the scene unfold before them.

The engineer opened the door when he saw blood on Garcia's neck, thinking there had been an accident. He was surprised when Garcia grabbed him and threw him into the passenger compartment atop Jack and Emily before closing the door behind him and locking it.

Jack tried to open the door, but it was secured, and Garcia was at the computer monitor in the engine compartment typing at the keyboard.

"How do we open that door?" Jack asked the engineer.

"We can't from this side, *señor*. He has total control," the engineer said.

Hey, wait a minute, Jack thought. Why is he speaking in Spanish? Aren't we in France? Emily's voice made him turn.

"There is nothing we can do?" Emily asked.

"*Nada*," he replied.

The train began to speed up, rapidly attaining its maximum speed of 186 miles per hour. Inside Garcia slumped over the computer console. The poison had finally reached his heart.

"Let's go," Jack said. "I need to get to the command console."

The train continued to pick up speed. Emily and Jack had a hard time maintaining their balance as the passenger cars rocked violently. The passengers inside continued to sit quietly as Jack and Emily tried to open the engine compartment door.

What the hell? Jack thought, puzzled by their composure.

"Jack, we are going too fast. It feels like this train is going to crash. What did Garcia do?" Emily asked.

"He probably disabled some safety override that controls the speed. We have to get the engine uncoupled and quickly!" Jack said.

"Is there a manual override to uncouple the engine?" Jack asked the engineer.

"*Si*, there is a manual lever behind us," the engineer replied.

They went back inside the accordion passage behind them. The engineer opened a panel and threw a lever. Nothing happened.

"Why didn't it work?" Jack shouted above the wind.

"It is controlled by a computer inside the cab to prevent inadvertent uncoupling of the engine," he informed them. "Normally it is set to the off position once the train is in motion. He must have turned it on."

Pulling out his pistol, Jack aimed at the lock.

"Jack, no!" Emily yelled above the howling of the locomotive reaching top speed.

The round ricocheted past Emily, who took out her pistol and shot out the window to the control room. Reaching inside, she unlatched the lock and opened the door.

Pushing the body of Garcia off the console, Jack explained quickly, "Emily, this is a maglev train. It uses magnetic levitation to suspend, guide, and propel vehicles from magnets rather than using mechanical methods. In addition, the magnets create both lift and thrust, only a few inches above the rail," Jack explained. "There is no need for an operator, since all these systems are computer controlled. Besides, at the extremely high speeds of these systems, no human operator could react fast enough to slow down or stop in time." How did I know that? Jack asked himself. This is getting scary, he thought.

"Wait, where did the engineer go?" Jack asked.

"He must have gone to the rear of the train. Jack, what are you getting at? We need to stop this train!" Emily said.

Then Jack suddenly started to tell Emily more about the train, to his own surprise. "Two maglev system microwave towers are in contact with an EMS vehicle at all times for two-way communication between the vehicle and the central command center's main operations computer. Garcia must have overrode the communications system too. We have no way of stopping this train unless I can find what he did in the computer console," Jack replied.

This time, Jack didn't have time to question himself. He just worked feverishly, going through all the menus on the console. He needed a password now, and he started to enter every word he could think of, but nothing worked.

"Jack, hurry! The train is approaching Toulouse too fast," Emily said.

"Toulouse? How can that happen? We just got on the train. We're still too far away," Jack said. How could this be? Jack wondered.

I can't access the system. I need to find that password, Jack thought. Wait! The past few weeks flashed in front of him, and he knew he had found the word. He typed OCCAM'S RAZOR in all caps, and a new menu popped up. "Got it," Jack said proudly. "If I can find the brake command, this thing will stop on a dime, but everything is in Spanish. Damn, I should have paid attention in class!" Jack said. Spanish? Isn't this a French train? Jack thought. What is going on?

Jack pressed several commands, finding the one to uncouple the cars behind them. The cars disconnected, but Jack and Emily couldn't get to the retreating car in time to jump to safety. Jack knew he had to stop this engine! But what about Emily? He had to get her to safety.

The train closed in on the station. Its platforms were crowded with commuters. Emily paced impatiently. "Jack, hurry!" she cried out. "We don't have time for this!"

Turning to the panel above the computer console, Emily opened the compartment. It was a mass of wires. Grabbing a handful, she yanked and pulled hard, and the computer screen went blank. The locomotive sped ahead, crashing into the crowded platform. Jack heard the sound of steel bending and glass shattering, and screams filled the air. And then Jack turned to see if Emily was alive.

The world came back into view through brilliant shards of light as Jack gradually was able to focus on Emily's angelic face.

"Jack, you're back. Thank God," Emily said.

"What happened? We were on the train, and I heard you scream as we were about to crash, and that's all I remember," Jack said.

"Jack, what are you talking about? What train?"

Jack was baffled. "The train that Garcia trapped us on. You know. You were there!"

"Jack, you have been in a coma for several months, ever since Garcia shot you at the bar," Emily said. "The doctors didn't think you would ever come out of it."

"Wait, Tommy is Tomas Garcia who shot you in the head. Am I going crazy? This did happen, didn't it?" Jack asked.

"Did what happen? Tommy never shot me, Jack. Apparently Garcia was robbing the High Tide when we saw him," Emily said. "You had a serious head wound. The doctors did not expect you to recover. The hospital thinks I live here because I'm here almost all the time"

"I am still confused. None of this happened? No Garcia, no Vargas, no Marie?" Jack asked.

"Who are Vargas and Marie? Unless I am going crazy, then no, whatever you are talking about never happened," Emily said.

Jack was rambling now. "Em, we saw Gisele. She was in a wheelchair. You killed her!"

"Jack, you're confused. Gisele is dead. You were probably in a coma-induced dream state," Emily replied.

"Wow, I can't believe none of this actually happened," Jack said. "You were a spy, working with me to save the world. It all seems so surreal now, almost like some spy movie!"

Kissing Jack on the forehead, Emily said, "I am unfortunately still working at the same company."

A woman with an eye patch appeared in the doorway of Jack's hospital room and leaned on her cane.

"Hi, can I help you?" Emily asked her.

"I am sorry to bother you," she said with a faint foreign accent. "When I heard that Jack was awake, I came as soon as I could."

"I'm sorry, but why would you be interested in Jack? Have you been hospitalized as long as he has? Do you know him?" Emily asked.

"Forgive me," the woman said, "but, if I am right, I believe Jack knows who I am, *n'est pas*, Jack?"

Emily watched as Jack's eyes lit up as if recognizing an old friend after years of being apart.

"Charlène?" Jack asked.

"Yes, Jack, I am Charlène... Charlène Shemesh," the woman said, closing the door to Jack's room behind her.

She approached Jack's bed with a pronounced limp and smiled at Emily. "Ah, *mes enfants*, I am glad to meet you both. We have much to discuss."

Familia

Early the next morning, Nigel Willingham, British *Chargé d'Affaires*, presented the group their official papers, designating them as citizens of the British Empire. For the two Americans, he produced similar papers designating them as members of the American ambassador's staff in Madrid. Everyone, including Charlène and André, was given clean fresh clothes for the train trip to Cadiz.

"Remember to present your papers should any Spanish officials ask you for them. Do not show your papers to anyone else. You will all travel on the same train, but I would separate into smaller groups. It's less conspicuous that way," the *Chargé d'Affaires* instructed.

"What about Sergio?" Robertson asked. "Won't he try something along the way?"

"I seriously doubt he would do anything while you are on the train. As a Nazi sympathizer, he would not want to attract the attention of the Spanish government," Willingham said, "especially since his alliances during the civil war were with the Republican government. If captured, he would be thrown into their worst jail to rot and die. If he were to try anything, it would be at Cadiz after you get off the train."

"Will we have difficulty crossing to Gibraltar?" Madeleine asked.

"No, I have informed the commander of the Gibraltar garrison that guests will be arriving tomorrow night," the *Chargé d'Affaires* said.

"The good thing is that, earlier this year, the situation changed. Gibraltar's installations were a prime target for sabotage by the Abwehr, using sympathetic anti-British Spanish workers. Just this past January, two Spanish workers, convicted of attempted sabotage, were executed. We have managed to use turned agents and sympathetic anti-Fascist Spaniards to uncover subsequent attacks," he said. "Recently, one of our double agents provided enough information to make a detailed protest to the Spanish government of the Abwehr operations near Gibraltar. As a result, the Spanish government declared its *strict neutrality*. The Abwehr operation in southern Spain has been closed down."

"Well that's good news. Should be clear sailing!" the lieutenant exclaimed.

"I hope for your sake it is, Lieutenant. Now you should all be off to the train station," Willingham instructed. "I have two cars waiting outside to take you there."

That day, as Javier pulled up to his shop after the long trip back from San Sebastian, he spied a window broken on the side alley as he drove in to park his truck. Cautiously opening the shop's back door, he peered inside, but nothing seemed amiss. *Niños*, he thought. They are always causing trouble in the streets. I'll have to fix that today, but first I need a nice cup of tea by the fire to relax.

Every trip taking *évadés* to the British was harrowing for him. Spies abounded everywhere and were always watching the comings and goings of vehicles and people into the embassy. He always watched if he was followed, normally losing those who tried anyway on the back roads if needed. But now Sergio's family had been threatened, and he hoped that the *évadés* would make a successful escape, even though he had betrayed them.

Time for that later, he mused. I need to contact Sergio to secure the safety of my *familia*. Once I can get them into hiding out of the country, if there is time, I can warn the British about Sergio's plans.

Entering the kitchen, he started the wood-burning stove, filled the teapot with water, and set it on the blackened top. Adjusting the wood logs to spark a flame, he went back to the cabinet and reached for the tea stored in a metal container. He felt a sharp pain in his lower back and instantly thought he pulled that muscle again. Annoyed with himself that he pulled his back out, he suddenly realized something warm and sticky was running down his leg. He reached down, touching the liquid. Bringing his hand back into view, he realized it was blood.

Sergio removed the knife from Javier's lower back and sliced across his neck with a quick flick of his wrist as Javier turned to face him. Javier, mortally wounded, grabbed his throat and fell to the floor, slowly bleeding to death.

Sergio reached into his coat pocket and dropped an identity card next to Javier.

As Javier's life slowly left his body, he watched as Sergio made bloody boot prints across his clean kitchen floor.

Two days later when the police were investigating the murder of Javier Gomez, they found an identity card belonging to Henri.

Further to the east, Emilio Diaz, a.k.a., John Smythe, stared blankly out the windshield of his truck, a bullet neatly drilled into his left temple. Later that week in the offices of MI-6 in Scotland, Major Scotty Smythe crumpled the telegram in his hand from the War Office, having received the news of his brother's demise in Spain.

At the train station, the *évadés* separated into three groups: Henri, Madeleine, and Charlène went as a family, Lieutenant Robertson, Antoinette, and André went as another, and Françoise and Sergeant Waldron acted as a young married couple. In each group they had one person who was fluent in Spanish as well as French. It was determined that they should all sit in the last coach car on the train, in case there was any trouble.

"I've never been on a train." Charlène hesitated at the steps.

"N'ais pas peur, ma chérie," Madeleine commented.

The conductor was holding out his hand.

They boarded, handing their tickets to the impatient and flustered conductor.

Madeleine and Henri both breathed a sigh of relief as they sought out a secluded section of the train.

Opening the door to their compartment, Madeleine closed the red-velvet curtains mounted on the doorway, while Henri peered out from behind the plush curtains, waiting for the others. Soon all the *évadés* were inside the same compartment, and Henri locked the door from the inside.

The tickets they had received were for a nonstop trip all the way to Algeciras in southeastern Spain, very close to Gibraltar. In Algeciras, they would be picked up by two cars belonging to the British Embassy Service and taken into Gibraltar. Once in those cars, they would not stop until they were safely inside the British Empire.

The group was relieved as the train only slowed down through Madrid, being redirected to another track. The sites of the ancient city were magnificent. Great Romanesque buildings passed by their window. World War II had not touched this place like it had London, Berlin, and Rotterdam; Madrid had remained untouched by the ravages of the war.

"C'est très beau," Madeleine sadly noted. "I hope Paris is beautiful once we have won the war."

They all stared in silence as the great city slowly passed from view, gradually revealing farmlands. As they made their way south, their spirits began to rise. They were now only hours away from true freedom from the oppression they had suffered in France. The trip took approximately ten hours, but the railcar compartment gave a sense of security to their flight.

Having driven all day and into the night to Taraguilla, a twelve-hour trip, Sergio had time to devise a plan.

Taraguilla was established in ancient Roman times where one of the Roman roads included in the so-called Antonine Route was situated. Now, almost two thousand years later, in 1944, it was a major railway hub in southern Spain.

With his 2,500 pesetas, Sergio secured enough materials to make a bomb to blow the river crossing over the Rio Guadarranque. Sergio knew he had only one chance to stop the *évadés* before they reached the safety of Gibraltar. Without stopping to rest, he climbed down the steep embankment with his backpack of explosives.

Down below, amid the steel piers that held up the bridge, Sergio found a set of piers and abutments made of wood. The government-run railroad company, Red Nacional de los Ferrocarriles Españoles, or RENFE for short, never finished the project of replacing all the wood supports with steel. This is going to be easy, he thought.

Planting explosives on a wooden pier and on the abutment, he tied the two together with fuse.

Patiently Sergio waited for the train to approach. According to the local tavern owner, they should be crossing the bridge at or around 10:00 AM. He planned to time the fuse so the explosives would blow the piers and abutment just as the locomotive crossed the midpoint of the bridge, so that there would be no survivors.

The train would approach the bridge on a sweeping curve to the east. From his viewpoint, Sergio could see the train long before it arrived.

The hot summer sun rose slowly as Sergio waited under the bridge by the riverbank. The explosives had been set, but they were sweating in the rising temperature of the unforgiving Spanish sun.

Sergio knew that over time the dynamite would sweat nitroglycerin. Crystals would form on the outside of the sticks causing them to be even more shock, friction, or temperature sensitive.

I knew I shouldn't have bought them from the black market, he thought. Old dynamite is very dangerous. Nevertheless, he thought, I have enough explosives here to cause the train to fall if there is one among them that fails me.

Off in the distance, Sergio heard a low rumble that got louder, and, seconds afterward, felt the tracks above him vibrate. Quickly glancing around the corner of the wooden abutment, he saw the locomotive heading for the bridge. He lit the fuses.

Charlène awoke as the train slowed to approach the village of Taraguilla, where the track split southeast to Gibraltar and southwest toward the coastal town of Algeciras. Up ahead a beautiful old wooden bridge appeared on the horizon stretching out and over the Rio Guadarranque.

Lieutenant Robertson took in the serene scene with a bit of melancholy. He had lost two people under his command.

Nothing he could do would bring back Tony or Armand. He must at least get the rest through. Almost dreamlike, he saw a great puff of smoke and timber rise up from the picturesque bridge and a section collapse in a cloud of dust below. Immediately the train lurched, sending those facing the bridge forward as the breaks of the train strained, squealing loudly, in an attempt to stop the forward motion.

"Everyone brace for impact!" Lieutenant Robertson yelled. "Get down on the floor. We may have a chance yet."

The engineer in the locomotive looked on in horror as the rails at mid bridge fell away before him, explosions echoing in his ears. He thought of his wife and children as the engine plummeted into the river, the g-forces of the impact ripping his body apart. Behind him the screams could be heard for miles.

The train's engine did not stop in time as it plummeted into the river below, the deafening explosion of cold water and steam shattering the cars that followed it into hundreds of pieces. The screams of the passengers could be heard over the snapping of steel and wood as the railroad cars approached the drop.

The train car in front of the escapee's coach car skidded to a stop sideways on what remained intact of the bridge. The car behind them slammed into the first, stopping its forward movement, but that action pushed that coach sideways and over the edge. The screams of the terrified passengers faded as the car tumbled into the river below. Their coach now careened off the track and tilted twenty-five degrees to the right, leaning precariously toward the embankment that dropped a few hundred feet below to the river.

Collecting themselves, seeing that no one was injured, they pulled open the door of their compartment and made their way to the back of the car. Seeing that the doorway was damaged, the door crumbled in the frame, Lieutenant Robertson went across to the left side of the coach car. Opening a door, he saw a well-dressed man in his seventies sitting there, eyes staring upward, head tilted at a grotesque angle, his neck obviously broken from the impact. Taking a nearby blanket, he quickly covered the man's face as he waved the group into the small room. Grabbing a metallic pitcher from the floor, he smashed open the damaged window and climbed out. As he did, the car slid slightly toward the embankment.

"Quickly, hand me Charlène!" the lieutenant commanded. "Everybody get out now!"

Billy Waldron stayed in the car assisting all the others out of the broken window.

"Come on, Billy, let's go," the lieutenant directed his sergeant. "Get out of there!"

"Sure, LT," Billy said with a smile and reached for Robertson's outstretched hand.

Everyone watched in horror as the coach car shuddered and fell. The lieutenant screamed as Billy's outstretched hand fell away with the mass of crumbling steel and glass to the river below.

Lieutenant Robertson sat against the embankment in shock for several minutes. Sergeant Billy Waldron, having miraculously survived battle after battle with him, was dead.

Antoinette came over and sat by Robbie, her head resting on his massive shoulder, softly crying.

"Let's get to Gibraltar," the lieutenant choked out.

***

Sergio watched in satisfaction from a distance as the locomotive plunged into the river, great rivulets of steam filling the river valley, the ground beneath his feet vibrating from the violent explosion. He beamed as the first passenger cars plunged into the river but was disappointed to see two of them survive. Hopefully they are all dead, he thought. But in case they survived, I should go to La Línea to prevent their escape to Gibraltar.

Driving away in his car, he got onto the main highway heading east to San Roque and then southeast through Puente Mayorga and into the city of La Línea de la Concepción, more commonly known simply as La Línea, or "boundary line," in Spanish. It was often referred to as the Gateway to Gibraltar.

***

Resting on the embankment, they watched as a crowd began to gather. On the nearby highway, cars and trucks began to stop to see the train wreck. Others who had survived were asking for rides into nearby La Línea to get to a local medical station.

"We should try to get a ride into La Línea and make our way to Gibraltar," Madeleine uttered.

"We need to get away from this wreck. If we are discovered, the game's up," the lieutenant said.

Madeleine led the group to a farmer's truck, apparently empty from having just delivered his goods to market. After a brief discussion, mainly pointing to Charlène, the driver looked as if in agreement with her.

Coming back to the group, she said with a smile, "This man will take us to La Línea. The main gate to Gibraltar lies at the southern end of that city."

"C'est bien," Henri proclaimed.

Waving them over, the farmer opened the back of his truck and motioned for everyone to climb in, signaling to Charlène and Madeleine to get in the cab with him.

The old truck rumbled to life as the farmer steered his truck back onto the highway headed east toward La Línea.

"You are with Americans, are you not?" the Spaniard asked Madeleine.

Stunned at their discovery, she tried to counter his accusation.

"It's OK, *amiga*," the Spaniard said in a heavy accent. "I am sympathetic. I fought on the side of the Republicans during the civil war. My name is Pablo Antonio Gomez.

"I can take you as far as my sister-in-law's house, only a few blocks from the gate to Gibraltar. I will remain hidden nearby. Driving to the gate will attract attention from Franco's men," Pablo said. "Your group can rest as long as you like before you walk to the main gate of Gibraltar, which is not very far."

"Gracias, señor," Madeleine replied, gazing back at the growing crowd by the train wreck.

"De nada," Pablo replied.

"Will we have any problems getting into Gibraltar?" Madeleine asked.

"You will not be harmed," Pablo informed her.

Pablo's sister-in-law's house was only a thirty-minute drive, the group arriving by the back door.

"Welcome to my home," a pretty Spanish woman with jet-black hair said. "My name is Adoncia Gomez. My husband's family is from La Línea. You all look exhausted. Please come in and cool yourselves."

Introducing everyone by name, Antoinette said, "Thank you for your hospitality, Adoncia. We need to rest before we can continue. We have been in a train accident."

"Yes, Pablo has already told me. I am happy you are safe," Adoncia said, smiling.

"And what about your husband?" Lieutenant Robertson asked. "Is he available? I would like to talk to him about getting in to Gibraltar."

"My husband is not here, señor. He was killed fighting Franco's army in 1937. Pablo and I can answer any questions you have about the gate at Gibraltar," Adoncia informed him.

"My apologies, Señora Adoncia. I didn't know," Lieutenant Robertson replied.

"He was a local hero, and I am treated well here," Adoncia said.

Adoncia excused herself to set up a room where the ladies could get refreshed and even take a bath. Pablo got out a washbasin and invited the men to wash off the grime from the trip and the accident.

As everyone was getting cleaned up, Adoncia put out fresh coffee, bread and butter, and a variety of cheeses. For Charlène and André, there was a pitcher of horchata, a delicious nonalcoholic drink with a very long history dating back to the period of Moorish rule in the area of Valencia and Sangria— an indispensable element of every Spanish fiesta, even for the adults.

"I love *orujo*," Pablo said to the lieutenant. "You Americans call that moonshine."

"What does the name mean?" Robertson asked.

"Umm, let me think. Ah yes, it means burning water in *inglés*," Pablo said.

"If it's anything like the moonshine back home, I bet it does!" the lieutenant said.

"*C'est comme notre eau-de-vie, n'est ce pas?* Can you translate, Madeleine?" Henri chuckled as he accepted a snifter of the strong brandy from Pablo.

"Pablo, why are you helping us?" Robertson asked bluntly. "You could have turned us in, probably for a reward."

"I could," Pablo said. "You see, I was a Republican fighter during the civil war and hate the Franco regime. Most of us in Spain do not agree with what Nazi Germany is doing to Europe and would have preferred to fight on the side of the Allies. We don't agree with General Franco. So you see, I do what I can in silent protest for those who need my help."

Pablo continued to explain, "My brother, an anti-Fascist as well, was taken to Mauthausen-Gusen concentration camp, a slave labor camp for the Nazis in Austria. He was intelligentsia, working for the cultural ministry in the former Republic. Franco saw him as an enemy of the state and sent him away to die in the labor camp. I have been closely watched since then, but I do what I can to fight against General Franco's regime."

"Much appreciated, partner," the lieutenant said.

"Now it is getting too late for you to cross over into Gibraltar. I suggest you make a fresh start in the morning. You are quite safe in La Línea, and my sister is quite well known for her cooking!" Pablo proclaimed.

"Pablo, hush!" Adoncia admonished her brother. "You're embarrassing me. I do what I can." She finished talking to Antoinette.

"She is humble, my friends, a good woman," Pablo said.

For now the group was safe. The Spanish government earlier that year had kicked out the Abwehr operations that spied on Gibraltar, which lessened the contingent of Spanish authorities keeping watch on the border area as well.

"On va boire à votre santé," Henri announced. "May we all remain safe and live to see the end of the war. *Vive la France! Viva España! Vive l'Amérique!"*

"Salud!" Pablo and Adoncia said.

"A votre santé!" the French guests replied.

"Here's mud in yer eye!" the lieutenant toasted.

"Mud?" Charlène asked. "America is such a strange place!"

"Just a saying, kid." The lieutenant laughed.

After dining, the group sat down in *el gabinete* to plan their final walk into Gibraltar. They were so close they could taste it in the salty air.

Everyone was relaxed and happy to be this close to freedom, far from Nazi rule.

"My friends," Adoncia addressed the group, "I need to go to the market. You're welcome to come with me."

"I am not so sure that's a good idea," Madeleine intoned. "What if we are caught, and so close to freedom?"

Madeleine did not miss the disappointment on Charlène's face.

"Charlène, we must remain hidden," she explained, trying to appease the child. "When we are truly free, I will take you to the market whenever you like."

"Madeleine, she will be fine with me. There is no danger here," Adoncia said. "If anyone asks, I will tell them she is my niece, visiting from Madrid."

"Please, Madeleine, I will be quiet. No one will notice," Charlène exclaimed excitedly.

"Let her go, Madeleine," Henri remarked. "We are safe here."

"*Mon Dieu.* You must talk to no one. *C'est entendu?*" Madeleine said to Charlène.

"*Oui, je promets,*" Charlène acknowledged.

The *évadés*, having eaten Adoncia's good food, sat by a crackling fire in Adoncia's *gabinete*. They made small talk about the war, Spanish versus French and American culture, and which country made the best brandy.

"I am fond of brandy from the Andalusian city of Jerez. It has deep, rich tones. It does not hurt that it tastes delicious too!" Pablo said.

"Times are tough in France. We normally drink eau-de-vie, made from our local fruits," Henri said. "But if I were able to acquire some, Cognac would be my choice."

"What about you, Lieutenant?" Pablo asked.

"Ever hear of tequila?" the lieutenant asked. "It's big back home in Texas. We call it ta-kill-ya."

"Sounds terrible," Henri said.

"It can be, Henri, trust me!" the lieutenant said.

Adoncia, carrying an oversized handbag, held Charlène's hand as they opened the front door. Both were dressed in matching black-and-white taffeta shawls, with Charlène carrying her backpack underneath.

"We will be back soon," Adoncia said.

"*Sois sage avec* Madame Adoncia, Charlène," Madeleine said.

"*Oui*, I will behave," she replied.

Walking up to the marketplace, Adoncia purchased some fruits and vegetables for her guests.

Charlène was delighted that, after such loss and injury to herself and friends, she was able to do something normal again.

The market was just closing down; most of the vendors had already departed. Adoncia paid the man behind the cart, who placed all the fruits and vegetables in the oversized handbag she carried.

"*Familia, señora?*" the man asked her.

"*Si, Carlos,*" Adoncia replied. "*Mi sobrina* from Madrid."

"She has your eyes," Carlos said.

"*Gracias, señor!*" Adoncia replied.

When Adoncia had finished purchasing the food, she led Charlène around back of the marketplace into an alley.

"Why are we going this way, *madame?*" Charlène asked.

"It's a shortcut," Adoncia said.

Out of the corner of her eye, Charlène saw Adoncia pull out a handkerchief to wipe her face, remembering how her mother would always embarrass her like that. But instead Adoncia held the handkerchief to Charlène's nose and pressed hard. Charlène suddenly felt very odd, like the world was spinning and fading from view.

Coming up the alley to Adoncia was her brother, Sergio Garcia. He grabbed a piece of fruit from her bag and nonchalantly munched on it.

"Nice work, *hermana*. Are they all at your house?" Sergio asked.

"*Si*, they suspect nothing," she answered.

"That is good. Go back and say I have her," he whispered.

"How shall I say you got her?" she asked. "I cannot go in and tell them you walked up and took her from me."

Turning to Adoncia, Sergio slapped her viciously across her face, splitting her lip. "This is how you were unable to stop me, *hermana!*" He then slammed her against the brick wall of the theater and tore the side of her dress open.

Pulling out a 9 mm Luger and holding it against her face, he said, "Now, tell Henri and Madeleine to meet me here, *si?*"

"*Si, hermano*, but remember, I am on your side," Adoncia said, angrily spitting blood on his shirt.

"Go now. I will have my revenge." Sergio grinned sadistically.

Walking back through the side streets so she wouldn't attract attention, Adoncia burst into the house sobbing. "Adoncia, who has done this to you?" Pablo exclaimed upon seeing her, running to her side to hold up the collapsing woman.

Battered and beaten, she lied about the kidnapping. "A man, named Sergio attacked us and took Charlène. He had a gun, and there was nothing I could do!" she cried.

"Sergio is here?" Henri exclaimed. "Nigel said he would follow us!"

"He wants only Henri and Madeleine to go. If anyone else comes, he said he will kill her," Adoncia sobbed. "I am sorry I could not stop that madman."

"I can follow you at a distance, Henri. He'll never know I am there," Lieutenant Robertson said.

"*Oui*, Lieutenant, just make sure he doesn't see you," Henri replied.

"Just make sure you remain hidden, Robbie," Madeleine said.

"Pablo, do you have any weapons they could use?" Madeleine asked.

"No, I am sorry. If anyone is caught hiding weapons, they are sent to concentration camps," Pablo explained. "But I do have a knife from my army days," he said as he rummaged in the kitchen drawer. He pulled out a wicked-looking blade, serrated on one end with a deep blood groove down the middle.

Tucking the blade in his belt, he said to Lieutenant Robertson, "I use it to cook. Let us go at once."

"Pablo, I am scared. Please stay here with me," Adoncia pleaded.

"They do not know the streets like I do, *hermana*. They need my help. You will be safe here," Pablo said.

"Adoncia, let me help you, *ma chère*," Antoinette said helping her up off the floor. "Do you have another dress? I can fix this one for you."

"I will remain with Adoncia also," Françoise said as she turned to André. "You must also stay, André."

A block away from the house, the four split off into two groups, with Pablo and Lieutenant Robertson making their way through the alley to get around behind the theater. Pablo gave Henri and Madeleine directions to the rendezvous point.

"We will circle from behind him. You two will be the decoys," Pablo explained.

After Henri and Madeleine were out of sight, he pointed down a side street. "Lieutenant, this way."

The lieutenant led the way. But, something was amiss, and the hairs stood on the back of his neck. He spun around just as

Pablo tried to embed the blade in his back. Instead, the blade cut into his arm. Slamming his fist into Pablo's face, he removed the blade from the Spaniard's hand, flipped it around, and plunged it into Pablo's heart.

They must be in this with Sergio! I should have known. We got that ride to La Línea much too easily. Garcia's spies must have watched us the whole time!

Lieutenant Robertson sprinted off down the dark back streets of La Línea.

Walking into the alley from the main street, Henri and Madeleine were confronted by a pistol-wielding Sergio.

"I thought I killed you in France, Sergio. I will not fail again," Henri said.

"No matter, as neither of you will live now," Sergio laughed manically, dropping Charlène behind him and awakening her. Groggily Charlène assessed the scene before her and reached for her backpack, which Sergio had removed earlier and now lay on the ground.

"You promised to let Charlène go," Madeleine demanded.

Sergio started to raise his pistol toward the couple, "Certainly. After you are dead, I will let her go back to Germany!"

Two shots rang out behind Sergio, and his body, suddenly appearing as if controlled by puppet strings, rose up and toward Madeleine and Henri.

Looking down in shock at the growing red stain soaking the front of his shirt, Sergio unconsciously squeezed the trigger of his pistol.

As Sergio fell, Madeleine felt his bullet pierce her chest. *Pas maintenant, pas ici,* she thought.

Sergio fell to his knees dropping the gun. *"Culpe a mi hermana!"*

From out of the shadows Lieutenant Robertson stepped in behind him and broke his neck, ending his life.

Picking up Sergio's gun, Robertson turned and slowly removed the pistol from Charlène's hand. It was the same pistol she had hidden in her backpack when they confronted the Carlingue in Saint-Girons. She said nothing but stared straight ahead, tears forming in her eyes.

Henri cried out to Madeleine, *"Mon Dieu,* Madeleine, *ne meurs pas!"* Henri cried out holding her body against his, blood staining her shirt.

"Henri, *mon amour, je t'aime,"* Madeleine said and died in his arms.

Charlène burst into tears, repeating *"Maman"* over and over until Lieutenant Robertson picked her up in his arms and cradled the sobbing child.

Weeping, Henri picked up Madeleine's body and slowly walked past Lieutenant Robertson and Charlène back toward Adoncia's house.

In the distance they could hear alarm bells ringing at what must have been the local *Policía* station.

***

Back at the house, Françoise and André sat by the fire. They nervously waited for their friends to return.

"When will they return?" André asked. "I am afraid for Charlène."

"*Ne t'inquiète pas.* They will be back soon," Antoinette said, trying to break the tension.

After Antoinette helped Adoncia to change, she went into the kitchen to make tea.

There was a thud against the kitchen door leading to the alley behind. Antoinette opened it and was surprised by the source of the noise.

When Adoncia entered the kitchen, Antoinette said to her, "It is strange, Adoncia. Pablo was so good to take us away from the train accident." Antoinette took cups from a cabinet and had her back turned as she continued to prepare the tea.

"What do you mean?" Adoncia was playing innocent.

"It is strange he was at the train with a truck and knew we wanted to escape to Gibraltar."

"We have done this before, Antoinette. We recognize those escaping Nazi tyranny," Adoncia said.

They had heard the gunshots in the distance, and now alarm bells were ringing in the town. Françoise ran into the kitchen with André close behind.

"What happened?" Françoise asked Antoinette.

"Maybe we should ask Adoncia," Antoinette said.

Realizing her cover was broken, Adoncia grabbed a kitchen knife from the counter. "You should have never come here," Adoncia growled, raising the blade to strike Antoinette.

Antoinette was quicker, pulling Pablo's military dagger from her apron and fatally plunging it into Adoncia.

Adoncia was in shock, only the hilt of the blade showing. "How did you get Pablo's knife?" she cried out, her life draining away.

"Lieutenant Robertson ran back as soon as he killed Pablo. He slipped it to me when he told me who you were. Now join *su familia* in hell!" Antoinette exclaimed.

Adoncia died on the kitchen floor.

EPILOGUE

Henri placed flowers by the grave of the woman he loved as he did every day that week in Gibraltar. They were free, but for him it was an empty and hollow feeling, having lost Madeleine. Someday, he thought, I will bring you back home, *mon chérie*.

Not far way, the newly promoted Captain Robertson was still debriefing his British allies on the escape and evasion route he had led the group on. MI-6 in Gibraltar was especially interested in the size and disposition of German troop movements in France. The loss of his team was looked upon poorly, but without their sacrifice, the *évadés* would have never made it, and the valuable secrets they held would have cost the Allies dearly.

Charlène was heartbroken at the loss of Madeleine, whom she considered her mother throughout this whole ordeal. Antoinette was quick to realize Charlène needed lots of attention to bring her back to normal, whatever that might be. The doctors in Gibraltar couldn't believe Charlène had broken bones and dismissed Antoinette's assurances that, indeed, she was very badly injured before they arrived at the convent in Nevers.

Months later, a ship pulled into New York, and the Statue of Liberty was the first thing Charlène saw as she held

Antoinette's hand, with Henri at their side. They would deliver Charlène to her Uncle David and Aunt Judith in December of that year in Virginia, just in time for the Hanukkah celebration. Henri and Antoinette stayed with David and Judith until the war was over, guests at their country estate near Williamsburg. Late in 1945, a young Captain Robertson paid a visit to the estate, proposing to Antoinette Gibert, which culminated in a grand Texas-sized wedding in June 1946.

In 1958, Henri passed away at the age of sixty-four from a heart attack while working the fields near Bergues, near his beloved rebuilt farmhouse. After his unexpected death, Antoinette and Robbie moved into the farmhouse, both passing away in their nineties after a long and happy marriage in the French countryside.

CPSIA information can be obtained
at www.ICGtesting.com
Printed in the USA
BVHW031156191021
619310BV00011B/60